LOST TIME

Bill Pezza

Dedicated to the twelve of us.

Fall, 2023

Do not go gentle into that good night,
Old age should burn and rave at close of day;
Rage, rage against the dying of the light.

Dylan Thomas

CHAPTER 1

Nick liked his psychiatrist. She had a calming demeanor that he supposed most psychiatrists possessed and a look that conveyed genuine empathy. She respected Nick for what he'd been through, so much so that when he broke off their sessions at the Veterans Administration years ago, she promised to squeeze him in quickly if he ever decided to resume. So, when Nick called, the receptionist gave him an appointment within four days.

Nick scanned Dr. Braun's inner office as he waited for her to arrive. He smiled at the warm surroundings. While much of the décor at the VA was drab and functional, someone saw the value of carving out a sanctuary of mahogany paneling, leather furniture, and thick carpeting as the proper setting to meet with patients.

Dr. Braun entered through a rear door. She had aged and allowed hints of gray to emerge undisturbed in her otherwise dark hair. She nonetheless possessed the attractive features Nick remembered from previous years. She dressed conservatively, with a dark suit and powder blue blouse. Despite her prim look, Nick often imagined her at one of those bars where professionals congregate to unwind at happy hour. The image helped him relax.

"Nick," she said brightly as she took the seat across from him without shaking hands. "It's good to see you after all this time."

"It's good to see you, Doctor."

She observed him for a moment and said, "You look fit. I mean, a few years have gone by, and honestly, you look better than I thought you would. That's meant as a compliment."

"Thank you. I started working out a few months ago. Not all the joints work the way I'd like, but I use light weights and isometrics, even some martial arts moves from the Green Beret days. It relieves stress."

"For sure," she said. "Healthy body, healthy mind. Where do you exercise?"

"In the basement of my friend's deli. He has equipment from when his son was in high school. One of the veterans I helped who served in Afghanistan is a weightlifter and trainer. He has me on a strength program and stops in now and then."

"Well, that's great." Changing the subject, she said, "I was pleased to learn that you asked to return for more sessions because I'm nearing retirement and have reduced my caseload."

"I asked for a session," Nick corrected politely, "not sessions."

Dr. Braun ignored that as she referred to the file on her lap. "I received the letter you sent in advance. I see three main points here: You think you've found something to live for. That's intriguing, and I'd like to discuss it more later." Turning back to the papers, she said, "You feel you've wasted precious years, decades really, and you want to make the most of the years you have left."

"That's an accurate summary, Doc."

Then, out of character, she smiled and offered a joke. "Well, I guess we're finished here then because that has been the goal all along, to get you to a place where you embrace a healthy life and an optimistic future."

Nick didn't respond.

"I'm kidding, of course. We're not nearly finished. But," she added, "it says in your file that you're seventy-one. For the record, none of us know how much time we have left. We might live to be ninety, but I suppose it's natural to begin to hear the clock ticking."

Nick said, "I guess it is because I do."

"I guess we all do at some point, but we try not to let it consume us."

She glanced at her notes again and said, "Let me review my observations from years ago. You were a Green Beret in Vietnam. You were awarded the Distinguished Service Cross for an incredibly heroic mission. You were shot, captured, and spent two years in a POW camp which was hell on earth. You suffered severe physical and psychological trauma which left you angry and withdrawn when you returned home. You limited yourself to a small circle of friends and became relatively unproductive, insecure, and isolated. My assessment was that you used a persona of what we call assumed disability as a defense mechanism against having to interact broadly with others. There was one exception, though. You advocated for veterans' groups, a cause for which you feel strongly. In fact, you were invited to speak at a congressional subcommittee hearing because of your extensive efforts. That's amazing."

Nick nodded. "Veterans needed a voice. They still do."

Dr. Braun took a long pause to reflect. "I agree, but Nick, that's what I've always struggled to understand about you. You are intelligent. I have your school and military records here. Your IQ is just under 130. Your army aptitude tests reveal strengths in several areas, and you had the courage to testify before Congress."

She shook her head as if perplexed. "And yet, aside from that testimony…I don't know. The years are empty."

□ Nick went back to her previous statement. "What's this assume disability stuff?"

"It's a defense mechanism," Braun repeated. "It's when a person conveys the notion of 'don't expect much from me because I have nothing to give'."

"Do you think I do that?" Nick asked.

Braun didn't respond directly, instead, she said, "How did you get to the VA hospital today?"

"My friend Jimmy drove me."

"So you're still not driving?"

Nick didn't answer.

Dr. Braun went on. "When was the last time you bought some new clothes?"

Nick didn't answer.

"How about technology? How many apps do you have on your phone?"

Again, Nick didn't respond.

Dr. Braun nodded. "Well, I haven't seen you in years, but it appears little has changed. So, yes, Nick. I think you purposefully put up a persona of disability, of detachment, of being out of step with an evolving world. You seem to have good hygiene, but you don't buy clothes frequently. You don't embrace technology. You don't drive, and you rarely venture out. Now, in contrast, you testified before a congressional committee on something important to you. That behavior is a contradiction. Social skills aren't something you gain or lose, turn on or turn off like that, normal in one area and abnormal in others. I don't want to be too presumptuous, but it wouldn't be far-fetched for someone to think that you might be faking a little in your daily routine."

Nick didn't respond.

"Am I off base, Nick?"

"Faking is a pretty strong word," Nick said.

Dr. Braun nodded. "Perhaps you could offer a better one." Nick flashed a pained expression. "I have a friend who said basically the same thing you're saying. She said that I crawled into this hole for so long when I got back to the States that I don't know how to get out of it."

"Interesting," Braun said. "Do you agree with her?" "She's a dear friend, sort of a family member, who loves me. In effect, she called me out. Scolded me for doing this to myself. She said I was afraid to face the real world and, as a result, I'm dragging down everyone around me, people who care about me."

Braun asked again, "Do you agree with her?"

Again, Nick didn't respond.

"Is that why you're here?" Braun asked. "Do you want to know whether I agree with her?"

Nick just looked at her.

"It doesn't work that way," Braun said. "At least not yet. What's important right now is not what she or I think, but what you think. So?"

Braun waited as silence filled the room. Finally, Nick said, "Yeah, I guess I do agree with her."

Dr. Braun exhaled deeply. "Admitting that is a big

breakthrough, Nick. That's important stuff."

She leaned forward for emphasis. "So, let's review. You say you found something to live for. You feel you've wasted precious time in your life. And you say in your letter that you want to make maximum use of the time you have left. Now you've added that you realize that somehow, you've been holding yourself back. Explain that part to me. We need to know the why."

Nick lowered his head. "I guess I'm afraid. Yeah, I guess I'm afraid that I won't know how to act normally if I try. Like my friend Carrie said, I guess I got in that hole so deep that I'm afraid to get out."

Dr. Braun nodded. "I'd like to make some points here. First, it was perfectly understandable for you to sink into that metaphorical hole you reference after what you went through. Your story is devastating. I was deeply disappointed when you terminated our sessions because we may have been able to help you with that. But that ship sailed."

Nick rubbed his eyes, and Dr. Braun asked if he'd like some water. He declined, and she continued. "Let's discuss that fear you mentioned. Everything in this file tells me that you had an amazing, outgoing personality and that you oozed confidence as a young man. Having those qualities is like riding a bike. People never forget how. They may be a little apprehensive about getting on again after a long break, but once they do…"

Nick looked at her hopefully, and she continued. "Once you've made the decision that you want your life back, you've won two-thirds of the battle. The rest will come easily if you take small steps and have confidence. Are you comfortable trying that?"

"I wouldn't say I'm comfortable, but I am willing, and I'm going to do it."

"That's wonderful news, Nick." She paused. "It seems that the impetus for all of this is that you've found something to live for."

Nick nodded.

"So, tell me about it."

Nick shook his head. "No."

"It's important, Nick. Talking about it might be helpful in many ways."

"Nope. Not gonna happen. I will tell you that I plan to pursue my goal. It's risky, and certainly not a baby step. But that's all I'll say."

Dr. Braun checked her watch. "We have time, Nick. "I really think…"

Nick interrupted. "Look, Doctor. I'm not entirely sure why I came here. I guess because I liked you before and I like you now. I appreciate all you did for me, and I apologize for bailing out before. I guess I came to get reaffirmation about what I was thinking anyway. I sort of did, so you did your job. Thank you."

Braun tried again. "Nick, this has been a good talk, but we're just getting started. We have plenty of time left."

Nick smiled. "Do we, Doc? You said earlier that none of us knows how much time we have."

Braun tried to clarify, but Nick added, "Someone once said, 'Live each day as if it's your last, and one day you'll be right."

Braun couldn't help herself and laughed out loud.

Nick looked pleased by her reaction and said, “I intend to do just that, and I hope I’m wrong for a long time. Thanks for seeing me.”

Dr. Braun gave in. “Will I see you again for another session?”

“If I’m successful, I won’t need one.”

She replied, “If it turns out disappointing, you know I’m here. I’m cheering for you, Nick.”

CHAPTER 2

Nick hated funerals. In his mind, most fell into two categories. Those for people to whom he was emotionally attached and everybody else: old classmates, neighbors, or casual friends. Fortunately, most who made up the first category were in the deli with him now, still alive and kicking. They’d been gathering in Angelo Marzo’s deli every day for almost forty-five years, ever since Nick and his friend Jimmy had returned from Nam.

Aside from occasional improvements to the spotless kitchen to satisfy code requirements, nothing had been done to the deli in the decades since Angelo’s parents left it to him. The hardwood floors had shrunk with age. Two refrigeration cases that stopped functioning years ago were simply unplugged and left in place. The wall clock no longer worked, and there were a handful of ads on the walls touting products that no longer existed. There was a single round wooden table off to the side, marred and scratched, surrounded by six folding chairs, only three of which matched.

Neighbors accepted the place for what it was, a quick, convenient stop to buy milk, bread, cigarettes, or lottery tickets. What kept Angelo in business, aside from the absence of a mortgage, was his exceptional cooking. Patrons ordered hot trays for small parties, as well as his famous cheesesteak, roast pork, and sausage and pepper sandwiches.

Yesterday's funeral was for a former classmate, Sam Defillipo. He and Nick were never close, but Nick knew him, and when he read that Sam had passed, the little voice inside him began whispering that he should attend the services. Nick tried to tune it out, but in the end, he went, just like always, and he dragged his buddy Jimmy along.

Nick and Jimmy had been inseparable since high school. While young Nick had been smart, confident, and outgoing, Jimmy had been slow, insecure, and introverted, a prime candidate to be picked on, but Nick took him under his wing and protected him through high school, and right up until Nick enlisted and Jimmy got drafted into the miserable, stinking war that was Vietnam. Jimmy was skinny, and the army, in its wisdom, made him a tunnel rat and ordered him into dark holes searching for VC among the rats, spiders, and whatever else lurked there. It was the first time Jimmy didn't have Nick to lean on. Terrified, he survived but returned home emotionally shattered, needing Nick's help and companionship more than ever. As it turned out, Nick wasn't around when Jimmy returned. He was still in treatment at Walter Reed recovering from two horrific years in a Viet Cong prisoner-of-war camp. When Nick finally came home a shell of the man he once was, Jimmy realized Nick would need him as much as he had always needed Nick.

Jimmy had a simple method of gauging Nick's mood. If he was caustic and insulting, it meant that he was doing okay. If he was quiet, it meant that he was possibly drifting, as Jimmy called it, sinking into a familiar place where he didn't want to be.

The deli was quiet, and all eyes were on Nick. Angelo stood behind the counter while Jimmy and another buddy, Big Frankie, shared the table where Nick sat. Jimmy had warned them that Nick had been quiet ever since yesterday's funeral and might need help. Nick's continued silence seemed to confirm it.

The four of them were an unlikely group to offer emotional support to anyone. They were quirky, some would say odd and dysfunctional, and each carried psychological baggage of their own. Angelo and Big Frankie's experiences, although different from their two military friends, nevertheless took a significant toll. Angelo was a draft dodger who had fled to Canada with his girlfriend, Donna during the war. They married in Canada, had a child, and returned when President Jimmy Carter pardoned everyone who fled. Frankie was a diabetic who had flunked his draft physical.

None of the four had recovered from the emotional impact of the war. For Angelo, it was the shame of leaving family, friends, and country to avoid service. For Big Frankie, it was the guilt of a medical exemption while his friends went off to fight. For Jimmy, it was the nightly reminder of the abject terror of crawling through pitch-black tunnels, barely larger than a storm drain. And for Nick, it was flashbacks of more than seven-hundred days of the worst torture and depravity one could imagine. But somehow, their bond offered more mutual support than any therapist could provide. Whenever one of them began to drift, as they called it, the others would jump in to offer help. Now it seemed as if it was Nick's turn to be helped.

Before Vietnam, Nick had been handsome, intelligent, and popular, a star athlete and a natural leader. He later excelled in the military, qualifying as a Green Beret and earning sergeant stripes. He volunteered to lead a team to liberate a captured American pilot from a Viet Cong village. The mission was a success. He'd ordered his team to move out while he and a team member stayed behind to provide cover. His team escaped along with the pilot, but Nick was wounded and eventually captured. His teammate was killed, and Nick endured two years of beatings, starvation, and isolation before his release. He spent months at the Walter Reed Army Medical Center where he underwent repeated surgeries and countless hours of rehabilitation. He was awarded a Distinguished Service Cross in a hospital ceremony and eventually returned to Bristol and his friends at Angelo Marzo's deli.

The confident and outgoing Nick everyone knew before the war was replaced by a reclusive, withdrawn, and moody individual uncertain of his place in the world. He worked sporadically at part-time jobs, but otherwise, lived off his disability pension and spent most of his ample free time at the deli.

The "treatment" method at the deli when guys were down was as unorthodox as the collection of eccentric characters who gathered there. There were no soothing words of encouragement, no quiet voices of understanding. Instead, the guys made liberal use of sarcasm, mockery, and good old-fashioned ball-breaking, anything to distract whoever was in distress.

Jimmy broke the silence. "I told you not to go to the funeral. Funerals are a pain in the ass. You don't handle them well. They always leave you feeling like crap. So why do you keep going?"

Nick stared at him for a few seconds before responding. "It's called respect, dimwit. Sam was a classmate, your classmate too."

Jimmy sighed. "We're seventy-one years old, Nick. We were classmates more than fifty years ago. We didn't even hang out with Sam."

Nick took a moment to study his friend. He exhaled deeply and said, "I'm tired of teaching you things, Jimmy. Respect is respect, regardless of how much time passes."

"You win, Nick. Go to every damn funeral in town, for every Tom, Dick, and Harry you read about in the obits."

"That's sexist, Jimmy. It's 2018. I go to female funerals too, not just Tom, Dick, and Harry's. Get with it, Man."

Jimmy saw Nick's sarcasm as a good sign. Maybe he had misread Nick's mood. Anything was better than silence, so he kept the exchange going.

"Great. Go to all of them. That'll give you more chances to come home in a funk." Jimmy paused, then added, "It's bad enough that you go," Jimmy said. "But you drag me along with you. I'm tired of it."

"Free country," Nick said. "Do what you want."

"That's not fair," Jimmy said dejectedly. "You know I do whatever you do." Then he turned to Big Frankie. "Do you think that's fair, Frankie? He knows I do whatever he does."

Frankie closed his eyes and rubbed his forehead. "What I think is that you guys should end this dumb-ass conversation. You're giving me a headache. Take a ride or something."

"That's a good idea, Nick," Jimmy said. "Let's cruise the town. You can bitch about people who don't cut their grass or bring their trash cans in on time. You love that. You can even send some anonymous letters to the Borough reporting them. That usually makes you smile."

"I'd like to," Nick said flatly, "but I can't."

"Why not?" Big Frankie said. "Sounds like fun."

"I'm waiting for someone."

"Who?" Jimmy asked.

Nick didn't reply.

"Who?' Jimmy repeated.

"He's waiting for my son, Johnny," Angelo said from behind the counter.

Jimmy perked up. "Johnny's coming. That's great. Why didn't you tell us?"

Angelo shrugged. "Nick asked me to call him. Said it was personal."

"Personal? That's bullshit," Jimmy said. "We haven't seen Johnny in a couple of weeks. If he's coming, I want to see him too. You're not going to hog him, Nick."

"Ditto," Big Frankie said.

"It is personal, but not private," Nick said. "You guys can stay, but I need to ask him a favor."

"What kind of favor?" Jimmy asked.

Nick smiled. "It's personal."

"Jesus!" Jimmy yelled. "Now you're just bustin' my chops."

"Sometimes you're a pain in the ass, Nick." Big Frankie added. He turned to Angelo. "So, what's the favor?"

"Don't know. Nick wouldn't tell me. Johnny's coming at five o'clock. We'll find out then. He's bringing Brian with him."

"Brian's coming too?" Big Frankie said. "Great. It'll be good to see them."

CHAPTER 3

By any objective standard, Johnny Marzo was a rock star and a Bristol legend. To the guys in the deli, he was a shining light in what could otherwise be a dark world. Angelo was the only guy from the deli who had a child, and when his wife Donna gave birth, Nick, Jimmy, and Big Frankie immediately became his adopted uncles when they returned from Canada. They doted on him and never missed a sporting event. They beamed with pride as he excelled both on the field and in the classroom. They all became Nittany Lions fans when he was accepted at Penn State and took pause when he joined the campus ROTC. Angelo wondered out loud whether his son's interest in the military was somehow an attempt to compensate for his father's flight to Canada. Johnny assured him that there was nothing to read into his decision except a desire to serve and lead.

They followed his progress as he went through paratrooper, desert, aquatic, and jungle survival training. Nick especially perked up at these milestones as they reminded him of the good parts of his military service, and the sense of accomplishment he once had. They prayed and worried as he was assigned to Afghanistan and sat together at the deli table to hear Angelo read his son's occasional letters. Finally, after four years of service, Johnny announced it was his last tour of duty. He'd be coming home to marry his high school sweetheart, Carrie, start a family, and consider a new career.

The guys sat in the last pew at the wedding, not because they weren't welcome upfront, but because they were quirky that way. They asked for a table in the back at the reception too and marveled at the beauty of the bride. Their hearts exploded when Carrie came to sit with them and made it clear that she considered them her uncles too. The gesture was genuine, and they loved her for it. Rather than be standoffish about their eccentric behavior, she reveled in it. She poked fun with the best of them and welcomed their rebuttals. If they loved her for the warmth she shared, they liked her even more for the wit and humor she brought to their relationship.

Later, when Gracie was born, Carrie never missed a chance to take her to the store to see her grandparents and adopted uncles. Nothing was a better reminder that there could be goodness and joy in people's lives, than Johnny Marzo and his family.

While Johnny was stationed in Afghanistan, Carrie joined the International Red Cross and was stationed in Kenya. She was on the scene in the aftermath of the deadly terrorist attack on the American Embassy there. She helped remove bodies from the rubble and was shocked by the grizzly experience. That, plus the equally horrific memory of 9-11, left her with no illusions about the need for constant diligence in the war on terror. So, knowing Johnny would never be happy with a desk job after his military experience, it was her idea to encourage him to apply to the FBI. He applied and was accepted. He excelled at Quantico and was eventually assigned to the anti-terror division of the Bureau and stationed in Philly. She wasn't pleased when she learned his assignment would include undercover work and was terrified when he was assigned to infiltrate right-wing militia groups.

He once tracked a would-be assassin across three states back to Philadelphia where he thwarted a planned attack on a Presidential candidate at the Constitution Center. Though the attempt was foiled, the assassin was on the loose. When a reporter recklessly broadcasted Johnny's name and hometown in the midday TV press coverage, the enraged assassin turned his attention to Johnny's family. Marzo was still on his tail and soon realized where he was heading. He tracked him to an abandoned power station in Bristol, where Johnny engaged him in a shootout and killed him. The widespread coverage of the episode, *FBI Agent Defends Hometown and Family,* made Johnny Marzo a local legend.

Brian Kelly and Johnny had been best friends since their school days when Brian demonstrated an amazing intellect. When he was ten, his uncle was flying home from Europe to be with Brian's family for Christmas. Brian was his only nephew, and his uncle had earlier purchased a life insurance policy for a million dollars naming Brian as the beneficiary. When his plane exploded over Lockerbie, Scotland as a result of a terror attack killing all on board, double indemnity kicked in and Brian had $2,000,000 dollars placed in his trust fund. He pledged to spend the rest of his life and fortune fighting terrorism. Using his intelligence, he easily more than doubled his money in the stock market and started an anti-terror think tank. His portfolio and reputation grew, and eventually, the FBI hired him as a consultant on selected cases. Occasionally, he and Johnny would work together.

Chapter 4

Nick checked the large clock on the deli wall. It read 7:10, the same time it read every minute for the past six years after it stopped working. Nick checked it habitually and cursed Angelo each time he did.

"Fix the damn clock, Angelo. It drives me crazy."

Angelo didn't look up from the paper he was reading. "Can't do it. I'd need a ladder and I don't have one. Probably can't be fixed, anyway. Besides, you were crazy long before the clock stopped working."

"Thanks, wiseass. Maybe it's time you borrow a ladder and hang a new clock."

"Can't do it. Gotta cut costs. Business has been slow the past few years. I think it's because you guys hang here."

"I think it's because the place is a dump," Nick replied. Then he added, "Hey, Jimmy, Christmas is a few months away. Let's chip in and give Angelo a clock."

"I don't need one. I wear a watch," Jimmy replied. "By the way, you're wearing a watch too."

Nick slammed his hand on the table. "That's not the point. The point is I keep glancing at the damn clock instead of my wrist. It's killing me."

"If it's that bad," Jimmy said, "maybe you can't wait until Christmas. Hey, Angelo, When's your birthday?"

Angelo's face was still buried in the newspaper, and he didn't reply.

Big Frankie decided that the concern about Nick drifting was a false alarm. As long as he was going back and forth with Jimmy and Angelo, he was fine. Maybe it was the thought that Johnny was coming that perked him up.

Big Frankie got up and helped himself to a three-pack of Tastykake cupcakes. He threw a dollar on the counter, opened the wrapper and devoured one in two bites. Digging inside the wrapper for another he said, "After all that, can someone tell me what time it is?"

Jimmy checked his watch. "It's twenty till five. Johnny should be here soon.

The door opened and a customer from the neighborhood came in. He made small talk with Angelo, purchased a lottery ticket and a pack of cigarettes, and left.

Nick was tired of waiting and began tapping his fingers on the table and Big Frankie snapped. "You're not going to do that until Johnny comes are you?"
"You should brace yourself," Jimmy said smiling. "I think he probably will."
Frankie ignored him and said, "You've got twenty minutes yet, Nick. Maybe you should take a walk."
"Good idea," Nick said. He went outside and walked across the street. He sat on the church steps and took out the letter he'd received three weeks earlier from Johnny's wife, Carrie. He'd read it several times and stared at the envelope contemplating whether to read it again. Of course, he knew he would. He opened the envelope, unfolded the letter, and began to read.

Dear Nick,
This is a very difficult letter to write, and it will be equally difficult for you to read, but I've kept my feelings bottled up too long, and can't any longer. You know I love you, but I'm also angry with you and have been for some time. Although it was before my time, I know that what you experienced was enough to crush any man. But enough is enough. I hate to be harsh, but I believe you are afraid to face the world as the Nick you once were and prefer instead to hide behind a façade that may be subconscious but is nevertheless disabling for you and everyone around you.

Everyone thinks you were a prisoner of war for two years, but in my view, you've been a prisoner for decades. In the first two years, you were imprisoned by the Vietnamese, but in the subsequent years, you've been imprisoned by yourself. I'm angry because of the joy that you unintentionally deny not only yourself, but Jimmy, Big Frankie, and my father-in-law, Angelo. In a sense, you all live in the same gray world.

One of the things that hurts me most is your relationship with our daughter, Gracie. She loves you so much, and you shine when she is around, but she's getting older and understands more. Some of her questions about you are heartbreaking. I don't want her to see you deteriorate further. You need to do something, Nick. For your own good and the good of all who love you, you need to do something.

I consider this letter confidential. You may do what you wish with it, but I will never share it. When you see me, none of this will be apparent in my demeanor, but you'll know what I'm thinking.

Love,

Carrie

Nick folded the letter and returned it to the envelope. He walked back to the deli and continued to wait for Johnny.

Moments later, Big Frankie looked out the window and saw Johnny's car pull up. "Here he is!"

Nick and Jimmy jumped up and moved toward the door as Johnny and Brian came in.

"There they are!" Nick said smiling.

"Here we go," Jimmy said and gave out a whistle. "J. Edgar Marzo, in person."

Johnny laughed. It was the same greeting he received each time he came. He shook hands with Big Frankie who was closest and then leaned over the counter to hug his father. "How ya doing, Pop? You look good."

"I'm good, son. Never been better. You're looking good yourself. How are Carrie and Gracie?"

"They're great. Carrie said they're going to visit you Sunday."

Angelo beamed. "Can't wait to see my little girl."

Johnny shared hugs with Nick, and Jimmy and Brian followed suit.

Angelo looked hopefully at Johnny and said, "Can you guys eat?"

"Yup. If you're cooking, we're eating. I told Carrie we'd have dinner here tonight, and Brian did the same with Jenny."

"Perfect!" Angelo replied. He stepped around the counter, turned the sign on the door from open to closed, and said, "Jimmy, get us some beers."

Jimmy left for the back room and Angelo said, "I've got some chicken cutlets warming with some penne. It's left over from a lunch I catered for today. I'll open some olives and peppers for appetizers. Nick, get us two more folding chairs."

"Got it," Nick said as he left for the back room.

Angelo smiled at the thought that a simple visit from Johnny could lift the room's spirits so quickly.

Everyone took a seat at the table while Angelo worked in the kitchen. Jimmy handed out the beers, and Frankie proposed a toast, "To our superhero guests," and they clinked glasses and drank.

Jimmy wiped his mouth and asked, "So what have you guys been up to?"

"Standard stuff," Johnny said smiling. "Nothing we can tell you until you get your security clearances."

"I thought we had them already," Nick joked.

Johnny looked at Brian and winked. "Brian's taking care of it. He's shooting for the highest clearance."

"Any day now," Brian said.

Big Frankie said, "Speaking of Brian, tell us something we don't know, something only really smart people know."

Brian scratched his chin. "That's a tough one. You guys know a lot."

He glanced at Angelo in the kitchen and said, "Here's one. We'll stick to useless trivia. Angelo doesn't wear a chef's hat. But if he did, an authentic one has exactly one hundred pleats, allegedly representing one hundred ways to cook an egg."

"That's it?" Jimmy kidded. "That's the best you can do? I already knew that."

Brian smiled. "Like I said, you guys know a lot." He thought for a moment and added, "Do you know the formal name for a chef's hat?"

Jimmy stared blankly.

Brian waited briefly and then added, "A chef's hat is officially known as a toque. In case you're ever asked."

"Bingo!" Nick shouted. "He got your ass, Jimmy."

Jimmy laughed. "Yes, he did. I'll drink to that."

They clinked glasses again as Angelo put out bread and olive oil. "For the record, I'm a cook, not a chef. Chefs have the guts to serve a meal the size of a deck of cards because it's supposed to be special. Me, I feed people. I mean, really fed them. When I cater, I fill the plates and there's plenty left for seconds."

"Great speech," Nick said. "Wish I had videoed that for Facebook. Post it like a commercial and generate some business so you could fix the place up."

"Shut up and eat," Angelo said.

They ate and drank and laughed for over an hour until Johnny said, "This has been great. We really have to do this more often."

"Count me in," Brian added. "Loved the food, Mr. Marzo, and the jokes were just as good."

Johnny turned to Nick and said, "Okay. Pop called to say you needed a personal favor. So here we are. What's up?"

Nick turned serious, thought for a moment, and said, "I really can't remember."

The room erupted, and Jimmy screamed, "Are you shitting me? After all of this…"

Nick burst out laughing, then gathered himself and said, "Sorry. Just kidding. I really do need a favor."

Big Frankie rapped his knuckles on the table for attention and everyone stopped talking. He said softly, "Listen Nick. It's time to stop jerking around. We're all worried about you. You've been different all day. If there's something that's getting you down, we want to hear it. Jimmy thinks it had something to do with the funeral you went to. Whatever it is, get it out. We want to help."

Nick nodded. "Thank you, Frankie. I appreciate that. I appreciate all of you. The truth is, I'm good. I'm very good, better than I've been in a long time."

Frankie looked skeptical but went along. “That’s good to hear. So, what’s the big favor you need from these guys?”

Nick smiled. “I need you to help me find someone.”

“Sure, “Johnny said. “What’s the person’s name?”

“Liz.”

“Okay. What’s her last name?”

“See, that’s the thing,” Nick said sheepishly. “I don’t know.”

Surprisingly, the guys knew enough to keep quiet and let Johnny do the talking.

“Do you know her well? When was the last time you saw her?”

“It’s been more than forty-five years.”

Something registered on Big Frankie’s face, but Johnny hadn’t yet made the connection. He took a deep breath and exhaled slowly. “Do you know where she lives?”

“I wish I did,” Nick said. “She used to work at Walter Reed when I was there, so maybe Washington or Maryland.”

Big Frankie smiled. “I’ve got it. Is this the nurse we saw when we visited you? The cute one?”

“That’s the one,” Nick said.

“I remember her,” Jimmy said, smiling.” She seemed nice.”

“She was damn nice. Better than nice, Nick said. “Super nice.”

“Now we’re getting somewhere,” Johnny said. We’ve got a place of employment and the dates when you were there.”

Brian nodded and Johnny continued. “Liz is kind of a nickname. Like Betty for Elizabeth or Joe for Joseph. Do you know her formal first name?”

Nick shook his head. “I would have called the Medical Center myself, but I knew all I’d get would be bureaucratic bullshit. ‘Can’t divulge personal information. Records don’t go back that far,’ stuff like that.”

Brian leaned forward. "We'll find her, Nick. We've got an employer, a general date of employment while you were there, and the beginning of a name. We'll find her. As long as…" he caught himself, but Nick finished for him.

"As long as she's alive."

Brian nodded. "It's been decades. There's always that possibility."

"I know," Nick said. "But she's alive. I can feel it."

"Then that's good enough for us," Johnny said. "There are records, lots of records. We'll locate Liz. Brian has some avenues available to him that I don't."

Johnny scanned the faces at the table, then he said, "Nick, there's something I bet everyone in the room is thinking."

Nick said, "Well not everyone, because Jimmy doesn't think."

Everyone laughed and Jimmy gave him a playful tap on the arm. "Trust me. You don't want to know what I think."

Johnny went on. "I certainly get your interest in finding a nurse who helped you, but why now after all these years?"

Nick had no intention of sharing the impact Carrie's letter had on him. Besides, he had enough to share without it. "Good question," Nick said. "I've been kicking it around for a few weeks. I even visited my shrink and hinted about it. But the tipping point was when Jimmy made me go to a funeral with him."

"Hey!" Jimmy said. "There you go again."

Nick smiled. "I'm just bustin' on ya. This table is way too serious right now. It's making me nervous."

Johnny thought back to the scrapbook his father had shown him about the guys' high school days, some of which featured Nick as a football star, class president, and prom king. It was storybook stuff. There was a photo of all the guys helping the Rotary deliver Thanksgiving baskets to the needy. There was a photo of a smiling Nick on the day he earned his Green Beret, and a clipping about his release as a POW. It broke Johnny's heart to see what the war had done to all of them, especially Nick and Jimmy.

"I get it, Nick," Johnny said. "Just relax and take your time. So why now?"

Nick straightened up and cleared his throat. "It was the recent funeral I attended. There was a long line waiting to get in to pay their respects. So, I got talking to the guy in front of me, Chip Romanski, another classmate. Jimmy was talking to someone else. Anyway, he was telling me a story about needing to buy new shoes. He told his wife he was going to do that, and she said, 'You better get a good pair because they'll probably be your last ones.'"

"Seriously?" Big Frankie asked. "She said that?"

"Yes. They have a great relationship, and she didn't mean anything bad by it. She just meant, a good pair of shoes can last for years and given his age... Makes sense."

Nick continued. "So, it got me thinking. Given my age, one more good pair of shoes might be my last too."

Brian said gently, "Come on, Nick. That's a pretty sad way to look at things."

Nick smiled. "You've got me all wrong. I didn't see it as a sad thing. I saw it as a wake-up call. Heck, it's reality. When you're my age," he looked at his friends and added, "our age, you've only got so much time left. Maybe five or ten years. That story about the shoes reminded me that I've been jerking around with my life, wasting it. I've been angry at what those friggin' gooks did to me, to my mind and my body, and it's like I've been letting them do it to me over and over in my head every day since. I figure I may have one more good pair of shoes left, and I want to use them. " He paused and looked at Johnny. "So that's the answer to why now? That's why I want to find Liz."

Nick could see Johnny struggling to stay composed. Angelo was less successful as a tear ran down his face. The others looked emotional too.

"Hey, come on guys. It's all good. My knees hurt, I can barely use my shoulder and my neck is really screwed up because of the stuff those bastard gooks did to me. But I don't give a shit. I've got some quality time left and I'm gonna use it."

Brian smiled and nodded. "Kind of like a bucket list, huh?"

The guys moaned and Nick shouted, "Hell no!"

Brian was taken aback by the response. "Wait, did I say something wrong?"

Big Frankie answered. "Nick and Jimmy hate references to bucket lists. I think we all do.

Nick jumped in before Brian could ask why. "I'm so sick of hearing people who live soft, cushy lives say stuff like, 'before I die, I want to skydive, or do the polar bear plunge and jump in the ocean for thirty seconds in January, or fight a paintball war, or have lunch with some candyass movie star. It's insulting."

Jimmy jumped in. "If people are looking for excitement, a real challenge, they should jump out of a plane when it counts, with full military gear while people on the ground are shooting real bullets at them, or crawl through a dark, rat-infested tunnel and kill or be killed at the end. Bucket list, my ass. When you're holding a dying soldier in your arms, he's not saying, 'damn, I never got to see the Grand Canyon. He's saying he wants to go home, see his loved ones again."

Nick put his hand on Jimmy's arm to stop him. "We're sorry, Brian. None of that was directed at you. You didn't deserve that. It's a common term. It's just that we're a little crazy."

Brian exhaled slowly and said, "No problem, and no need to apologize. I fully get it. Let's get back to Liz. Assuming we locate her, and we will, how do you plan to correspond with her?"

"I plan to surprise her," Nick said. "I'm going to go to her home and knock on her door. Wherever she is. Bam, that's it."

"Really? No phone call first? No letter?"

"Nope. What I have to say has to be said face to face."

"And what's that, Uncle Nick?" Johnny asked. "What will you say?"

"That's easy. I've had forty-five years to imagine it, to play it out in my mind. What I wanted to say all along but didn't have the urgency until now, until the shoe story."

He took a breath, gathered himself and said, "I'll say hello. I'll tell her my name and say that she was my nurse over forty-five years ago at Walter Reed and that I hoped she remembered me. I'll tell her she saved my life. Not the way the doctors did with surgeries and prescriptions. She saved it in other ways.

"I'll remind her that when I came to the hospital, I had several broken bones that had never been treated and had healed improperly. Some had to be rebroken and reset. I'll remind her that I was too weak to stand or walk. I was grossly malnourished and couldn't keep food down. I had jungle parasites that invaded my body. I'll tell her that once I slowly gained enough strength, I wanted to kill myself. Each day I'd hide my painkillers under my tongue, pretend to swallow them, and then spit them out and save them in a drawer next to my bed. I wanted to save enough to be sure they'd do the trick when I finally took them all at once.

"I'll tell her that in the midst of that, you came into my room one morning and announced you were my new nurse. You opened the curtains to let the light in and when I said I preferred it dark, you said 'not anymore.' You came to my bed, held my hand, and gave me the most amazing smile I had ever seen. You said you heard about my story of being a hero and rescuing the pilot. Then you said you were going to be a hero too by rescuing me from Walter Reed and getting me home.

"I'll say that each day you visited you lit up the room with your smile and kindness. You sat with me and made me tell you stories about my life. One day I told you about the pills in my drawer and asked you to throw them away. You cried when you saw them and gave me a hug. I fell in love with you. I didn't just love what you were doing for me, I loved YOU. I wanted to tell you, but I thought it might scare you away, so I settled on just cherishing your visits.

"When the doctors decided I was well enough to go home after five months, you gathered every nurse, orderly, custodian, and even some doctors. They lined both sides of the hallway and clapped as I was wheeled by. You were the last person in line waiting there with that terrific smile. It was the strangest feeling. I was going home. I knew my best friends were waiting for me, but a part of me didn't want to leave. I mean, who doesn't want to leave Walter Reed? I didn't want to leave you. I wasn't sure if I could make it in the world without your support. You must have read it in my face because you stopped clapping, leaned over to give me a hug, and whispered 'You're going to do great.'

That was it. They wheeled me away and I never saw you again."

Nick paused and Johnny said, "Damn, Uncle Nick." No one else spoke until Nick said, "There's more."

"I'll tell her I wished you knew me before I was broken mentally and physically. I thought maybe if you did, we'd have a chance together.

I'll say I've thought about you every day since. Every day for all these years. Then a few years ago, I started thinking that I had to see you, even if just for five minutes. I wanted to do three things, I wanted to hug you, I wanted to tell you I love you, and give you one innocent kiss. But I couldn't bring myself to find you because I knew that regardless of how I felt about you, deep inside I knew that you probably didn't feel the same about me. You were just a nice person doing your job and hundreds of guys who relied upon you in their worst times probably reacted to you in the same way. But now I realized that time is running out. If I didn't take my shot soon, I'd never get the chance. So, here I am."

It remained quiet as Nick scanned the guys at the table. He took a breath and said, "That's what I plan to say to her."

Finally, Big Frankie said, "That's powerful, Nick. Not sure about these guys, but I had no idea."

"I never told anyone, not even Jimmy. I was too embarrassed. Now, I don't care."

Angelo said softly, "It's risky, Nick, to invest yourself like that. She may not be around."

"She might be married," Big Frankie said. "Most likely she is."

Angelo added, "I don't know, Nick. Can you just tell a woman you haven't seen for decades that you want to kiss her? We just don't want you to be disappointed."

"It's what I'm doing," Nick said flatly.

Finally, Jimmy said, "Hey, if this is what Nick wants to do, then I support him. I'm in."

There was more silence, and then Angelo said, "Me too, Nick."

Big Frankie nodded. "Not sure you need a group decision, but if this is what you want, then go get the girl. For what it's worth, I'm in."

Nick smiled and looked at Johnny and Brian.

"Well, Uncle Nick. Looks like Brian and I have a girl to find."

CHAPTER 5

On the way home, Brian told Johnny he'd handle the search. "You'd have a lot more red tape to go through than I would. I'll start with the IRS and Social Security databases. Don't worry. I have no intention of violating anyone's privacy. I'll get a list of all Walter Reed w-2 forms from 1971 and 1972. I don't need their taxes, just names. We'll do a digital sort. Next, we'll sort by gender. There are seven thousand employees today. Assuming a similar staff back then, we may have three thousand five hundred names after the gender sorting. The big sort will come by age. Nick guessed Liz was his age at the time, so I'm thinking sort out the 22 to 26-year-olds. From there, I think it's prudent to do the rest of the search manually, one at a time.

"While I'm doing that, can you focus on nursing certificates issued in Maryland between, let's say 1966 and 1972. Since Nick says they are the same age, she couldn't have been certified prior to sixty-six or later than 1972 when Nick arrived. Can you use your credentials or call in a favor from the Baltimore field office to contact the Maryland Department of State? I have no idea how many that would be. Fortunately, Maryland is one of the smaller states. Probably a couple of thousand, if they've digitized their records, we should search by first names pretty quickly and maybe get lucky.

"Sounds like a plan," Johnny said. "I have one more idea. I'll take a vacation day and drive to Walter Reed and visit the Human Resources department. I'll get a clearance letter from Nick to circumvent the HIPPA protections. I'll do the FBI thing, show Nick's letter, and ask to see Nick's records. Maybe Liz had to sign off on something. Meds administered, or something that would require her name."

"Sounds good," Brian said. "Are we missing anything else?"

"I'm sure we are, so keep thinking."

CHAPTER 6

"Go easy on the brakes. You almost put me through the windshield," Jimmy said.
"It's the damn pedal," Nick said. "It's too stiff."
"They work fine for me. You just have to get used to them. Let me see you come to a smooth stop ahead."
Nick hit the brakes so hard that Jimmy had to use his hand to brace himself against the dashboard. "That's much better," Jimmy said, patiently. "But we still have a way to go."
"Much better?" Big Frankie shouted from the back seat. "You wrenched my damn neck! Get behind the wheel, Jimmy, before he kills us."
Nick turned to face Frankie, took his foot off the brake, and the car began to coast.
"Nick! The brake!" Jimmy shouted.
Nick hit the brake harder this time and Frankie spilled the beer he was holding.
"Jesus!" Frankie said, "Get me out of this car."
"Screw you, Frankie," Nick said. "You shouldn't be here anyway. Who sits in the back seat during a driving lesson? You're making me nervous."
"Is that what this is? A driving lesson? We haven't left the parking lot yet. This isn't going to work."

Jimmy reached over and turned off the ignition. "Put it in park, Nick."

Nick put the car in park and looked straight ahead as he spoke. "Jimmy, we double-dated at the prom. I drove, remember?"

"Of course, I remember, but that was nineteen sixty-five. You haven't driven since we left for Nam."

"That's because when I got home, I could barely use my hip or foot. Then, after I healed better, I was just not interested."

"I know, Nick. We all know, and I've been happy to drive you ever since., We're a team. But this… Look, I offered to lend you my car. I offered to help you practice. But we're not thinking it through. Your license expired decades ago. You don't have a learner's permit. There's no way you're ready to drive on an actual street."

Nick shook his head. "It's been almost two days since we told Johnny and Brian. What if they call with an address? I have to be ready to go."

Frankie leaned over the seat. "It's breaking my heart to say this, Nick, but if that call comes, and Liz still lives in the DC area… That's a three-hour drive. You're just not thinking it through. Jimmy's plan makes sense."

"He's right, Nick. I'll say it again. I will drive you, just like I've done all these years. I don't care if Liz is in Alaska. We get the call, and I will take you to her. And I'll stay out of the way once you're there. In the meantime, we'll keep practicing."

Nick pounded the steering wheel in frustration. "God damn Viet Cong."

Jimmy and Frankie waited for Nick to compose himself. When he did, he said, "I'm sorry. What would I have done without you guys?"

"Ditto, Nick," Jimmy said. "Works both ways."

"It's the leg," Nick said. "It's functional and getting better. I went back to physical therapy. I'm doing the exercises the therapist gave me. He said I have to work on muscle memory. You know, gas, brake, gas, brake. I can't do it as smoothly as I'd like, but I will."

"I know," Jimmy said softly.

They sat in silence until Nick said, "You'll drive me?"

"You're damn right I will."

Nick wiped his eyes and forced a smile. "I hope it's not Alaska." Then he looked at him sharply and said, "But if it is…"

"We're going!" Jimmy said before Nick could finish.

"Okay. Can we let Big Frankie drive home so I can break his balls from the back seat?"

CHAPTER 7

The search had been painstaking, and three days had passed with little progress. Brian had finally downloaded some databases and was assembling some of his private staff to review thousands of names. Johnny's progress had been slower because he had to go through official channels and deal with bureaucrats. He took a vacation day and was leaving for Bethesda, Maryland in the morning.

Carrie got home late from the office and found him at the dining room table looking over records.

"Hi, hon," he said, barely looking up from his work. "You're home late. I already dropped Gracie off at my parents. She's staying overnight so we can get an early start for Bethesda in the morning."

Carrie was a reporter for the *Bucks County Courier Times* and Gannett newspapers. She took the next day off to join Johnny on his trip.

"I had some unexpected work to do at the office."

He barely heard her as he continued to examine lists.

She left him to his work and returned with two glasses of wine and a file folder and sat next to him.

"You've been working hard, Johnny. Gracie's away. I think we need a date."

He looked up. "I'm sorry, Carrie. But I really can't go out tonight. There are some things I have to nail down before we leave tomorrow."

Carrie smiled and rubbed his arm. "That's not the kind of date I'm talking about, Big Guy."

Johnny smiled. "I suppose I could take an hour off before I get back to work."

"Have some wine, Johnny. We don't need to go to Maryland tomorrow."

Johnny sighed," Okay. Tell me what's going on."

"You're a great FBI agent, Johnny. But I'm a great reporter. I did a little research of my own. I was thinking, if I was the public relations person for Walter Reed and one of our patients, a war hero, was being awarded the Distinguished Service Cross while still in the hospital, I'd want it covered. I'd notify the local press. And if I was an editor of a local paper, I would assign a reporter to the event."

Johnny glanced at the folder she was holding and said, "You're beautiful."

"I know. There are two newspapers that could have covered it. The largest is the *Baltimore Sun*. But I took a crack at the *Montgomery County Sentinel* in Montgomery County Maryland, not Pennsylvania, where Walter Reed is located. I called your dad at the store because I knew he saved all of Nick's important stuff in his scrapbook. I figured if there was a certificate that accompanied the Distinguished Service Cross, he'd have it. He did, and he was able to give me the date it was awarded. I got online to search the paper's microfilm on past articles and searched for the day after the award."

She slid the folder across the table to him. "Here's your girl, Johnny, here's Liz."

Inside the folder was a grainy photograph, a screenshot from microfilm. The title above read "Walter Reed patient receives Distinguished Service Cross." The caption below identified the people in the photo. Brigadier General James F. Bradbury; Walter Reed Medical Center administrator, Dr. William Brady; Chief Surgeon, Dr. Angelo DeLuca, and attending nurse, Elizabeth Cherry.

Johnny looked at Carrie and beamed. Carrie rubbed his arm again. "Have some wine, Johnny. And I hope you have more than an hour to relax."

Once Johnny and Brian had the name, the rest became routine research from public records readily available. Within two more days, they had everything they needed. Brian prepared a narrative to present to Nick. It yielded some very surprising results.

Elizabeth Cherry, 68, grew up in Langhorne, Pennsylvania, just eight miles away, and was Baptized at Our Lady of Grace Church, Penndel. She attended the same elementary school and then Neshaminy High School in Langhorne where she graduated in 1967. She attended George Washington University in Maryland where she earned her BS in 1971 and a Master's Degree in Nursing in 1972. She was hired at Walter Reed at the same time Nick was admitted.

She married Dr. Peter Ambrose, who was on staff at the hospital in 1976. They bought a home in Bethesda and had two children, Peter and Kate. They divorced in 1984, shortly after Kate was born, and Elizabeth and the kids moved back to Langhorne, presumably to be near her family. Elizabeth took a job at the Veterans Hospital in Philadelphia. She retired from the VA in 1992 once her twenty years of combined work at Walter Reed and the VA made her eligible for a government pension. At age forty-three, she went to work at Aria-Jefferson Hospital in Langhorne until 2015 when she retired.

She resides at 169 Fairview Avenue in Langhorne and is a member of the Langhorne Arts Society.

"I'm not sure how Nick will react to this," Brian said.

"On the surface, it's all good news. She's alive, single, and nearby. We couldn't ask for more than that," Johnny said.

Brian agreed. "But..."

"But, knowing she's been this close all these years. Who knows? Let's call him and set up a visit."

They met that night at the deli, less than a week after promising to find her. Big Frankie was away visiting his daughter, but Nick, Jimmy, and Angelo were there when Johnny and Brian arrived. Nick looked at them and shook his head. "I can usually read people, but you guys have that FBI look on your faces. I'm nervous."

Johnny smiled. "It's good news, Nick."

Angelo was at the counter and asked Nick if he wanted some privacy.

"No," Nick said. "You've put up with my nerves all week. You should stay."

Nick sat at the table, and Brian handed him the envelope. "Here is Elizabeth from elementary school until today."

Nick took it warily. "She's alive?"

"She's alive."

Nick's hands shook as he unsealed the envelope. His lips moved as he read quietly. His facial expression ran the full spectrum of emotions with each line. When he finished, he handed the paper to Jimmy and buried his face in his hands.

Jimmy wasn't the smoothest reader. He said he was too nervous to read. He handed it to Angelo and asked him to read it out loud. Angelo did.

Nick looked up when he finished and Angelo said, "This is great news, Nick. My God. She's right here. You'll be able to see her easily."

"Yeah," Jimmy said. "And think of all the gas money we'll save not having to go to Washington. And the tolls. I've been thinking about that."'

Angelo glared at him. "You really are a dimwit, Jimmy."

Nick ignored them. “All this time,” he mumbled, barely audibly. “She’s been right here, just eight miles away, all this time. All those trips Jimmy and I took to the VA in Philly while she was working there. I may have passed her in the hallway at Aria. We’ve been there for stuff while she worked there.”

“That stinks, Uncle Nick, “Johnny said. “But you’ve got to shake it off. She’s here. You’ll see her. You deserve to be happy about that.”

“I know. And I will. It’s just a shock right now. I can’t thank you guys enough for finding her.”

“Don’t thank us,” Johnny said. “We were on it, but it was Carrie who made the breakthrough. The rest was easy.”

Nick thought of the letter again. “Beautiful and smart. I love that girl. You guys have to bring your wives around more often, and your kids.”

Brian had enclosed a screenshot of Elizabeth’s house taken from Google Earth.

Jimmy felt bad about his gas comment. “Wanna go see her, Nick? I can drive you now.”

“Thanks, Jimmy. Not yet. I need to let it all sink in.”

He picked up the image of the house. It was a modest, single-family, nicely manicured home, with a driveway, but no garage. “There’s no car in the driveway in this picture. Do you know what kind of car she drives? I want to make sure she’s home when I go. If there is a car, I want to be sure it’s hers and not a boyfriend or something.”

Brian smiled. “Good idea. Never thought of it. We’ll get it tomorrow from the DMV.”

Brian handed him a second envelope. “We found this on Google. We wanted to give you a chance to process things gradually. I think you’ll like it.”

Nick opened the envelope. It was a photo from a year earlier of four women from the Langhorne Arts Society at the dedication of a Thomas Hicks mural in town. The woman on the far right was identified as Liz Ambrose, secretary.

Nick studied the photo and smiled. “Damn, she looks great.” He handed the photo to Jimmy to pass around.

“She stayed trim,” Nick said. “The blond hair is gone, but I like it. What do you call that color?”

“Ash blond,” Johnny said.

“That’s it,” Nick said. “Ash blond. And look at that smile. The same beautiful smile.”

Angelo and Jimmy agreed.

Nick frowned and rubbed his face. He got quiet for a few seconds and then shook his head. “I can’t go. Forget it. Sorry for all the work you did, but I can’t do it. It was a bad idea.”

“No way, Nick,” Angelo said. “You’ve got to see her.”

Nick shook his head. “Look at her. She looks great. She’s active. She goes out. She has a house that she cares for. Me? I’m a friggin’ wreck and a misfit. Who was I kidding?”

The guys exchanged glances not knowing what to say. Finally, Johnny sat next to Nick and asked everyone to give them some privacy. The others nodded and Johnny waited for them to leave for the back room.

Nick said, “Don’t be mad, Johnny.” But instead of anger, tears were welling in Johnny’s eyes.

He cleared his throat and said, “Uncle Nick, you have been my idol all my life. I love my dad, and respect what he did, going to Canada. Looking back and reading about it, he was right. It was the most misguided war in history, a terrible mistake that cost so much, not just in lives lost, but in dreams shattered. If more felt the way he did earlier, maybe much of that suffering could have been avoided. I don't know.

"But like most of the country, you didn't know that then, at least early on. All you knew was that your country needed you and you volunteered. You were the best America had to offer- intelligent, athletic, a natural leader. I was an infant living in Canada when you went. But I've seen my dad's scrapbook of you guys, especially you, and you were someone I learned to admire. Football captain, National Honor Society, Prom King. I mean you can't make that stuff up. And your accomplishments in the military, a friggin' Green Beret for God's sake.

"The more I read about who you were and what you suffered, the more I grieved. But it inspired me too. I know that to this day my dad thinks I enlisted out of some deep psychological need to atone for his actions. That's not true. As I said, I think he was right for that war." Johnny emphasized the word that. But I also know that the world is a dangerous place, and the mistake in Vietnam doesn't change the fact that we need the best and brightest to serve. You were the reason I enlisted. You were my inspiration. "Each time I completed another phase of my training, jump school, desert survival, jungle warfare, any of it, I thought of you because I knew you went through it too.

"When I'd come home, and all you guys were here to greet me and congratulate me, I appreciated it, but I knew you were the only one who could fully appreciate what I did in special forces training."

Nick had tears in his eyes. He grabbed Johnny's arm and said, "Stop!"

Johnny brushed his hand away and said loudly, "No, you stop. I'm not finished."

"You have every right to be angry about what you went through, and what you're still going through. But the gooks, as you call them, didn't beat you. You beat them. You survived. The entire nation saluted you when you got off that POW plane.

"Two years ago you took a giant step when you started working out with weights and an exercise routine. I could see the difference it made in you. I was proud of you then, and I want to be proud of you now. I can accept your anger. I can understand a degree of self-pity. But I can't and I won't accept you being a quitter. You had a dream a couple of days ago, and I was more excited for you than I've been in years, maybe ever. But what I just heard today, calling yourself a wreck and a misfit, doubting yourself, I can't buy that.

"You were brave enough to volunteer to rescue that pilot, and you're afraid to face a woman you've thought about for years because you have a limp and have been cocooned in the deli for so long that you've forgotten how to talk with people. That's bullshit."

Johnny gave Nick a playful punch on the arm. "By the way, Carrie has seen the pictures of you when you were a young man. She thinks you're still ruggedly handsome."

Nick smiled. "Has she seen an optometrist lately?'

Johnny turned serious again. "Please, Uncle Nick. I need you to do it for me and for you. Do it. Go see the girl."

Nick exhaled deeply and rubbed his eyes. "I love you, Johnny."

Johnny nodded. "The girl?"

Nick paused and said quietly, "Okay." Then he smiled and said louder, "Okay. I'll go."

Chapter 8

Nick checked his phone and told Jimmy to turn left at the stop sign.

"It says here, we're a mile away. This app that Johnny installed is pretty neat."

Nick had been thinking about the cocoon reference ever since Johnny raised it. He loved the guys at the deli and the security the deli offered, but he was realizing how isolated he had been.

"Maybe Johnny had a point about the cocoon," Nick said, more to himself.

"Huh?" Jimmy said.

"Never mind. I was just thinking out loud."

"Well, that thing is amazing," Jimmy said. "You don't have to worry about where you're going."

"Yes, the app works well, but I am very worried about where I'm going."

"That doesn't make sense."

"I was speaking metaphorically about life."

"I have no idea what you're talking about."

"Doesn't matter. Make another left up ahead. We're just a mile away. Remember, slow enough so we can check things out, but fast enough that we don't look suspicious. And if you get a flat, keep going. I don't care if you ride on the rim. We can't stop at her house."

"I've got it," Jimmy said. "Remember, it was my idea to do a test run. What kind of car does she have again?"

"A two thousand seventeen Camry. Okay, here's the street. Her house is number 169. Go slow until we catch the numbers."

He checked the mailboxes. "There's 135, 139, ok, we're going the right way. Keep this speed. Just watch where you're going while I check the numbers."

Jimmy kept his eyes straight.

"There's 157. Slow down just a little. 165, 167, 169. There it is."

Nick slid down in the seat a little as they went by. The house looked just like the photo he'd seen, only better. More cheerful. A silver Camry was in the driveway.

They drove to the end of the street and turned. Nick said, "Pull over. I need to get my breath."

Jimmy glided the car to the curb and parked. He looked at Nick and smiled. "We did it, but can I ask you a question? Why did you slide down in the seat when we went by? Did you think Liz would look out the window and say, 'That guy in the car looks like a patient I had back in 1972?'"

"Wiseass. I was nervous. Natural reaction."

"Then it's good we took this dry run to get the jitters out."The whole thing didn't feel right to Nick. He was acting like a high school kid driving past his girlfriend's house hoping to see her, instead of a seventy-plus-year-old combat veteran scoping out a woman who hadn't seen him in decades.

Nick thought for a moment and said, "This is schoolboy stuff, Jimmy. Maybe I should just go back right now and ring the doorbell. Get it over with."

"No!" Jimmy snapped. Then in a more even voice, he said, "No."

"Why not?"

Now Jimmy was nervous. "They said..."
"Who said?"
"Nobody. Nobody said anything."
Nick looked at him. "What's up, Jimmy? "
"Nothing. I have to go to the bathroom really bad. Check the phone and tell me how to get back."
"Okay. I guess it's better to let this sink in first. Plan it out."
"Right," Jimmy said, looking relieved.

When they arrived at the deli, Nick was surprised to see the closed sign on the door. Angelo never closed on Saturday. Jimmy said, "Angelo probably forgot to flip it this morning." He tried the door. It was unlocked. Jimmy held it open and said, "After you."
Nick walked in and was greeted with a chorus of "Surprise!" Donna, Angelo's wife, was behind the counter. Carrie and her daughter, Gracie, were there, and Brian's wife, Jenny, with their daughter, Stella. There was one other woman Nick didn't know.
Everyone cheered and little Gracie ran up and hugged Nick's legs. "Surprise, Uncle Nick!"
"Thank you, honey." He kissed the top of her head and then greeted the others who had lined up to give him a hug. Carrie was last and said, "Hello, Handsome," and gave him a peck on the cheek.
There was food on the table and pitchers of mimosas and Bloody Marys.
"What's all this? Where are the guys?"
"You're spending some time with the girls today. The guys are at the Little League field watching a game."

She turned to Jimmy and said, “Good job, Jimmy. You can join them now.” Jimmy eyed the food. Carrie laughed and said, “Take a sandwich with you.”

Nick said to Jimmy, “You knew this?”

“Yeah. I didn’t really have to go to the bathroom. I still don’t. Have fun.”

He wrapped a sandwich in a napkin and left.

“So, what’s all this? Nick asked.

“Honestly,” Carrie said. “We know about Liz and we’re excited. We’re here to help you spruce up a little.”

“And” Jenny added, “it wouldn’t hurt to be around women a little.”

“I’m embarrassed,” Nick said.

“Well, you’ll have to get over it. We’re your friends and we’re cheering for you. Let’s start with a drink. We have a couple of beers on ice, too.”

As everyone moved to the table, Carrie led Nick toward a woman who had been waiting in the background. “Nick, this is my friend, Christine. She’s my hair stylist.”

Christine shook his hand and said, “You’re right, Carrie, he is handsome.”

Nick stammered, and Carrie said, “She’s here to do your hair.”

“My hair! No way.”

Christine laughed. “Maybe ‘do your hair’ isn’t the right term. We’re just going to do a little trim..”

“I cut my own hair,” Nick protested. “Sometimes Jimmy helps me.”

Jenny smiled. “We know. That’s why Christine is here.”

“I could go to a barber if I have to.”

“No worries, Nick,” Christine said. “One-third of the customers in my shop are men. Things have changed.

You've got great, thick hair. We're not going to change your look. We're just going to trim it, clean it up, and give you a sharp but natural look "

Nick stopped protesting.

Carrie handed him a beer. "Here, relax a little before we talk about your nails."

"Nails!" Nick exploded. "No way you're going near my nails."

Now everyone laughed. "No offense, Nick, but your nails are crooked, maybe chewed a little, and you look as if you just changed the oil on Jimmy's car. We thought as long as Christine was here, she'd clean and file them and buff them up."

Nick looked at Donna and said, "You better make sure that door stays locked. When are the guys coming back?"

Donna smiled. "Don't worry, Nick. They're going to Itri after the game for pizza, wings, and beer. But I'll guard the door for you."

They sat at the table and had drinks and sandwiches. Nick loosened up and started telling jokes. After a while, Carrie said, "The girls have some gifts for you."

Gracie and Stella went to the corner to gather boxes.

Nick melted every time he saw the girls, especially Gracie, who he saw more often. "These are from Amazon" Gracie said, "so you can return them if they don't fit or if you don't like the colors. Uncle Jimmy got us all of your sizes."

Nick didn't want to hurt the girls' feelings, but he wasn't sure he liked the idea of people picking out clothes for him.

Carrie read his face and said, "Don't worry Nick. We're not changing you. These are the clothes you already wear, just a little newer, and maybe with a trimmer, more contemporary cut."

Gracie giggled. "She means no more baggy-butt pants."

Nick grinned. "Is that what I wear?"

"Well..."

"Then I guess I'm glad you got me new ones."

The girls unpacked each box. There was a pair of Khakis, two pairs of jeans, a dress shirt with a button-down collar, a plaid shirt, a navy blue short-sleeved golf shirt, and a woven belt.

"What do you think, Nick. Nothing crazy, huh?" Carrie said with a smile.

"Not at all. I like them. The pants look comfortable too."

"Are the shirts okay," Jenny asked? "The colors?"

"They're perfect. You guys are so kind. This has been fun."

"In case you think we've forgotten," Carrie said. "it's time for the hair and nails."

Nick mimicked a moan. "Okay, let's get it over with."

"Wait!" Gracie said. "We forgot the other box." She ran to get the remaining box from the corner and gave it to Nick.

Nick opened the box and took out a pair of new shoes. He was momentarily stunned. His smile faded, but he recovered quickly. He hoped no one noticed. Still, his hands shook slightly as he removed them from the box and he stared at them without speaking.

Gracie was excited. "We wanted to dress you from head to toe, but mom said you didn't like hats. So, I said, let's at least do the toes."

Carrie laughed. "This was all Gracie's idea."

"Do you love them, Uncle Nick?"

Nick stammered. "They're very nice honey."

"Do you want to try them on?"

He struggled to control his shaking as he checked the size. "They're my size, Gracie. I'm sure they'll fit. I'm just not sure I'm ready for new shoes yet."

Carrie wasn't sure why Nick was acting strangely, but he'd been a good sport all afternoon, and she didn't want to push it.

"Amazon gives customers thirty days to return items. You can keep them for now and decide later if you like."

"Yes," Nick said blankly, "Let's do that. I'll decide later."

CHAPTER 9

The young woman seemed a bit surprised when she entered the deli. It must not have been the setting she was anticipating for the interview.

Angelo was behind the counter, and she introduced herself. "Hi, I'm Mallory Baldwin from Temple University. I'm supposed to meet Nick Hardings here."

Angelo directed her to the table where Nick was sitting. Nick stood when she approached.

She extended her hand and introduced herself. "I want to thank you again for allowing me this interview."

"My pleasure," Nick said. "Please have a seat. Can I get you something to eat? Angelo makes an incredible cheesesteak."

She looked as if she existed on kale salads and grilled chicken. She was slender and smartly dressed, with brown hair with red highlights that reached her shoulders. She declined the sandwich but accepted a bottle of water that Angelo placed in front of her.

"May I record this? I'd rather focus on our conversation than take notes while you're speaking."
"Sure."
She placed a small device on the table and began.
"So, by way of review, I am a second-year graduate student in a Master's program at the Temple University School of Journalism. My professor is constantly searching for authentic and timely stories on which we can find primary source individuals to interview on the topic.

"As you may know, recently there was a prisoner-of-war exchange in the Middle East. My professor thought it would be a good idea to locate an actual former prisoner of war to get his perspective."
"And you found me."
"Yes. I began my search expecting to find POWs from the Iraq or Afghan wars, but when your name came up in my search, I became fascinated by your story, especially the twist it took in 2016."
Nick nodded.
"If you don't mind, I'd like to go back to the beginning in 1971 to make sure I have my facts correct."
She reviewed the mission to free the downed pilot from captivity in the Viet Cong village, the wounds Nick suffered, his capture, two-year captivity, release, return to America, his long ordeal at Walter Reed, the awarding of the Distinguished Service Cross, and his eventual return to civilian life. She was on the money for each phase of the story, and Nick was impressed.
"You've done your homework, young lady. I wish all journalists were as accurate."

She smiled briefly and moved on. "First, I want to thank you for your service and sacrifice."

"The service was voluntary, but I didn't have much choice with the sacrifice part."

"No, I suppose not."

"Do you know what became of the pilot you freed?"

"No, I don't. Maybe that could be your next assignment."

"What would you say to him if you had the chance?"

Nick thought for a while. "I guess I'd say that I hope he led a healthy and productive life."

"Are you disappointed that he never contacted you?"

Nick shrugged. "I never thought about it. I think each of us, you, me, him, we all just try to survive. Who knows what he might have been going through?"

"So it never bothered you?"

"I don't know. Maybe a little."

She paused as if weighing whether to ask the next question.

"What if you ever came face to face with your captors, the people who tortured you?"

"Off the record?"

"Why?"

"Because there are two little girls in my life who I wouldn't want reading it. And because off the record is the only way you'll hear me say it."

"Okay, off the record." She switched off the recorder.

"If I ever came face to face with my captors, they wouldn't leave the room alive."

She raised her eyebrows. "Wow. That was abrupt."

Nick shrugged, "Not much to think about on that point."

"No room for forgiveness? Reconciliation? Some things have been written about American World War II POWs who suffered brutal, sadistic treatment at the hands of their Japanese captors and forgave them years later."

Nick shook his head. "I guess those guys were better men than me. What my captives did to me and the others with me is unforgivable. Don't get me wrong. I don't obsess about them and certainly never wanted to go looking for them, but if we were in the same room..."

"Let's go back to 2016." She switched on the tape recorder "I found so much about your original story, but then virtually nothing for the next forty-five years or so until 2016. Why was that?"

"I came home physically and emotionally shattered. I was angry over the years I lost, the torture I endured, the lingering effects, and the persistent nightmares. I had nothing to say."

"I did find a couple of stories about Vietnam POWs in which you declined comment."

"Like I said, I had nothing to say."

"So, what changed in 2016?"

"You know what changed."

"I do, but I'd rather hear it from you."

"It's an old story. Everyone knows about the Trump-McCain thing. It's not worth retelling."

"But they don't know it from the perspective of another POW."

Nick smiled. "So that's the hook. That's your ticket to an A in the course?"

She smiled. "Hopefully, if it's written well."

"I have no doubt it will be." He exhaled and said, "I'll make you a deal. I'll talk about the 2016 mess if you promise to do a subsequent piece sometime about the substandard treatment veterans and their survivors still receive when they return."

"That's a deal if I can count on your help with it."

"Done."

She cleared her throat. "Okay. Now back to 2016. How about if you just tell the story and then I'll follow up with questions?"

"Okay, but it's one you already know. Trump was gearing up to run for president, and it was no secret he and John McCain had no love for each other. At one point in an interview with a reporter, he called John McCain a loser. It was in the context of the previous time McCain ran for president and lost, but nevertheless, he called him a loser. I thought it was very disrespectful. McCain was a former Navy combat pilot. He was shot down by a surface-to-air missile over North Vietnam. He was able to eject, but when he did so he broke a leg and both arms. The VC watched him descend and then beat him mercilessly before taking him to captivity."

Nick paused and looked at Mallory as if to ensure she was getting this.

"He was held in captivity for five years! Tortured, nearly starved, suffering from illness and injuries that went untreated. Five years! And Trump had the audacity to call him a loser."

He sat back and lowered his tone. "That disrespect coming from a guy who missed the war because of some chicken-shit story about bone spurs; it got me. But then, the reporter said something like, 'you're calling a war hero a loser.' And Trump said, 'He wasn't a war hero. All he did was get captured.'"

Nick leaned forward and said it louder. "All he did was get captured! He said that, and I saw red. But that wasn't enough for Trump. He added, 'I like the guys who don't get captured.' Should I say that again?" He leaned even closer, and Mallory flinched. "Should I repeat that?"

Mallory said softly, "No, Mr. Hardings. I got it."

"Call me Nick, and I didn't mean to startle you."

"No worries, Nick. I completely understand."

Nick shook his head. "Do you?"

Mallory looked embarrassed. "I apologize. I guess that sounded dumb. I want to understand. I guess it's different."

He nodded his agreement. "I know you do, and I appreciate it. Should I go on?"

"Please do."

"Look, I'm not saying all POWs are heroes. I certainly wasn't."

"Let me interrupt you," Mallory said. "You may not have been a hero just because you were captured, but you were a hero doing what caused you to get captured. You won the Distinguished Service Cross."

"That's kind of you, but I don't see it that way. I was just doing my job."

"A job you volunteered for."

Nick waved her off. "Back to McCain. He may not have been a hero just because he was shot down and captured, but he was certainly a hero for what he did after being captured."

The statement seemed to surprise her as if what was coming would be new. "McCain's father was an admiral in the U.S. Navy, " Nick said. "After nearly two years in captivity, the North Vietnamese offered to release him as a courtesy to the father. Of course, the real reason was for the propaganda benefit of being able to tell other prisoners that McCain went home because he was special, an admiral's son. But guess what? McCain refused, adhering instead to the honored practice of releasing prisoners in the order they were captured. McCain told them others were captured before him and they should be released first. This infuriated the Vietnamese and the beatings intensified."

He paused again and looked at her. "That is what a hero does, and for Trump to dismiss it turned my stomach."

"Everyone already knows what I've said. You knew it. And a lot of people thought, damn, that's not nice to say about John McCain, and it wasn't. It was an outrage. But what about all the other POWs? Can you imagine them, me, hearing that? That son-of-a bitch who wraps himself in the flag like some big patriot demeaned every American serviceman who was ever captured."

Mallory shook her head. "I have to admit, I'm ashamed to say I never thought of it that way."

"Not many did. I want you to imagine what it was like for a former POW to hear that. Imagine the mother of, wife of, child of, or sibling of a former POW hearing that.

But that's still not the worst part."

Mallory sat back wondering what was to come.

"I thought to myself, it's terrible, but he's finished. This country would never tolerate such a statement about men in uniform from a person who wants to be commander-in-chief. But guess what?"

Mallory put her head in her hands. Of course, she knew what was coming next, but Nick had to say it.

"I'm sorry Mallory, to do justice to this story you have to feel it, not just know it."
Mallory nodded and Nick went on.
"The country didn't abandon him, it embraced him. People flocked to his rallies, with stars and stripes everywhere. They cheered wildly and then voted for him. That, Mallory Baldwin, was the worst part. That was the part that broke my heart, and I'm sure the hearts of others. The only thing worse than the isolation of a prison camp is to be abandoned at home."
He took a deep breath and said, "That's why I spoke out in 2016, for all the good it did. Are there any other questions I can answer for you?"
Tears welled in Mallory's eyes as she shook her head. "I'm so sorry, Nick. Let me know when you're ready for that other story we agreed upon. I'm in." She reached over and turned off the recorder.

Chapter 10

Nick selected the day fro his visit and everyone gathered at the deli for the sendoff. Carrie pulled Nick into the corner for a quiet moment.
"Having everyone here is making me nervous," Nick said.
"I know. Jimmy had the right intention by inviting everyone, but I agree with you."
"She might turn me away and when I come back everyone will know it. I'll be embarrassed."

"She might, Nick. I'm not going to lie to you. But I have a feeling she won't."
Nick had shared his planned speech with Carrie earlier.
"That speech is the best I've heard since Tom Cruise's speech to Renee Zellweger in the Jerry McGuire movie."
"I don't know it."
"Trust me. Every woman in America from Liz's era knows it and loves it."
"I do trust you. "
She smiled. "I will say it is a bit unorthodox to ring a person's doorbell and say, 'Can I kiss you?' but who knows. Just remember, no matter what happens you have a room full of people who love you. You told me so many times that you love Teddy Roosevelt's Man in the Arena speech. It may be a little corny to say so, but to paraphrase, if you have a good outcome, wow, it will be awesome, and if you fail, you'll fail while daring greatly, That's you today. You are daring greatly, and everyone respects you for it."

She eyed him up and down. He wore a new pair of jeans, the plaid shirt untucked, and he'd polished a pair of loafers he had in the closet. He held a small box of candy. He'd told Carrie he didn't know what to do with his hands while he spoke to Liz, and she suggested holding a box of sweets might do the trick. He liked the idea.

"You look great, Nick." She adjusted his collar and patted his chest. Then she gave him a kiss on the cheek. He looked over his shoulder to make sure they were alone. Then he looked at her and said softly, "Thank you for the letter."

She smiled and said, "Good luck. Don't let Jimmy eat the candy on the way."

Jimmy bumped the curb as he parked across the street and one house away from Liz's. "Sorry, Nick. My nerves."
They were relieved to see the Camry was in the driveway.
"Good luck, Nick"
"Thanks for waiting. This might take two minutes or two hours."
"I'll be here."
Nick nodded. He seemed more confident than Jimmy expected. He opened the door and left. Jimmy felt his limp was less pronounced as he watched him walk to the house. Jimmy had hidden a pair of small binoculars he'd won at a carnival. They worked over short distances. He brought them out now and focused on Nick as he approached Liz's door.
Jimmy had heard the speech several times. He thought of it as being in three parts. First Nick would reintroduce himself. Then all the stuff about how much he appreciated what Liz had done for him, and finally the big stuff at the end.
Jimmy watched as Nick rang the bell and waited.
Several seconds passed before Liz appeared at the doorway and Nick started talking. Soon her hands went to her mouth as Jimmy imagined he told her who he was. Jimmy thought she must have remembered if she reacted that way. Then, her hands returned to her side and she just stood there and listened. Finally, when Jimmy assumed Nick had made it to the end, without saying a word, she took a step forward, put her arms around his neck, and kissed him.

Nick was holding the box of chocolates, but he hugged her with one hand. When they parted, she still hadn't spoken, but she took him by the hand and led him inside.

Jimmy was floored. It went just as Nick had hoped. Even better. He slid the binoculars back under the seat, took out a comic book, and settled in for the wait.

Ten minutes passed, maybe fifteen, when Jimmy noticed movement at the house. Liz had come out and was walking toward his car. She crossed the street and came toward him. He tried to lower the window but had to start the car first. He started the car, and she laughed as he finally lowered it.

"You're Jimmy," she said with a million-dollar smile.

Jimmy tried to say yes, but his mouth wasn't working.

"Please come inside for coffee. Nick and I have a lot of catching up to do."

CHAPTER 11

Jimmy said he was tired from so much driving. "I checked the speedometer. We drove sixteen miles round trip."

"Odometer," Nick said.

"Huh?"

"A speedometer measures speed. An odometer measures distance."

"Whatever, I'm tired "

"You've had a long day. Why don't you drop me off at the deli and go get some rest?"

"Yeah, I think I'll do that."

Privately, Nick was relieved. A little less noise was fine by him.

Nick got out and thanked Jimmy for driving.

Nick entered the deli and was relieved to see it empty except for Angelo who was doing food prep behind the counter.

"Hey, Angelo. Where is everyone?"

"Carrie sent them all home. She thought you'd want some privacy when you got back."

"She was right," Nick said.

Angelo nodded. "I agree. I don't want to bug you about details. I'd settle for a simple thumb up or thumb down over how it went."

Nick gave him two thumbs up but didn't smile."

"Good," Angelo said, not sure how to read the mixed signal. "Carrie left you her number in case you wanted to talk."

"Yeah, I think I do."

"Grab a beer from the back room and talk there if you want some privacy."

"Thanks, I will. She already put her number in the phone Johnny got me."

Carrie answered on the first ring. Hoping for the best but fearful of the worst, her voice was neutral. "Hi, Nick."

"How did you know it was me?"

"You're on my contact list, so your name comes up when you call."

Nick cursed to himself. During his self-imposed isolation, his cocoon life as Johnny called it, he'd made himself a

"So, for starters, go to dinner. Don't worry about the big picture. If you miss her when you're apart, see her more often. If things don't turn out the way you thought, see her less. Maybe just be friends or maybe something much more. Just get started and see where things take you."
"That's all good from my end, but what if we end up wanting different things? What if it turns out that one of us wants more or less than the other? Then what?"

"You poor, poor boy," she said mockingly. "You don't know how things are going to turn out. That's what everyone thinks about when they consider a relationship. Welcome to the universe."
Nick didn't respond. Carrie added. "I dated Johnny for two years in high school. During our senior year, my father was transferred to Italy, and we had to move. Johnny and I were devastated. As far as Dad knew, we'd be there for at least three years. Right before we left, after a couple of weeks of tears and long talks, I broke up with him because I thought it was the responsible thing to do. Johnny wanted to stay together, although we'd be an ocean apart, which was crazy. It broke my heart, but I told him it had to be over. I went to Italy, moved on, and eventually sent him a letter saying I had a new boyfriend and I hoped he'd find someone to be happy with.

"As soon as Johnny graduated, Brian paid for him and Brian to come to Italy. He had my address from my letter and went to our home. My mom always liked him and was shocked to see him. She told him I usually went to the fountain in the town plaza after school. It was where all the kids gathered. He went there and found me with my new boyfriend. I was stunned. He said he wanted to talk with me. He'd traveled so far, and I thought I owed him that, but Nunzio, my boyfriend, said no. Johnny tried to be polite, but Nunzio was a bit arrogant and said somewhat obnoxious. Johnny warned him, but Nunzio didn't back off. Johnny warned him again, I knew what was coming and begged Nunzio to back off and for Johnny to leave him alone. When Nunzio got in his face again, Johnny picked him up and threw him in the fountain, humiliating him and me in front of all my new friends. Johnny looked at the guy fully clothed and struggling to get up with a soaking wet coat and backpack and said, 'stay there until I'm gone.' He turned to me and said, 'That didn't work out the way I planned. I love you, and we'll be together soon.' Then he and Brian left. I was furious with him, but at the same time, I thought it was the most romantic thing ever."

Nick laughed aloud. "Johnny told me that once. He left out some of the details, but he told me about the fountain. I loved it. That's Johnny."

"My point, Nick is that relationships are complicated. People may want different things at different times. People evolve. You can't be afraid of being hurt or hurting someone else. Just be honest whenever you can and roll with whatever comes along."

"I guess you're right," Nick said reluctantly.

"So will you go to dinner?"

"Definitely."

Chapter 12

Nick sat across from Johnny and Carrie at a table at the King George Inn overlooking the Delaware River and boat docks.

"I want to thank you both for doing this."

"Our pleasure," Carrie said. "Although I'm sure this is not necessary."

Nick had asked them to do an out-to-dinner dry run in advance of his dinner date with Liz that weekend.

"How long has it been since you last went out to dinner, a couple of months? Longer?"

Nick stared at her blankly.

"A year?" Carrie asked "Two?"

"You don't want to know."

"It doesn't matter," Johnny said. "We're just curious."

"It was sometime in 1969. I was on R and R with my unit, and we went to a restaurant in Saigon."

Johnny reflected on that. "Wow, you were a soldier in Saigon, and I was an infant in Montreal with my expatriate parents who were hoping for the chance to come home. Thank God for Jimmy Carter. Without his pardon, we would have never met."

Normally, mentioning draft dodgers in front of a combat vet wouldn't go over well, but Johnny knew that wasn't the case with Nick about Angelo.

Nick laughed. "You'd be up there freezing your ass off and cheering against the Flyers."

"Back to dinner," Carrie said. "When was the last time you went out to dinner in the states?"

Nick shook his head as if they didn't get what he was saying.

"The first time I walked in the deli after being released from Walter Reed, Johnny's grandfather, Angelo's father, welcomed me home and said, "From now on, you eat here as our guest."

Nick smiled and added, "I guess I took him literally. Fortunately, he was a great cook. So is Angelo."

Carrie looked stunned. "Are you saying you never...?

Nick smiled. "I have not eaten in what you'd call a restaurant since Saigon. We did Burger King and years ago we'd get pancakes on Saturdays at the Radcliffe Cafe, but other than that, nothing like this."

Carrie said, "Wow. Every time I think I know all there is to know about you, I learn something else. I mean, I saw you eating at the deli a thousand times, but I never assumed it was the only place you ate."

"Don't get me wrong. I haven't been sponging off the Marzos. I mean, I have, but it wasn't the money. The Marzos suffered so much when Angelo went to Canada. Some people were angry thinking their sons were in Vietnam while Angelo was safe, so business dropped off. They were stigmatized. Today, I think he did the right thing, but back then, they suffered a lot and carried a lot of guilt, just as your dad does today no matter how much I tell him he shouldn't."

Neither Carrie nor Johnny spoke so Nick continued.

"When I returned and they saw how mangled I was, their guilt was compounded. They actually needed to feed me. They got relief from it. I hated seeing people I loved in pain like that. So, in a strange way, I needed to eat there, to accept their kindness as my way of saying everything was okay."

Their waiter came with water and menus and took their drink orders. Nick ordered a beer, Carrie a white wine, and Johnny a Jack and ginger.

Carrie used the break to change the subject. As much as Johnny insisted that his military service was not driven out of a need to atone for his father, she still believed that had to be a part of it. She thought it best to move on.

"Okay," she said brightly, "so, let's think of your dinner with Liz as special in a couple of ways. It will be your first in a very long time, and a first for the two of you together."

Nick looked downcast. "It's crazy, isn't it? I'm so angry with myself. I've wasted so much time by shutting myself off from so much. I prided myself in not participating in the world around me, even scoffing at it. Looking back, I think I understand why, but it was foolish. I have a lot of catching up to do."

Carrie covered his hand with hers. "Maybe you did what you had to do, and maybe you overdid it a little, well, more than a little. But hearing you say you want to catch up is the best news."

Okay," Johnny said." Let's get down to business. Whether it's Saigon or breakfast at the Radcliffe Cafe, things haven't changed much. You've got a menu, a waiter, food, drink and the tip."

"Unless they have an electronic menu," Carrie added.

Nick's eyes shot up. "What's that?"

"You hold your phone up to a QR code, a circle with dots and lines, and the menu pops up on your screen."

"Holy shit!"

Carrie laughed. "Don't worry about it. I'm sure you'll pick a place with paper menus," Johnny jumped in. "Now, you're on a date, and the assumption is still that the man will pay. But some women resent that now. You do not discuss it, especially on a first date. That would be tacky. But, you send a subtle message that you're paying and that she can order whatever she wants. Again, you can't come right out and say that because it would sound condescending. So, here's what you do. You check out the menu, notice one of the most expensive items and say something like, "I heard the king crab is good here. That lets her know she doesn't need to be concerned about what she chooses. If when the bill comes and she tries to pay it or split it, you can let her know you'd like to see her again by saying. 'Why don't you get the next one if you like.'"

Nick smiled. "You're smooth, Johnny boy."

Carrie laughed out loud. "All that changed after we got married. Now he picks up the menu and says, 'Damn, this place is expensive.'" Then she added, "Here's another tip. Never, ever, ever, eat off her plate if she doesn't finish. Even if she has a delicious looking piece of steak left that's calling your name. Never say, are you going to eat that?"

"Got it."

"And most important," Carrie said, "be more interested in her than you are in yourself. Ask her about herself. Be interested in what she's saying and let her finish when she speaks."

"Geeze," Nick said. "I should have brought a notebook."

"You'll be fine," Johnny said. "Now let's decide what we want before the waiter comes back."
Nick grinned and said, "I hear the surf and turf is good here."

CHAPTER 13

Nick was honest with Liz about his driving. When he returned from Vietnam his leg was too severely injured for him to drive, so he never renewed his license or bought a car. Jimmy drove him wherever he had to go, but he had no intention of having Jimmy drive him on their date. Liz offered to pick him up, but he politely declined. He told her his friend Johnny had downloaded the Uber app to his phone and worked with him until he was confident using it.
Liz said an Uber was silly and that she'd gladly pick him up. But Nick was insistent. Sensing it was important to him, she agreed and offered a compromise. He'd take an Uber to her house, and they'd walk a couple of blocks to the Langhorne Hotel for dinner. It was a casual place with good food.

Nick arrived on time, closed out the Uber transaction, and found Liz waiting by the front door smiling. "Look at you, all cool after your first Uber ride. Congratulations."
Nick laughed. "I'm embarrassed about accomplishing something any high school kid could do."

She draped her arm through his and started to walk. "Technology is learned behavior. You just decided to start learning late. It will come easily to you."

The conversation was light as they walked. They discussed the weather, which was beautiful, and she gave a brief overview of her hometown of Langhorne.

The dining room of the Langhorne Hotel was a rustic, casual place with ceiling beams and a sign that read, *Established 1704.* A guy with an acoustic guitar was singing softly in the far corner and there was light chatter at the bar. Liz asked Nick if the place was okay, and he said it was perfect.

The hostess led them to their table. Nick's smile faded when he noticed a small cardboard tent with a QR code. Liz noticed his expression, followed his eyes, and laughed out loud.

"Oh, no. Nick won't be able to eat tonight."

Before he could respond she said, "This will be fun. Take out your phone."

He did, and she showed him how to interface with the image. She giggled as he missed the connection twice. When he suggested that she better do it, she said, "Heck no. If you don't do it, then we don't eat. Simple as that!"

The third time was a charm and she cheered softly when the menu appeared on his screen. "Okay, now scroll through and tell me the appetizers. "

They giggled a little as Nick read them out. When he finished, she said, "Would you scroll back up and read them again? I can't decide." Then she smiled and said, "Just kidding. What sounds good to you?"

When Nick said he didn't have a preference, she said, "We're not in any hurry, right?"

"I've got all the time in the world."

"Let's nibble on a cheese board before we order the rest."

Nick said that sounded good. He didn't share that he had never heard of a cheeseboard. He never saw one at Angelo's or on TV.

The waitress came and they ordered drinks. Then she looked at Nick. When he didn't respond, Liz said, "We'll have a cheese board for now."

Nick smiled and sat back. He thought he'd be nervous, but instead, he couldn't remember being this relaxed. She made things easy.

She returned his smile and said, "So what are you thinking?"

"I'm thinking you are fun, and I'm very glad I'm here."

"Me too." She checked her watch. "It's seven-twenty, and this place closes at eleven. We've got decades to catch up on, so you better get started."

"Me?"

"Yes. You're going first."

He thought about Carrie's advice, and said, "I'm more interested in your story."

Liz leaned forward and said playfully, "Listen, Buddy, you won the Uber dispute, so I get this one. That or else I'll sit at the bar and wait for some handsome twenty-something who likes cougars to buy me a drink."

"Fair enough," Nick said.

At that moment, it all came back to him. Forty-five years ago, he was alone in a dark hospital room planning to take his life when a young nurse swept into the room, threw open the curtains, and changed his life. Now so many years later, she was just as cute, perky, cheerful, and funny as she was then, with a self-confidence that was contagious. Then and now, it was impossible to be down when he was around her.

Their drinks and cheeseboard came, and Nick learned that it was simply a board with chunks of cheese and small piles of assorted peppers, olives, and things he didn't recognize. She introduced him to hummus, and Nick decided it was just okay. He liked the cheese and olives better and felt okay saying it.

She checked her watch. "Time is moving. You better get started."

CHAPTER 14

"Okay, I'll start, but it won't take long."

"We'll see about that because I have some questions."

"Fine, jump in whenever you like." He took a deep breath and began. "When the doctors decided I was well enough to be released, they were saying my life was no longer in danger, but I was in no way good."

"No, you were not," Liz said. "Maybe this would be a good time to tell you that I've always kept a journal. I don't make entries each day, but I do when something seems important enough.

"By far, the most important part of my career was the time I spent at Walter Reed during the war. I mean, I've treated patients all my life, but none impacted me more than the guys returning from Vietnam in such terrible condition. And no one impacted me more than you."

Nick smiled and said, "I bet you said that to all the guys."

Liz didn't return the smile. Instead, her voice turned more serious. "You were the only POW I ever treated, and that had a special impact on me. Most guys who came in wounded had been evacuated quickly and sent to medical institutions throughout the States. Maybe a week or two lapsed between their injury and when I got to treat them. But in your case as a POW, I knew many of your untreated injuries were two years old, and there were others more recent, obviously the result of recurring abuse and torture. That got to me. But that was the physical part. But I also couldn't imagine what the isolation was like. To be a wounded and malnourished prisoner, ten thousand miles from home, alone for two years and with no idea, when, if ever, you'd be released. So yes, Nick, no one impacted me more than you."

Nick nodded. "I'm sorry," he said softly. That was a dumb comment. Just trying to be funny. "

"I know. Don't worry about it." She went on. "So, I had several journal entries about you, and they changed over time. At first, the theme was the compassion I felt. Then there was heartache when I discovered you considered suicide. But in time, my entries changed to something difficult to describe. As your condition improved, your intellect and sense of humor became more apparent, and I felt an attachment to you. From there, I struggled between my attraction to you and my responsibility to maintain professional standards.

"Over the past decades, I would go back occasionally to read my journals from the Vietnam years. Sometimes I might read them five years apart, and sometimes more frequently. So, I want you to know that when you showed up at my door, I wasn't seeing a stranger. I was seeing someone very much alive in my memory."

Nick took a deep, slow breath and rubbed his eyes before speaking. "To think that all of these years while I thought of you, while you were doing the same thing.... I don't know what to say, except that it adds to a feeling of lost time and lost opportunity."

Their food arrived and neither looked at it.

Liz looked to have wiped away a tear. She said, "So what happened to you all of these years?"

"I went back to a deli owned by the parents of one of my friends and four of us gathered there every day since. Let me say that again. Four of us have gathered there every day since, including today. We made up quite a bunch, a draft dodger, a person who failed his army physical, a former army tunnel rat, and me."

Nick gave her a brief rundown of Angelo, Big Frankie, and Jimmy.

"Those guys and the deli became my refuge. They saved me. I guess we all saved each other."

Liz said, "I'd love to meet them sometime."

Nick kidded, "Be careful what you wish for."

He sipped his beer and continued. "My parents were divorced when I was young, and my father disappeared. My mother died while I was in prison camp."

Liz put a hand to her mouth. "My God, Nick. I knew she was deceased from when the hospital tried to contact her, but I had no idea it happened while you were in captivity."

Nick shrugged. “It was a long time ago, and I’ve got no more tears left for her, just good memories. So anyway, I returned to Bristol with no living relatives. I rented a one-bedroom, four-hundred-square-foot shoebox of an apartment to sleep in and went to the deli each day.

“Whatever good feelings I had when I was around you faded quickly once I was home. I was angry, angry at my condition, angry at the loss of my mother, angry that Jimmy was drafted when someone of his mental capacity should never have been, angry that they sent him down in VC tunnels, angry that a nice kid of limited capacity, the closest person I had to a brother, came home marred for life. I was angry because Angelo carried even worse guilt because he went to Canada while I was alive and fighting.

“I didn’t know any of this when I was in the hospital with you. Because of you, I was feeling better emotionally. I didn’t know what was happening to the other guys. When I got home, everyone I knew was screwed up because of the stinkin’ war. And then,” he gathered himself before finishing, “and then, we lost.”

He paused and said softly. “We friggin’ lost. What was it all for?”

Liz hated seeing him this upset and considered stopping him but decided it might be therapeutic and let him go. She was relieved to see he grew calmer when he continued.

“Then I watched as the new battle started, the battle by veterans to get the treatment and benefits they were entitled to. To keep my sanity, I focused on my physical therapy and improved.”

He felt he was going on too long and asked if he should stop.

“Absolutely not. Please go on.”

He did.

"My disability pension wasn't nearly enough to live on, even with my simple lifestyle and Angelo's generosity in the kitchen. When my condition improved enough, I went to work part-time in a wood shop owned by a classmate. He paid me under the table so it wouldn't affect my pension.

"Eventually, I channeled my anger into helping veterans and their families get the treatment and benefits they deserved. I'd write a letter to my congressman and the VA every day about a different family or hardship that came to my attention. As word got out, people from the area came to the deli to ask for help. I studied the law and became an advocate when other official avenues were too backed up to help. Helping others gave me a sense of purpose, but it was depressing work because each case was so sad. I guess it's a lot like being a nurse and seeing what you see."

He paused and looked at her food. "Please eat while I babble on. I'm not hungry anymore."

She pushed her plate aside and said, "I'm not either. Please go on."

"By now it's the 1990s. I'm still at the deli every day. Still working part-time and helping Angelo with little things. Then, veterans from the first Iraq war start coming home, and the stories began all over, especially the government's refusal to recognize the effects of what was later called Gulf War Syndrome. It was sad."

He chuckled a little and said, "Then something interesting happened. The congressman I'd been writing to was on the Veterans Affairs Committee. He would use his staff to help vets whenever he could. What I didn't know was that he had ordered his staff to save the letters and told them to let him know when the file reached one thousand.

When it did, I received notice that he was inviting me to testify before the committee at an upcoming hearing. He had asked his colleagues if, as a courtesy, they would allow a constituent who was a former POW and Distinguished Service Cross recipient to testify briefly, and they agreed. There were some heavy hitters from the VA and pentagon scheduled to testify, but they gave me five minutes before the main witnesses went on."

Liz flashed a big smile. "No way! That's amazing."

Nick continued. "I have a classmate who is an undertaker. He drove his limo and Jimmy, Big Frankie, Angelo and I went."

"Talk about being nervous," Liz said.

"Nope. Strangely, I wasn't. The whole time I spoke, I thought about all the stories I'd heard." He paused and wiped his eyes. "Did you know that if a married soldier whose family lived in military housing on the base was killed in action, the family would be evicted in 45 days?"

Liz's jaw dropped.

"Congress didn't know either. So no, I wasn't nervous. I was allotted five minutes, but I wish I had five hours."

He took a sip of his beer and said, "So that's it. I went back to my relatively reclusive life with one addition. A while back I began lifting weights, upper body only, and I enjoy it. Makes me feel a little more like the guy I was before Nam. I'm doing more physical therapy on my legs too. And now, with this Uber crap hanging over my head, I will be highly motivated to get this leg to the point where I can drive and buy a car!"

Liz smiled. "There you go! I believe you will." Then she turned serious and said, "That's quite a story, but you left out something important."
"What's that?"
"How and why did you find me?"

Nick didn't respond. He took a long pull of his beer, and said, "Okay."
He drank again before starting. "The why part is easy because I already told you. I sort of fell in love with you at the hospital and have thought about you every day since. I know that sounds crazy. At times I wondered whether it's a medical version of the Stockholm Syndrome, you know, the psychological condition in which hostages develop an emotional bond with their captors. I mean, I needed someone and you were there, but that bond never faded. Seeing you now... I don't know how to finish except to say again that I'm really glad to be here and I hope this isn't too awkward for you."
She smiled without answering. "So, how did you find me?"
"Do you want the long or short version?"
"The full story."
Nick shrugged. "Okay, full story. I used the FBI...
Liz interrupted. "FBI! Come on, Nick. Stop the kidding."
"I'm not. I have a nephew who..."
Liz interrupted again. "A nephew?' I thought you were an only child."
"I am. Angelo's son calls all of us uncles, and we consider him an adopted nephew. His name is Johnny Marzo. He's an FBI agent."
"Really?"

"Yes, really. I called him and said I needed his help, you know, unofficially to find someone. He said sure. I told him your name was Liz and you were a nurse at Walter Reed forty-five years ago. He asked for a last name, and I said I didn't have one."

Liz laughed. "You didn't know my last name?"

"Nope. You wore a brass plate that said, 'Liz.' That was it."

"Wow, the FBI. So, what happened?"

"Johnny is as straight as an arrow. He hoped all he had to do was call Walter Reed and ask them to give him a last name for a Liz who worked in 1971. Their records didn't go back that far, which meant he'd have to search tax and social security records of the hospital from that time."

"Geeze," Liz said.

"Johnny couldn't do that because it wasn't an official case, so he contacted his friend, Brian Kelly, a private anti-terror contractor who had "access" to databases."

She smiled. "Are you sure you aren't pulling my leg?"

"They were mulling over how to find you without breaking any laws when Johnny's wife found you for them."

"How?"

"She's a reporter, and she had a hunch. She got the date of the Distinguished Service Cross ceremony at the hospital. She thought that was a newsworthy event that a newspaper might cover. She did a microfilm search of the local paper for the day after the ceremony. She thought if any hospital official was mentioned, they could track that person down in hopes he or she was still alive and would know your name. Instead, she struck gold."

Liz perked up, "The photo! I remember now. I was at the ceremony, and they invited me to be part of the picture with the general and the doctor."

"Bingo. The caption identified you. Once they had your name, it was easy to track you to the present."

"Wow. Amazing. That took some effort."

"And some luck," Nick said. "So, I told you why I wanted to find you and how I found you, but you never asked why now after all these years?"

"I didn't have to. It's because you could hear the life clock ticking. Guess, what? So can I."

"Yup. So you got the full version. Now it's your turn."

The waitress came to check on their drinks and asked if everyone was okay when she noticed they hadn't touched their food. Liz said everything was fine and ordered another wine. Nick ordered another beer, winked at Liz, and said, "What the heck, I'm not driving."

Liz told her to leave the food because they might pick at it, and then the waitress was gone.

Nick checked his watch and said, "I left you plenty of time, but you better get started."

She was about to when he cleared his throat and said he had something to add before she got to her story. He popped a cold french-fry into his mouth and waited to swallow.

"My friend, Carrie, the one who found your photo, gave me some advice when she knew I'd see you. She said, be perfectly honest. Liz might not like what you say, but she should respect you for being truthful."

"Please don't tell me you're a murderer or bank robber. I'm having a nice time, and that would ruin it for me."

"It's nothing like that. I told you that Carrie found that newspaper photo of you along with your maiden name."

"Right."
"And I said once Johnny and Brian had your name, it was easy from there."
Liz nodded.
"So, to find you today, and separate you from maybe a hundred other Liz or Elizabeth Cherrys, they did it step by step. So first you marry and become Liz Ambrose, then Liz Ambrose has a child, then, years later, Liz has a second child, then she is divorced. In other words, they trace vital records which are public, to follow you to today."
Liz agreed, "I'm a member of the Langhorne Arts Society. That's how we would do a genealogy search. So where are you going with this?"
"I'm saying I know the milestones of your life, and I didn't want to sit here pretending I didn't while you told your story."
"I assumed as much, and honestly, it felt a little invasive when you first said it. But that's how it's done. So, I'm okay."
"So, I know the milestones, and I'm looking forward to hearing the why and how of your story."
"Before I start, since it's full disclosure time, I have something of my own to share. The day after we agreed to meet for dinner, I took a ride to the Margaret R. Grundy Library in Bristol and pulled the yearbook from your class. You were quite the big man at Bristol High, all-conference football, national merit scholar, pretty impressive. And prom king! So, tell me about Patti Weber. Pretty cute. Prom king and queen. Were you a thing? Are you in contact with her?"
Nick shrugged. "We were a thing until we weren't. I haven't seen or heard from her since. I don't know where she is."
"Will you be using your private team of agents to find her?"

Nick laughed. "Not a chance."

Liz said she had another question. "Why no college? You weren't just in the National Honor Society, you were a National Merit Scholar. "

"Biggest mistake of my life. Mom and I had no money. I had some small schools interested in me for football, and my counselor said I could get an academic scholarship. But I was attracted to the military. I was wrapped up in the patriotic thing about the war. A recruiter said with my creds I would be a candidate for officer candidate school. Plus, I'd start receiving a paycheck as soon as I was in.

"Once I got in and went through basic training, I got more interested in the macho thing and became a Green Beret sergeant. Then, I volunteered to rescue a pilot, and you know the rest."

"I'm glad I checked the yearbook. I hope you don't mind. The only Nick I knew was the guy in a hospital bed. Now I know more." She laughed and added, "But for a scholar, you're pretty much a dumb ass when it comes to the world around you."

Nick laughed too. "Like I said, I've been living in a cocoon. For some strange reason, I wanted it that way."

She took one of his French-fries and said, "I'm glad you just used the past tense, wanted, instead of want."

She paused and said," I'll start with my so-called marriage. Dr. Peter Ambrose joined the hospital about three years after you were discharged. He was young and handsome, with all the aura of a confident doctor. All the girls were gaga over him, and he didn't discourage it. He'd flirt with them all. I was flattered when he started paying most of his attention to me. We started dating and it was fun. It was obvious that he came from money that supplemented his already generous paycheck. His nice car, club membership, and fancy restaurants made it easy for me to overlook his arrogance. He taught me to sail and had season tickets to the Kennedy Center. We married after a brief engagement.

"Talk about a big mistake. His arrogance permeated every aspect of our lives. He was making all of the decisions when he was courting me, but I thought it was cute. I thought he enjoyed surprising me with restaurant choices, trips, whatever we did, but I soon learned that he expected to make decisions about everything.

"I expected to have children. We never discussed children, but I just assumed we'd have them. I was surprised to learn that he didn't want any. On that issue, I insisted, and he reluctantly gave in. I thought he would change after Peter was born, but instead, he saw the baby as a major intrusion into his lifestyle. As far as he was concerned, one was enough. But seven years later we had a second child, this time by accident, and Peter blamed me, said I had intentionally stopped my birth control pills. Our relationship got worse. He started leaving the house more often, and in time I learned that he was seeing other women. The marriage fell apart, and I learned that most of his finances were shielded from me. I didn't care. All I wanted was the children, and that decision was easy for him. He put forty-thousand dollars in escrow for their education with the understanding that would be it. He'd have no visitation rights or support payments. We divorced, and I decided to move back to Bucks County to be closer to my parents who would help with the kids. I applied for, and took a job with the Veterans Administration hospital in Philadelphia.

"From there, my professional life was uneventful. I didn't care for the work at the VA as much. At Reed, the patients were mostly trauma victims, and there was a sense of urgency and much more fulfillment for me as I treated them. Don't get me wrong, the work at the VA was no less important to the patients who received it, but it was more or less the general type of cases that you see in any hospital.

"I worked there for a few years, commuting from Langhorne until I finally transferred to Aria or Aria-Jefferson as you may know it. It was closer to home and actually paid better. Fast forward. I stayed there until I retired and began part-time work at a doctor's office."

Nick said, "Did any doctors sweep you off your feet?"

"As I said, my professional life was rather uneventful. I focused on my kids growing up and basically became a soccer mom."

"Where are your kids now? "

"Peter is a pharmacist working in Colorado. Privately, I think he has something to do with the legalized marijuana laws there. He's a bright guy and has always been ambitious, so I wouldn't doubt it. Kate has a nursing degree and lives in Falls Township."

She went on. "As you know, I'm involved with the Arts Society in town. I take yoga lessons and teach it occasionally. I do just enough to give my life meaning without being too busy."

Then she smiled and said, "And that, my friend, is a summary of my contented but uneventful life."

"I doubt it, " Nick said.

Liz looked surprised and Nick explained. “When I decided to visit you without calling first, I did it to guarantee myself one chance to tell you what I was feeling, face-to-face. I was afraid that if I called or mailed you, it would be easier for you to turn me away. But, still, I worried. Did you have a boyfriend? Were you engaged? Were you living with someone? I didn’t know what to expect when I knocked on the door, but I decided to take the chance.”
She waited for more, and he continued.

“You are a very attractive woman, far more so than most your age. You’re smart you’re upbeat, and fun to be around. So,” he said jokingly, “I have a hard time believing that there isn’t a guy in your life who might shoot me when he finds out I’m around.”
He smiled and added, “So I think I at least deserve a warning.”

Liz laughed and said, “You’re very flattering, but don’t worry. No one’s going to shoot you. I’ve dated men during these years, but nothing ever came of it. There were a couple of relationships that could’ve gotten serious, but I got the sense that they were frightened off by the prospect of raising someone else’s little kids. And there were a couple of other guys who seemed promising at first, but the more I got to know them the less interested I became. By the time the kids were grown, I’d settled into a comfortable life that didn’t include men. As I said, I’m involved in my community. I do yoga and play cards with the girls, and that is it.”
The waitress showed up, eyed the unfinished food, and asked if there would be anything else.

“I think we’re finished,”Liz said.

The waitress left a check and Nick reached for his wallet.

“We’re splitting this,” Liz said.

“Nope. I’ve got it.”

Liz reached for her bag and said, “No, really, I want to split it.”

“Tell you what,” Nick replied, “if it’s that important to you, why don’t you take the next one?”

Liz grinned and said playfully, “Oh, have we decided there will be a next one?”

Nick did an exaggerated exhale. He shook his head and said smiling. “I don’t know if you’re fun or more trouble than you’re worth.”

“It’s 2018, Nikki boy. Gender roles have changed since you’ve been exiled into that cocoon as you call it. I’ll make you a deal. We’re at the point in the night where there is sexual tension.”

Nick played along. “Really?”

“Yes. We’re going to walk home and summon your Uber along the way. Now, in the old days, and by that I mean your days, during the walk the guy would be wondering if it would be all right to kiss the girl. I mean, he’d want to, but he’d be wondering how to pull it off. Meanwhile, the girl, a passive participant, would be hoping he would. Well, like I said, times have changed, so here’s the deal. You’ll pay the check tonight and when we get to my house, I will kiss you. If that kiss is as nice as our first one, and I hear bells ringing and see shooting stars, then we’ll have another date and I’ll pay. If not, then it’s back to the cocoon for you and yoga lessons for me. “

Chapter 15

Nick's nerves were shot. Things were moving fast, too fast, and he needed the advice of the guys. They were gathered around the table at the deli. Angelo locked the door, produced beers for everyone, and reminded them that the coffee can in the back room was short a few bucks from the monthly beer contribution.

"I don't want to name names, but, I'm not running a damn charity here."

In fact, he was. He'd been feeding them for years and enjoyed doing it. But the beer thing was a sacred monthly ritual that had to be paid.

All eyes turned to Jimmy.

"Why do you guys always think it's me?"

"Because it's always you," Big Frankie said.

Jimmy lowered his eyes and confessed. "I've had extra expenses this month. I'm burning gas driving Nick to Langhorne to see his honey."

"She's not my honey, and you only did that twice," Nick said. "And I gave you gas money!"

"Yeah, but what about wear and tear on the tires? The oil? Windshield washer? Remember we drove through that construction zone and I had to clean the windshield?"

Big Frankie rolled his eyes, took out a ten from his wallet, and gave it to Angelo. "I paid for you last month, and I'm doing it again. But that's it. If you don't pay next month you're flagged."

"It won't happen again, Frankie. I'm getting my finances in order, and Nick said he's getting his learner's permit. Then he'll get his license and then a car, and I'll get some breathing room."

Everyone knew Jimmy could pay. After Vietnam, he worked at the steel mill for twenty-five years before they downsized. He collected a pension and social security.

"Why don't you just admit that you're cheap, Jimmy, Nick said. "You still have the First Communion money your relatives gave you."

Big Frankie winked at Nick and said, "That's not fair, Nick. You have to pass the test on the catechism to make your First Communion. No way Jimmy made it."

"Yes, I did," Jimmy protested." I just needed a little help from Sister Clara."

"I need proof," Frankie said. "Bring in a picture of you in the white communion suit."

Angelo had enough. "Knock it off. I have to reopen the store soon." He turned to Nick. "So, what kind of advice are you looking for?"

Nick took out his phone. "I got a text message from Liz."

"I knew it," Jimmy said, "Complications. Relationships have complications."

Nick ignored him and unlocked his phone.

"Let me read you this" He cleared his throat. "Hi, Nick. I hope things are good. As I told you, I'm on the board of the Langhorne Arts Society. We're having our annual cocktail party fundraiser, and I'd like you to be my date. Change that. I expect you to be my date. The event is next Saturday, and I'll give you more details later. In the meantime, read up on artist Edward Hicks in whose honor the event is held. I don't want my date to be tongue-tied as we mingle with the Langhorne elite. Ha. Can't wait to see you there. I've attached the invitation." He paused and looked at the guys. "I can't open the attachment."

Big Frankie took the phone from Nick and opened the attachment. He read for a moment and laughed. Then he checked it again and laughed louder. "This is going to be special," he said, handing back the phone and still trying to suppress a laugh. "It looks like it's going to be a very nice event, especially the part about black-tie, optional"

He burst out laughing again, and Jimmy said, "What's black tie, optional?"

"It means that Nick is going to look like a penguin that night. "

Nick was stunned. "A tuxedo?"

"It's optional," Big Frankie said. "But it certainly means you'll have to wear at least a suit"

"Complications," Jimmy said. "I called it."

Nick mumbled, "A suit?"

"I have one that might fit you," Angelo said. "But forget the suit for a minute. Let's talk about the invitation. She expects you to go?" Angelo emphasized *expects*. "I mean, is that a joke or is this girl a little pushy?"

"Nah, that's her way of being funny. She's not pushy; she's just really confident."

"This sounds serious," Jimmy said. "Is it serious Nick?"

"How can it be serious?" Nick said. "I've only been with her twice."

"Well," Angelo said. "Looks like number three will be you wearing a suit mingling with the elite of Langhorne, whatever that means, and sipping cocktails, while you talk about some artist named Edward Hicks. I'd say that's damn serious."

Nick thought back to his conversation with Dr. Braun. She had suggested baby steps. This wasn't baby steps, Nick thought. This was a leap. This was a bigger leap than Neil Armstrong on the moon, and Nick shook his head.

"Look," Angelo said. "Do you like this girl?'

"Yes," Nick said, without hesitation.

"Do you like to drink a little?"

"Yeah, sometimes I like to drink a lot. "

"Are you smart enough to do some reading and bullshit a little about whoever this artist is?"

"Yeah, I can do that."

"Then put on a damn suit and give it a shot," Angelo said.

Jimmy shook his head and said, "Complications."

"Better think it through," Frankie said.

Nick's head was spinning.

Big Frankie felt bad enjoying Nick's discomfort, but he couldn't resist one more playful jab. "You better Google this Edward Hicks guy if you go. You'll be representing Bristol before Langhorne society."

Chapter 16

Angelo was behind the counter when a woman walked in. She was wearing a pink jogging suit with purple sneakers. Her hair was pulled back in a ponytail. She was spry and attractive and looked to be in her late sixties. She reminded Angelo of Geena Davis. She flashed a broad smile and said, "Is Nick Hardings here?"

Angelo and Jimmy were seated at the table with their backs to her. They turned when they heard her voice, and Jimmy's jaw dropped.

"Liz!" He said before Angelo could reply.

She recognized him from his earlier visit and said, "Hi Jimmy."

Jimmy stammered. "What are you doing here?"

"I'm looking for Nick. I know he hangs out here. I hoped I could surprise him."

Jimmy was speechless, so Angelo introduced himself. "I'm Angelo Marzo."

She shook his hand and said, "Of course, of Marzo's deli. It's how I found you."

Angelo noticed that she'd been taken aback by the condition of the deli, but she recovered quickly, and her smile never faded. He thought that was gracious.

After Big Frankie introduced himself, Angelo said, "Nick's in the basement doing his workout. We thought we'd play a little pinochle when he's finished."

Liz made a motion of counting heads. "Well, there are only three of you. I'd love to play. Would you mind dealing me in as a fourth until Nick shows up?"

"It's pinochle," Jimmy said.

"Right," Liz said smiling. "I got it."

"Can you play pinochle?" Jimmy asked.

"Absolutely. My grandfather taught me when I was twelve "

She sat at the table and began shuffling the cards. "It would be a shame to waste a chance for a good card game"

Big Frankie shrugged. "What the heck," he sat at the table and Jimmy, his normal partner, sat across from him. Angelo, who normally partnered with Nick, glanced at the empty chair, and then at, Liz. He said, "You better be good. I hate to lose. "

Liz smiled and said, “Funny, I was thinking the same thing about you.”

Nick came upstairs thirty minutes later to the sound of laughter and stopped dead.

No one noticed him, and Angelo boasted to Liz, “You were loaded in spades, partner.”

“I had six,” Liz said. “Double Ace, ten, and a marriage. I just missed a run by the Jack. “

“We didn’t need it. Good game.” They clinked bottles and Liz took a long pull of her beer while Jimmy and Big Frankie slumped in their chairs.

Angelo saw Nick standing by the basement doorway dripping with sweat from his workout. Nick scratched his head trying to process the scene, and Angelo said, “Hey, Nick. Liz just gave Frankie and Jimmy a lesson in pinochle.”

Liz laughed and said, “I just drew some lucky cards.” Then she added nonchalantly, “Hi Nick. Did you have a good workout?”

“I did,” Nick said without smiling. “I’m a little surprised you’re here. “

“Well,” she said, “let me explain. I’m an old-fashioned girl, and I respect the old tradition of asking your family for permission before going on a big date. I sent you that text message today asking you to go to the cocktail party. I know that these guys are the closest thing you have to family, so I thought, out of respect, I would ask them for permission to see you.”

The guys looked around. “You get my vote, “Big Frankie said.

“Hell yes, “Jimmy said.

Angelo slapped his hand on the table and said, "I guess I'll make it unanimous. You can date Nick whenever you want. He's all yours!"

Chapter 17

Nick took Liz by the hand and led her out of the deli. They crossed the street without speaking and sat on the church steps.

When Nick didn't speak Liz said, "You're upset with me."

Nick turned to face her. "What was that?"

"I thought it would be fun to meet your friends and see where you hang out."

"But you didn't think you should ask me first."

Liz said softly, "I wanted to surprise you. I guess on second thought it wasn't a good idea. I'm sorry."

Nick waited to respond. He didn't want to sound angry. "Well, you did surprise me, but not in the way you intended. I thought you knew what I'd been like before finding you. I thought you knew that I was making small steps because I've been living in a shell while you've been," he paused, "I don't know, shouting from a mountaintop or something. Today was hard for me on lots of levels. Tuxedo, cocktails, art. But most upsetting was finding you in the hole in the wall where I spent half my life. Not to mention finding you playing cards and drinking beer with guys who in many ways are as messed up as I am. I wanted to prepare you for that, ease you into it. It's all overwhelming."

She draped her arm through his and said, "I'm really sorry, Nick. I wasn't thinking. I intruded upon your space. Please don't be mad."

Nick forced a smile. “I love your personality. I admire your spunk and your confidence. I feel good around you.”
She started to speak, but he interrupted. “I feel good around you, but not today. I’m not sure what we are right now, you and me, but whatever it is, it wasn’t that today. Today I felt like…I don’t know, maybe a circus act.”
Now Liz interrupted. “No, Nick,” she pleaded, ”Please don’t see it like that.”
Nick shook his head. “It felt like I was being trained. Wear a tux, mingle with people, and discuss art. I’ve been broken all these years, Liz, but I’m still a man, and I have pride.”
Liz said, “Boy, I really screwed this up. Things were going so well.”

Nick rubbed his eyes and turned to face her more squarely. “I have to ask you something. You just said you screwed this up. I need to know what this is. What is it exactly that we’re doing together?”

Liz’s eyes were getting moist. “I don’t know. We’re doing something nice together. I know that. It’s been the best three weeks. It’s fun, and it’s nice, or at least it was until I ruined it.”

Nick took her hand. “You didn’t ruin anything. You just overshot a little today.” He smiled and added, “overshot a lot.”
She smiled back.

“But I still need some answers. One actually. Why me? I mean, you are very attractive. The guys in the deli are obviously Gaga over you. You’ve got an amazing personality. You’re funny. You’re confident. You’ve got energy. I don't want to seem like a loser or anything, but I don't see you falling for a train wreck like me. There must be other men in your life."

She put her index finger to his lips to silence him and said, "Of all the flattering things you just said about me, most of which were exaggerated, you left out assertive. Now it's my turn to talk, so please listen. There were other men. I had a husband, remember? He turned out to be a creep and we got divorced. There were a couple of other guys soon after. As I told you, they didn't work out. Then, I did what millions of divorced women do, I settled on to a life without men. It was easy, really. I had two kids who filled my life. I had my career. My parents were still alive. I had a nice circle of friends, many of whom were divorced or widowed women.

"It was good, and then you rang my doorbell. I told you before, I had so many patients at Walter Reed, and I cared about all of them, but not like I cared about you. You were young, handsome, and obviously very brave, and I cared for you in a way that was unprofessional for a nurse. I had mixed feelings the day you left, very mixed feelings. I was happy that you had recovered to the point where you could be released, sad that I'd never see you again, but relieved that I hadn't said or done anything to jeopardize my career. Remember, I was a kid, a rookie.

"Over the years, I would think about you now and then and wonder how you were. I'd even fantasize a little about what it would be like to see you. Then, you rang the doorbell. I recognized you right away. More than forty years later, I recognized you. Then you said the most romantic thing I ever heard. "

He started to speak, but she put her finger to his lips again.

"Wait, let me finish," she said. "This is the important part. You might think I was trying to change you today, and I know now I overdid it. I had the best of intentions, but I overdid it. But what you don't know, is that you changed me. I had, as I said, settled into a life that was comfortable, nothing more. But at that moment, I realized I didn't want to settle for comfortable. I wanted to be excited, and I was. I felt like a schoolgirl. That kiss seemed like my first ever.

"As for my personality, my behavior is not like it was before you came. You opened me up. Before, I guess I was friendly and reserved. So, what you may see as bubbly or perky now is the person inside of me that you brought out. You talk about your wasted years. I realized I had wasted years of my own.

"It hurts to hear you say that I wanted to dress you up like a circus act. Or like I was like being Henry Higgins in my fair lady, showing people that you were my project, that I could change you. No. It was the opposite! I wanted to bring you to that party because I wanted my friends to see the man that I'm developing strong feelings for. I read once that lonely people move quickly when they find happiness. I wasn't lonely, but I was alone."

She wiped a tear from her cheek.

"You asked me to tell you what this is we're doing. Well, I don't know for sure except to say, it is awfully nice and I hope to God I didn't ruin it before finding out what it really is. So, let's forget the cocktail party, but I hope we can still see each other. A hamburger at a diner would be good enough for me."

She forced another smile as she wiped away a tear again. "The old me would feel awkward about sitting on church steps in broad daylight. The new me wants to kiss you right here, right now."

Nick didn't give her the chance. He leaned in and kissed her gently. When they parted, he said, "we're going to that party. And I'll wear a friggin tux if I can find one. And I'll know more about Edward Hicks than he did about himself. Now wave to my wonderful, idiotic, crazy friends. I'm sure they're watching through the window."

Chapter 18

Liz explained that Black Tie Optional was just that, optional and that most men who attended past events simply wore suits. Nick was fine with that, but he had no intention of buying a new one. He had gone with Jimmy to a Salvation Army store once when Jimmy was looking for snow boots. The store had a large used clothing section, but Nick noticed a separate, "Another Chance" section of gently used professional clothing donated to assist people of limited means who needed to dress for a job interview or similar event. Nick wanted to try it.

Jimmy drove and Nick swore him to silence. The store had a large selection of suits, and Nick found a grey wool that was his size. There were no set prices on the garments. Instead, each was tagged with a message inviting shoppers to leave a donation in an amount of their choice. He went to the counter where he was greeted by a hip-looking, young, African-American girl with streaks of red in her hair, large hoop earrings, and a red, black, and green striped sweater.

She eyed Nick and Jimmy and gave them an easy smile. "How's it going, Pops? Find something that works for you?"

Nick didn't like the Pops reference but didn't think it was meant to be derogatory. "Yes, I'll take this suit." He handed her a twenty-dollar bill for the donation. She thanked him and put it in the register. She handled the suit and said, "This is real nice. Some hotshot lawyer probably wore it a few times, put on a few pounds until it didn't fit, and was kind enough to drop it off here. I'm glad you can use it. Most people don't know about this opportunity or take advantage of it." She eyed him skeptically and said, "Job interview?"

Nick smiled. "I guess some people might see it that way, but no, not a job interview." She seemed in a playful mood. "Wedding, right? You're going to a wedding."

"Not yet," Jimmy interjected.

Nick gave Jimmy an elbow and said, "No, not a wedding."

"Not yet?" she said grinning. "Did the man say, not yet?" Nick was ready to leave, but the girl said, "Wait. Don't tell me you're going on a date?"

Jimmy blurted, "next weekend."

Nick looked ready to kill him. The girl said," A date! Well, I'll be damned. You handsome devil, you. That's great. How about if I help you pick out a tie from that rack over there? They're free."

"No thanks," Nick said sheepishly, "I'm not wearing a tie. I'll just leave the collar open."

"No tie? Cool. This man knows what he wants." Then she snapped her finger and said, "I have a suggestion. Did you ever watch the cop show Miami Vice?"

"Never heard of it," Nick said.

"It's really old, nineteen-eighties, I think. I used to watch reruns with my grandmom. Two young, cool cops, one white and one black. The black guy was really hot, which is why she watched it. Anyway, they wore suits with no ties, but instead of open-collar shirts, they wore crewnecks. Dressed but casual. Very cool. My advice, get yourself a nice black crewneck. It will look good with the grey." She lowered her voice and said, "Don't get the shirt here, "

Nick listened.

"Yup, get yourself a nice black crewneck and put a black handkerchief in the breast pocket. Not all fluffy like the guidos do it, just a tasteful, subtle peak of it. That look will be sic."
Nick gave her a blank look and she laughed. "Sic, you know, cool." Nick nodded. "Yeah, that would be sick."

She wasn't finished. "And please, please don't douse yourself with cologne. You old guys tend to do that. Just shower with a nice AXE body wash and leave it at that."

Nick grinned. "Right, no cologne. Thank you. You've been very helpful. He turned to leave and she called after him. "Hey, Pops, be sure to use protection. That girl's gonna be all over you, and you don't want to be making no babies at your age."

Chapter 19

They stopped at the Levittown Walmart, and Nick bought the crewneck shirt, black handkerchief, and socks. Then they drove to the dry cleaners on Pond Street where Nick dropped off the suit after being assured it would be ready on time. The next stop was the Elizabeth R. Grundy Library on Radcliffe Street. Nick had reserved a session with the librarian to tutor him on firing up a computer, navigating the screen, and doing a Google search. Nick was surprised to learn how much easier it was compared to what he feared.

Within twenty minutes he was reading about Edward Hicks while Jimmy scanned magazines in the lounge area.

On the day of Liz's event, he found himself counting the hours until he'd see her. It reminded him of his high school football days when he'd count the hours before a game or the army when he'd measure the time before a mission commenced. He felt very much alive at those times, exhilarated even, and he admitted that he felt the same now, even if he felt less prepared than he was for any game or mission he undertook.

He laid out his clothes, suit; shirt; handkerchief, which he had since learned was called a pocket square; socks, belt, and underwear. Then he checked the shoes at the bottom of his closet. There were two older pairs and the new pair Carrie and Jenny had bought him. The new pair would work perfectly for the night. He reached for them and then paused, and shook his head no. He wasn't ready for that countdown, not yet. He checked his watch and decided he had enough time to polish an old pair before heading in to shower with his new body wash.

He had arranged his Uber pickup at the deli for his first trip but planned on skipping that idea this time because he didn't want to deal with the abuse he'd take. But in the end, he stuck with the deli pickup. It sounded crazy, but he knew the guys would be hurt if he didn't stop in first.

As he walked the two blocks from his apartment, he thought about the time he testified before Congress. As an unofficial advocate for veterans, over several years he'd written over one thousand letters to his congressman on behalf of veterans or their widows. The congressman directed his staff to look into each request and save a copy. He was deeply impressed by the persistent efforts of the former Distinguished Service Cross recipient to help Vietnam, and later Iraqi, war veterans. But when the file grew by the hundreds, he told his staff, without telling Nick, that if the file ever reached one thousand he would invite Nick to testify briefly during one of their Veteran's Affairs subcommittee hearings, which he eventually did.

On the morning of the hearing, Nick walked to the deli in the early morning darkness to meet the guys. When he arrived everyone was excited, including Ralph McGinnis, a high school classmate and undertaker in town. Angelo closed the store for the day, and they all piled in Ralph's funeral limo for the ride to Washington.

Nick choked up at the memory. He loved the guys like brothers and he definitely owed them a visit tonight, even if it meant he'd get his balls busted royally.

He took out his phone and dialed Angelo's number. "Tell those assholes I'm coming over. If they say one word, I swear I'll punch them in the eye." He hung up and smiled. He was about to get destroyed.

Chapter 20

It was another nice night, and Liz and Nick agreed that he would Uber to her house, and they would walk the three blocks to the Arts Society Building.

Liz came out when she saw him exit the vehicle.

"Damn," he said, louder than he intended. "You look beautiful." Liz had relied upon her natural attributes without overdoing it. She wore a simple, above-the-knee, black spaghetti strap dress. Her hair was as she always wore it, and she used just a hint more makeup than usual.

He took both of her hands in his and said, "Did it hurt much?"

She looked perplexed. "Did what hurt?"

Nick said straight-faced, "Did it hurt much when you fell from heaven?"

Liz laughed out loud. "Oh, my God! Where did you get that cheesy line?"

Nick laughed with her. "I googled it."

"Googled it! How?"

"I searched for things to say to women when they look good. "

She laughed again and they released their hands. "That might be the worst line I've ever heard, but I appreciate the effort." She paused, laughed more and added, "Google? You googled what to say to a woman? Priceless."

"I only used it because it's true."

"Is that the only one you found?"

"Heck no. Want another?"

"I can't wait."

"Are you a parking ticket? Because you have fine written all over you."

"Oh, brother."

Nick was having too much fun to stop. "I must be in a museum because you are truly a work of art."

"Okay," she said, "that's enough."

"Nope, not even close. Someone better call God, because he's missing an angel."

"Please!" She begged, still laughing.

"Okay. That last one was a little redundant. He turned serious and said, "Here's one not from Google. "You look exceptionally nice tonight."

She smiled. "Thank you." She took a step back and eyed him up and down. "Look at you. I love that suit."

Nick shrugged. "Just something I had in the closet."

Liz doubted that but let it go. "Well, you'll be the most handsome guy there. Let's go. We're a little late."

She draped her arm through his and they walked.

"So, tell me about the Arts society,"

"It's a nice group of people. Our mission is obviously to promote the arts, but were also interested in the history of Langhorne, including the preservation of our historic buildings. We have a few events throughout the year. We participate in Historic Langhorne day in the fall with craft tents and vendors. We do a tea in the spring."

"Now that sounds exciting. Can I come?"

She poked him. "No!"

"Just kidding. I'm sure it's nice."

"It's not, actually. It's boring, but it's an annual tradition."

"Are there many men in the club?"

"Hardley any, but a couple of them know Langhorne inside and out. It's important to preserve our past."

Nick knew what she meant but thought that some things in the past are best not preserved.

"So, what's the deal tonight?"

"We have one big fundraiser a year, and this is it. We have bills to pay, utilities, insurance, and maintenance. Tonight's the night we pay for it."

"What's it have to do with this Hicks guy?"

"Edward Hicks was a renowned 17th-century artist from Langhorne. We claim him as our most famous citizen. This year we're featuring his life and work as a draw for our donors. We'll have lots of non-members tonight, hopefully with their checkbooks, doctors, lawyers, engineers, bank officials, business leaders, and other civic-minded citizens with means."

They reached the Arts Society building, It was a red brick structure with arched windows on the second floor, an ample yard, and surrounded by a beautifully ornate iron fence.

They stopped before entering and Liz asked Nick if he had learned anything about Edward Hicks.

"I wanted to," Nick said. "But never got the chance. No problem. I'll just lay low."

He took her by the arm and led her in.

A quick scan of the room revealed about a quarter of the men were in tuxedos and the rest in suits with one exception, a seemingly eccentric man wearing jeans and an untucked denim shirt, with disheveled hair and a straggly beard. The women appeared to range from nineteen to ninety. Most were tastefully dressed, although there were a few exceptions who must have thought it was a nineteenth-century ball.

"Where's the bar," Nick asked.

"Not yet. I want you to meet my friend Julie."

She led him through the crowd, exchanging greetings with several people as they passed.

A woman was adjusting a Arts Society display and stopped when she saw them. "Liz! You're finally here." Then she added, "And you must be Nick."

Nick deadpanned, "I'm John." He turned to Liz, feigned annoyance, and said, "Who's Nick?"

Liz gave him a jab on the arm and said, "Sorry, Julie, Nick seems to have developed a sense of humor tonight."

Nick put out his hand and said, "Sorry Julie, just a little nervous energy, I guess. I don't know anyone here, except Liz"

"No problem," Julie said. As she took his hand, she looked at Liz and said, "I like him already." Turning back, she said "Well, Nick, now you know two people. Thank you for coming."

"is one of my yoga partners and I told her a little about you."

Nick said, "Yoga seems to fit you both very well."

"Thank you. Liz is the one who keeps me going, but we love it. I hope we can all spend some time together once I tidy up this display. "

As they made their way to the bar, Nick said, "Julie seems nice. A little on the younger side than what I'd expect from your yoga partner."

"She's more than that. She's my best friend. She's pushing fifty. She lost her husband fifteen years ago in Afghanistan around 2003."

Nick shook his head.

"He was a captain, a long-timer. He was planning to leave the military, but then, the twin towers came down, and he extended his time. He left her with two boys. They were six and eight at the time. Rob is out of college now and working and living in the city. Paul is 21 and a senior at Temple. He's supposed to be here tonight, so you may meet him."

"I'd like to. I hope Julie got all the help she needed when she lost her husband."

"At times it was a struggle. I'm convinced she's active here just to fill the time."

They got their drinks and were ready to move to the appetizers when Liz whispered, "Oh, no. There is Seth Wagner. Stay here a minute. I'm hoping he doesn't see us."

"What's his problem?"

"Nothing, really. He's our speaker tonight and a pompous blowhard. I'm sure he'll want to drone on later. I just don't enjoy his company."

Nick gave her a look that said he expected more.

"He's a big donor, but a bit full of himself."

"Too bad," Nick said. "He's spotted you and is on the way over."

"Liz!" Wagner said louder than necessary. I was wondering if you arrived yet. You look ravishing." He gave her a hug that lasted longer than Nick thought it should, while Liz rolled her eyes behind his back. And ravishing? Really? Nick shook his head. His angel lines were no worse.

When they broke the embrace, Liz said, “Seth Wagner, this is my friend, Nick Hardings.”

Wagner gave him a dismissive look, and a perfunctory handshake before turning back to Liz.

Nick thought to himself, that he’d met two people so far, one he liked and one he didn’t.

“We have an exceptionally large turnout tonight,” Wagner said. He didn’t add that the crowd was there to listen to him, but it was implicit.

Liz, obviously with a large booster check in mind, said with as much excitement as she could muster, “Seth is our speaker tonight.”

“I’m looking forward to your talk,” Nick lied.

“Good. Do you know of Edward Hicks?”

“I think everyone does,” Nick replied.

Liz looked worried. She didn’t want Nick to be caught faking it.

“Your thoughts?” Wagner asked.

“They’re mixed,” Nick said.

Now, Liz was near panic mode. “We should let Seth go, I’m sure he has lots of people he needs to see.”

Wagner ignored her and focused on Nick. “Mixed, you say, how so?”

Liz would have pulled a fire alarm if there was one nearby. Anything to end this conversation.

Nick said, “I’ve always admired art that depicts biblical references or stories, especially the Renaissance masters. So, Hicks distinguished himself in that regard by providing the world with a distinctive early American version. His Peaceable Kingdom, clearly inspired by Isaiah, Chapter 11 is a Masterpiece.”

"Yes, Isiah," Wagner said. He was about to recite the verse, when Nick beat him to it.

"If I recall, it's something like, 'The wolf also shall dwell with the lamb, and the leopard shall lie down with the kid; and the calf and the young lion and the fatling together; and a little child shall lead them.'"

Liz almost burst out laughing and chugged her drink instead.

Wagner was on his heels and needed to recover. "So, you said you had mixed thoughts about Hicks."

A waiter passed by with a tray of drinks, and Liz snatched one. She'd punish Nick later for fooling her, but right now, she was happy to hear where this was going.

Nick said, "I guess this is where the subjective part of art comes in. Peaceable Kingdom does a great job of depicting the verse, but in my view, it is too busy. He's depicted lions and lambs and infants and tigers, all in harmony, in peace. That's fine, but then he throws in William Penn. And as if that weren't enough. He's got Native Americans and Quakers meeting in the background. It's a lot."

Wagner had to salvage something and decided to try history. "But don't you agree that the Quakers were such an integral part of early American thought and should be depicted?"

Nick smiled. "Hicks obviously did. I get why he did it. After all, his Uncle was a leading Quaker who created a split in the movement with his inner light teachings. Regardless, I feel the painting is too busy, I guess that's why we have chocolate and vanilla."

It was everything Liz could do to keep her jaw from dropping.

Wagner was fading and said, "As you said, Hicks obviously valued it. He painted multiple versions of Peaceable Kingdom."

"Yes," Nick replied. "Multiple versions is an understatement. He painted sixty versions in all. Sixty. I've always felt that was strange."

Liz suppressed a smile at Nick's reference to what he always felt about Hicks since he most likely had never heard of him a week earlier.

Wagner was in full retreat now. "It's been a pleasure. I intend to focus my remarks more on his early life, before he turned to the type of art we're discussing."

Nick couldn't resist one last shot before Wager left. "I'm glad. That's the part I like, his early days as a sign painter and later as a custom painter of carriages, a middle-class guy, struggling to make an honest living. I'm looking forward to your remarks."

Wagner nodded. He couldn't retreat fast enough. He smiled at Liz, turned, and left.

Liz watched him go. Then she draped her arm through his again, and whispered, "Right this moment, you are the sexiest man alive. That was so awesome."

"Now a bad circus act, huh?" He said kiddingly.

"Stop it with that. You obviously did a lot of reading."

"I didn't want to embarrass my date."

She gave him a peck on the cheek and said, "You could never do that."

"I hope I didn't just cost the society money. He didn't look happy."

"I think the opposite. He's such a pompous ass who needs to be admired. He feels deflated and upstaged by that conversation. He'll compensate with an even larger check that everyone will gush over."

They circulated among the guests, and it was obvious Liz was well-liked. Her friends greeted him warmly and he felt comfortable in their presence. When the time came for Wagner's talk, they lingered in the back as he confirmed his penchant for droning on.

As he was winding down, Julie appeared beside them. "It's finally over. Did he see you guys?"

Nick smiled. "I don't think I'm his favorite person."

Julie said to Liz, "Does he know?" She knew immediately from Liz's expression that she made a mistake.

"Know what?" Nick asked.

"I'm sorry, Liz," Julie said. "That was dumb."

Liz shrugged. "It's okay. There's nothing to hide. You tell him."

Julie exhaled. "Wagner has a thing for Liz. It's harmless but annoying. She avoids him like the plague."

"He's borderline inappropriate, no big deal." Liz added. "Just annoying. He's a widower and a little creepy."

"I can fix that," Nick said.

"Absolutely not," Liz said. "There's nothing to fix."

"She's right," Julie said. "I made it sound like something that it isn't."

Nick looked doubtful but smiled and said, "If you say so."

Julie's son and girlfriend approached, and her son said, "Hi, Mom."

"Ronnie, so glad you came. Hi Mallory.

"Hi, sorry we're late. Traffic on 95 was bad."

Ronnie said hi to Liz, and said both women looked nice.

Liz introduced Nick to the couple, and Ronnie shook Nick's hand. Mallory smiled and said, "Hello, Mr. Hardings."

That sounded strange since Liz hadn't used Nick's last name when she introduced him. Nick looked at the girl and said, "I feel as though I know you."

Mallory smiled politely as Nick tried to place her. "I'm Mallory Baldwin from the Temple School of Journalism."

"Yes," Nick said enthusiastically. "Of course."

Julie smiled. "You know each other?"

"I interviewed Mr. Hardings for a major project I was doing on prisoners of war."

Nicked cringed because he didn't know what Liz had told Julie about him.

Mallory went on. "He was fantastic. He blasted Donald Trump for the derogatory things he said about John McCain not being a hero and then for disparaging POWs in general."

There's the double whammy, Nick thought. He didn't know Liz's feelings about Trump and didn't want politics to enter into their relationship. Now it was too late.

"I hope you did well on it," Nick said.

"I did very, very well. First I had to present it to the class for critique. There were two veterans in the class. They actually clapped when I got to the parts you asked me to quote. The paper was published in the department journal."

"I hope you got the "A" we discussed."

"Nope," Mallory said beaming. "A plus."

"Good for you," Liz said as she draped her arm inside Nick's and gave him an affectionate squeeze.

"Yes," Julie added. "Congratulations. Maybe your next article can be about how he treats women and brags about it."

Nick relaxed. He had no interest in injecting politics into their relationship, but it was still good to know where they stood on something important to him.

"Stick around, everyone," Julie said. "I have to wrap this up."

She left, and Liz explained that Julie was this year's program chair. She said to Ronnie, "Your mom did a terrific job, as usual. I'm sure she's thrilled you could be here."

Julie took the stage and thanked everyone for coming. She recognized the board of directors and the various committee members and mentioned how nice it was to celebrate Edward Hicks, Langhorne's favorite son. She reminded the gathering of the rising costs of maintaining the building. "Which is why we're so happy to announce our most successful fundraising event ever."

The audience applauded. "That's due to your collective generosity, and especially the generosity of the 2018 donor of the year, Seth Wagner, of First Langhorne Savings and Loan, who doubled his contribution from last year."

Again there was wide applause and some cheers as Wagner took the stage.

Liz whispered to Nick, "See, I told you. Thanks for your help, Big Guy."

"And finally," Julie continued, "Our last business of the evening, the Volunteer of the Year Award. The board always has a difficult job selecting from so many worthy candidates, but I'm pleased to announce that this year's winner is Liz Ambrose."

Liz seemed embarrassed as she made her way to the stage to accept her plaque.
Nick watched Liz grimace as Wager put his arm around her waist while they posed for the photograph.

Chapter 21

Liz drove to town and picked Nick up in front of the deli. They drove to Mill Street and parked in the lot behind the street. As they left the car, Liz said, “So tell me again about this restaurant. I wanted to check out their website but must have spelled it wrong.”
Nick said, “It’s called Itri Wood Fired. It’s one of the newest places in town. For a while, Cesare’s, about a mile from here, and the King George Inn down the street were pretty much the only games in town and are still very popular. I practically grew up at Cesare’s, and King George was the preferred spot for special occasions. Beyond them, this street was practically on life support for a long time, but now there are new businesses, bars, and restaurants popping up. Everyone has their favorite, but Johnny wanted to try this place tonight.”
“I hope we try them all,” Liz said. “What’s with the name?”
“Itri is a town in Italy. The grandfather of the owner’s family was born there. A person with the same last name was a revolutionary in the Itri area who fought against the French occupation around 1800. He became a folk hero and was

so feared by the French that they called him Fra Diablo, of the devil."

"I hope the food is as good as the story."

"I'm told it is, "Nick said.

"Tell me more about Johnny."

Nick smiled at the thought. "He is truly the all-American boy. High school football star, Penn State graduate, special forces captain, served in Afghanistan and Iraq, and currently in the FBI. All of that can be normal dinner conversation when you meet him, with one exception."

"I think I know what that is. I remember the news stories from several years ago because it happened around here," Liz said. "What exactly happened?"

"We're coming up on the tenth anniversary. A deadly criminal was on his way to Bristol to attack Johnny's family for revenge after Johnny foiled a planned attack in Philadelphia. Johnny tracked him to an abandoned industrial site where he killed him in a shootout. Johnny became a regional hero, and Carrie remains terrified of the memory."

"Understandable. So, I get it. That conversation is off-limits. What about Brian?"

"Brian is a genius, and I mean that literally. He collected two million dollars as a young boy as the beneficiary of his uncle whose plane was brought down in a terror attack. As soon as he was old enough, he put his brains to work with investments and increased his wealth several times over. He started a private, anti-terror agency that does consulting work for the FBI. He occasionally works with Johnny."

They reached the door to Itri, and Nick added. “Brian will buy dinner tonight. No use trying to stop him. He gets upset. So just enjoy it.”

Liz loved the feel of the restaurant. It had a small, fully stocked bar, distressed brick walls, just the right amount of eclectic art on the walls, and a team of young, hustling servers. It reminded Liz of the kind of place one would find in Brooklyn.

Johnny and the others were already seated at a corner table in the adjacent dining room. Everyone stood and exchanged hugs as Nick made the introductions. The waitress came and took drink orders and referred them to the QR code on the table linked to the menu. Liz winked at Nick and Nick smiled. “No need to keep a secret, Liz. We’re with friends here, and everyone knows I’ve been in a cave,” Nick said. “Let me try it.” He held his phone to the circle, nailed it on the first try, and cheered.

Carrie said, “I love the new Nick as much as I loved the old.”

Nick nodded. “One step at a time.”

Johnny said, “So you’re the long-lost Liz. It’s so nice to meet you.”

“It’s so nice to be found. Thanks to both of you for doing that.”

“It wasn’t us,” Johnny said, “although we were trying like heck. It was Carrie.”

“Really?” Liz said.

Johnny retold the story of Carrie and the newspaper article. At the end, Carrie said, kiddingly, “These boys were working so hard, day and night, with the full force of the FBI and the most famous private agency in America behind them, and they were getting frustrated. I thought they needed the help of a woman, so here we are."

Liz laughed and said, "Well, I'm very glad you did."

The drinks came and Brian's wife, Jenny, offered a toast. "To our newly found friend." Then she looked at Nick and added, "Make that two newly found friends."

They decided to order a sampling of menu items, assorted wood-fired pizzas, truffle fries, brussel sprouts, wings, and a cheese board. The conversation was light. Liz asked about the careers of the other women, their children, and how the couples met.

The food arrived and they enjoyed sharing reactions to the various offerings. Truffle fries were a unanimous first choice, but all received high marks.

They ordered another round, and Liz asked about Nick's bond to Jimmy, Big Frankie, and Angelo. Nick told stories that dated back to high school friendships.

Even though Nick was a generation older than Johnny, Brian, and their wives, he was always comfortable around them. In fact, they brought him out of his shell, and he was pleased now that Liz was blending in so well.

Jenny said to Liz, "We've been monopolizing the conversation about our lives. I'd love to hear about you.

Liz started with a brief review of her medical training, her assignment at Walter Reed, and how she met Nick. She mentioned her marriage and divorce. At that point she noticed Johnny and Brian exchanging uncomfortable looks. She wondered what it was, and then it hit her. "Wait," she said smiling, "you guys know this already. You found me."

Johnny looked sheepish. "We only know the parts that helped trace you. Vital records which are public information detailed your marriage, births, and divorce. Brian helped with other things, not so public, like employment records, and where you lived."

"They were doing me a favor," Nick said, apologetically.

"I know," Liz said, and I'm glad they did."

Brian said, "We really don't know anything about your kids except their ages. So, as Jenny said, we'd love to know more about your life"

Liz smiled. "My son, Peter, is a pharmacist who lives in Colorado," she said proudly. "He's very smart. In that regard, I guess he inherited the one good trait his otherwise creepy father possesses. He's a great son who dutifully stays in contact with his mom. He's making a lot of money, and I think he's part of the growing legal marijuana industry in that state."

"Good for him," Jenny said.

"If that's the case," Brian said, "then he's riding the early wave of what is to come across the country. It won't take long."

Jenny asked if Liz's son was married, and Liz said that he wasn't.

"And your daughter," Carrie asked?

There was a slight change in Liz's expression. Then she seemed to force a smile and said, "Her name is Kate. She's a nurse at Aria-Jefferson Hospital and she lives in Falls Township. Unfortunately, I guess she inherited her mother's trait of marrying the wrong guy. She and her beautiful daughter Addie are going through a difficult time. I'm not sure the marriage will last. She's trying to make it work, but it's not going as smoothly as she'd like."

"I'm sorry to intrude, "Carrie said, "and I'm sorry for what you're going through."

"That's quite all right," Liz said forcing another smile. "It's just difficult to talk about right now."

Everyone seemed more than eager to change the topic, so Nick suggested another round of drinks and waived down a server. They ordered and the conversation shifted to a comparison of Bristol and Langhorne, as two of Bucks County's oldest towns. Nick told the group about Liz's recent award from the Langhorne Arts Society, and they all agreed to have lunch and tour Langhorne soon.

Then Liz turned to Johnny and Brian and said, "I'm sure there's a lot about your jobs that you can't talk about, but I'm really intrigued by the work you guys do, especially Brian's private company."

Nick chimed in and said proudly, "Like the old comic books used to say, they fight for truth, justice, and the American way."

Johnny ignored Nick's hyperbole and said. "You're right, Liz, there's a lot we can't talk about, but we can certainly tell you everything that Nick and our wives already know."

The drinks arrived, and he waited as the server passed them around. When they were alone again, he said, "I work for the domestic anti-terror division in the Philadelphia regional office of the FBI. "

Brian spoke next. "And I run a private company that specializes in domestic terror threats here at home. We focus on tracking hate groups, and the threats they present."

"That's interesting," Liz said. "When I think of terrorism, I think of foreigners who want to harm our country."

Brian nodded, “Up until a few years ago you would be right. My uncle was killed when a terrorist blew up the plane he was on while flying from overseas to visit our family for the Christmas holiday. That’s what got me involved in the first place and of course after 911 that was our country’s primary focus, and it remains extremely important today. But thanks to an influx of tremendous resources and a growing understanding of how to do the job better, we’ve got a pretty good handle on foreign threats. That’s not the case nearly as much with domestic terrorists.”

Brian looked at Johnny, inviting him to take over. Johnny said, “Today, without question, right-wing extremist and hate groups pose the greatest threat to our safety. Most, like the newest phenomenon we’ve looked at, the incels, live strictly on the internet. Others have gathering places or actually create encampments in sparsely populated wooded areas.”

Liz said, “What or who are the incels?”

Brian said, “It’s an abbreviation for involuntary celibates, heterosexual men who self-describe as unable to attract women as sexual partners. They share hostile tendencies toward women and even other men who are sexually active. Somehow, they blame society for their misfortune and often share violent rhetoric on the internet.”

Johnny continued. “But that’s just the newest group to keep an eye on. There are growing numbers of good old-fashioned white supremacists, usually angry men who feel society has left them behind economically and blame it on blacks and immigrants who they feel get all the benefits. They envision a day when whites will be in the minority and the country will be ruined.”

Brian continued, "The radical wing nuts and militia groups are often well-armed, near fanatical in their beliefs, and emboldened by some of the very politicians who should know better. They offer a smorgasbord of anti-government, racist, anti-Semitic, homophobic, misogynistic, and disaffected individuals. And that's a mouthful, I know."

Brian checked with Johnny to see if he had anything to add. Johnny shrugged and said, "Anyway, they're all out there, living on the radical fringe and usually protected by their first amendment right to think and say what they want. It's the ones who intend to cross the line from thought and speech to action that we have to be vigilant about."

There was a long, silent pause as everyone took in what was said. It wasn't so much that they hadn't heard it before. It just seemed more real hearing it from two people they knew who were so deeply involved.
Finally, Brian said cheerfully, "Hey, I guess we know how to ruin a good time. Talk about a buzz killer, wow. How about if we return to a lighter topic?"
"I'll drink to that," Jenny said.
They laughed and raised their glasses in a toast. As they did, Nick saw a look on Liz's face he hadn't seen before, and she wasn't smiling.

Chapter 22

Nick kept both hands on the steering wheel as he drove.
"You're paying for gas, right?" Jimmy asked.

"I said I would."

"I have some questions, but keep your eyes on the road while you answer."

"Fire away," Nick said.

"Are you getting married?"

Nick shot him a look and said, "Jesus, Jimmy. What kind of question is that?"

"Eyes on the road," Jimmy said. "Answer the question."

Nick laughed. "No, Jimmy, I'm not getting married. It's a dumb question."

"You've been seeing a lot of Liz lately."

Nick summoned his best Groucho Marx imitation and said with a smile, "I'd like to see more of her."

"I'm serious," Jimmy said.

Nick said calmly, "I've seen her six times in three weeks. That's it."

"That's six times more than you've dated any woman since you came back from Nam."

Nick smiled. "You've got a point there, but no, I'm not getting married. Next question."

"Are you moving to Langhorne?"

Nick sighed. "No, I'm not moving to Langhorne."

"We're on our way to get your driver's license. You've been practicing and even paying me for gas. Will you buy a car if you pass?"

"Probably."

"So, you plan to commute to Langhorne every day."

Nick laughed. "No, I don't plan to commute to Langhorne every day."

"Then why get your license and a car?"

"Because I'm seventy-one and it's ridiculous that I haven't driven all of these years."

"You were hurt. Your leg was bad."

"I was, but it improved enough over time. See, I'm driving. The leg isn't great, but it's good enough." Nick paused and added, "Plus, I think maybe I was faking a little without knowing it."

"You can't fake something without knowing it. You're not a faker. You're a hero."

"I'm not a hero. I just did my job. And my shrink says maybe deep down inside, I wanted sympathy, so I didn't do things as well as I could."

"That's just shrink bullshit."

Nick shrugged. "Maybe. "

"But you are different lately," Jimmy said.

"I know. I can't explain it. I just feel better inside. Not all the time, but a lot more than I used to."

"It's the girl. You're a lot different since Liz came along."

"I don't know," Nick said. "I'm sure that's part of it." He thought back to the letter he received from Carrie. "It could be a lot of things. I don't think I would have tried to find Liz unless I was feeling a little different already. But anyway, you're right. I'm different. I feel a little better. I guess Liz just adds to it. She's fun."

"I know, "Jimmy said. " She was fun that time we played cards and drank beer. Maybe she should hang out at the deli. Maybe not though. I could tell you were pissed off."

"I was just a little surprised, but no, Jimmy. That's our place. She can visit whenever she wants, but it wouldn't work to hang there."

It was quiet for a moment, and then Jimmy said, "We've been friends a long time."

Nick smiled. "Since kindergarten."

Nick looked at him and winked. Then they said together, "The longest friendship in human history." It was a thing they always did when they talked about their time together. They laughed and then Jimmy turned serious again. "Remember when I made that big catch in the Morrisville game?"

"Like it was yesterday, Jimmy. It set up our winning touchdown. I never saw anyone get hit any harder after a catch."

"Do you remember what you said when I got back to the huddle?"

Nick knew where this was going and decided to let Jimmy play it out his way. "I said, 'They hit you so hard that you have snot coming out of your nose.'"

"Do you remember what you said after that?"

Nick nodded. "I said, 'But you held on to the football."

Jimmy rubbed his eyes with his fists. "It made me so proud when you said that. You've always been my idol."

Nick's eyes began to tear. "Ditto, Jimmy. After what you went through in Nam, you're the hero for surviving."

"Nam was the only time we were ever apart. We were always together. You always looked after me. Then, I was alone in Nam and that son-of-a-bitch lieutenant kept making me go into those tunnels, over and over. I was scared shitless each time. I did't want to go. They said I had to because I was small. Those friggin tunnels, sometimes I hardly fit. They were dark. I could feel the spider webs. I wondered about snakes. I wondered whether there would be VC waiting to kill me when I reached the cave. Sometimes I wet my pants because I was so scared. Once the lieutenant laughed. Timmer was his name. The son of a bitch thought it was funny. I thought about shooting him right then. But I didn't. A lot of times I thought, if Nick were here, he'd do something."

Nick had heard the story countless times. It broke his heart each time, but he knew it was important for him to tell it.

"The army called us tunnel rats. I wasn't a rat. I was a person, but that's what they called us. The tunnels were so dark. That's why I still sleep with the light on. It doesn't matter though because I dream about those tunnels every night, and they're still dark."

"I know, Jimmy. But it's over. You survived. You've got to keep telling yourself that."

Nick knew there was more.

"I couldn't wait to tell you what they did. But when I finally got home, I found out you were a prisoner of war. We worried about you every day. We watched the news every day about that stinking war. Then they announced you were coming home. We all watched it on TV. We saw the POWs getting off the plane. When I saw how banged up you were, I wanted to kill someone. I wanted to go back to Vietnam and kill as many of them as I could. Not in the tunnels, but out in the open. But I was so glad you were home."

Nick said, "And I was so glad when you guys came to see me at Walter Reed."

Jimmy said, "I'm glad Liz took care of you, and I'm glad you found her after all this time."

Nick just nodded and Jimmy said, "I have something to tell you."

"I'm listening," Nick said.

"I think I might be dying."

Nick looked at his friend and Jimmy said, "Keep your eyes on the road. If I die, I'm leaving you this car. It's in my will, but it's no use if you have an accident."

Nick summoned his patience. "What makes you think you're dying?"

"You know how I've been complaining about my thumb not moving sometimes, like it's locked? I tried to go to the VA and couldn't get an appointment for weeks, so I went to a regular doctor one day while you were with Liz."

"And what happened?"

"He said it's like a thing called trigger finger, only sometimes it affects your thumb. So, it's trigger thumb. Comes from an inflamed tendon."

"You don't die from that, Jimmy."

"I didn't think so either, but he said I hadn't seen a doctor in five years, and he wanted me to get a blood test."

"That's standard procedure, Jimmy. What did the doctor say?"

"He said it was standard procedure. I asked him if it meant I was dying, and he said no. The blood test was standard, like he said, standard procedure."

"There you go," Nick said brightly. "Nothing to worry about."

"I hope not. I don't always trust what people say. Anyway, it got me thinking. What happens when I do get sick, you know, really sick? The only time we've been apart is when we were in Nam, and that was really bad."

"That was in the past. Nothing to worry about now."

"I was thinking about Liz. What if I needed something and you were busy with Liz?"

Nick took a long breath. "Jimmy, I don't know what I'm doing with Liz. I mean I really like her and I'm glad I found her, but I'm not even sure what it is we're doing except having some fun, and I'm sure she doesn't know either. But it doesn't matter. If you ever needed me, you better know I'd be there. Do you believe that?"

Jimmy smiled. "Yes, I believe that."

"Good," Nick said. "And I hope you'd be there for me too."

"You know I will," Jimmy said.

Nick thought a moment and said. "You know how you've been wanting to go target shooting and I haven't felt like it?"

"We used to go a lot. It was fun, but you stopped."

"I know. Tell you what. Are the guns in good shape?"

"All clean and oiled," Jimmy said.

"Why don't we go one day this week, just like old times?"

Jimmy grinned. "That would be great."

"Ok," Nick said. "We'll do it."

Chapter 23

Liz called and Nick briefly considered letting it ring four or five times before answering. He'd seen that in a movie once as a way to avoid appearing too eager, but instead, he answered on the second ring.

He also considered using a humorous opening, like Harding Enterprises or Hanoi Hilton, instead he settled on an enthusiastic, "Hi Liz."

"Hi, Nick. How are you?" He loved hearing her voice.

He thought back to Patti Weber, the last girl he dated. It was the Spring of their senior year. He'd asked her to the prom in early April even though the prom wasn't scheduled until mid-May. She was the prettiest girl in the class, and he wanted to get his request in early. Like most of the kids, he didn't want to make the request cold. No one wanted the risk of being shot down. Instead, he used Big Frankie as an emissary. His job was to casually mention to Patti that he thought Nick was thinking about asking her to the prom. If the response was positive, Nick would make the call. If not, Nick had plausible deniability that he was ever interested.

The result was predictable. Nick was handsome, popular, a star athlete, and a strong student. He and Patti had exchanged enough smiles and pleasant small talk beforehand to make Nick confident. Still, he followed the process. Big Frankie reported a positive response, and Nick called her the next day.

They started dating right away. It was the most wonderful spring of his life. The sun was shining, the birds were chirping, the flowers were blooming, and Patti was great to be with.

Spring of any senior year was also a time of mixed emotions. The proms, yearbook exchanges, and looming graduation were bonding experiences as students struggled to hold on to what was familiar while anticipating what was to come.

Nick and Patti saw each other every day, virtually every minute of every day. He'd walk her home after school. They'd go out at night, sometimes with friends, more often alone. Nick couldn't afford a car, so they often used Patti's.

At night, after their dates, he'd call her and they'd talk until they fell asleep or Patti's mom told her to hang up.

They tried not to think about the fall. Patti was heading to the University of Pittsburgh. Her parents had gone there, and, as a legacy applicant and a good student, she'd been accepted in January. Nick's single Mom couldn't afford an expensive school, so he accepted a partial scholarship to play football at West Chester State College. But even with the scholarship and student loans, it wasn't clear how Nick and his mom would afford the balance.

As graduation approached, their sense of pending separation grew. They held hands a little tighter, kissed with a bit more urgency, and laughed a little less. Then, three nights before graduation, he dropped a bombshell that shocked Patti, his mother, his guidance counselor, and his friends.

Nick and Patti had gone parking. She had tears in her eyes as she talked about the five-hour drive between West Chester and Pitt and how they'd try to make it work. She'd find a way to West Chester during football season when Nick couldn't get away and then he could find a way to get to Pitt in the winter. She was looking into bus schedules and talking about hitching rides with students going home for the weekend.

Finally, Nick summoned the courage to tell her that he'd been talking to a recruiter and decided to join the army.

Patti flipped out. He tried to explain that sooner or later he'd be drafted anyway, especially with growing talk that Washington might end student deferments. Besides, he believed in the war and thought it was better to fight communism in Asia before we had to fight it at home. He didn't like the fact that guys his age were living in a jungle and fighting and dying while he was preparing to live in a dorm and enjoy college life. He said he'd be out in two years and could use the GI Bill to pay for college. He could even apply to Pitt.

None of this mattered to Patti. She was hysterical. She screamed, cried, and beat his chest. How could he do this without talking about it first? Then she laid into him about Vietnam. They'd never discussed it, but she told him now how much she hated the war. We had no business being involved in what she saw as a civil war. She wondered how someone as smart as Nick could be sucked into the war machine propaganda.

Nick had never seen her like this.

The most wonderful ten weeks of his life changed into three weeks of misery. By the time Patti left for her two-week family vacation in early July, they were finished. He wrote to her once from Vietnambut never received a reply.

Over the years, he blocked out the miserable way the relationship ended. But somewhere in the back of his mind, he held on to what it felt like to be happy, to look forward to being with someone special, or just hearing her voice. He admitted that he was feeling that again, and he liked it.

His thoughts came back to the present. "I'm good. How about you?"

"I was wondering if you are busy today?"

"I'm very busy," Nick kidded. "I'm on the board of directors at our local bank. We have our monthly meeting this morning. Then I have a power luncheon with a group of investors who want my input on a project. Then…"

Liz laughed and repeated, "Nick, are you busy today?"

"Right now I'm at the deli reading the sports page and sipping Angelo's terrible coffee. After this my day is open. What's up?"

"I have my annual eye exam at 2 o'clock at my doctor's office which happens to be on Mill Street. It's a beautiful day and I thought if I came to Bristol early, we could take a walk along the river and maybe have lunch."

"Works for me. Where would you like to have lunch? "

"I was thinking maybe I could bring something in, and we could eat on a park bench somewhere."

"That sounds perfect."

She parked at the doctor's office which was a block from the King George, and he was waiting for her. She held a small bag which she said held their surprise lunch. They walked to the riverfront. It was a mild day, the sun felt good, and Nick noticed he was more aware of birds chirping.

He wanted to show off Bristol's new docks and pier. They passed under the wharf pavilion and walked to the pier that protruded over the river. It was late in the season, but some boaters were docked. The wind was stronger on the pier, and it blew her hair. She looked great.

"I absolutely love this spot," she gushed. "You're right. Langhorne is a beautiful town, but we don't have a river."

"I wanted you to see this. It was just finished two months ago."

They left the pier, and he led her for a walk along the river and past Bristol's row of ethnic monuments.

Closest to the wharf was the Columbus monument. Nick said it was commissioned as a tribute to the Italian immigrants who came to America at the turn of the previous century and those who settled in Bristol. It tells a story of their contributions to America and the region.

"History is complicated," Nick said. "And people are more aware of the more controversial side of Columbus now. But the statue was commissioned and paid for by Bristol residents with the best of intentions." He took her by the hand and led her closer to the monument. "Let me show you something you may find interesting." He scanned the list of names engraved in the granite until he found Angelo Marzo's parents.

"That's so cool," Liz said. "I'm sure these families take great pride in their ancestry."

"Yes," Nick said, deciding to keep hold of her hand. "But we're not all Italian." He walked her to the next monument and Liz said, "Wow. A Celtic Cross. The crosses first emerged in Ireland and Great Britain in the Early Middle Ages. It's beautiful."

"Hey," Nick said, I guess Miss Arts Society knows more than just the history of Langhorne."

"I love art and history of all kinds," she replied. She saw inscribed names and asked if Nick's family was included. Nick said it wasn't. "It cost a few bucks to get on. It was a reasonable amount, but it didn't fit in my mom's budget."

Next was the Puerto Rican monument replicating El Morro, the watchtower from the Fort at Old San Juan. "Look at the roof shaped like a bell. Very well done." They stepped closer to read the dedication and learned that the fortress dated back to the late sixteenth century. "This is all so tasteful," she said.

Last in the row of monuments was a sculpture of the African-American tribute to Harriet Tubman. "No need to

read anything here," Liz said. "Everyone knows about Harriet Tubman. That statue is so powerful."
"She's pointing to the North Star," Nick said. "With a pistol tucked inside her belt. She was not a person to be messed with."
"That's for sure. The detail of the sculpture is amazing."
"There are people in town today who trace their ancestry back to her."
"No way!"
"Yes," Nick said, "really."
"Thanks for sharing this, Nick. These monuments are a wonderful celebration of your town's diversity."
She checked her watch and said, "We'd better start lunch, or I'll miss my appointment."
Nick asked if she'd like to have lunch on one of the benches near the river.
"Perfect," she said as she draped her arm through his and said, "lead the way."
They sat and Nick commented on the bag she was carrying. "Are you sure you have two lunches in there?"
"Positive," she said smiling. "Keep an open mind."
She opened the bag and produced two cups of yogurt and plastic spoons.
Nick looked despondent. "This is lunch?"
"Look," she said with exaggerated enthusiasm. "The lid has crushed nuts. You mix it with the yogurt. And, if you're still hungry," she reached into the bag and produced an apple and pear. "Take your pick. "
"I could never eat all of this," Nick deadpanned.
Liz was undeterred. "I've watched what you eat for lunch, especially at the deli. You just can't eat a cheesesteak

every day. I'm sure you don't realize how bad that makes you feel."

Nick looked at his yogurt and said, "I'm feeling pretty bad right now."

Liz laughed out loud. "You look like you're going to cry. Look, we can get you a burger right now if you want, but trust me, if you ate a lighter lunch for a week you'd feel so much better. But" she added playfully, "you may not be tough enough to do it."

"Tough enough? I can do the yogurt, but you realize I eat with the guys at the deli each day. I'm not sure I'm tough enough to eat yogurt in front of them."

She smiled. "Worry about that later. Let's dig in."

They ate and watched a Boston Whaler dock and four boaters disembark.

"This is really nice," Liz said. "We should do it again."

There was a gentle breeze, and the midday sun felt good on Nick's face. Liz looked great and Nick felt more relaxed than he could remember. At that moment he felt he could sit on that bench forever.

"Yes. Let's do it again."

They finished the yogurt and passed on the fruit. "I'm stuffed," Nick said.

She smiled.

Nick turned serious. "Can I ask you something?"

"Sure. What's up? "

"Last week when we went to Itri with the others, you asked Johnny and Brian about their jobs."

"I remember," she said without expression.

"They were describing the various hate groups out there. It's not a pleasant topic, I admit, but I saw a look on your face I hadn't seen before."

Liz shrugged. "It was no big deal. Like you said, it's not a pleasant topic."
"I know, but what I saw looked more like apprehension than just unease."
"Nope, whatever you saw, you misread it. I'm fine."
"Okay. Sorry to bring it up."
The Burlington-Bristol Bridge had opened earlier, indicating a large ship was coming. Now a cargo ship came into view.
"Nice," Liz said. How often does that happen?"
"A couple times a day. They usually head to the port in Falls Township."
Liz kept her eyes on the ship.
"That's where your daughter lives, right?"
Liz nodded.
"I hope things are working out for her."
"Me too," Liz said. She checked her watch and said, "Better go. It's time for my eye appointment."

Chapter 24

It was the biggest pinochle tournament of the year and attracted the sixteen best players in town. This was not to be a friendly afternoon of cards. The one hundred dollar entrance fee ensured that participants were playing to win the thousand-dollar prize.
Angelo closed the Deli to host the event. Seating was tight and reminiscent of the old boxing clubs where spectators crowded in to view the contest. He set up four card tables with four players per table. Ralph McGinnis from the funeral parlor loaned him sixteen padded chairs for the players and another twenty for spectators who paid twenty dollars each

to crowd in for unlimited beer and buffet, as well as the chance to join in the ball-breaking between games.

Angelo and Big Frankie were registered to play, as were Nick and Jimmy. Interest in the spectator seats was so high that Angelo conducted a lottery to determine who was eligible to purchase. He reserved two for Johnny and Brian and easily sold the remaining eighteen.

It was his father's tournament and from the time he was seven, Johnny would serve beers to players who wanted a drink while they were playing. Just for fun, he continued serving right into adulthood whenever he was in town for the event. It was an honor for the players to be served by a hometown hero, and they continued to tip him a dollar, just as they did when he was a kid. Part of the joke of the day was that he kept it.

Once, someone wondered out loud where all the entrance fees and ticket money went, implying that Angelo was gouging them. That person almost got a chair broken over his head and was banned for life from the tournament. Only one other person had ever been banned for life. Tom Getti had left in the middle of the tournament when his wife called saying he was needed at home because the kids were acting up. From that day on, all cell phones were turned off and collected at the door.

Angelo didn't want the controversy over the money to happen again, so after the first incident, he gave everyone a breakdown of where the money went. He collected $1600 from player fees and $500 from spectators totaling $2100. From that, $1000 went to the winning team, and $200 went to the runner-up. Angelo provided each player with a black golf shirt embroidered by Great IDs by Anne with the words "Marzo Invitational 2018." Anyone who knew cards knew it was a mark of distinction to wear the shirts throughout the year. The shirts cost $400. That left $500 for beer and food for thirty-six people, which amounted to less than $15 per person. Anyone who thought that was too much could kiss Angelo's ass and be banned for life. One final financial note, Donnie Pit from Cesare's donated $50 each year for the winning team's trophies.

History was being made in 2018 because it was the first time a woman entered the tournament. It wasn't that women were banned, it was just that no one had ever bought a ticket as a spectator or registered to compete. But Janet Tyler had been taught pinochle by her grandfather, the legendary Bill "Cards" Brady, himself a two-time winner before his passing. She was damn good and she and her husband were in it to win.

When Angelo cautioned her that there would probably be a fair share of cussing going on, she just flipped him the bird. That put everyone's mind at ease.

It was a double-elimination tournament, and play began at 10 AM. With breaks, the event was expected to last until early evening. Last year's winners, "Sheets" Bedford and Bobby Radds, were favored to repeat, but all teams were confident. By mid-afternoon, four teams had been eliminated and Angelo removed two tables so spectators could gather closer around the four teams in the semi-finals. Table one featured Angelo and Big Frankie against Tim and Janet Tyler. Table two matched Nick and Jimmy against "Sheets" and Bobby Radds. Both tables went to three games. Jimmy dreamed of an all Deli final, but it wasn't to be as Angelo and Big Frankie lost to the Tylers two games to one. In a thrilling upset, Nick and Jimmy defeated "Sheets" and Radds by the same margin.

The final game was a nail-biter. It came down to the last hand and the Tyler's led 114- to 108, with 121 needed to win. It was Jimmy's turn to deal, which meant he would bid last, and Janet would bid first. She passed, which was a good sign. Like any card game, skill was important, but you had to have good cards. Janet was good, so passing indicated she didn't have much to play with. Nick was next. He didn't love his hand, but he bid the minimum of twenty-one just to save his partner. He sighed with relief when Tim passed also. Then Jimmy surprised everyone by bidding one better than his partner. Nick was concerned, but his concern turned to elation when Jimmy called trump and laid down a run in spades. Not only did that pretty much assure they would make their bid, but what Jimmy didn't know was that Nick had four spades of his own. If played right, they would sail through the final hand and win the game and the tournament. But their luck didn't end there. It turned out that Jimmy was trumping diamonds and Nick was trumping hearts. The Tylers were helpless to stop the crossfire that followed, and the hand became a romp. In the end, there was no need to count the points. Jimmy and Nick were the Marzo Invitational 2018 champions. The room erupted and Janet Tyler jokingly flipped the winners the bird and said, "Good game."

Some of the crowd lingered for another hour or so, making sure they got their money's worth, but eventually the guys were alone. They helped Angelo clean up. When they were finished, Big Frankie said he was exhausted. He congratulated Nick and Jimmy one more time and left. Angelo was locking up the rear and Nick and Jimmy were left alone at the table with one more beer.

Nick said, “You did a great job, Jimmy.”

“I got some good cards, didn’t I Nick?

“You did,” Nick replied, “and you played them well.”

“We did it,” Jimmy said softly. “We did it, and we were partners.”

“Yup,” Nick said. “We always were, and we always will be.”

Chapter 25

Nick and Liz were sitting on her back patio sipping wine and discussing Nick’s new truck that he bought from Big Frankie. Frankie was a retired cabinet maker but still did occasional small jobs. He decided he wanted to trade in his ten-year-old Ford F-10 pickup for a new one.

He wasn’t pleased with the trade-in offer, so he offered to sell it to Nick cheaply. Knowing how well Frankie cared for the truck, Nick took the offer and used his pinochle winnings as a down payment. Jimmy offered to give Nick his share to help with the purchase, but Nick declined.

It was raining and chilly under the patio overhang, so Liz had gotten them a blanket to share on the twin glider. Nick was quiet, and Liz felt he seemed a little distant.

“I love the rain, as long as I can be cozy and comfortable,” she said. I wish it would thunder.”

Nick thought about the monsoon season he spent in a bamboo cage when he was drenched for days at a time. " I'm not a big fan of rain," he said softly.

She tried again, " Are you liking your truck?"

Nick nodded. "Yes. It could be a little newer, I guess."

Liz said, "I thought you'd be a tad more excited about owning your first vehicle in over fifty years."

"Ever," Nick replied.

"Ever?"

"It's the first vehicle I've ever owned. I didn't have one in high school and nothing after the army."

They both got quiet and then Liz placed her glass back on the side table next to her and said, "Are you okay, Nick."

Nick shrugged. "Yeah. I guess I'm drifting a little."

Liz turned to face him. She looked concerned. "Drifting away?"

"No." He had his arm around her shoulder and pulled her a little closer. "No, not away. More like drifting back."

"To what?"

Nick shook his head. "I'm not sure. Sadness, I guess. I think having that old truck reminds me that I didn't for all those years. Don't get me wrong, it's not a material thing for me. I couldn't care less. But not being able to afford a new one reminds me that I hardly ever worked. I did a few years of under-the-table work in a wood shop, but never a steady job. Jimmy, in spite of all his troubles, worked at the steel mill for twenty-five years. He made good money and collects a pension. Big Frankie became one of the best cabinet makers in Bristol. Angelo ran the store when it was a real business, busy. He still caters small events. Me, I just collected my disability pension and lived like a hermit in an apartment about the size of this patio."

He looked off in the distance. It was raining harder now. "Why did I do that? I mean I know I had physical ailments and was in a bad place mentally, but why did I waste all of those years?"

Liz snuggled closer and rubbed his chest. "You helped all those veterans and their families," she said reassuringly. "That's something."

"I did," Nick admitted. "But that's not enough. I'm angry with myself, especially since I'm not sure why."

Liz looked as if she were pondering something. She said, "I'll be right back. I have to get something." She pulled off the blanket and went into the house. She returned a few minutes later, holding a small brown book. It looked like a diary with the date 1972 in gold letters on the front and a leather strap to tie it shut.

"Remember I told you I keep a journal? It was something my grandmother encouraged and it stayed with me. Remember after you arrived, I told you that every couple of years I'd write an entry wondering what became of you? "

Nick wasn't sure where she was going with this. "Yes, he said, " I wondered about you too, a lot, but only in my head. I didn't write anything down."

"When I was playing cards with the guys, and by the way," she kidded, "I would have won that tournament had I been invited."

Nick smiled. "Maybe. But Jimmy needed that day. Just him and me. It turned out better than I expected."

"I agree. Like I said, I was kidding. But, in the future, I might bring my friend, Julie. She plays too. How would that be if two women from Langhorne won the Marzo Invitational?"

Nick frowned at the thought. "That wouldn't be good. We'd probably have to lock you both in the basement and say it never happened."

Liz laughed. Then her eyes went to her journal.

"So, when I was playing cards with the guys before you came up from your workout, I told them it was nice meeting them. Big Frankie looked at me, scratched his head and said that we may have met before. He said when you had recovered enough for them to drive to Washington to visit you, there was a nurse in the room. She told Nick his visitors had arrived, smiled and left the room. It got me thinking that maybe it was me. So, I went way back in my journal to the time it may have been, and found out that it was."

She untied the string and opened it to a page she had marked. "Would you like to read this entry?"

Nick looked apprehensive. "No, you read it."

"I thought it was obviously significant when I found it but decided to let it go because you are doing so well. But now I think it might be helpful."

Liz turned to an entry dated July 21, 1973, and read. "Nick Hardings in room 118 had visitors from home today. Knowing they were coming had boosted his spirits for three days. I was in the room briefly when they arrived, and Nick was smiling from ear to ear. I thought this would be a catalyst for something good, a breakthrough. But when I returned after they left, he was despondent, far worse than before. When I asked what was wrong, he wouldn't answer. It was obvious he'd been crying. At times in his sleep, he would be restless and mumble, Johnny."

Nick stiffened when he heard the name.

Liz turned a few pages to an entry on July 27. "Nick Hardings is calmer now. But he is not the same as he was when he was improving. He seems stoic. When I asked again what had happened, he still refused to discuss it. I made an entry on his chart and decided to drop it for fear of upsetting him more."

She closed the book and looked at him.

"Who's Johnny, Nick? It obviously wasn't Johnny Marzo. He wasn't born yet. So who is Johnny, and what happened that day?"

Nick stared at a puddle that was forming at the edge of the patio.

"Johnny was our friend who was killed in Vietnam. Angelo and Donna named young Johnny Marzo after him." Tears began to well in his eyes. "He was an amazing kid. That's what we were when I saw him last, kids. He was a natural leader among the guys. He always knew the coolest new music and the coolest stuff to wear. He had a little mischief in him and had amazing enthusiasm. It was infectious. If he said it would be fun to do something, we'd all be on board. We all hung out at his mother's house, Anna. Of course, we called her Mrs. Francelli. She was incredible. She was a widow and loved having us around, even though we'd be in his finished basement most of the time."

He sniffled and rubbed his eyes at the memory. "I guess the last big caper we did with him was crashing a wedding. It was great. Years earlier, he talked us all into going to see President Kennedy lie in state at the Capitol after the assassination."

"No way!" Liz said.

"Yeah," Nick said, thinking back. "It was spur of the moment. He talked his sister into stealing his mom's car, totally out of character for him, but he really loved Kennedy. We all piled in and went. Totally oblivious to what we were doing. We chipped in for gas and thought we'd be gone seven hours. Three hours down, one hour at the capital, and three hours back. We'd park the car, and no one would know. Turns out we waited in line all night to walk by the casket, but we got to see it. I'll never forget it. It was one of the most moving moments of my life, and it wouldn't have happened if it weren't for Johnny."

"That's an amazing story," Liz said. "Sounds like an incredible guy."

"We were all very tight. We played football together, but Big Frankie was his best friend. Anyway, soon after I enlisted, Big Frankie got his notice to report for his draft physical. He was despondent. Johnny hated seeing him that way and he enlisted after being told by a recruiter that they could go in on the buddy system, same basic training and everything. He wanted to surprise Frankie. The day Johnny told him, Frankie was notified that he was 4F. He had flunked his physical because they discovered he was diabetic."

Liz put her hand to her mouth, "Oh my God! "

Nick nodded. "Johnny went in, and Big Frankie didn't. Johnny was killed while rescuing a wounded friend."

Nick wiped away a tear and said, "Big Frankie hasn't been right since."

Liz seemed stunned. "I'm so sorry, Nick. So, the day the guys came to see you at Walter Reed…"

Nick finished for her. "I saw them, and then I said, 'Where's Johnny?' That's when they told me. So one way or another, broken maybe, but we all made it through the war except Johnny."

They sat quietly for a while, listening to the rain. There was a crack of lightning in the distance. Finally, Liz said softly, “Have you ever heard of survivor’s guilt?”

Nick looked at her. “Yeah. I guess I have.”

“I think that deli has the worst case of collective survivor’s guilt one can imagine.”

She reached for the wine bottle and poured some for herself. Then, she said, “Give me your glass.”

“I can’t,” Nick said. “I have to drive.”

“No, you don’t, Nick. You’re staying with me tonight.”

Chapter 26

 Jimmy called Nick and said, “Bring the box when you come. We have another one. Big Frankie is here, so he can enter it as soon as you’re finished.”

Nick said he’d be right over. He arrived twenty minutes later with an old sneaker box tucked under his arm. Jimmy was seated at the table nervously tapping the edge of an envelope. Frankie was next to him hunched over a laptop. Angelo was cooking.

Nick sat, and Jimmy handed him the unopened envelope. Frankie said, “I looked him up based on his return address. It’s not a new case. You helped him six months ago. He’s Corporal Joe Dillon. Afghanistan. It was a mental health case.”

Nick opened the envelope and saw it held a thank you card. He read the message and smiled. “His was a PTSD case. He wanted treatment and couldn’t get in to see anyone.”

Big Frankie nodded. "I remember. He was in pretty bad shape. It's here in the database."

"The note said he finally got placed," Nick said. "He's been getting therapy for a couple of months and says he's doing better. He says the most important thing is that he doesn't feel helpless anymore."

Jimmy smiled. "Good job, Nick."

Nick said to Frankie, "Do you have what you need?"

"Yup. I have notes on his initial letter, your follow-up, and now his current status. We already had his address, email and phone."

Nick opened the box and gazed at the contents. It represented every correspondence he ever received from veterans needing help."

"What did that guy say in that Jaws movie? 'I think we're gonna need a bigger boat'? I think we're gonna need a bigger box."

He dropped the envelope in the box and gave the contents one last look before closing the top. Frankie closed the laptop as well.

Twenty years earlier, Frankie fell for Jane, a waitress at the diner who was slightly more than half his age. She had a rough life and struggled with two young kids and little money. Frankie and Jane were an unlikely pair, but they started dating. Frankie was generous to the girl and kind to the children who grew increasingly attached to him. He offered the most stability they'd had in years. The relationship became more serious, and they began to discuss the possibility of marriage. When Frankie said he wanted to adopt the kids, it sealed the deal, and soon they married. Less than a year later, Frankie suffered the second major blow of his life when Jane abandoned them all and disappeared. She broke his heart, but the kids saved his life and he saved theirs. He loved them both and raised them as a single dad. He still had his personal demons to deal with, but the kids gave him something to live for when he'd often thought there wasn't. The kids were grown now, and his son followed his work to a job in Ohio. He bought Frankie a laptop and insisted that he learn how to email and exchange photos with the grandkids. Frankie took an interest. Once, when Frankie told him about Nick's box, his son sent him a link to a YouTube tutorial on using spreadsheets. He suggested they make a digital record of future correspondence instead of storing them in a box under a bed. Frankie was absorbed by the idea and mastered it to the point where he told Nick they could enter information from the letters into a spreadsheet. Nick agreed to let him do it but insisted on keeping the hard copies in the box as he always had done.

□ Everyone who knew Nick or read the newspaper accounts was well aware of the unlikely invitation to speak before a congressional committee. What started as a brief courtesy gesture to Nick, caught the attention of the media in a big way. The comments of an enlisted combat veteran, a Green Beret, a Distinguished Service Cross recipient, and a former prisoner of war testifying about the inadequacies of veterans' services proved far more newsworthy than the mundane, statistical testimony of VA bureaucrats. Nick became a bit of a hero among veteran advocacy groups. His testimony led in part to increased funding for congressmen to add staff with specific duties to deal with veterans navigating an unresponsive system. In time, he developed by phone or letter a personal relationship with staffers, not only in Bucks County but throughout the region.

The whole database exercise was cathartic for the guys at the deli, Angelo included. It captured Nick's work in a tangible way and opened the door to new ideas. With the contact information they gathered, they could create a newsletter urging action on pending veterans' legislation or form support groups, any number of things. Maybe just a picnic for those who lived close enough.

Their records included a handful of very old men from World War II and Korea, and still a surprisingly large number from Vietnam. But most now were from Afghanistan and the two wars in Iraq. Their stories ranged from vets denied benefits, to those navigating the hospital system, to the most outrageous as far as Nick was concerned, families of dead soldiers being evicted much too soon from military housing when their husbands were killed in combat. More recently, the records included the struggles of female veterans as their ranks in the military grew.

Big Frankie's database was a good idea, but Nick still clung to his box of original correspondence. They humanized the stories for him. Carrie even suggested they might make interesting material for a book.

Nick thought back to his conversation with Liz on her patio. At times when he drifted and thought of a life wasted, the box reminded him that there had been some purpose after all.

Chapter 27

Sergeant Bill Applegate was a high school teammate of Johnny Marzo before they eventually went their separate ways in law enforcement, Johnny, of course, to the FBI and Applegate to the local police department. Applegate knew the guys at Marzo's Deli, and was aware of Jimmy's service record so he wanted to help. He called the deli, told Angelo that Jimmy was at the police station, and suggested someone come to the station to see him. That was all he would say on the phone.

Nick and Big Frankie were in the deli when the call came in. Angelo closed the store, and the three of them climbed into Big Frankie's truck and raced to the station. Sergeant Applegate met them in the foyer and thanked them for coming.

"Thank you for calling," Angelo said. "Is Jimmy okay? Is he hurt?"

"He's fine physically, but he was very agitated."

Nick had met Sergeant Applegate several times and took the lead. "Is he under arrest, Bill?"

"No, but he could have been. We helped him out a little."

Big Frankie asked what happened, and Applegate shook his head. "He coldcocked a guy in the checkout line at the grocery store. He said he was tired of being disrespected. That's it. That's all he would say."

Big Frankie said, "So he actually hit a guy?"

"He sure did, and it wasn't a love tap. He really whacked him."

Applegate was met with silence as the guys let that sink in. He waited and then continued. "I have no plans to arrest him, and I'll explain in a minute how we pulled that off. But to be honest, I'm not comfortable releasing him until I'm assured there's not a mental health crisis going on with him right now, some triggers that would cause something like this."

The guys shook their heads, and Nick replied, "Bill, I think you know me well enough to know I'm a straight shooter and we all want what's best for Jimmy. If we thought he needed help we would tell you. But honestly. I'm not aware of anything, and from my perspective, he's been great lately."

Applegate eyed the others, and Angelo and Big Frankie agreed.

"Where is he now?" Nick had visions of Jimmy in a jail cell and was concerned about how that confinement might set off the former tunnel rat who hated close quarters.

"Don't worry. He's not in a cell. I have him in an interrogation room and I left my partner Jake to stay with him. Jake is good at defusing situations."

Nick looked relieved. "So, he's not under arrest?"

Applegate smiled and added, "The other guy won't be pressing charges. My partner and I separated them outside and spoke to them privately. The other guy was a young punk in his twenties, high as a kite. I ran his ID and found he was on parole. He also had a penknife in his pocket, which I consider a weapon. I told him I was in a forgiving mood and would cut him some slack. I gave him an option. Leave and forget it happened or press charges and I do all the paperwork, which would include notifying his parole officer, doing a urine test for drugs, and also dealing with the knife. Just for fun, I also suggested it wouldn't look good to his buddies if this story went further and they found out he'd been flattened by a man in his seventies. The guy thanked me profusely and walked away the minute I stopped talking."

Nick thanked him and Applegate said, "I don't do this for just anyone. Johnny and I go way back, and I know Johnny loves the guy. But hey, you guys can't say anything or my ass will be in a sling. Same thing with my partner who's doing me a big favor. And any signs that Jimmy has something serious going on, I want a call and I'll recommend a mental health eval."

"Got it," Nick said. "You have my word."

Angelo said, "Can we see him?"

"Follow me."

Applegate led them down a corridor to the interrogation room. Before opening the door, he said, "Talk to him. Try to find out what happened. As soon as you think he's calm enough, you can take him." Then he opened the door and told Jimmy he had visitors.

Jimmy and Applegate' partner had dollar bills in their hands, and it was obvious they'd been playing liar's poker, a simple game involving betting on the digits of the serial numbers on the bills.

They put the bills away. The officer stood, patted Jimmy on the back, wished him luck, squeezed by the others and left.

Applegate said, "I'm turning you over to these guys, Jimmy, but first, tell me you understand that you can't go around punching people in grocery stores."

Jimmy looked apologetic in front of his friends. He said, "I understand, Bill. It's just that he got me so mad and I…"

Applegate cut them off. "Don't even tell me, Jimmy. You can tell your friends here. Let's just call this a bad experience and move on."
Applegate winked at the guys. "You're welcome to the room for as long as you need it if you like." With that, he turned and left.

The guys pulled up some chairs and sat. Jimmy said sheepishly "Don't be mad at me. The creep had it coming."
"We're not mad, "Nick said. "We just don't know what the heck happened."
Angelo said, "Take a breath. Gather your thoughts and tell us what happened step by step."
Jimmy leaned forward in his chair. "So, I'm in the self-checkout line at the store…"
Angelo rolled his eyes and Frankie said, "Oh, boy, that means trouble."
Jimmy hated lines and was determined to learn to use the self-check aisle. It had been a challenge.
"Self-checkout shouldn't mean trouble," Jimmy protested. "I'm getting pretty good at it, and I'd like to use it. I have the right to use it."
Nick didn't want to agitate him again and said, "You absolutely do, Jimmy. But what happened? Did you hit a snag?"
"Exactly! "Jimmy said. "Things were going good. I was zipping through my stuff, and then I hit a snag. I couldn't find a barcode on this one thing. I kept looking, and it really pissed me off because I could hear the guy behind me

making noises like he was impatient. And I looked back and saw this sad excuse for a man, tattoos all over the place and his jeans down so low on his ass that you could see a good four inches of his underwear. His skin was pasty white like he was some kind of an addict. He caught my eye, gave me a smart-ass grin, and said, 'Let's go, Boomer.'"

Jimmy's statement got everyone's attention because they knew what was coming. They deferred to Nick who always handled Jimmy best. Nick knew Jimmy hated derogatory statements about the Baby Boomer generation, people in Jimmy's age group who were born after World War II. The insulting comments had become a fad popular with younger people.

"That's it?" Nick asked. "That's all he said?"

"That was enough," Jimmy said. "Something inside of me snapped. I flattened him. Right then. One shot and he was down. He looked at me like I was crazy and made it clear that he was going to stay down." Then he added, "I only hit him once. I'm small, Nick. But what was that term you used once to describe me?"

"Strong and wiry."

"That's it! I'm strong and wiry."

Nick visualized the scene and tried to suppress a smile. Angelo and Big Frankie were grinning as well.

Jimmy relaxed and grinned himself. "The place went crazy. Some lady was screaming. It happened so fast that hardly anyone actually saw it happen. I remember hearing one person tell another that she thought the creep fainted. I guess that was good because it turns out Sergeant Applegate and his partner were on break at the snack bar, and they came rushing over. They hustled us both out of there and separated us. That's when I recognized Bill Applegate as one of Johnny Marzo's friends, and I thought maybe I would get a break."

"You got a big break," Nick said. "If it wasn't for Bill, you could be in a great deal of trouble right now. It's aggravated assault. And so, we may be smiling a little at the thought of you dropping this guy, but we want to make sure you understand that you just can't do it. So, promise us this won't happen again."

Jimmy shook his head. "I'm sorry, but I can't promise that. If somebody else gives me that 'Okay, Boomer' bullshit, I'm gonna pop him too."

Nick shook his head. "Where is all this coming from, Jimmy? I know the term pisses you off, but this is a pretty strong reaction. It's not a big deal, Jimmy. Hardly anybody uses it."

"Oh, really?" Jimmy looked defiant again. "Hey, Angelo, remember when Gracie was over a couple of weeks ago, and I asked her to look it up and she showed you how to do it on your phone."

Angelo said he did.

"Do me a favor. Look it up. Go ahead, type Ok Boomer on that magic look-up line and see what pops up."

Angelo did and passed the phone to Jimmy who read the definition.

"Okay Boomer is a catchphrase used by Millennials and Gen Z to mock attitudes typically associated with Baby Boomers. It is intended to be cutting and dismissive and attack against older people considered to be out of touch and close-minded about current values and opinions."

Jimmy had stumbled reading but got through it well enough to look up proudly and say, "See. This guy doesn't know me, but he makes assumptions about who I am and what I believe, what my attitudes are, and where I've been. He does all of that because I'm older and can't find a friggin' barcode."

It was tough to argue with that, and no one did, so Jimmy went on. "I've had enough," he said defiantly. "I'm tired of people dismissing older guys like us, like we've had it, like we're done, washed up. What the hell are we supposed to do, roll up and die because we got a little older?"

He took a breath and went on. "When I saw that guy, I saw every wise-ass millennial who doesn't know us, doesn't know me, doesn't know what we've done with our lives, and just dismisses us as irrelevant. Yeah, maybe I don't know some tech stuff. Maybe we're not cool enough, or whatever. I say that's bullshit."

His voice was rising now, and Nick hoped Sergeant Applegate didn't hear him. "I fought in Vietnam, Nick. I saw guys with their faces blown off. I crawled in goddamn tunnels. When I wasn't busy trying to kill people because President Johnson drafted me, I was trying to change the world for the same causes these candy-ass millennials want now. We, all of us at this table, admired Martin Luther King and watched his big speech. Our generation supported civil rights. We protested to protect the environment. We admired Kennedy. Remember when we all snuck off without our parents' permission and drove to Washington, so we could walk by Kennedy's coffin when he was shot?"

Nick said quietly, "We'll never forget it."

"Damn right," Jimmy said. "We were inspired by him. Do these little jerks know that when they write us off?"

Jimmy went on. “After the army, I worked in the steel mill for twenty-five years, sweating and busting my ass at the blast furnace. That was when America made shit out of the steel we produced like cars, bridges, and skyscrapers. We were number one. Today, all we make are freaking video games. The guy I popped probably lives in his parent's, basement playing games and getting high till the middle of the night and then sleeping half the day. What friggin right did he have to dismiss me or you or anyone else our age?”
“None,” Nick said just as softly as before. No one else spoke, as they processed what Jimmy said. A tear ran down Jimmy's cheek and he wiped it away before offering one more thought. “I'm a man, and I deserve respect. I'm getting up in years, and I might croak tomorrow. Heck, we all might, and I don't know about you, but until I do, I will not be brushed aside by people like him.”
Jimmy's comments had struck a nerve with all of them.
“I know I'm not smart, and I can't say things as good as you guys, but that's how I feel.”

“We respect that,” Big Frankie said. “We just don't want to see you get in trouble. This isn't like you. When was the last time you hit someone?”
Jimmy scratched his head. “I guess it was about fifty years ago when I cracked a gook in the face with my rifle butt after I ran out of ammo.” He reflected on that and said, “Just once in fifty years. Heck, that damn near makes me a pacifist. But I swear to God, the next guy who dismisses me with a Boomer wisecrack will be on the floor.”

Big Frankie drove everyone to Jimmy's vehicle in the grocery store lot. From there, Nick stayed with Jimmy for the ride to Nick's apartment. Along the way, Nick said, "It's been a pretty eventful morning."

"Yeah, I guess so. Thanks again for picking me up. I guess I was lucky Bill Applegate was there. Maybe I'll buy him a six-pack."

"That's a nice thought, but I think I'd just leave it alone. He really stuck his neck out. Just disappear for now. Someday you'll see him in a bar, and you can buy him a drink."

"Okay," Jimmy said. "I'll lie low for a while. Maybe pick a different grocery store too."

Nick nodded and changed the subject. "I have something important to tell you, so tune in."

"You've got me."

Nick said, "I want you to know I understand exactly what you were feeling today, both at the grocery store and the police station. I mean, I don't get that bothered by Boomer comments, although after listening to you, I may be changing my mind about that. But besides that, the real issue for me, and I think for you, is that we're getting older, and we don't know what to do about it."

Every so often, Nick had quiet talks with Jimmy, talks about things that mattered, without the usual banter and jokes. Jimmy always welcomed the attention, and he could tell from Nick's voice that this would be one of those talks.

Nick waited a few seconds and said, "For starters, I've conflicting emotions I'm trying to sort out. Like most older people, I miss our youth. Hanging out with the guys, playing football, and even basic training in the army. I miss rising to the physical challenge."

"We were tough," Jimmy said.

"Damn tough," Nick replied.

"At least you still lift weights," Jimmy said. "Maybe I should do that."

"That's up to you, but I can tell you it makes me feel good mentally. So, anyway, I miss the physical challenge, the competition. I also miss having something important to do, being someone who others depend upon."

"You help the vets," Jimmy said. "That's important."

Nick nodded. "It is, and I'm glad I have that. When I'm with those guys, either one-on- one or in small groups, I feel like a million bucks. They know me in a certain way. They know what I can do. The last thing on their minds is that, 'hey, this guy is old.' But when I'm not with them, I feel like people just see an old man. So, in a way, it's kind of like your boomer thing.

"As we get older and our knees hurt, and our backs are stiff, and we don't remember things like we used to, it's natural to think we're on the way out. Then something or someone reminds us of it, like your Boomer punk, and it can get us down, or like you today, it can get us angry."

Jimmy looked focused as Nick continued. "We're getting old, Jimmy. It's not good, and that's the reality. But, lately, I've been looking at it differently. I've been thinking about a poem I studied in high school."

"A poem," Jimmy said. "Geeze, we're gonna talk about a poem. You were always so damn smart," he said with genuine admiration. "We were in different classes. You were with the brains. We didn't do any poems in the classes I was in. We might make up our own in the cafeteria like, roses are red, violets are blue…"

"Shut up, Jimmy. We're almost at the house and I want to finish."

Jimmy smiled. "Sorry. I forgot this was an important talk. So what's the poem?"

"It's called, 'Do Not Go Gentle into That Good Night,' by Dylan Thomas."

"The folk singer? Is it a song?"

"You're thinking of Bob Dylan. Dylan Thomas is a poet."

"Oh, so what's the poem about?"

"The thing about poetry is that people can have different opinions about it. I remember in high school, Mr. Fran explained it as a poem about not giving into old age, and, you know, thinking about the grim reaper coming. Stuff like that. Anyway, I remembered a little bit about it and looked it up a few weeks ago.

"I memorized the first verse and I'm going to recite it now. If you laugh, I'm going to smack you in the head. I don't care how strong and wiry you are."

Jimmy smiled and said, "I won't laugh. I know this is an important talk."

"Okay. Here goes.

"Do not go gentle into that good night,

Old age should burn and rave at close of day;

Rage, rage against the dying of the light."

Jimmy scratched his head. “That was nice. What the heck does it mean?”

“I think it means that there is a light inside of us that can grow dimmer with old age, and instead of just accepting it and fading away, we should burn and rave against it, fight it, brighten it by living life to the fullest and putting passion into everything we do in the time we have left.”

Jimmy shrugged. “I guess I get that.”

Nick said, “When you hit that guy this morning, you were sort of doing what Dylan Thomas was saying. The punk made a comment about your age, and you burned and raved against it by hitting him.”

Jimmy broke in to a broad smile. “I did what the guy in the poem was saying?”

“I think so. Maybe not the punch, but at that moment, you were showing your passion for life and not giving in to people or things that get in the way.”

“Damn right I was,” Jimmy said proudly.

Nick smiled. “Liz has been a big help to me in forgetting how old I am. I feel younger. I look forward to things. I'm not interested in slowing down.”

“Yeah, Liz is great. Good card player too.”

Jimmy pulled up to the curb at Nick's apartment. Nick turned to Jimmy, put a hand on his shoulder, and said, “Jimmy, how about if you and I make a pact? Let's promise each other that we'll stop feeling sorry for ourselves and the hand life dealt us. Let's start living life to the fullest.”

Jimmy smiled. "I'm in, Nick. We've gotta keep moving. Let's have some fun. We'll go to ballgames, movies."

"We'll do all of that, Jimmy, but I need more than that. I want to accomplish something. I want to do something good besides helping vets. I don't know what it is yet, but I want to do it."

"Me too, Nick. I want to do it with you."

Chapter 28

Nick was about to take a shower when his cell phone rang. He was pleased to see the caller was Liz. He was always pleased when the caller was Liz. He answered right away.
"Hey, Liz. What's up?"
"Am I interrupting anything?"
"I was meeting with my stockbroker and financial advisor, but we were just breaking up." He loosely cupped his hand over the speaker and said to no one, "Okay, guys, that's it for today. We'll pick it up Tuesday."

Liz laughed out loud. "Any tips you can give me?"
He was tempted to say, "Viagra stocks are rising," but thought it would be in bad taste. He considered saying, "Depends" and letting the double meaning hang there, but he dismissed that as well. Instead, he said, "For now, we've decided to keep our money under the bed." He paused and said, "So, what's new with you?"
Liz said, "Do you like popcorn?"

Nick thought that was a strange question. "Popcorn? I've never considered that as an investment option. I don't think anyone has."

She laughed again. "Can we get off the stock market thing for a minute? I'm asking you whether you like to eat popcorn."

"Only if it's drenched in butter, and if there's dental floss nearby. It should be a law, if you sell someone popcorn you have to include dental floss. The stuff is impossible to eat without getting at least one kernel stuck somewhere."

"You are exhausting, Nick. Most people would answer that question with a simple yes or no."

"See, Jimmy was right. You try to have a nice, simple relationship, and pretty soon complications set in. People try to stifle you. Pretty soon you're not yourself anymore."

"Nick!" She interrupted.

"Yes?

She paused after each word for emphasis.

"Do, you, like, popcorn? Yes or no?"

"Yes!"

"Phew, that took some effort. I've almost forgotten why I asked."

"Listen," Nick said. "You don't have to tell me if you don't want to. Unlike you, I don't believe in adding stress to a relationship. Maybe in time you'll feel differently and want to open up, but…"

"Shut up, Nick. I think I'm going to start taking a Tylenol each time I call you."

"Buy a big bottle because I hope you call a lot."

"That's sweet, Nick. Thanks." She paused and said, "I'm going to hang up now, and then call you right back. When I do, after we say hi, I'll say, 'Do you like popcorn?'

Then you'll say, 'Sure, everyone does, why?' Then I'll say, 'I'm watching my granddaughter tonight and we're going to rent a movie. I was wondering if you'd like to come over to watch with us and have some popcorn.' Then you'll say, 'Sounds like fun. I'd love to.'"

Nick paused and mumbled, "Then I'll say....wait, can you repeat that? I'm trying to write it down, but you went pretty fast."

Liz exhaled slowly and said, "Nick, would you like to come?"

"Yes. I'd love to come and meet your granddaughter."

"That's great. Can you make it by 5:30? I'll make dinner and then we'll watch it. I can't keep her up too late."

"Do you have her overnight?"

"Yes."

"That's nice. What's the occasion?"

Liz's tone changed. "Nothing special. I just have her."

It was the second time Nick detected a change in demeanor when the topic involved her daughter, or in this case, her granddaughter.

He decided not to push it. "Sounds good. Can we watch *Rocky*?"

"She's seven."

"How about *Jaws*?"

"She's seven. Our choices are *Benji* or *Coco*. One is about a dog that helps hold a family together. The other is about a little boy who loves music, but his family has a mysterious ban on it. Addie hasn't decided yet."

"Those are tough choices. I'm sure she'll pick a good one. I'll see you at 5:30."

"Great," Liz said. "I'll make sure the popcorn has lots of butter. Just don't lick your fingers in front of her. I'm teaching her to use a napkin."
Nick smiled to himself. "I guess we'll learn together."
"Just one more thing," Liz said. "She's very smart and very perceptive."
"Sounds like her grandmom."

Chapter 29

Nick arrived at 5:20 and Liz's granddaughter greeted him at the door before he could ring the bell. Cute kid, Nick thought. He saw traces of Liz's features, even more so when she smiled.
"Are you Nick?" She asked before saying hello.
"Hi," Nick said. "Yes, I am."
"Hi, I'm Addie." She stepped aside and said, "You can come in."
Nick stepped inside and Addie said, "Mommy-Liz is in the kitchen."
Nick grinned at the Mommy-Liz reference and promised himself to have fun with that later.
Addie sat in an armchair, and Nick sat on the loveseat across from her. "Mommy-Liz said to entertain you while she finished dinner."
Nick smiled.
"So, would you like me to sing, dance or tell jokes?"
Nick didn't know how to answer. Addie smiled and said, "I was just kidding. I know what she meant. We should have a conversation." She looked at Nick as if she was waiting for him to start.
Finally, he said, "What grade are you in?"

"Second. I skipped first grade." Then, without hesitation, she added "Are you Mommy-Liz's boyfriend."

Nick was caught off guard and stammered. "We're ah ..."

Addie laughed and said, "That's funny. Mommy-Liz answered the same way."

Nick laughed, and Addie continued. "It's not fair."

"What's that? "Nick asked.

"Sometimes Mommy and Mommy-Liz ask me if there is a boy in my class that I like. I say no and they say stuff like, 'There must be someone you like, someone you think is cute.' I say, there isn't and they say, 'I think there probably is, and you're just too shy to say it.' So it's not fair that they can ask me, but I can't get an answer out of adults."

"You've got a good point there," Nick replied. "I'll tell you what, I'll tell you if you tell me, deal?"

"Deal." She reached out her hand to shake, and Nick did the same.

Liz stuck her head out of the kitchen doorway and said, "Hi, Nick. Sorry for the delay. Dinner will be ready in five minutes. I hope you two are getting to know each other."

Nick winked at Addie and said, "We are."

Addie added, "We're entertaining each other."

"Great," Liz replied. "Give me five more minutes."

Liz left and Nick said, "Okay, you go first. Is there a boy in your class that you like? Someone you think is cute?"

Addie said, "You go first."

Nick shook his head. "Sorry, Kiddo, I said I'd tell you IF you tell me. You said we had a deal and we shook on it."

Addie smiled. "You tricked me. You shouldn't trick a kid. I'm seven. You must be forty or fifty or something."

Nick liked this kid. “Something like that. Anyway, we have a deal. What’s your answer?”

She thought for a minute and said, “No. None of the boys are cute and I don’t like any of them.”

“Really?” Nick said. “Not one?”

“Really,” she said. Then she added shyly, “Maybe one.”

Nick smiled. “Tell me about him.”

“His name is Andrew. He’s a little cute. Sometimes he comes up to me in the schoolyard. He looks at me and smiles and then runs away.”

“That’s it?”

“That’s it. He just smiles and runs away.”

“Well, he must like you, because you are very likable.”

“Please don’t tell Mommy-Liz. She’ll get all excited and ask me a thousand questions that I don’t feel like answering.”

“I won’t,” Nick said. “I promise. Maybe you should invite him to a movie night. “

“No way!” She said, “Oh, my gosh. If the kids at recess found out, they would go crazy. No. I will never do that.” She paused. “Now it’s your turn. Are you Mommy-Liz’s boyfriend?”

Nick scratched his head. “I don’t know how to answer that.”

“Yes or no will work just fine.”

Nick laughed. “Being someone’s boyfriend is a big deal I guess. Besides, you’d have to know if the other person wanted to be your girlfriend.”

Addie shook her head. “When Mommy-Liz said you were coming tonight, I asked her to tell me about you. She said you were nice and that you were very smart. The smart part must not be true because anyone could tell she wants to be your girlfriend.”

Nick loved her spunk. “How?” he asked.

“She’s all excited about you coming tonight. She’s been cooking all afternoon and playing her favorite music. And she’s happy all the time now. Before, she was just normal, now, she’s happy all the time, except when she’s sad about my mom.”

Nick just looked at her.

“Like when she picked me up from school today, and I could tell she was sad. She said I was sleeping over because my dad was coming over to talk with my mom. Except they never talk. They yell. Him mostly. He’s not the same as he used to be. It’s scary sometimes. So, Mommy-Liz was sad. But then she said she had an idea. How about if she invited you over for a movie night? I said, sure, and she got happy.”

Nick didn’t say anything. He wanted to know more about her concerns but didn’t want to pry.

“Anyway, you should be Mommy-Liz’s boyfriend because you make her happy. I wish my dad made my mom happy, but he doesn’t. He makes us both sad, and he’s mad all the time.”

Liz came into the room and said, “Sorry that took so long, but it’s time to eat. I hope you two like octopus.”

They both shot her a look, and she laughed. “Just kidding.

Chapter 30

The table was set nicely, and it was obvious Liz had put considerable care into the dinner. She served cantaloupe with prosciutto for an appetizer. Nick had never eaten a real meal with a child before and was interested in observing her eating habits. Addie ate the cantaloupe but passed on the meat. Next came a small Caesar's salad. The dressing was perfect, and Addie nibbled. The main course was chicken parm with stuffed shells and spinach casserole, but Liz had made Addie buttered noodles instead.

Nick complimented Liz on the food and joked with Addie about the buttered noodles. "Your noodles look delicious," he said. "I hope Mommy-Liz saved enough butter for the popcorn tonight."

Addie looked hopefully at her grandmother, and Liz assured her that she did.

Nick asked, "Who does the dishes around here when Addie visits?"

"I load the dishwasher and Mommy-Liz does the pots and pans."

"I'll be happy to do that tonight if you girls would like to rest, especially Mommy-Liz since she worked so hard making dinner." He grinned at Liz each time he called her Mommy-Liz.

Addie said, "I don't think you know how to do dishes. I never saw a man do dishes."

"Of course, I do. My friend owns a deli, and I always help him."

Addie asked what a deli was, and Nick said it was like a small restaurant.

"Can we go there sometime?"

Liz noticed her reference to "we" and thought it was sweet how Addie was warming up to Nick. She used the opportunity to poke him. "It's a special kind of place," Liz said. "You have to be invited to go. Sometimes a certain person gets mad if you go without asking."

Nick caught the reference and was about to respond, but Addie lost interest.

She said, "Why don't we all do the dishes together? Then we can start the movie."

"Good idea," Liz said.

Nick asked the name of the movie they'd be watching.

"I couldn't decide between *Benji* and *Coco*. It was a hard choice, but I chose Benji. It's about a dog."

"I have a surprise, Addie," Liz said, trying to sound upbeat. "Mommy called and asked if you could stay another night. So, we can watch *Coco* tomorrow."

Nick noticed that Addie looked concerned.

"She called? Addie asked. "Can I call her back?"

"She's busy, honey. We'll call her tomorrow morning before I drive you to school."

Addie looked disappointed but said okay and left for the kitchen. When she left, Liz let her concern show. She whispered, "I have some things to tell you later."

After the movie and popcorn, Liz took Addie up to bed, but not before Addie gave Nick a warm hug goodnight. Nick waited for Liz to tuck her in and stay until the little girl fell asleep.

When Liz came downstairs, she poured herself a glass of wine and offered one to Nick. He declined, and she joined him on the couch.

Nick said, "She's a great kid."

"She really is," Liz said. "And she certainly took a liking to you."

Nick grinned and said, "I loved the Mommy-Liz thing."

Liz smiled but had too much on her mind to joke.

She sipped her wine and said, "Thanks for being here tonight. I invited you for fun, but it turns out I needed you for more than that."

"I really enjoyed it. It was a lot of fun, but…"

Liz finished for him, "But you'd like to know what's going on."

"It's not my business, and I don't want to pry, but something is bothering you and I'm concerned."

Liz turned to him, "You are not prying at all. You've been reading me for a while and it's not fair for me to be so secretive. I appreciate your concern."

"You don't have to tell me anything, but I'm here if you want to."

"I want to." Liz took another sip of her wine and put the glass on the coffee table.

"Let me start by saying I'm a wreck tonight, and the story I'll be sharing spans three years. It may sound disjointed at times as I try to piece things together from memory. So, forgive me if I ramble and please stop me when you've heard enough."

"Take your time, Liz," Nick said. "Just do the best you can."

Liz straightened in her seat, cleared her throat, and began. "As I told you, Kate is having a difficult time with her husband. Change that. Make it an impossible time."

She paused, thought a moment, and said, "Maybe I should take you all the way back, so you have a better understanding of how she ended up with such a guy."

"Makes sense," Nick said.

Liz took a sip of wine and began. "Growing up, Kate was a rebellious kid, very bright, but a handful. I'm sure being raised by a single divorced mother didn't help. Knowing her father left when she was just a year old had to play havoc with her head, especially since he was gone and showed no interest in reuniting with her.

"After high school, she didn't want to go to college, but I forced her, which was a mistake. She hung around for a year and a half, said it wasn't for her, and dropped out. She took off to live in Oregon with two girlfriends where she took some online mixology courses and got a job tending bar. She's cute and can be flirtatious and ended up making decent money. We'd talk now and then, and I tried to be as supportive as I could, hoping someday she'd grow out of whatever she was looking for and return home. She'd visit twice a year at Christmas and Mother's Day, and I'd fly there for a couple of days in midsummer. I learned that the less judgmental and more accepting I was, the closer we'd get. She stayed on the West Coast four years and finally returned home. I tried pitching college again, but she resisted. She got an apartment and took another job bartending. She met Tom at the bar when she was 26 and they started dating.

"The more I saw him, which was infrequently, the less I liked him. I found him to be arrogant and self-centered. I tried to gently share my concerns with Kate but backed off when she reacted in typical fashion, especially when she implied that I might not be the most qualified to give advice about choosing partners. That hurt, but I knew she'd had a difficult life because of my divorce, so I backed off. Kate became pregnant when she was 27 and decided to keep the baby. She and Tom married and Addie was born when Kate was twenty-eight.

"The baby brought us closer. Tom's family was not around, and I helped as much as I could. Gradually, as she depended upon me more, she became less quarrelsome. She finally decided that bartending was not an ideal job for the mother of an infant. I was thrilled when she decided to become a nurse like her mother. She took as many on-line courses as possible and face-to-face when she had to. Tom wasn't crazy about it, but as long as I was paying tuition, he tolerated it. It took her four years to graduate. When she finished, I couldn't have been prouder. She was 33 and beginning a new career."

"Good for her," Nick said. "That had to be difficult."
"As I said, I was very proud. I still am. But now, let me tell you about Tom. I was never crazy about the guy in the first place, but I just couldn't put my finger on it. He was gruff at times, and a little too domineering for my taste, but I told myself I was probably overreacting to my own marriage and the baggage I carried from that. I decided that he was okay, not great, but okay. Besides, Kate loved him, so that was that."

Nick seemed to be fully engaged, so Liz continued.

"About two years ago, things began to change for the worse. He was a union laborer. He thought he was in line for an apprenticeship and would eventually become a skilled pipe fitter. "Instead, things went the other way. He was passed over and swore it was because they gave the spot to a Latino. They were still doing okay financially. Liz was working full-time, and they lived comfortably with their two salaries. Not great, but comfortable.

"But instead of being grateful for the money she brought in, he resented it. He said it was a man's job to support his wife and child. He grew increasingly angry and lashed out relentlessly at minority groups he believed were ruining America- Blacks, Hispanics, and immigrants.

"Then, along came 2016 and Hillary ran for president. Kate had never been into politics much. She had moderately liberal views but wasn't active beyond voting. But, like so many women, she was excited about a woman having a good chance to get elected, especially a woman she agreed with on the issues. She sent in a twenty-five-dollar donation and received a Hillary for President Tee shirt.

"When Tom saw the credit card bill he became enraged. He rattled off a list of special treatments that women received in business loan preference, hiring practices, college acceptance, and even union membership. He said Hillary and her policies represented all that was wrong with America. He told her to get rid of the shirt because he'd be embarrassed if she wore, in his words, 'that bitch's shirt' in public."

Nick shook his head. "It doesn't sound as if this is heading in a good direction."

"That's an understatement," Kate said. She went on to explain that something happened to her at that moment. After years of putting up with his ranting and political lecturing, the argument represented the proverbial straw that broke the camel's back. Kate said it had little to do with the shirt or her support of Hillary. She wouldn't disrupt her marriage over that. She told me she'd been, 'dominated' throughout her marriage, and this disagreement simply represented a tipping point. She'd had enough of his anger and verbal abuse. She told him she could support whomever she wanted, and he could do the same.

Kate said she never saw him so angry. She told him she loved him, but he would have to show her more respect as a woman. He ignored that and responded by virtually ransacking the house to find the shirt. She watched in horror as he searched drawers and closets, cursing, yelling, and slamming doors and drawers as he did. He didn't think to look in the laundry basket because she always washes new clothes before wearing them.

"When she wouldn't tell him where it was, he stormed out of the house. That outburst and others like it terrified Kate, especially because they increasingly happened in front of Addie and upset her so much. Tom had always been a good father who doted on his daughter. But as he became angrier with the world, he showed less interest in Addie.

"Soon he began using racial and ethnic slurs around the house, even in front of Addie. Kate told him he'd have to stop, He said he would, said he loved Addie so much and was sorry. Things would improve slightly and then deteriorate again.

"When I gently suggested she might be better off without him, she told me she was trying to rediscover the man she fell in love with. It's a common response from women in abusive relationships. I recommended they undergo counseling, but when she suggested it to him, he said he didn't need to hear that psychobabble. Besides, he said, therapists always side with the women."

Liz stopped at that point and asked Nick again if he'd like some wine. He said he'd take a beer instead. She left for the kitchen and Nick spent the time gathering his thoughts. He considered the sweet little girl who was sleeping peacefully upstairs but living in such a tumultuous household. He felt his own anger build.

Liz returned with his beer and sat next to him. "I'm sorry to dump all of this on you."

"You're not dumping anything on me. That kid upstairs doesn't deserve this, and, although I've never met your daughter, she obviously doesn't either. No one does. So please go on."

She took a breath and continued. "He began spending less time in the house. Sometimes he'd be gone overnight."

Nick asked if she thought he was seeing someone else.

"Kate doesn't think so. It was more guy stuff. He'd always owned a gun, which Kate wasn't thrilled with, but he bought two more, a handgun and some kind of automatic rifle. He'd go off to a shooting range to practice. He also mentioned a friend who had a cabin in the Jersey Pines. Apparently, they'd go there to shoot as well.

"She confided to me that their sex life had become non-existent. She had trouble being interested in a man who was verbally abusive and increasingly misogynistic. Their once-happy home had become a very sad place, and she hated the way it was affecting Addie. She was finally seriously considering a breakup.

"Like many of us, she was shocked when Hillary lost. But Hillary's loss had a strange impact on their marriage. After a brief period of gloating, Tom became calmer. He felt that the things that angered him so much, the perceived injustices against white working men would somehow be fixed. They'd build a big wall to keep out immigrants, ban Muslims from entering the country, and push back on special privileges for minorities. In some strange way, he felt empowered.

"Kate thought it was all poppycock, but her's wasn't the only marriage where husband and wife held widely opposing views. They agreed to disagree, and their marriage improved. He still went off shooting with his friends and smirking at liberal views, but the tirades were gone."

Nick took a pull on his beer and asked why he sensed tension now.

"Things are falling apart again. The wall never got built, and experts are predicting a possible major sweep for Democrats in the November congressional elections. A win by Democrats would virtually kill Trump's agenda for the next two years. Sensing this will be the case, Tom's tirades have returned."

Nick sensed there was more to the story than what he was being told, and asked about the phone call Liz received that night.

"Kate called and asked if I'd pick up Addie from school today because she and Tom had some things to work out. Then, while I was cooking dinner she called and asked if I could keep Addie another night. I asked her why and she said she'd explain later. That's it."

"Okay. I want to know what I can do for you."

"Nothing right now, just listen."
"Sorry, Liz," Nick said. "That's not enough."

Liz cupped her face in her hands and sobbed. Nick wasn't sure what to say, so he just rubbed her back gently while trying to console her. She opened her hands and wiped away her tears.

"I'm so sorry Nick. It's not fair to bring you into this."

"You have nothing to be sorry about. I told you, I'm here if you need me."

"It's just that I'm so afraid. When Kate asked me to watch her tonight, I was hopeful, foolishly hopeful, that something good was happening, that she and Tom were reconciling and looking for some quality private time together. But her phone call tonight made it clear that it was nothing like that. I mean, she didn't say much, but the tension in her voice was clear. This will not end well."

Nick was pretty sure she was right but didn't know how to say it.

"My biggest fear is Addie. What will happen to her if they split up? I can't imagine If there is a custody issue."

Nick had been thinking the same thing.

Liz continued. "I'm a worrier, Nick, and it's hard not to inject myself into Kate's life. But we're talking about my daughter and only grandchild. I can't sit back and wait for things to unfold. I've been wanting to consult with an attorney privately about how the law works, just for my own understanding. I know a few from the Arts Society. I know they are bound by confidentiality, but it's a small town and I'm embarrassed because it's really not my place to get involved. Not only that, but it's probably expensive."

Nick gave her a reassuring smile. He asked Liz if she'd mind if he contacted Johnny's friend Brian for help. She resisted. She certainly wanted help but felt awkward asking. "I've only met Brian once. I really don't know him."
Nick smiled and said, "That's right. You don't really know him. If you did, you'd know he loves helping people. Please trust me on this."

Chapter 31

Tom Baron's stereotypical image of a militia leader was someone who was bearded and brawny, with lots of body ink and maybe a denim jacket with cut-off sleeves. Richard Raymond Rogers, or R3 as the men called him, was none of that. He was trim, toned but not muscular, clean-shaven, and his clothing of choice was a flannel shirt with jeans. He had piercing blue eyes and an aura of leadership. He spoke with passion and clarity, and people listened. He was the owner of the Three R Shooting Range and president of the Pineland Patriots.

The shooting range was located midway between the Route 72 traffic circle and Long Beach Island, in the heart of the Jersey Pinelands. On the surface, it was a legitimate business. Locals came for target practice or to buy ammo. R3 knew how to diversify. He offered lessons to new shooters, rented quads to drivers to use on the dirt trails that wove through the Pinelands, and had a snack bar and a shot and beer bar. He was open six days a week and closed Mondays.

Mondays were special. His invited guests would gather in the large back room of the shooting range office for smoked brisket, beer, and a gripe session. They affectionately called the gathering, Brisket, Beer, and Bullshit.

The men arranged their chairs around the perimeter of the room. The brisket had been smoked for ten hours and was well worth the wait. The beer was a strong IPA that worked well with the beef, but the food wasn't the main attraction; Richard Raymond Rogers was.
They ate and drank and shared their complaints about whatever was stoking their anger that week. One by one, in no established order, they'd go off about immigration, Blacks, Jews, women, government oppression, whatever had pushed their buttons recently. R3 would sit back and let their anger build as each speaker tried to outdo the others with a level of outrage. Then he would wait until the right time to jump in. He'd start off slowly to take each of the pieces of their grievances and connect them into one broad message about what was wrong with America and what needed to be done to save their country.

Week after week he'd remind them that it was white Christian men who built the country, blue-collar men. The same men who were getting squeezed today. He'd remind them that manhood itself was under attack. Women were getting all of the breaks in society, getting promotions just because they were women. Men were portrayed as buffoons in TV shows, commercials, movies, and literature. He'd remind them that Jews and gays controlled Hollywood, the news media, and many colleges. He warned of the growing influence of gays on children. He spoke of corrupt government officials lining their pockets through special deals while catering to minorities and enacting policies that weaken America. He blasted China and elected officials who were losing the war to the "chinks," as he called them.

In every attack, he wove in just enough facts to give his words authority. When he didn't have facts, he created his own and shared them so convincingly that the men in the room believed he had all the answers. Like most charismatic figures, he became more passionate as he spoke and allowed his voice to rise. He'd scan their faces to ensure he still had their attention. He always did. Near the end, he'd speak reverently about their guns and how the second amendment would save America.

Always cautious about the potential for informants, and careful not to cross the line publicly with specifics that may be illegal, he'd close with vague references about big changes coming, and that the Pineland Patriots and other groups like them would be in the vanguard. In the meantime, R3 gave them a sense of belonging, a feeling of empowerment, and a vision for a better America. His men would leave energized and confident they would have a place in that change.

Tom Baron finished his beef and took a sip of beer. He agreed with every word R3 said. Change was coming and

Tom was determined to be a part of it. It hadn't been easy for him to get invited to the gatherings. It had taken over a month of frequent trips to the shooting range and conversations with R3 as he bought his ammo, before R3 finally invited Tom to a meeting. After a few meetings, Tom had the sense that there were other, more exclusive gatherings, something like a tight inner circle that discussed the specifics of the real plan, whatever that was. Eventually, he told R3 he wanted to be more involved, but R3 waited. He was cautious, a bit paranoid about the FBI's ability to infiltrate. Tom waited, made friends, and slowly gained the confidence of the group. Then he moved into a cabin with another regular looking for a roommate to help pay his bills. Now, he was getting signals that R3 might be feeling more comfortable about him. He hoped so.

R3's concern about the FBI was well-founded. Across the room from Tom sat Gabe Kramer, an FBI informant. Gabe had been a multiple-time loser with a long rap sheet of minor drug infractions, an occasional assault, and a robbery which resulted in a short stint in prison. Judges were losing their patience with the repeat offender. When he was caught driving a truckload of meth, the Feds knew they had something good to work with. They strung together a series of charges and parole violations that would have put him away for more than twenty-five years. Then they offered a deal. He would infiltrate the Pineland Patriots and become an informant in exchange for parole that could be revoked at any time. Gabe didn't like either choice and knew the dangers of fooling with a militia, but twenty-five years in prison was out of the question. He took the deal.

The process took months. He was trained in using a firearm and schooled in the lingo of weapons and ammo. Gabe had always been non-political. He didn't care about any of the issues that bothered the men he was going to deal with, so a crash course in militia ideology was necessary as well. He was given a new identity, rehearsed in the fabricated biography that went with it and was finally declared ready to go.

He went to the range frequently, interacted with the regulars, said the right things, and slowly worked his way onto the meeting list. His weekly messages to his FBI handlers were consistent. There was nothing of substance to report. Robert Rivers never went beyond his usual rhetoric to say something unlawful, and Kramer didn't see an opening to what everyone suspected was an inner group. Besides that, his instincts told him things were heating up. He had no evidence, no proof, but his gut said things were happening. His instructions were to keep attending the meetings, keep his ears open, and give the FBI updates on any new members.

Chapter 32

Johnny Marzo sat at the breakfast table with Carrie and Gracie. Gracie was thrilled that her dad had time to make his famous pancakes that morning. It wasn't that she ate much. In fact, she ate like a bird, but she loved helping to pour the ingredients into the bowl and watching them cook on the griddle. She also enjoyed applying her butter and syrup when the pancakes were ready. She'd take three or four bites, nurse down a couple more at her parents' urging, and then declare herself finished.

Johnny and Carrie worried about her appetite, but the pediatrician advised against making her eating an issue. She was a healthy, happy nine-year-old, just slightly below the average weight for a girl her age. The doctor recommended giving her a steady offering of the foods she likes best, plus a vitamin supplement, and she would be fine.

Gracie was in third grade, and the class was doing a social studies unit on communities. Johnny had just explained the concept of public services offered by firemen, policemen, mail carriers, and sanitation workers and was pleased that Gracie got the concept. She was a bright kid. Like most kids, she craved time with her busy parents, and they did their best to provide it, but there was always a nagging level of guilt they both felt below the surface that they weren't giving enough. Their time off was precious, and they planned things they knew she would love over the upcoming Christmas vacation, including an overnight trip to New York.

Johnny's phone pinged and he saw a text message from his supervisor at the Bureau. As always, it was short and to the point. MY OFFICE 0:800 MONDAY. DON'T SHAVE.

Johnny slid the phone to Carrie who turned from her sudoku to read it. She frowned and slid it back. The DON'T SHAVE reference was a euphemism for "You're going undercover," and he would receive a full briefing Monday.

She shook her head and glanced at Gracie to ensure she was occupied by her pancakes. Then she turned to Johnny and whispered, “It’s Christmas season.” Johnny shrugged and said quietly, “Let’s see what he says Monday.”

Carrie never approved of her husband’s undercover work and the danger it presented, but experience taught her to respect it. She was relieved that in recent years Johnny’s undercover assignments had shrunk to less than ten percent of his work and most were just one or two-day stints. Still, she worried. She looked at Gracie and hoped this assignment would be a short one.

Chapter 33

Brian called Liz the day after her talk with Nick and got right to the point. “I’m so sorry to hear what you are going through. I want to assure you that everything Nick told me will be strictly confidential. I also know that you’re not comfortable asking for help, so please let me tell you something about myself. Years ago I inherited a sizable amount of money when my uncle died in a terror attack. On top of that, God blessed me with a pretty good brain, and I used it to make a lot more money by investing in the stock market. It came so easily to me that I don’t often feel that I’ve earned it.

“As for my uncle, I’ve dedicated my life and resources to fighting terrorism and helping people.”

Liz knew some of this from what Nick told her.

“It’s very satisfying when my private company can assist the FBI in tracking down bad guys or thwarting an attack. But, all of that is part of a pretty dark world. It may prevent sorrow, but it doesn't do much to spread happiness. Sure, we like to buy dinner for friends and even treat for an occasional vacation. But that's not the way I want to honor my uncle. So, Jenny and I donate to charity, which is nice, but what gives us the most satisfaction is when we can help people we actually know. So you would be doing us both a favor if you'd allow us to help."

Chapter 34

Andrew Ertz was the most sought-after divorce and child custody lawyer in Bucks County. As a full partner in one of the county's most prominent firms, he commanded a fee of five hundred dollars per hour, and he produced results.

Nick went with Liz to the law office and was pleased by the old-school surroundings. He knew it was just superficial, but he was a traditionalist when it came to what a law office should look like- dark wood, deep, rich colors, floor-to-ceiling bookcases, leather furniture, and, of course, an antique desk. By contrast, he frowned on the modern law offices depicted on current TV with their sleek, minimalist furnishings, and glass walls on upper floors overlooking a city skyline. In his view, the latter version was more about selling representation to a client, while the former depicted quiet confidence.

Andrew Ertz stood to greet them when they were ushered into his office. He was sixty-ish, trim, and impeccably dressed. He invited them to take the chairs in front of his desk. He asked if he could get them water or coffee. When they declined, he sat and said, "It's nice to meet you. I've done a lot of work for Brian Kelly over the years before focusing my practice solely on divorce and custody issues."

"We appreciate your seeing us," Liz said. "We won't take much of your time. I'm grateful for the chance to have a consultation about my daughter and granddaughter."

"Yes. Brian filled me in on the information he received from Mr. Hardings. By the way, it's an honor to meet a Distinguished Service Cross recipient. Thank you for your service and sacrifice."

Nick nodded and said, "Please call me Nick."

"Good. Nick, it is." Turning back to Liz, Ertz said, "As for my time, Brian Kelly has retained my services for you from this meeting to anything you may need moving forward, your filings, depositions, trials, private investigators, appeals, anything. Those services extend to you, your daughter, and your granddaughter as long as those interests don't conflict in the future. Of course, you may fire me at any time. Finally, we've been instructed that all billing goes directly to Mr. Kelly."

Liz was shocked by Brian's generosity and intimidated by the mention of hearings, depositions, and appeals. She swallowed hard and said, "Thank you."

Nick wasn't surprised by anything he'd just heard. He'd learned to expect Brian's generosity long ago and knew this legal process could get nasty.

Ertz leaned forward and jotted something on a legal pad. "I don't want us to get ahead of ourselves here. The best scenario is that the couple's differences are resolved, and they all live happily ever after, but if not, there are issues of property, custody, and even grandparent visitation rights.

He explained a little of each. Then he said, “But, for purposes of our meeting today, there are things you and your daughter need to know right away, and they will be disappointing to you.”

Nick reached for Liz’s hand and she took it.

“Pennsylvania makes very little legal distinction regarding gender when considering custody rights. The days of a child belongs with his or her mother being the default mode are long gone. Men and women are viewed equally. In fact, and this is important, judges frown on any attempt,” he paused for emphasis, “I’ll repeat, any attempt by a spouse or family member to turn a child against the other parent. Now, if it can be proven that a parent is a criminal, addicted to drugs, or physically abusive, then things are different. But until then, being a creep or not a nice guy is not enough for a spouse to lose custody.”

Liz reached for a tissue on Ertz’s desk and wiped her eyes.

Ertz continued. “Is there a criminal history?”

Liz shook her head.

“Drug use?”

“Not that I’m aware of.”

Ertz wrote on his pad. “With your permission, I’d like to use the firm’s investigator to do a background check.”

Liz looked at Nick. “I don’t know what to do. I mean, Kate doesn’t even know I’m here. It doesn’t feel right.”

Nick’s silence told her he agreed with Ertz.

Ertz said, “This first step can be fairly simple. There may be something on his record that you or your daughter are not aware of. It will be quiet and discreet. It’s your call.”

Nick nodded, and Liz said, “Okay.”

Ertz made another note. Then he placed his pen on his desk and leaned back. “Is there any evidence of physical abuse?”

Liz dabbed at her eyes with the tissue and said, “No. I’ve never seen anything like that.”

“Maybe when you’re not around?”

“No, Kate and I are very close now. She would have told me.”

Ertz said, “I understand, but experience has taught me that many women, especially educated women, are embarrassed to admit that they made a choice to marry someone who later becomes an abuser. They often try to conceal it while they seek a solution. I’m not saying that’s the case here. I’m just gathering information.”

Liz decided she would find a way to ask Kate once they were alone.

“Again,” Ertz said, “let’s not get ahead of ourselves. This is all preliminary and hopefully, things will improve, and the couple will rediscover happiness.”

Liz wanted to believe that, but her head said otherwise.

Ertz stood and said, “That’s enough for now, but let me remind you not in any way to try to turn Addie against her father. When a judge interviews a child, the judge will accept a child’s independent assessment that a parent is bad or mean or has some other negative attribute. But if a judge feels a child has been coached to resent another parent or shares something like, ‘Mommy says that Daddy is…’ Trust me, judges come down hard on that.”

Chapter 35

Tom nursed a hot dog and coke at the snack bar until R3 was alone and went to the ammo counter where R3 was working.

R3 liked Tom. He was a good customer and a regular at the weekly Beef, Beer and Bullshit meetings. Judging by the things Tom said at the meetings, he was either a true believer or a damn good actor with an even better script writer.

R3 flashed him a smile. “Hey, Tom, how’s it going? What can I get you? “

“I’m good, R3.” He hesitated and said, “Actually I was hoping to get a few minutes alone with you.”

R3’s antenna went up. As much as he’d developed a good feeling about Tom, he was always cautious about informants. The FBI was all over militias and R3 knew that a taped private conversation was the FBI’s favorite tool.

“Sure,” R3 said. “Is there a problem with your monthly bill? Short on cash? I can work with you.”

“Nothing like that. I’m good.” He stammered, stared at the ground as if he was weighing whether to go on. Then he raised his head, looked R3 in the eyes snd said, “I’d like to get more involved.”

R3 knew what he meant, but conducted each conversation as if he were being recorded. “Involved with what?”

“You know. The things we talk about. The political things.”

R3 faked s smile. “That’s great. That’s the point of my speeches, to get people more involved. It’s easy. You can call your congressman, tell him what you think. You can write letters to the editor. If you’re serious enough you can send a donation to one of the groups fighting to save America.”

Tom realized what R3 was doing. Without saying a word, he unbuttoned his shirt and spread it apart to reveal he wore no wire.

R3 nodded and took it as an invitation to do a more thorough search. He patted him down, examined his ears and motioned for him to put the contents of his pockets on the counter- keys, a wallet, cigarettes and a lighter. R3 went behind the counter, removed a lead box from the shelf and placed Tom's items inside.

He said, "What did you have in mind?"

Tom rebuttoned his shirt before replying. "Whatever you think I can do. I get the sense there are meetings that are more private than the one's I can attend. Something bigger."

R3 didn't reply, and Tom went on. "Look, I can tell by your speeches that you can never be satisfied with just talk week after week. There's gotta be more. I want in because I'm not satisfied with just talk either."

R3 believed him. He'd rate his trust at maybe eighty percent, which is the maximum trust R3 gave anyone. Still, he remained guarded.

"Groups like ours have expenses. We print literature, support other organizations, purchase certain materials. We need money. I guess you could say there are guys who help with that. They bring in money, they get to hear more things." R3 didn't mention bribes paid to sympathetic law enforcement officials. The informant thing worked both ways.

Tom thought he was hearing an opening. "Makes sense. What kind of money are we talking about?"

R3 shrugged. Most guys come in at around $20,000-$25,000."

Tom raised his eyebrows. "That's a lot of money."

R3 shrugged again. "Some guys talk like they want to be one of the big boys; others do something about it."

Tom was thinking about where he could get that amount of money.

R3 read his thoughts. "I guarantee you they don't get it by going to a rich uncle. They just get it, and we don't care how. We don't just need money. We need people who demonstrate they're resourceful."

A customer pulled into the gravel parking lot and R3 indicated their conversation was over.

Chapter 36

Nick was driving home after leaving Liz's house. Liz hadn't slept well in days. The meeting with Andrew Ertz had drained her physically and emotionally and she needed a nap. He reassured her before he left that things would work out, but privately, he was convinced that they would get as bad as she feared.

After Addie's second night of sleeping over, Liz dropped her off at school with the understanding that Kate would pick her up at the end of the school day. So, except for a brief phone call to ensure the plan hadn't changed, Liz had still not had a real conversation with her daughter.

Alone in the truck now, Nick found himself drifting. He'd learned long ago that apprehension about something could snowball into anxiety in other areas. His concern over events of the past couple of days, and especially the conversation in Ertz's office, were triggers that brought some of his own demons to the surface. He felt them coming on but was helpless to stop them. They were gripping him like a vine growing over his body, tightening over his arms, legs, and chest to the point where it took all of his effort to drive. His breathing became shallow, and he felt lightheaded.

The first demon had been with him since he was fourteen. It happened before his parents' divorce. The couple would fight constantly, and Nick would escape to his room to shut it out. But on a couple of occasions, his father had crossed the line. He remembered once looking from his slightly open bedroom door as his father grabbed his mother and shook her violently before storming out of the house. There was another time during an argument when he squeezed her arm so tightly that she cried out in pain. That attack left a bruise that lasted for days. Neither parent was aware that Nick had seen these episodes, but he did see them, and he felt ashamed for not coming to his mother's aid. He told himself that he was only fourteen, and there was nothing he could have done. But he was a big kid. He should have at least cried out for his father to stop, even if it earned him some roughing up of his own. The fact that he didn't haunted him. Fortunately, his father left soon after and never came back. Nick had never seen him hit his mother, and she and Nick never spoke of it, but the shame of not intervening never left him, and the thought of men abusing women always brought that shame to the surface.

Nick's second demon was born six years later while he was imprisoned in Vietnam. In most cases, captured Americans were sent to Hanoi, and imprisoned in what Americans sarcastically called the Hanoi Hilton. But occasionally, a village would keep a captured American for their own vengeful pleasure, sometimes even concealing that they held a prisoner at all. Years later, Nick would learn that in some cases, it was suspected that the men imprisoned in these villages were never returned, even after the war ended. Men who had been listed as MIA, or missing in action, and later presumed dead, were actually alive and held captive.

The North Vietnamese government knew of some instances where villagers kept prisoners rather than send them to Hanoi and allowed it to continue for the duration of the war as morale-boosting compensation for what they had suffered. Later, when a prisoner exchange became one of the conditions to end the war, the North Vietnamese ordered all outlying prisoners back to Hanoi. Fortunately, the village that held Nick complied with the order, but not before he had endured two years of utter hell.

In the hierarchy of ranking prisoners by the hatred the Viets held toward them, Nick was ranked second, only behind captured pilots. He had freed a pilot from their captivity, and pilots were the most hated of all Americans. Pilots followed orders to bomb and strafe suspected enemy villages. Pilots had followed orders to drop deadly napalm, the chemical agent that acted as an incendiary device that burned humans and vegetation alike. In addition to destroying their intended targets, these actions often killed women and children. Moreover, as the war dragged on, the likelihood that villagers had lost a loved one increased and Nick would endure the intensified wrath of the villagers.

In time, Nick came to understand the treatment he received, the lack of medical care, long stretches without food, and regular torture and beatings. He hated it. He feared it. He wanted to die to escape it, but he understood the anger that provoked it.

The villagers would take turns visiting the cage, sometimes to deliver a bowl of rice and some water, just enough to keep him alive, because they didn't want their prize to die. When Nick went on a hunger strike in the hope it would accelerate his death, they held him down and force-fed him. He gagged and choked as they jammed rice into his mouth and washed it down with water. Eventually, he decided to eat. On some days, women and children would gather outside his cage to scoff and jeer and jab him with bamboo sticks.

The worst visits of all were the men who took turns beating him. His leg was tethered to a pole in the cage to limit his movement. They would enter the cage with bamboo poles and beat him from a distance which would keep them out of his reach. At first, when he still had his strength, he would lunge at them and try to grasp the pole. Later, when his strength was gone, he would simply curl in a ball to reduce his size as a target and wait for the beating to end.

Gradually, he learned their names. The most sadistic and feared of them all was named Duong. His visits were the most frequent, lasted the longest and left the most pain. He struck his blows where he knew Nick had not yet healed from the previous day. But worse than that, he was the only visitor who realized that he could inflict more pain by jabbing than by striking. He would ram the stick into Nick's kidneys, his spleen, his testicles, and even his Adam's apple, wherever he saw an opening that Nick couldn't protect.

Ironically, if Nick was shown any kindness by his captors, it came from Duong's wife, Mai. When she brought food, her eyes revealed a hint of compassion and shame. That was the extent of it, but it came to mean something. If he spoke Vietnamese, he would have asked her to poison him, choke him, or maybe bring a knife to slit his wrist, anything to end his suffering.

Once, during one of Duong's longest and most brutal tortures, Mai showed up to plead with him to stop. But Duong was in a rage. He turned and slapped her so hard that she fell to the ground. Then he grabbed a handful of her smock to pull her up. When she regained her balance, he punched her full in the face, knocking her unconscious. Other villagers came, calmed the raging Duong, and led him away while other women tended to Mai.

Nick had never seen a woman actually hit before. The references to abuse in Ertz's office reminded him of Mai, which reminded him of Duong, which brought him to a mental place he didn't want to experience again.

Nick agreed with Andrew Ertz. There was no need for any of them to get ahead of themselves. Maybe things would work out fine for Addie, Kate, and Liz. But if they didn't... He'd been too afraid to act against his father when he was fourteen and too weak and battered to help Mai six years later, but he vowed he would never stand by and watch as anyone abused a woman again.

Chapter 37

There was nothing gradual about Nick's panic attacks. They came suddenly. He'd feel a twinge in his chest, and within seconds he'd be overcome by a general sense of unease, accompanied by physical sensations that were virtually incapacitating. His arms and legs would feel like lead and his breathing shallow.

He was alone in his truck halfway between Langhorne and Bristol heading home when this one hit. He knew he shouldn't drive but forced himself to try. He reduced his speed and focused as much as possible. The remaining four miles passed slowly but when he reached Old Route 13, just a mile from home, his shaking hands were sweating, and palpitations were so severe that he had no choice but to pull over.

He needed to gather himself, to practice the techniques Dr. Braun had taught him. Breathe in slowly through the nose and exhale gently through the mouth. Close your eyes and focus on something other than the sense of foreboding. Nick was fighting to do it, but it wasn't working. His mind drifted to distractions. He considered the possibility that maybe this wasn't an anxiety attack. Maybe it was his heart. He thought about being found dead in his truck in an empty auto repair parking lot. He shrugged off the thought. He'd had enough anxiety attacks to know that's what this was.

He closed his eyes to meditate, but his thoughts drifted to Duong. The sadistic bastard was grinning, showing his rotten teeth, jabbing at him with his bamboo pole.
Nick pounded the steering wheel and tried again. He focused on his breathing, four long seconds in and three long seconds out. Four in and three out. He wished he had the meditation cassette Dr. Braun had given to him. The speaker had a soothing voice. But the truck didn't have a cassette player so he left the tape in his apartment.

He continued his deep breathing and tried focusing on his feet. It was another technique Dr. Braun had shared. She told him it was impossible to think of two things at once. The mind could only handle one thing at a time. If he focused on his feet touching the floorboard, he could blot out Duong. He concentrated and resumed his rhythmic breathing. Slowly, very slowly, he felt better. He wiped the sweat from his brow. His pulse was slowing. The palpitations were easing, and his hands were no longer shaking.

It took another ten minutes or so, but he recovered enough to drive. He put the truck in gear and left the parking lot. He was drained, but he didn't want to go to his apartment. As badly as he needed sleep, he needed his friends more. He headed for the deli.

He parked out front and sat looking at the windows. It was dusk, and the shades were drawn. Nick found the lights inside reassuring. He knew how the guys would react if they knew he was having trouble. The store had been his home for decades and the men inside were the only family he had. He gave himself more time to recover, at least to the point where he could function. Then he left the truck and walked inside.

Jimmy saw him first and shouted, "There he is!"
Angelo was scrubbing a pot and said, "If you're gonna be absent this long, you need a doctor's note."
"Not a doctor's note," Jimmy said jokingly, "A note from Liz."
Nick wasn't smiling. Big Frankie noticed it first and put his hand up for everyone to stop.
The room got quiet, and Frankie said, "What's up, Nick?"
Nick just shook his head. He took a deep breath and said, "Nothing special, just having a bad day."
Frankie pulled out a chair for Nick to sit.
Jimmy said softly, "What's wrong, Nick? Get a visitor today?"
Getting a visitor was code for having a flashback.
"Yeah," Nick said. "And I'm having a hard time getting him to leave."
"Son of a bitch," Jimmy replied. "It will pass, Nick. Just hang in."
Angelo took a bottle of Jack Daniels from behind the counter and placed a shot glass in front of Nick. The other guys looked at Angelo expectantly and Angelo said, "What are you looking at? I have a friend in the dumps and I have to give all of you free booze?"

"It's the polite thing to do," Jimmy said.

Angelo thought for a moment. "Who the hell are you? That lady?"

"What lady," Jimmy asked.

"That lady, Martha Stewart. Always telling people how to cook stuff and entertain guests. I mean, who the hell does she think she is?"

"This goes back long before her," Jimmy said. "The Indians used to smoke a peace pipe around the fire. If you offered it to one, everybody got a toot."

Nick was concentrating on following the conversation, and Big Frankie thought he saw the hint of a smile developing.

"Tell you what, wise guy," Angelo said, "how about if I give anyone a free shot who is paid up in beer money?" Angelo grinned and added, "Yeah. I like that. "

"Not that again with the beer money!" Jimmy said.

The guys were masters at deflection, and they were doing their best now to deflect Nick from whatever he was thinking.

"What's he owe?" Big Frankie asked, sounding disgusted.

"Three-fifty for the month, just like everybody else. Only you guys pay. He doesn't."

Nick finally spoke. "Jesus, I'm dying over here. Can I get a shot of Jack?"

"Guess I'm paying for Jimmy again," Frankie said.

"Again?" Jimmy sounded indignant. "Did you ever pay before?"

Frankie just looked at him and threw five dollars on the table.

"That's more like it," Angelo said. He went back behind the counter and produced three more glasses. He filled them all and asked, "What should we drink to?"

They all looked at Nick for an answer.
Nick thought about Liz, Addie, Kate and her husband for a moment. He raised his glass and said, "Peace." Then he added, "And if not peace, then strength."
They weren't sure what that meant, but they joined him in knocking back their shots.
Angelo began to gather the glasses, and Jimmy said, "Just one. That's it?"
Nick finally broke a full smile. "What the heck. Let's do one more, Angelo. I'm buying."
"No need, Nick. It's on me. But I get to make the toast."
He poured another round, raised his glass, and said, "To our friend, Jimmy the dimwit."
Everyone, including Jimmy, repeated it. After they drank, Big Frankie said, "What can we do for you, Nick?"
Nick said, "What I really want right now is for Jimmy and me to beat you and Angelo in a game of pinochle. I have some things to tell you guys between hands."

Chapter 38

Nick's phone rang on October 28. When Donna Marzo's name appeared on the screen, he knew immediately why she was calling. He tried to sound as upbeat as possible.

"Hi, Donna. How are you?"

"Hi, Nick. I'm okay, I guess, as good as can be expected." There was a pause before she added, "He's doing it again, Nick. Tomorrow afternoon, four o'clock."

Nick nodded as if Donna could see him. "I was hoping last year would have been the end of it, but after what happened in Pittsburgh this week, this is no surprise."

"Not at all," she said. "You know how important things like this are to him. I don't want him to be embarrassed. Can you round up some people?"

"Of course, I will. Do you think he'll follow the same format?"

"I'm pretty sure he will. I wish he wouldn't because it might make some people think it's a joke. Of course, we know it isn't."

"Don'tworry about it, Donna. I think people judge his sincerity."

"I hope so. He's always been this way with issues he cares about. You know that as well as anyone."

"I do," Nick said. "And I respect him for it. Have you told Jimmy and Big Frankie?"

"I was hoping you would. They probably know, but I'm hoping you'll poke them to reach out to others. I want to support him."

"Donna, you've been supporting him since Canada, and you've paid a price for it. No one thinks you'll stop supporting him now." He wanted to give her more assurance. "I've always thought this was important in past years, but the more I think about it, the prouder I am that he's doing it again now. Please don't worry. We'll get through this."

Angelo Marzo had always stood up for the principles he valued, as far back as the Vietnam War when he made the decision to flee to Canada rather than face the military draft and support a war he felt was unjust. Many said he was a coward for doing so, that he took the easy way out. But those close to him knew the price he and his parents paid as a result. When he decided to go, Donna, his girlfriend at the time, held equally strong feelings against the war and was emphatic that she go with him. By leaving, they separated themselves from their friends and families for eight years until President Carter pardoned draft dodgers in 1977. Angelo's parents, who had supported his decision, paid a price beyond their separation from their son. They were ostracized by town members whose sons went off to war and their business suffered considerably. Of course, the greatest price of all was the lifetime of guilt Angelo carried for fleeing while his friends did not.

Angelo's commitment to issues like black civil rights and women's equality was strong, but after the Sandy Hook Elementary School massacre, nothing mattered more to him than gun regulation. Six years earlier, Angelo watched in horror as details were released of the 2012 mass killing of twenty-six people, including twenty six and seven-year-olds while at school in Newtown, Connecticut, slaughtered by a crazed gunman with an automatic weapon. Like so much of the country, Angelo was certain that the heartbreaking event would prompt a level of outrage that would ensure legislation including sweeping reforms and an assault weapons ban.

The outrage came, but the legislation didn't. When almost a year passed without any progress, Angelo began an unusual ritual that he repeated every year.

As in past years, a day or two before Halloween, he put a bucket of small candy bars on a milk crate in front of the store, flipped the sign on the door to read closed, and turned to face the people who had assembled in the deli. There were roughly twenty present. Unlike the arrangement for the pinochle tournament, the only chairs available were the six that surrounded the only table in the room. Everyone else stood. Angelo preferred it that way. He once said, if the press ever showed up to cover the event, they would have to report that the crowd was standing room only. Angelo invited the press every year. They never came.

Angelo scanned the gathering. He saw Donna, his son Johnny and Carrie, Nick, Big Frankie, Jimmy, Brian and Jenny, the postal carrier, the bread delivery driver, and a history teacher from Bristol High who came every year. This year he brought three of his senior students. The rest were a handful of customers from the neighborhood who also came every year.

Angelo cleared his throat and began his speech. "Good afternoon and thank you for coming. As most of you know, this is the sixth time I've arranged this meeting during the Halloween season. I select this time to draw attention to the fact that we have politicians on all levels of government who masquerade as responsible public officials, but in fact, do absolutely nothing to combat the scourge of mass shootings across the country. I repeat, inexplicably, they do nothing.

"I began these meetings in the aftermath of Sandy Hook. Any parent, grandparent, aunt, uncle, or any human being for that matter, who sees the photos of the smiling faces of those adorable little kids and then imagines what those horrible moments must have been like at the end..." He paused to gather himself and shook his head before continuing. "They were riddled by so many bullets that DNA tests were required to identify the bodies. Any person in elected office who does nothing, I repeat, nothing, to prevent the next slaughter should never hold elected office. I don't care how many roads they pave or bridges they build, or how much they rant against taxes. If they don't take action, they should not be in office period."

The crowd applauded.

Angelo went on. "Every year at this time, I give my SOS report which is short for State of the Slaughter. In 2018, as of this month, three hundred and eleven people have been killed, and one thousand one hundred and eighteen have been injured in mass shootings. Mass shootings are defined as four or more people, not including the shooter. Nothing has been done."

"I won't go back over the long list of shootings over the past couple of years. We don't need to. We only need to go back to three days ago when eleven people were murdered and seven others wounded in a mass shooting at a synagogue in Pittsburgh. Will anything be done? You know the answer. But it doesn't have to be this way. We don't need to feel helpless. What we're doing tonight, this small gathering, should be taking place in every neighborhood in America. The number of groups such as this should grow.

The intensity of our correspondence with the masqueraders should increase.

“Tonight, I invite you to do the same things I ask each year. One, sign the petition I will read now, and two, reach out to others to do what we are doing.

“As always, the petition calls for the following reforms. Ban the sale of assault weapons. Develop an up-to-date national database and require background checks for all gun purchases. Pass red flag laws that will allow the removal of weapons from individuals deemed to be a danger to themselves or others. Make it lawful to file suits against gun manufacturers just as we can sue any other corporation in America.

“I hope you'll sign the petition. I will then forward copies to every elected official on all levels who represent us. It is easy to feel that this is a worthless effort, that nothing will come of it, or that I am foolish for asking you to come. So far, that has been true. But we have to start somewhere. I know I can go to bed tonight knowing I tried something to end this scourge in America. Maybe instead of seeing the haunting smiles of those kids from Sandy Hook, maybe, just maybe, I'll sleep a little better tonight.

“Thank you for coming, and please reach out to others.”

That was it. It was over in fifteen minutes. Donna hugged her husband, and of the people leaving, no one thought Angelo was foolish.

Chapter 40

A few days later the guys were watching the Congressional mid-term election results on CNN. They were political junkies and usually made a party of it on big news nights. Angelo put out a bucket of beers and a tray of cheese, pepperoni, and bruschetta with garlic bread. Long-time CNN anchor, Wolf Blitzer, was referring to charts and graphs behind him, highlighting close races across the nation.

Jimmy said, "I wish my name was Wolf."

That took everyone by surprise. After a pause, Angelo said, "That figures. I read somewhere that most children don't like their names at some point and want to change them. How old are you, seventy-one, seventy-two? You're right on par with a little kid."

Jimmy stayed with it. "I'm serious. I wish my name was Wolf."

Angelo shook his head. "Would you like to tell us why?"

"I just think it's a neat name. There aren't many people named Wolf. There are plenty of people named Jimmy."

"That's for sure."

Nick jumped in. "I have to admit, Angelo, I went through a time as a kid when I secretly wanted my name to be Scott."

Angelo laughed out loud. "Scott! Where did that come from?"

"Remember Scott Shaffer?"

"No."

"He played Little League with us."

"Still no."

Nick shrugged. "Anyway. He was a decent player. But I remember he had a pretty nice dad, one of those upbeat guys who was always encouraging, not just of his son, but the whole team. He drove a decent car and they lived in a nice house on West Circle. There was a time when I thought it would be nice to be Scott, name, and all. Keep my mom but have Scott's dad as my dad, live in Scott's house, drive in Scott's father's car."

Angelo deadpanned. "That's deep, Nick. Very deep. Do we need to talk about it? I'm glad you feel comfortable enough to share that."

"Kiss my ass," Nick replied flatly. "It lasted a week or two. I'm just saying kids go through that kind of stuff."

Angelo ignored him and turned to Big Frankie. "How about you, Big Frankie? Ever wish you had a different name?"

"Absolutely."

Angelo was surprised by the response. "So let's hear it."

"I wanted to be Little Frankie."

Jimmy almost fell off his chair laughing.

"It's not funny. Know what it's like being the biggest oaf in the class? Standing in the back for the class pictures and towering over everyone? Special desk in elementary school? Wasn't easy. Still isn't."

In a rare show of sympathy, Jimmy said, "Your size got you to be first-team all-league offensive and defensive tackle."

"Yeah, that was nice, but it's still a pain in the ass to be this big all your life."

There was no sympathy from Angelo who said with mock sincerity, "Thanks for sharing your feelings too. I want you to know we never viewed you as a big oaf. I little clumsy maybe..."

"Screw you, Angelo. I'm serious. When I was a kid, I got sad every time I heard a song by Little Anthony and the Imperials, or Little Caesar and the Roman's, even Little Stevie Wonder, which is what they called him when he first broke in. I'd get sad every time."

"How about Little Eva and the Locomotion?" Angelo asked sarcastically, "Did she make you sad?"

"Nah. She was a girl."

"That's a break. Could have told old Coach Lukins, 'Big Frankie wishes he was Little Eva."

There were more chuckles. Frankie said, "What about you, Wise Ass, ever wish you had a different name?"

Everyone expected Angelo to say no. But after a pause, he said, "There was a time when I wanted my name to be Cosmo."

Angelo waited patiently for the laughter to stop. He suppressed a grin and said, "I didn't just want a different first name. I wanted to change the whole thing, first and last. I wanted my name to be Cosmo Lacavazzi."

Nick scratched his head. "Sounds familiar."

"Yup," Angelo added. "He was a great fullback for Princeton when we were kids."

"That's it," Nick said. "I remember. Tough as nails."

"That's him," Angelo said. "I used to watch the games on TV. Every time the announcer said, Cos-Mo La-ca-vazzi and emphasized each syllable, I thought, 'Damn, I love that name.'"

Nick agreed. "I have to admit that is a cool name. It kind of flows. Cos-Mo La-ca-vazzi. I like it. Do you want us to call you that?"

"No. Now that my son became a hero, I'll stick with Marzo."

"Good move," Nick said. "Johnny Marzo is the man."

CNN returned from commercial break and Wolf Blitzer was animated. "If you just joined us, to recap the night's events, we're watching a smashing victory for Democrats across the nation. Let's go now to our election night board room for an update."

The screen went to a reporter who was providing details. "While analysts predicted democratic gains, no one expected results of this magnitude. While the Republicans retained control of the Senate by a slim margin, Democrats picked up a whopping forty seats in the House to gain control of the United States House of Representatives. There was a strong Democratic victory on the state level as well, where Democrats gained seven governorships and flipped three hundred and fifty seats in state legislatures across the nation. Analysts like to say that off-year congressional elections are often seen as a referendum, a type of report card, if you will, on the party in the White House. If that's true, then tonight's results are a strong rebuke of the current Trump administration."

The reporter went on, as he moved through several map screens behind him showing results of various races. But Nick's thoughts turned to what Liz had said about Tom's earlier mood swings. He'd been improving but slipped back to his old ways as defeat in the November elections seemed more likely. He wondered how tonight's results would affect things now. He was pretty sure he knew the answer.

Chapter 41

Liz and Kate met for lunch at Panera Bread on Route1, midway between their homes. Kate asked that they meet early so she could do some food shopping after and still be on time to pick up Addie from school.

They ordered online in advance, and Liz arrived first, picked up the food order, and chose a table in the back corner. Kate arrived a few minutes later and found her there. Liz was stunned by her daughter's appearance. Her eyes were red and puffy, and her normally impeccable hair was unkempt. Liz made it a point not to comment on Kate's appearance and asked about Addie instead.

"She's okay, I guess, considering." Then she changed her mind and said, "She's not okay. She tries to conceal it, but she's upset and is trying to figure out what's going on between Tom and me."

"That goes for me too," Liz said. "So why don't you start at the beginning?"

Kate took a sip of her drink. "I'm not sure where the beginning is. You know Tom has mood swings. He always has."

Liz started to speak, and Kate stopped her. "Please don't lecture me, Mom, not now. I know you never liked Tom when we were dating. Yes, he had his moments, but he could also be kind and fun. I was a different person then, with some flaws of my own that you're well aware of. But I thought marriage would change him, that I would change him. I was wrong. As he experienced more disappointment with his position in life, his jobs, his personality turned worse."

Liz reached across the table and put her hand on Kate's. "Honey I'm not here to lecture you or judge. My only interest is your happiness and the happiness and safety of you and Addie. So please just do your best to tell me what's going on."

Liz removed her hand and patted her eye with her napkin. Kate said, "Well, you know most of this, so I'll just talk about the last couple of weeks. He's grown increasingly angry. His racism is rampant. He uses racial slurs, and foul language constantly, even in front of Addie, which he never did before. He's convinced that our country is being destroyed and wants to do something about it, whatever that means. He goes missing for days at a time presumably to visit his friend in the Jersey Pines for shooting practice and to do, as he says, guy stuff.

"I really don't think that he's seeing another woman or that romance has anything to do with it. I confided in you before that our sex life is virtually over. The other night when I asked you to watch Addie it was because he said he had things to discuss and wanted to be alone.

"I thought maybe he wanted to begin another one of those makeup cycles where he wanted to work things out. I've learned not to trust them to last very long, but at that point, I was exhausted, and I hoped he was on that kick again because I needed the rest.

"Instead, he went on a tirade about everything, race, politics, his boss, gays, immigrants, everything. He had me so frightened that I told him I didn't think our marriage would last unless we seriously sought counseling. With that, he exploded again."

Liz wanted badly to tell her daughter that she was describing the classic abuser routine- abuse, seek forgiveness, be nice, and abuse again. But she knew her daughter knew that. Besides, she'd promised not to lecture. Instead, she asked why Kate asked for a second sleepover night.

"As I said, I was way off base with my expectations. He came home drunk and immediately launched into the same old routine. Usually, when he drinks, he just keeps drinking until he passes out. So, I was afraid this would be going on more the next day when he awakened, which is why I asked for a second sleepover. It's good that I did because his next rant included a diatribe against women. He even criticized Addie. Thank God she wasn't there. He said Addie always sided with me, and she was becoming like the rest of us, not knowing our place. When his criticism mentioned Addie, I reached the breaking point. I knew then that I wanted a divorce."

"What did he say to that?"

"I didn't tell him because I'm too afraid. Right now, I actually think he's dangerous. I think I'm better off waiting a few days or even a couple of weeks until he cools off."

"But can you tolerate him that long?"

"Yes," Kate said with conviction. " As long as I know there is an end in sight and that I'm determined to see things through for my good and the good of Addie, then I can handle anything in the short term."

Chapter 42

Nick and Liz planned to have dinner at Liz's house. Nick insisted on selecting a surprise menu and doing the cooking. He showed up with hotdogs, tater tots, and a recipe for a three-bean casserole he got from Angelo.

Liz folded her arms and smiled as he unpacked the casserole ingredients: kidney beans, Cannellini beans, white beans, bacon, brown sugar, vinegar, cumin, and hot sauce. He unfolded the recipe, flattened it out on the counter, and scratched his head.

“I thought it would be fun to cook this for you, but now I’m thinking it might be even more fun if we cook it together.”

Liz laughed out loud. “I agree. Start by opening the cans.”

“It’s a busy world,” Nick said. “I mean, who has time to cook, right? I thought I’d embrace a quick meal. This should take like ten minutes to prepare.”

Liz smiled again. “Yes, if you just want hot dogs, but the casserole will need to cook for an hour and a half.”

Nick looked deflated. “Really, that long?”

“That’s what the recipe says. It’s no big deal. Are you in a hurry?”

“Nope.”

“Then let’s put this on, grab some drinks and get under a blanket on the patio. You can light the gas heater.”

They snuggled on the loveseat. She rested her head on his shoulder and placed her hand on his chest. She’d been stressing over Kate and needed an escape. She felt content with Nick, safe. She thought about the man he must have been before his capture, what he endured, and what he was experiencing now. She struggled to find the right word that defined the now part. She settled on rebirth. It wasn’t the perfect word, but it would do.

She adjusted their blanket, moved closer, and said, “Tell me about it.”

“About what?”

“What happened in Vietnam.”

"No," Nick said flatly.

"I care about you, and I want to know."

"Absolutely not." He said it softly as if there was no need for emphasis. There was no chance of it happening.

She didn't respond. They sat in silence, appreciating the warmth of the fire and blanket against the brisk November air.

Nick said, "I'm getting hungry. I wonder how the beans are coming."

"It's only been fifteen minutes; we have over an hour yet." She paused and added, "Plenty of time for you to tell me."

Nick shook his head and said calmly, "I'm sorry, Liz. It's not gonna happen. Next topic."

Liz waited and then said, "That's not fair."

Nick stiffened and Liz removed her head from his shoulder. "You're a hero, and aside from some vague understanding that you did something heroic, I have no idea what you actually did. It's part of who you are, and I feel I should know." She hesitated before adding, "Then you spent over seven hundred days in captivity, it shaped who you are or were for the next forty years. I need to know. "

Nick said firmly, "I told you before not to call me a hero. I mean, who knows what a hero is? Right? Maybe a hero is a guy who goes through shit like I did and doesn't waste the next forty years of his life. Maybe that's what a hero is."

"Okay," Liz conceded. "I guess hero is a subjective term. But the army awarded you the Distinguished Cross, the second highest medal behind the Medal of Honor. That's not subjective, and I was there when they pinned it on you, remember?"

Her voice was rising, and Nick understood her frustration. This wasn't just idle curiosity. She had been there and she was heavily invested in his well-being. Still, he had no intention of sharing what she wanted to know. He wanted to ease the tension in the best way he knew how. “The cross reminds me of a story.”

Liz relaxed. She felt she was getting somewhere.

Nick started. “Little Johnny is in fifth grade and he’s flunking math. His parents work with him, but he still flunks. They meet with his teacher and get him a tutor, but nothing helps. He’s still flunking. Finally, they pull him out of the public school and put him in the local Catholic school. He starts bringing home math tests and they are all A’s. Then his report card comes and he gets an A in math! His parents are thrilled and tell him they don’t understand what changed. Johnny said, “Every room in the school had a big plus sign on the wall, and they all had a man nailed to it. I figured these people take math seriously so I better learn it.”

Liz didn’t smile. She shook her head and said, “You can’t joke your way through everything. I know that’s what you and your friends, who I love, by the way, it’s what you all do. But I don’t function that way.”

Nick tried to smile. “Didn’t you get it? He confused the cross for a plus sign.”

“Stop it!” she shouted. She threw off her blanket and stood glaring at him with her arms folded.

Nick said softly, “I’m sorry, Liz. Please sit down.”

She stood there, looking defiant. He said again, “I’m sorry. I know this is important to you. Please sit down.”

She did and reached for her wine. Nick did the same with his beer.

He thought he saw a hint of a smile developing before she said, “That’s an old joke and not a very good one. If you’re going to annoy me, the least you can do is come up with better material."

"I have more if you..."

"No, I don't want to hear more," she said firmly. "I told you what I want."

Nick fell silent. His focus seemed to be someplace other than Liz's patio. Finally, he said, "Why would you want to know that stuff? It's ugly."

"I know. But let me make an analogy. And I'm not saying that the two are anywhere near the same, but you know my ugly stuff about Kate, and it helps me. It helps me to know that you know. And I think it helps you too to be here for me. I think it makes us closer."

Nick exhaled, put down his glass, and rubbed his face. "Okay. I'll tell you."

Liz nodded and Nick began.

"Headquarters learned that a pilot had been shot down. The other pilots in the raid made note of where the plane went down or more importantly, where the parachute was heading when the pilot ejected. Subsequent reconnaissance flights came back with a high level of confidence that they knew the village where the pilot, if still alive, would probably be held. They asked for volunteers for a four-man Green Beret team to approach the area, survey it, and, if he was alive and held, execute a rescue mission. I volunteered."

He paused and looked off in the distance. Liz assumed he was wondering what his life would've been like if he hadn't made that decision. She was wondering the same thing before he continued.

"We had a helicopter drop ten miles from the village and made our approach on foot. Understand, it wasn't a military base. It was just an unfortified village that was fairly easy to get close to, and we saw a bamboo cage holding a prisoner."

He took a long pull of his beer and went on.

"We drafted a plan. Two team members would circle to opposite sides of the village. They would have flash grenades and other explosives and would synchronize the time to set off the explosives as a diversion while I and another team member, Corporal Mitchell, entered the village to free the pilot. There was chaos everywhere as the other team members sprayed the village with gunfire and the villagers scrambled to their huts to grab whatever weapons they had. The pilot was unable to walk, so Corporal Mitchell threw him over his shoulder, and we exited."

Liz looked stunned. "This is terrifying. Why didn't they send more men on the mission?"

Nick nodded. "That's something I spent two years thinking about. But at the time it was thought that the element of surprise outweighed a larger force with a greater risk of detection."

Liz didn't respond, and Nick continued.

"We radioed the helicopter to meet at a preordained extraction point a mile away. The two men who had created the initial diversion set off timed explosions to keep the villager's attention in that direction and then regrouped at our original starting point. I ordered them to carry the pilot to the helicopter. To give them time, Mitchell and I stayed behind to hold off anyone who came in our direction. The plan was we would then break for the 'copter as well. It wasn't a great plan, but we had a pilot who couldn't walk."

Nick drank again. Whatever reluctance he had to tell the story was gone. He was fully engaged.

"The villagers were better armed than we anticipated, and they finally came at us. By then it was obvious the 'copter had to evacuate while we stayed and fought. I radioed our coordinates and ordered the chopper to leave. Fortunately, our attackers were armed but not trained. We took them out, maybe ten or twelve of them, but Mitchell was badly wounded in the fight."

At that moment it occurred to Nick that he had just told Liz that he had killed, probably multiple times. He assumed it had always been implicit that he'd done so, but now it was clear. Liz remained expressionless, and he went on.

"I was able to drag Mitchell to a cave, where we hid for two days, trying to figure out how we could escape and what the army's plan for our extraction would be. On the second day, a VC search party found us, and a second firefight ensued. This time, it didn't go well. A grenade knocked me unconscious. When I awakened, Mitchel was gone, and I was in a bamboo cage with multiple wounds and my leg tethered to a pole embedded in the ground. That's where I stayed for two years."

Liz sat stunned. Neither spoke for some time until Liz asked what happened to Corporal Mitchell.

" After I got back to the States, I learned that the VC transported him to the prison camp in Hanoi. He was in bad shape and died a couple of weeks later, but not before he told our story to other American prisoners who shared it with the army when they were released. That's how I was awarded the Distinguished Cross. It should have gone to Mitchell."

Liz asked, "Why did they send Mitchell to Hanoi and keep you at the village?"

"That's another good question. All I've got is speculation. Here's my best guess. Hanoi wanted all prisoners sent to them. They would later use them as bargaining chips toward American disengagement. But locals, like the villagers I encountered, liked to keep them for torture in retribution for the loss of loved ones. Our best guess is that they caught two, turned one in, and kept the other for fun." He snickered at the last reference.

Nick saw tears on Liz's cheeks and took her hand. She said, "How were you freed?"

Nick took a deep breath. "It was truly by the grace of God, and I mean that. There are stories of guys held captive in these villages who may have never been freed, even after the war ended. American families whose loved ones are officially listed as Missing in Action but may have been kept in captivity. In later years, long after the war, the Vietnamese government did take steps to account for as many MIAs as possible."

"So, what happened to you?"

"A couple of months before the cease-fire was reached, a North Vietnam unit was passing through the village and discovered me. The commander ordered me sent to Hanoi. I've thought about that a lot. It's a good thing that the commander was a rule follower. Another leader could have just as easily thought, 'What the hell, these people have been through hell, I'll let them keep their toy.'"

Liz shuddered at the thought.

"Thank God he didn't."
Nick smiled. "I already have."

Liz sipped her wine. "I'm glad you told me, Nick. I'm sure it was hard for you, but I feel..." She paused, shook her head, and said, "I don't know what I feel except to say it was hard for me to hear too, but somehow, I feel better, closer."

"I'm glad I told you too, and you're right. It wasn't easy."

Liz said, "I want to know more."

"More? There is no more."

"There's a lot more," Liz said. "There are seven-hundred days of more. I want to know how you survived more than two years in that cage."

Nick sighed. "I'd give you a flat no, but I already lost on that once. So, I'm giving you an emphatic no. Seriously, ask me again and I'm in the house checking on the beans."

Liz held up her palms in surrender. "Okay. I'm sorry. I won't ask again."

"Good," Nick said. "Let's check on the beans."

Liz checked the patio clock. "We still have time and I have one more request."

Nick eyed her warily.

"I love your friends. I really do. And I admire the bond you have. But there's something about Jimmy that I sense makes him just a little more important to you."

Nick nodded his agreement. "You're right, and it's more than just a little. It's obvious that Jimmy has some limitations. I've watched over him since high school, except one time, one tragic time."

"Vietnam, right?"

"Yes," Nick said almost inaudibly. "Viet friggin' Nam. I failed him on that small point."

"That wasn't your fault. There was nothing you could have done."

"Yes, there was. I should have put his ass on a bus to Canada when Angelo and Donna left. I should have done it, but I can't escape the thought that I didn't because I was naïve enough to believe that they would never draft someone with his limitations. Not only did they draft him, but they gave him the worst job imaginable."

"And you feel responsible."

"I do. There is no logical way I am responsible, but yes, I feel responsible. They shattered his psyche."

"So, what was his job?"

Nick looked fatigued. He wasn't relishing another story, but agreed she should know.

"Short version. Very short."

"Okay."

"Jimmy was a tunnel rat."

Liz crunched her face, "Tunnel Rat? What's that?"

"The Viet Cong had an elaborate system of tunnels in the jungle that dated back to their fighting against the earlier French occupation."

Liz realized she didn't know much about Vietnamese history but didn't want to interrupt him.

"They would use the tunnels to store weapons and even hide until nighttime when they would appear seemingly out of nowhere and stage a raid, only to disappear as quickly as they arrived. Sometimes the tunnel entrances were as narrow as a manhole cover concealed with vegetation and remained that narrow for several feet until they opened to a wider cavern capable of holding men or stockpiles of weapons."

Liz asked, "Okay, but what exactly is a tunnel rat?"

"When American patrols discovered a tunnel entrance, they would send slightly built men into the tunnel to ensure there were no weapons or, worse yet, enemy hiding. It was terrifying. Pitch black, spider webs, bats, and the uncertainty of what one would find at the cavern. Many tunnels were boobytrapped, so there was that too. If the tunnel rat found an arms cache, he would set a time-delayed charge to destroy it and crawl out before it detonated."

Liz put her hand to her mouth. "My God. That's horrible. What if the tunnel rat encountered men in the cavern?"

Nick let his silence answer her question.

"Fortunately, Jimmy never encountered men, just weapons. But he had a sadistic Lieutenant who didn't like him and selected him over and over to go in. Fortunately, the Lieutenant was eventually killed by a sniper, and Jimmy's days in the tunnels were over."

"Poor Jimmy," was all Liz could mumble.

"Jimmy is seventy-one years old. He's tough as nails, but to this day he hates bugs, will not sleep with the light out, or tolerate a tight space. I let him down, Liz. But he knows I will never do that again. I'll be there for him and there's no doubt he will always be there for me. No doubt."

Nick looked at the patio clock and said, "Enough talking. I'm hungry."

Chapter 43

Nick dialed Liz's number and smiled when Addie answered.

"Hi, Nick!"

"Hi, Addie. How are you?"

"I'm good. Mommy-Liz let me answer when the caller ID said it was you."

"I'm glad you did because we haven't talked for a while. How is school?"

"Good. Tomorrow we're making turkeys out of paper plates and construction paper. It's art."

Nick always enjoyed Johnny Marzo's daughter, Gracie, but he didn't get to talk to her as frequently as Addie. He was finding it enjoyable, maybe relaxing was the word, to have a little friend, especially one as smart and outgoing as Addie.

"That sounds like fun."

"Better than looking at real art like Mommy-Liz shows me at her society. It's better when you get to do it yourself."

Nick wondered whether Addie had her own lesson about Edward Hicks. That reminded him to ask Liz if the guy he met at the fundraiser was still around. He couldn't remember his name.

Addie brought him back to the present. "Did you know the Native Americans called corn maize?"

"Yes," Nick said. "I learned that when I was in school. It sounds like you're learning some things about Thanksgiving."

Addie was ready to move on. "If you're calling to see if you can come over tonight, you can't."

Nick heard Liz whisper in the background that it was rude to say that and that she should explain.

"Sorry, Nick," Addie said innocently. "I have to practice for my recital tonight and Mommy-Liz is going to help me."

"That's fine, Addie. I just called to tell Mommy-Liz something but tell me about your recital first. What are you going to do?"
"I'm singing all by myself. That's why I have to practice. If you come over, I'd be too shy or nervous."
"I understand."
"You can't come to the recital either."
Nick heard Liz chide her again to explain.
"I wanted you to come, but we had to reserve tickets a long time ago, before I met you. We only have three for Mommy, Daddy, and Mommy-Liz."
Nick was touched by her wanting him to go. "I wish I could see you perform. What are you singing?"
"I'm singing 'How Far I'll Go.'"
"I don't know that song."
"Silly, It's from *Moana."*
"I'm afraid I don't know *Moana* either."
Addie giggled. "Nick, are you teasing me? Everyone knows *Moana*."
Nick heard Liz coach her. "Maybe Nick doesn't. I'll tell him."
"No, Mommy-Liz. Let me."
Nick heard Liz say okay.
Addie said, "Nick, are you sure you're not teasing me about *Moana*?"
"Honest, Addie. I don't know her or the song."
"Well, everyone else does. *Moana* has been my favorite movie since I was five. She's a Polynesian princess and a hero for her village. She's brave and strong. Mommy-Liz says she's a good role model for girls."
"Sounds like she was quite a girl, and Mommy-Liz is right. What's the song about?"

"Moana loved the ocean. She went off on a canoe with a sail for an adventure to help her people. She didn't know how far she would be going, but she was willing to go as far as she had to."

Nick smiled to himself. "You said you skipped first grade, huh."

"Yes, the teachers said I'd be bored."

"Are you bored in second grade?"

"A little. Sometimes I already know the stuff we're studying."

Nick wasn't surprised. "When I was bored in school, I'd read extra books that I liked."

"Mommy-Liz said you were smart, but I don't know how you never heard of Moana. I guess you just know other stuff."

Nick absorbed the reprimand and decided he'd ask the guys at the deli to watch the movie together. He smiled at the thought.

"Anyway, I wish I could see your show. I'm sure you'll be great, and you won't be nervous."

"I know I won't be nervous. I like singing on a stage with people there. I did it before. I just get nervous if there's just one person listening unless it's Mommy or Mommy-Liz. So, I'd be nervous singing if it was just you listening. I'd feel funny."

"Well, I'd better let you go practice. But I have an idea. Why don't we ask Mommy-Liz to film you so I can watch it later?"

"Good idea, Nick! Mommy-Liz is nodding her head."

"Perfect. Let me talk to Mommy-Liz for a minute and then you can practice."

"Bye, Nick."

"Bye, Addie. Nice talking with you."

Liz came on the phone and Nick said, “That is one smart little girl. I love talking with her.”

Liz chuckled. “It’s obvious the feeling is mutual. It’s good to have you around, Nick. She’s going through a tough time at home.”

Nick had considered how to approach the news he was about to share. Should he dance around to lead up to it or just plunge in? Liz’s comment about Addie having a tough time made the decision clear.

“That’s why I wanted to talk to you. Brian called. The investigator for the law firm found something that he thought warranted a closer look. You remember you authorized Ertz to share information with Brian.”

Liz said, “That’s fair since he’s paying the bills.”

“That’s not it,” Nick replied. “Brian doesn’t care about the bills. Trust me on that. He just wants to help. The arrangement in the law office was that Ertz would contact Brian if he thought Brian’s connections were needed to dig deeper into something. Ertz and his investigator decided they were and contacted Brian. Brian’s company did some more digging and now he wants to set up a meeting.”

Liz’s voice cracked as she said, “I can already feel my anxiety kicking in. Please try to get a meeting as soon as you can.”

Nick’s anxiety was kicking in as well. Brian wouldn’t ask for a meeting unless there was something significant to report. Most likely, the news wouldn’t be good. “I will,” he said reassuringly “In the meantime, don’t let your imagination run wild. Let’s just see what he has to say.”

“I’ll try,” Liz said, not sounding very confident. “There’s one other thing that concerns me. I’ve never been comfortable doing this whole lawyer thing without telling Kate. I know I had to leave her out of it at first, but I'm still worried about how she'll react once she knows. Maybe I should invite her to this meeting and get it over with."

Nick didn't think it was a good idea, at least not yet, but he didn't want to intrude too much in her decision-making. He went lightly with his next comment. "I understand what you're saying about Kate not knowing. At some point, you'll have to address it. Most likely she'll be upset. But hopefully, she'll recognize you're just trying to protect her and Addie. It's totally your call, but you might want to find out what Brian has to say and then give yourself some time to figure out the best way to share it all with Kate."

A few seconds passed before Liz said, "Yeah, I guess that's the best way to do it."

Nick took a breath. "Now go enjoy your granddaughter."

Chapter 44

They met in a conference room at Andrew Ertz's law office. Ertz was away at court, but his receptionist handled things efficiently. She led them to the spare conference room where they found Brian and his investigator. The receptionist had put out coffee and assorted pastries.

Brian stood when they entered the room and shook hands with Liz and Nick.

The windowless room was functional with an oak table and eight padded chairs, but it lacked the character, deep colors, and wall hangings of the outer office. Nick concluded this was not the room used when dealing with potential clients seeking million-dollar settlements. But they weren't there for the ambiance.

Brian introduced his investigator, Sam Culligan, who stood to greet them as well.

Culligan didn't match the stereotypical disheveled private investigator Nick envisioned. He was trim, well-groomed, and smartly dressed in a deep blue suit and striped tie and carried himself in a manner that suggested ex-military. They sat, and the receptionist referred them to the tray of coffee and pastries before leaving. No one touched it so Brian began.

In the few times she had been in Brian's presence, he had always been a fun-loving, the drinks-are-on-me, kind of guy. That demeanor was absent today. He was all business.

"It's good to see you, Liz, and I apologize for the mystery behind this request for a meeting. When we do research and report to the client, we prefer to roll out the information in one coherent package rather than piecemeal it."

Liz said, "I understand."

Brian glanced at the coffee and pastry and said, "Are you sure either of you wouldn't like something before we begin?"

They both declined again, and Brian moved on.

"By way of review, you authorized Andrew Ertz to use his investigator to gather background with the understanding that he would call us in if the initial investigation indicated a deeper dive from my office was warranted."
Liz agreed that was her understanding.
"That deeper dive was warranted. I want to stress that Sam Culligan has been with me for seven years. He's our most thorough investigator with contacts that open doors for us that would otherwise be closed. He's a former Army Ranger and operates with the highest level of integrity and confidentiality. What is discussed between us stays between us."

Liz appreciated that and nodded her approval, even as she dreaded what might follow. Nick put his hand on hers briefly to offer support.
Brian nodded to Culligan to take over.
"Good morning, Ma'am and Sergeant Hardings."
"Please call me Nick."
"Good morning, Nick. Mr. Kelly told me your story. Thank you for your service."
The reference stung a little, and Nick realized that for the first time in memory, he didn't want to be defined as a combat vet and POW. He was becoming more than that. But he knew Culligan meant well, and Nick thanked him for his service as well.
Culligan turned his attention to Liz and said, "Tell me what you know about your son-in-law's military service."
"There's nothing to tell. Tom was never in the military."

Culligan showed her the short form front page of Thomas Baron's military file.

Liz was stunned. His photo was in the top left corner of the paper, so there was no chance of a mix-up with a different Tom Baron.

"So, we can assume your daughter never shared this information with you."

"No, she didn't, but it's not like her to keep a secret like this. Besides, there's nothing to hide about being in the military, so why would she hide it?"

Culligan nodded. "Which means at this point, at least, we cannot assume Kate knew either."

"That would be my guess," Liz said. "But why the secret?"

Culligan said, "Check the bottom of the page."

Nick had slid the paper closer between him and Liz so he could get a better look and saw the item Culligan was referring to just as Liz did. Tom Baron had been dishonorably discharged. Liz slid the paper away, sat back in her chair, and didn't speak.

Nick said to Culligan, "Do we know the reason."

Culligan looked at Brian and Brian nodded.

Culligan said, "Several things, insubordination, fighting, racial slurs, race-baiting, and resisting orders from female officers. He spent time in the brig. He was stripped of his rank although he never climbed above Private Second class so there wasn't much to strip. He once believed he was passed over for squad leader in favor of a Latino and made a stink about that. The army finally had enough and discharged him."

Liz looked at the paper again, reluctantly as if it were toxic, and noted Tom was discharged the year before he met Kate.

Culligan turned to Liz with a look that conveyed regret that there was more coming. "I'm sorry I have to ask this. Are you familiar with a group called Pineland Patriots?"

Liz said she wasn't.

"Who does the bookkeeping in Kate's household?"

"I'm pretty sure it's Kate, why?"

Culligan hesitated and then said, "I can't divulge how I know, but there is a one-hundred-dollar automatic transfer from Kate and Tom's account to Pineland Patriots on the first of every month."

Liz asked who they were.

"On the surface, they are a hunting and shooting club."

Culligan paused, and Liz asked the obvious question. "And below the surface?"

"They are considered a militia on the watch list as a hate group with possible violent intentions. I can't tell you everything because there is intermittent law enforcement surveillance that we can't interfere with, but it's not a good group. The Southern Poverty Law Center tracks these radical militia groups, and there are several in New Jersey. As I said, the Pinelands Patriots are on the list."

Culligan saw Liz's pained expression and wanted to ease off slightly. "It's possible Tom is just a member of the shooting club and not involved deeper. I hope that is the case, but given your concerns that prompted this investigation, and his military record, I think there is cause for concern."

Liz turned to Nick and said, "I think it's time we talk to Kate."

Brian broke his silence. "I agree. But we need a plan for that. As I've said, we sometimes use tactics and resources that should not be available to us. Until we know

Kate's mindset, we can't share the military record. But a simple search on the Internet would tell you everything we just told you about the Pineland Patriots except the part that they are under surveillance. I think we should start there."

Liz nodded and Nick agreed.

"There's one more thing," Brian said. "And I don't want to offend."

Nick remained quiet and Liz said, "You're trying to be helpful. You won't offend."

Brian said, "We rely upon data when we analyze best law enforcement practices. Unfortunately, for a variety of reasons, the data tells us that women in toxic relationships often do not react to things the way most of us would expect. Many become defensive of their partner even though he may be the source of their abuse."

Liz began to protest, but Brian raised his hand to interrupt. "I'm not suggesting this is the case with your daughter, I suspect it is not, and abuse might be too strong a word. But we cannot share all of this with her right away, not until we have a better feel for how she will react. Will she defend him and lash out over our intrusion into his privacy? As unlikely as that may seem to you, she may. From what you said about her political leanings, we're comfortable that she isn't sympathetic to what the Pineland Patriots stand for or that she even knows what they stand for. But, to protect the integrity of the undercover investigation of the group, you'll have to share this piecemeal until you have a good feeling of how she will react."

Liz seemed dazed but managed to ask, "What do you suggest?"

"Let's review how we got here," Brian said. "First, tell her that given the events she's told you about, you were concerned that the marriage was heading for a breakup or separation, and you wanted to know the law regarding custody. She might be upset that you didn't tell her first, but she'll appreciate your motivation."

"I think you're right on both counts," Liz replied.

"Second, ugly as it may seem, you were advised by your attorney to investigate Tom for anything that could be used against him in a custody battle."

Liz nodded. "Nasty, but it still makes sense."

"Next you reveal that the investigation raised questions about his involvement in the gun and hunting club. A simple search on the Internet revealed that the Pineland Patriots were listed as a militia hate group. Make no mention of law enforcement or any on-going criminal investigation, ever. Again, this is all readily available on the internet.

Nick said, "You could even suggest to Kate that she do an Internet search on it herself."

Liz agreed. Brian did too and then continued. "At that point, gauge Kate's reaction. If she's at all defensive of her husband, and you have to prepare yourself for that possibility, then stop right there and we'll regroup to plan a strategy. If instead, the information drives her further away from her spouse, then tell her about the dishonorable discharge."

Liz looked at Nick who nodded his agreement and said to her, "Sounds like a plan."

They all stood, and she turned to Brian and extended her hand, "Thank you both for your help and advice." She shook Culligan's hand and said, "I fully understand. Nick and I will work it out."

Chapter 45

Nick had a decision to make, and by the time he arrived at the school, he still hadn't settled on a plan to get into Addie's recital without a ticket. The first option was to lie his way in. He'd learned long ago that older people could get away with lying much easier. People were usually less suspicious of them, considered them more trustworthy, extended them more courtesy, and gave them the benefit of the doubt more readily. He hated to exploit that benefit of age society bestowed, but he really wanted to see Addie. The kid had grown on him, just like her grandmother had.

For the past several decades he had developed an extraordinary bond with the guys at the deli. They had saved him from his worst nightmares, just as he had saved them. For that, they would have his unshakable loyalty, and he was certain he would have theirs. But in all of that time, he had never, not once, experienced female companionship. He'd gone from being one of the most popular guys in school who never lacked for a pretty and equally popular girl to the relative recluse he became when he returned home. Liz was changing that, and he was grateful, resentful of what he'd deprived himself of all these years, but grateful just the same.

His exposure to kids had been limited as well. He loved his adopted niece, Gracie. She was a bundle of energy who gave him unconditional love each time she visited. But her visits to the deli were infrequent and rarely lasted more than an hour or so, during which he shared her with her grandparents, Angelo and Donna, and the other guys.

Then there was Addie. The mere thought of her brought a smile to his face. Although he didn't have a point of comparison, he was sure that her intelligence and effusive personality were exceptional. The one-on-one time he'd spent with her, either in person or on the phone, was more enjoyable than he could have imagined just a few weeks earlier. She was precocious, insightful, and just fun to be around. He wanted to see her on stage without being intrusive, but he didn't have a ticket.

As he parked his truck in the school lot, he thought about what he would say when he reached the ticket taker. He thought of saying he had already gone in but went back out to the car to get something and now couldn't find his ticket. He also just considered saying flat-out that he lost his ticket. That he thought he had it with him but didn't. Those lines wouldn't work for younger people, but for an older guy, no one would ever think that he would have the audacity to make that up. He ended up rejecting both stories because he remembered that Addie had to supply names of who was coming and they might check the names off at the gate. He wouldn't be on the ticket list so those lines wouldn't work.

He considered just telling the truth. He didn't have a ticket but just wanted to stand in the back. There was a risk in that. He knew if he ran into a rigid hard ass, he'd never get in.

In the end, he decided on a hybrid of half-lie and half-truth. The question was who to share the lie with? He would only have a few seconds between when he entered the building to when he approached the ticket table. He had to find the right person.

He entered and did a quick scan. The first thing he saw was a large sign that read, SOLD OUT. NO ADMITTANCE WITHOUT AN ADVANCE TICKET. That wasn't good. The ticket table was twenty feet away in the auditorium lobby. The ticket taker was a thirty-something phys ed type. He wore a lanyard indicating he was a faculty member. Approaching him would never work. Guys like him were too uptight, too rigid, too much like the drill sergeants he had in the military.

Nick sensed defeat until he saw the security guard. He looked to be in his late sixties, slightly paunchy, with his best years behind him, maybe an ex-cop, maybe ex-military, probably making thirty bucks for the night for what would be a useless presence if any real trouble broke out. But then what trouble could there be at an elementary school recital? Unless they declare a winner, in which case a fight could break out between parents.

This was going to be Nick's shot. He approached the guard and said hello. The guard was bored and liked the attention.

Nick said, "I'm hoping you can help me." Nick knew that everyone needs to feel important, and a security assignment at an elementary school recital probably made the guard feel anything but important. He perked up.

"What do you need?"

"I'm checking in to the VA hospital in Philly tomorrow for some tests on my lungs."

Nick thought mentioning the VA rather than just a generic hospital would be a subtle way of conveying he was ex-military. If he was lucky, the guard was too. If not, the reference might still earn him some respect.

"VA, which branch were you in?"

"Army, Vietnam. I'm spooked this might be from Agent Orange exposure." Nick hated to exploit what was a serious condition for so many, but he really wanted to see Addie.

"Terrible, the guard said. "I wish you well. I'm a Navy man. We were off the coast of Nam during the evacuation. What a shit show."

"Yup. Washington made us fight, but they wouldn't really let us take the gloves off and win."

The guard nodded his agreement. "So, what can I do for you?"

"I don't have a ticket and I really want to see my grandkid before I check in tomorrow. I was supposed to go to the VA three days ago, which is why she never reserved me a ticket. But then they bumped me back a week, so here I am. To tell you the truth, I'm a little worried about what they'll find."

What Nick was really worried about was bad karma for faking a possible affliction that others had for real, but he felt he'd done enough good for veterans over the years, to entitle him to an innocent lie for a good cause. He really wanted to see Addie.

"I'll just stand in the back and leave early because she's in second grade and they go in order."

"That's it? That's all you need?"

"That's it," Nick said.

"Hell," the guard said, puffing out his chest. "Come with me."

He walked by the ticket table with Nick in tow, told the phys ed guy he'd be right back, and, without explanation, escorted Nick to the auditorium door. The ticket taker shrugged and gave his attention to the people in line.

When they reached the door, the guard said, "Thank you for your service. Enjoy your granddaughter, and good luck tomorrow."

Nick felt a pang of guilt but shrugged it off. He thanked the guard and went in.

He stood in the back corner and surveyed the room. It was three-quarters full with latecomers making their way to their seats. He hoped Liz was already there so he wouldn't be seen if she arrived late. He was relieved to find her sitting in the fourth row with a woman he assumed to be Kate. The seat next to Kate was empty. He hoped Addie's father would show up because he didn't want her to be disappointed, but given the time, it seemed unlikely.

A female usher approached him and asked if she could show him to his seat because the performance would begin soon. He thanked her but explained that he had recent back surgery and could not sit for an extended period. He didn't want to disturb the show by having to get up in the middle of it. The woman smiled and said she hoped he enjoyed the show. As she left he felt that Karma thing again, and did a couple of back stretches.

The lights dimmed and Nick noticed that Addie's father's seat remained empty. He cursed the man he had never met and his dislike grew. The director appeared and made the bubbly obligatory comments about how excited the kids were and how hard they had worked to prepare for the show. Nick imagined Addie backstage, bursting with nervous energy. He wondered what she'd wear. She didn't impress him as a frilly kind of kid.

He scanned the audience of parents, grandparents, and friends, some held flower bouquets to present to their young stars. Others had cameras or cell phones ready to record the event. He was glad to see Kate holding a bouquet on her lap. All of this was a reminder of how much he had missed in his life. He felt a brief stir of anxiety, but he shook it off as the show began.

By the time the first graders were finished, Nick was grateful Addie's class was next. Watching his special performer would be great, but watching an endless stream of other kids, not so much.

Finally, it was Addie's turn. He watched her take the stage, a little girl all alone in front of a full house. She wore a simple dress, not frilly, but cute. He was sure Addie had significant input in the choice. She looked nervous, but he saw her take a deep breath to gather herself. Then she nodded to someone off-stage, and the background music began.

She closed her eyes for a moment as the intro to "How Far I'll Go" played.

Earlier that week, Nick had paid for the streaming service so the guys could watch Moana together in the deli. They protested strongly at first, but Nick knew they'd do it for him if he insisted. He did insist and they watched. When the movie ended, the consensus was that it was pretty good, and more watchable than they had feared. Later, Nick played Addie's song a few more times to learn the words. He wanted to soak up as much of her performance as possible.

As the first verse began, her voice rang out clear and strong. She obviously remembered Mommy-Liz's advice to project her voice and enunciate each word clearly. The singing wasn't that good, but she sang with passion, putting all her heart and soul into the performance. Nick admired her spunk.

As the song reached its climax, Addie closed her eyes once again, belting out the final notes with all her might. When the last note faded away, the audience erupted into applause, and Addie took a bow, feeling proud of herself. She searched the audience for her family and waved when she spotted her mom.

There was a brief intermission between each grade so the kids could go to their parents. Kate and Mommy-Liz ran up to her, hugging her tightly and apparently telling her how amazing she was. Addie beamed with happiness. Her smile faded when she must have asked where her father was, and he saw Kate kneel in front of her and most likely say something reassuring. Her smile returned and she took her flowers and disappeared backstage again.

Nick wiped a tear from his cheek and considered how much he'd like to kick Tom Baron's ass if he met him. Tom was much younger, and Nick didn't know his size or what shape he was in. Nick might get his own ass kicked instead, but he promised himself he'd get the first good shot in if the situation ever presented itself.

He crossed the lobby and waved to the guard as he headed for the door. The guard wished him good luck as he left the building.

Chapter 46

Nick saw that Liz was calling and he answered right away, only to find it was Addie calling again.

"Hi, Nick. It's me," Addie gushed. "I'm using Mommy-Liz's phone."

Hi, Addie," Nick said. "Thanks for calling."

"We just got to the playground near my house. It's my Monday treat. Mommy-Liz picks me up from school, buys me ice cream, and takes me to the playground near my house. She reads a book while I play. Then she takes me home."

"That sounds like a nice afternoon. What kind of ice cream do you like?"

"I always get Cookie Monster. It's my favorite."

"I've never had it. I'll have to..,"

Addie cut him off. "I can't talk long, I have to go play. But I called for a special reason. I had my recital Saturday and

Mommy-Liz recorded it. She said I can invite you over to her house tomorrow for pizza and we can watch it. Can you come?" Nick had forgotten about his request to record it. He paused for a second and said, "I'd love to. Are you sleeping over?"

" No, I'm going home after dinner. Okay. I have to go. Here's Mommy Liz." She was gone before Nick could say goodbye.

Liz took the phone and said, "Hi, Nick. She insisted on calling you."
Nick laughed. "I'm glad she did, but that was an abrupt ending."
Liz said, "I've learned that when she's finished, she's finished."
"It's okay. I think it's cute. It just takes me by surprise when she does it."
"Me too," Liz laughed again. "So, can you come for pizza? She was really cute in the play and wants you to see the video."
"Pizza and video. I'm in. I have a confession to make though. Strictly confidential. Promise?"
Liz's mind raced over what Nick was about to tell her now. The last meeting with Brian was bad news enough. She didn't need more. But Nick's voice sounded light, not ominous. She took a breath and said, "I promise."
Nick said, "I was there."
"You were where?"
"At Addie's recital."
"I don't understand what you're saying. How were you there?"

"I wanted to see her, but I didn't have a ticket. I went anyway and talked my way in. I stood in the back corner and left after she sang. She was great."

"Nick, are you teasing me? Were you really there?"

Nick told her what Addie wore, where Liz and Kate sat, and that they presented her with flowers.

"Wow," Liz said. "I believe you. That was so nice of you to come. I'm beginning to think you might enjoy Addie's company more than mine."

"It's a tie," Nick said flatly, "but for totally different reasons. You might be a pretty face and good arm candy when we go out, but sometimes a person needs some intellectual dialogue. That's where Addie comes in."

Liz smiled into the phone, but let the comment go. "Anyway, I'm glad you got to see her in person. You must have seen that we had an empty seat next to us. You should have joined us."

Liz detected a change in Nick's tone when he spoke again. "I saw the empty seat, and I had some not-so-pleasant thoughts about the intended occupant. I felt bad for Addie that he didn't show."

"She was very disappointed. But Kate talked to her, and she bounded back. She didn't let it ruin her day. She's very resilient."

"She might be," Nick conceded, "but I don't know how long she can bounce back when she's hurt. As for taking the seat, I would never do that. It was saved for her father, and he should have been there. I've never met this guy, but I'm liking him less and less."

"Me too," Liz replied. "Which is another reason why I wanted to talk with you. We have to tell Kate, and I'm not sure how to do it."

"I agree it's time to tell Kate, but let's discuss your use of the word, 'we.' I'm not trying to be a coward here, but you should talk to Kate alone. I've never even met her. It would be like, 'I'd like you to meet my new boyfriend. He knows more about your husband than you do.' I don't think that's wise."

Liz paused and then said coyly, "Are you my boyfriend?"

Nick regretted using the word. "You know what I mean. We've already discussed that we don't know what we are. Something nice, but who knows? Regardless, Kate will see it that way. It's not a good idea."

Liz turned serious. "I was trying to keep it light with the boyfriend reference, Nick, but you're right. This is serious. It's serious about Kate and serious about you and me. You said it, you know more about my daughter's husband than she knows because I confided in you. I've needed you during this, and you were there for me."

Liz paused, and when Nick didn't respond she went on. "Let me straighten out a couple of things. First, that coward reference you just made is ridiculous. I think you've proven your valor quite clearly."

Nick said, "You know what I meant, I…"

"Be quiet," Liz interjected. "I've got something to say."

Nick didn't speak, and she went on. "It's true you've never met Kate, but I assure you that you're not a stranger to her. Addie adores you and talks about you all the time."

"That's very nice, but it may not be wise."

Liz knew what he meant and said, "She does it when her father isn't around. She has a type of built-in danger sensor and perception skills beyond her age. It's terrible when a little girl needs to move gingerly around her own dad.

"She repeatedly refers to you as my boyfriend. So, Kate is eager to meet you."

"That's really nice, Liz. Please do us a favor. Give it more thought and we'll talk again soon."

Chapter 47

Nick answered the phone and said, "Hi, Addie."

Liz replied, "Wise guy, it's me."

Nick feigned confusion. "The voice is familiar. Let me think. Lucy? Loretta? Liz? That's it! Is this Liz?"

Liz said," I don't have time to play. I have news."

Nick turned serious. "Sorry. What kind of news?"

"I told her. I told Kate."

After their last conversation, Nick was convinced Liz wouldn't tell her daughter without him with her.

"You told her by yourself?"

"Yes. I thought about what you said. I imagined myself in her shoes hearing it, and decided you were right. I told her this morning."

Nick said, "Good. You did the right thing." He braced himself before asking the next question. "How did it go?"

"It turns out I was right too about how she would react to you and our investigation of Tom. She wants to meet you. Addie has left her with a very good vibe about you. As for the part about Tom. I did it in stages, deciding to gauge her reaction to each piece before going on."

"That was a good idea. So how far did you get? "

"I was able to tell her the whole thing. Everything we know and a lot about how we know."

Liz knew Nick was concerned about protecting Brian's role, and

she added, "I said I couldn't tell her everything about how the information was gotten. She was okay with that. She didn't push back."

Nick thanked her for doing that and Liz went on.

"She wasn't angry that we did it. I'd say she was more surprised than angry, and grateful too. She didn't know what to do. She was embarrassed that someone she didn't know was paying for it, but she realizes there is no other option."

Nick said, "So, she's okay with me being around and wants to meet. She tolerated the process. That leaves us with the big question of how she reacted to the stuff about Tom."

"I was saving that. She was surprisingly calm in some ways and frightened in other ways. She had already decided she wanted to end their relationship. There was no more happiness. Plus, she was growing more concerned about how Addie was sensing their relationship and Tom's changed personality. "

Nick agreed. "A kid that smart picks up a lot more than people might realize."

Liz said, "Kate is frightened about the possibility Tom might be in something very dangerous. She doesn't want to jump the gun on that until she knows more, but I think in her heart she knows. Anyway, she wants out and doesn't know how to do it safely."

Nick's thoughts hung on her last word, safely.

Liz continued. "She'd like to meet with you, Brian, and anyone else you think we should include. Can you set that up?"

"I'll call him right away." He paused and added, "I know that was difficult, and it will get more difficult now, but you're doing the right thing."
Liz didn't need reassurance. "After speaking with Kate, I know I am."

Chapter 48

Liz decided it would be best for Nick and Kate to meet over lunch before their meeting with the others at the law office. The three of them met at the Langhorne Hotel and sat at the same table Nick and Liz had shared on their first date. Nick liked Kate right away. She was outgoing and gracious like her mom and shared her physical features. She was slim and attractive, with dark hair that reached her shoulders and slightly more pronounced cheekbones than Liz. Nick felt her expression reflected someone trying bravely to be cheerful for their meeting while fighting back emotional pain, and he respected her effort.

They ordered drinks and a light lunch. When the waitress left, Kate put Nick's concerns to rest in one statement. "I know this can be awkward for you, so let me get this out of the way. I am thrilled that you and Mom are seeing each other. She deserves someone she can spend time with. She's an upbeat person, but since she reconnected with you her smile is broader, and she just seems rejuvenated. So welcome to our lives."
Nick thanked her, and Kate continued, "I also want to tell you that showing up at Mom's doorstep the way you did was something straight out of Hollywood. That was pretty cool, Nick."

Nick started to respond, but Kate held up her hand and asked him to wait. “I have one more thing to add. My daughter is absolutely obsessed with you and mentions you frequently. Winning Addie’s approval might be the hardest test anyone can face, and you’ve passed with flying colors.”

Nick thanked her again and said how much he enjoyed Addie and how happy he was to be spending time with Liz.

Kate said, “Now that we have the social piece out of the way, I guess it’s time to address the darker side of our lives and what you guys have uncovered.”
Her cheerful façade evaporated, and her lip quivered slightly. She paused to compose herself and then said, “First, I have no problem with what Mom did. She has always been my best friend, even when I was a young, rebellious pain in the neck, she was there for me. So, I know she did what she did with the best of intentions, and, as it turns out, it’s a good thing she did.”
She smiled at her mother and addressed Nick. “As for including you in what would normally be a private family thing, I fully understand her doing that too. I trust her judgment about you and realize this wasn’t something she could do alone. So, thank you for being there for her. I guess I should add thank you for being there for me.”
Nick smiled. “You have no idea how relieved I am to hear that.” Turning to Liz, he added, “Your family has three generations of females I like.”
Liz put her hand on Kate’s and said, “You’re gonna like this guy. Nick is good to have around.”

Kate said she could see that already. Her eyes began to fill, and she wiped away a tear. "I've been trying to hold it together, but this whole thing is just overwhelming. So, I'm not just being polite when I say I'm truly glad you're both involved with my problem." She paused and added with more emphasis, "I need you to be involved."

Nick cleared his throat before replying. "I don't want to be presumptions or speak for your mom, but I think we're both here for as long as you need us."

Liz squeezed Kate's hand in agreement.

Their food arrived, but no one felt much like eating. Liz asked the waitress if she would box it for them. The waitress shrugged, took the food she had just delivered, and left.

Nick said, "While you're going through this, as bad as it gets, just try to imagine a future life where you and Addie are happy and secure. It will help you cope."

Liz wondered if that advice stemmed from his POW days.

Kate said, "I don't see how happiness and safety are possible with Tom around. Addie and I need a new life."

Liz said, "You'll like the people we're going to meet with. I have confidence in the attorney and the men working on what Tom is up to. They'll make a plan."

Nick cautioned both women again that things might get uglier before they get better.

Kate straightened in her chair and replied, "I'm sure they will." She checked her watch and said, "I guess we should get going. For the record, I'm terrified, but as they say, it's either fight or flight. With your help, I'm ready for option one."

Chapter 49

On the way to the law office, Liz explained that they would meet with Brian first for an update on Tom's activities, followed by a session with Andrew Ertz.

They started in the same bland conference room they used before. Once again, Brain and Sam Culligan were already seated and stood while Nick introduced Kate.
When they took their seats, Kate said, "Before we begin, I just want to say how humbled and grateful I am for your generous support, especially for someone you've never met before."
"It's our pleasure," Brian said. "You are a friend of a friend and that's good enough for us. As I told your mother, my wife Jennifer and I have been blessed with wealth too easily obtained and we love giving back in this way. We actually budget for it. You have enough things in your life to worry about. Don't let finances be one of them."

Kate smiled. "You are incredibly generous, and I'm very grateful. I hope I can meet Jennifer one day."
"We'll make it a point," Brian replied. "As Liz can attest, we like to have a good time. I know having a good time might seem a bit far-fetched right now, but stay strong, put whatever you need to do behind you, and know that better times will come."

Kate was encouraged by Brian's words and prayed he was right. One thing was clear to her, she was in good hands. She said, "I have one more thing to say. I know from my mom that there was concern about looking into my marriage without my knowledge. I want you to know that I'm fine with that too, and glad you did, even though the results are not pleasant."

Brian nodded. "At the time, we were working for your mom. Now, we're working for you. We'll go as far as you like and stop whenever you like." Then he nodded toward Nick and said, "I've known this guy since I was a kid. We wouldn't be here if it weren't for him. I know you haven't known each other too long but..."

Kate interrupted and said kiddingly, "How about forty-five minutes?"

Everyone laughed and Brian said, "Then let me tell you. He is as solid as a rock."

Liz said," I can vouch for that,"

Kate added, "That's becoming obvious."

Brian said, "Let's get started. We have three things to share, none of which are pleasant. I'm told you already know some of this, so I'll be brief."

"Sounds good," Kate said.

Liz knew Kate was struggling to keep her emotions in check while she was dying inside, and she admired her daughter's strength.

Culligan took a sheet from the file folder in front of him and slid it across the table to Kate. "First, here is the information I shared with Liz and Nick at our last meeting. It's a copy of Thomas Baron's military service record, including his dishonorable discharge."

Brian took over. "He has a record of racism, misogyny, violence, and resistance to authority. I don't know how or if

these traits manifested themselves with you, but that's the army's assessment."
Kate reflected on that and saw the parallels, especially in recent months. She glanced at the paper but chose not to touch it.

When she didn't respond, Brian looked at Nick and Liz and said, "At our previous meeting we said that Baron frequents a shooting range in New Jersey that happens to be owned by a white nationalist militia leader. At that time, we said we had no evidence of any involvement by Baron beyond target shooting. We had reason to believe that since the Three R Shooting Range has numerous customers who are unaware of the owner's white nationalist ideology and simply use it to practice shooting or buy ammo. We were hoping that was the case with your husband. Unfortunately, we now know that Thomas Baron is more deeply involved, is aware of the owner's philosophy, and has participated in private meetings."
Liz was saddened by this development but not surprised. She had resigned herself to as much before the meeting began.
"None of what I just described about Tom is illegal. It constitutes free speech and freedom of association. It only becomes illegal if they cross the line from talking to planning or conspiring to commit a crime, or worse case, actually committing one."
Kate kept her eyes straight and listened.
Brian paused a few seconds before adding, "Legal or not, it's important to consider what type of man chooses to associate with a group that stands for the garbage these guys preach."

Kate responded by saying she didn't want herself or her daughter to be part of that life. "I just wish I understood the attraction, the motivation behind those who do."

Brian said, "That brings us to the third part of our discussion. The profile of members of these groups is that they are angry with their lack of achievement in life. Instead of analyzing their own shortcomings, they point to government policies and evolving norms that give preference to Blacks, Latinos, women, and immigrants. They also point to Jews who they believe do nothing but serve themselves financially. In their view, it's impossible to make it in America if you're in line behind all of that."

Kate had flashbacks of Tom's rants and nodded her understanding of what Brian was saying.

Brian went on. "They cloak their grievances in patriotism. Theirs is not a selfish mission as they see it. Their goal isn't to help themselves; it is to save America. They see the population trends. Each year America is becoming less white. The Black, Latino, and immigrant populations are growing at a faster rate, and the white nationalists use them as scapegoats for the ills of society."

Culligan removed another sheet from his folder and shared it with Kate.
"There are hundreds of hate or militia groups in America. The map you are looking at was developed by the Southern Poverty Law Center. It shows their locations across the nation. Notice there are twenty-two in New

Jersey alone. The numbers are supported by the FBI and other law enforcement agencies. I'm not telling you anything secret here. You can find it all online."
Liz said, "I had no idea of the extent of this. How do they get together?"
"Good question," Brian said, "Instead of brooding alone, they find comfort in numbers. They gain a sense of belonging when they join a group."
"Makes sense," Nick said. "Losers attracting other losers."
Brian nodded and added, "But they are not all losers. Another aspect of these groups is that they often have a charismatic leader, someone who is just a little smarter than they are, someone who is a good speaker and has crafted a message that captures their grievances and offers them a path, much like a televangelist does with his followers."

It was Culligan's turn again. "Often, these leaders don't fit the profile Mr. Kelly just laid out. They are successful in business but have such deep-seated racism that they want to play an active role in preserving America as a white-dominated society. That is the case with Richard Raymond Rogers, aka R3. He has a very successful business, but he is an avowed racist who works hard to attract like-minded followers.

"Once they convince themselves that their cause is noble, then anything they do in support of the cause can be justified, even criminal activity. Many groups are involved in anything from cooking meth, to theft to scamming people to fund the cause."

Brian said, "Let me summarize to wrap this up. I want to make it clear that we're not talking about strong, mainstream conservatism here, people who believe in self-reliance, traditional values, and less government. We're talking about extremist groups, hate groups, groups that advocate white supremacy at the expense of minorities. Again, they have the right to freedom of thought and speech. Our interest is when they crossover from rhetoric to illegal action. That's why we monitor them."

Kate, Liz, and Nick remained silent, and Brian added, "I think you've gotten the message, but since we've come this far, I'll throw in one more point. These militia groups don't just exist in isolation. There is an online network of organizations that communicate frequently with a dream that they will someday rise up together and take back America."

He checked his watch and said, "On that pleasant note, I think Mr. Ertz is expecting you now. Please reach out if there is anything you need. I mean that. Nick, please make sure Kate and Liz know I mean that."
Nick said he would. They stood, Kate and Liz thanked them again and then left for Andrew Ertz's office.

Kate was immediately struck by the contrast of the two rooms. The handsome, well-groomed, and stylishly dressed attorney obviously preferred the trappings of a richly furnished, classic office. Kate was both impressed and intimidated by the surroundings.

Ertz stood to greet them and shook hands with Kate. He smiled briefly before getting down to business. “As with all of my clients, I’m sorry you are going through this, but we have to make some things clear from the beginning. I will represent you to the fullest of my ability. But I need to know first exactly what it is you want. Is it reconciliation? Separation? Divorce? Partial custody? Full custody? What about financial settlements? I don’t expect you to know any of that right now. I’m sure you are filled with conflicting and overwhelming emotions. So I will ask some questions, lay out some alternatives, and then we’ll meet again. Now the first...”

Kate said, “Excuse me for interrupting, but I know exactly what I want.” She took a long breath and said, “I want a divorce and full custody of my daughter. I will not have Addie raised by him, not after what I know now. That is exactly what I want.”

Ertz nodded. “I appreciate your conviction, but experience tells me I can’t fully accept it, at least not yet.”
Kate looked surprised and Ertz explained. “Very often, a spouse will come to my office with the same resolve you are displaying now, and then after mountains of paperwork and hours of time they choose to kiss and make up. Don’t misunderstand me. The courts like nothing more than a happy reconciliation in marriage conflicts. It’s just better if we’re sure from the outset. I should add that experience also tells me that most reconciliations fail later.”

Kate listened and then said firmly, “My daughter will not be raised by a neo-Nazi or whatever the hell he thinks he is. I want a divorce and full custody. We can talk about property, but that's not my priority now."

Ertz nodded and made a note on his legal pad. "Okay. Take your time and walk us through your relationship. Anything you feel might be relevant."
Kate spoke for fifteen minutes straight while Ertz made an occasional note. She finished with Tom's recent absence from the house.

"At first he'd be gone for a couple of days at a time, supposedly to stay at a friend's cabin in the Pinelands to target shoot. Now he's been gone for over a week. He even missed Thanksgiving. No note, no phone call. He doesn't answer when I call. At times I can tell he's been in the house while I'm working to pick up clothes, I guess. As far as I'm concerned, he's abandoned us."

Ertz shook his head slightly. "No doubt he has abandoned you physically and emotionally, but not legally. In a legal sense, he would have to be gone for a year for reasons you did not agree to. And, if he comes back for a reasonable time and then leaves, the clock starts ticking all over again."
Kate raised her eyebrows in surprise. "A year?"
"Yes. So, abandonment as a reason for at-fault divorce is not an issue here. At least not yet. From what you told me, you may be able to make an at fault case for cruelty or the lesser standard of indignity. You may be very uncomfortable around him, but you've never been in any real danger as far as I can tell."
"He shook me once. That's it. The rest was verbal."

“Shaking could escalate into something else. But honestly, if you want out quickly, then I recommend a no- fault filing. It’s easier and faster. If he agrees, and that’s often a big if, especially with a child involved. On the other hand, an at fault divorce could help you with visitation rights and custody issues, which, of course, are your main con.”

Kate was about to ask a question when her phone pinged. She said, “Please excuse me. I just need to check that it’s not the school messaging about my daughter.”
Ertz said, “Of course.”

Kate checked her phone and frowned. Most of her bills were scheduled for automatic payment from the bank. Half were due on the first of the month with the others scheduled for the fifteenth. It was December 2 and her message indicated there were insufficient funds for her mortgage payment. Then she noticed an earlier message. She had missed an electric bill payment for the same reason.

She looked red faced and said, “I’m very sorry. This is crazy. The bank is saying I have insufficient funds for automatic payments. I always leave enough in my checking account to cover the bills. I’ll have to call them later.”
Ertz look concerned. “Do you and your husband share a joint banking account?”
The implications of the question were clear to everyone. Kate wore a panicked look as she said they did.
“Then please call the bank right away. We’ll wait.”
Liz looked terrified for her daughter as Kate searched for the number and dialed. As Kate went through the protocols

to verify who she was, Nick was already resigned to what the answer would be.

Kate listened and shook her head in disbelief. She covered the phone and said to the others, "He emptied the checking account three days ago."

Kate asked if it was possible fraud. The bank official assured her it was not, "We would never release an amount like that without verification. Thomas Baron showed up in person, presented his driver's license, and wrote a check for the amount."

Kate was stunned. They had three other accounts, a joint savings, a joint vacation club and an IRA for each of them. Kate inquired about all of them. The two savings accounts were empty. Kate's IRA was untouched. Only she had access to it, and the bank official couldn't divulge anything about Tom's IRA.

Kate disconnected and remained silent as the others waited for news. Then she mumbled, "He emptied all of our joint accounts." She paused again and added, "Fifty-two thousand dollars. Everything we had besides our IRAs." Tears were streaming down her face and Ertz handed her a tissue. Liz was crying too and reached for her own. Nick's fists were clenched so tightly that his knuckles hurt.

Kate wiped her eyes and asked in a choked voice, "Can he do that?"

Reluctantly, Ertz said that he could if they were joint accounts. "Do you have direct deposit of your paycheck into this account?"

Kate said that she did.

"Then call your HR department immediately and cancel it."

Nick struggled to control the rage he was feeling as Kate slumped in her chair and sobbed.

Ertz pressed the button on his desk to summon his personal assistant. When she arrived, he said, "Open a checking account at my bank in the name of Katherine Baron. Her information is in her file. Deposit $10,000 from the firm's account and bill it to Brian Kelly."

Kate began to protest, but Ertz stopped her. "Brian said any and all expenses. I assure you I'll clear it with him today. That's for this month. We'll revisit later."

Kate was too numb to speak. Ertz said, "This changes things. Let's get this son of a bitch."

Nick couldn't have agreed more.

Chapter 50

For the first time in years, Tom Baron felt the end to his frustrations was coming. The tide was changing, and he felt he'd be in the vanguard of the change. He had watched helplessly as the country he loved was coming apart piece by piece, and the people who once were its backbone, men, white men, blue-collar white men, were being cast aside by Blacks, Latinos, Asians, and immigrants of all types. Soon, if not already, whites would be in the minority. As if that weren't bad enough, women were trampling men. They get all the breaks in hiring, raises, and perks. There was also an all-out assault on men who were now portrayed as dumbos in TV commercials and situation comedies.

Even some men were part of the problem. They were the elites, the pretty boys who were bankers, lawyers, stockbrokers, men who went to spas and used hair stylists and got manicures and pedicures, men who drove cars worth more than the average annual blue-collar salary and paid country club fees higher than most people's mortgages. They led their smug lifestyles and enjoyed the benefits of the American economic system without ever lifting a weapon to defend it and would crap in their pants if they ever had to.

He thought about his wife and daughter. He loved Addie. She was a good kid, cute, smart, and fun to be with, but the writing was on the wall. She was her mother's daughter and would grow up to be just like her and her liberal causes. It hurt him to cut ties, but he knew things would only get worse at the house and he didn't want Addie to learn to hate him, especially if he decided to seek full custody in the future.

As for Kate, he loved her once but eventually found their relationship was doomed. Kate's mother never accepted him, which didn't help. When he got screwed out of his promotion which went to an underqualified Guatemalan, Kate showed disappointment over the loss of extra income, but instead of sharing his anger, she made politically correct comments about companies wanting to promote social justice. She didn't come right out and say it, but it seemed she was sympathetic to the idea of blatantly discriminating against white men to satisfy some liberal cause. Adding to his humiliation. Kate was making good money and even spoke of a possible promotion of her own. He was supposed to be the main breadwinner of the family, not her.

Then, instead of recognizing what was going on in the world around her, she supported Hillary for president. America's stature in the world was sinking like a rock, and Kate apparently wanted a president who would speed up the process. Tension grew when he found out she supported gay marriage. How could any sensible person support gay marriage? When he said if every marriage was a gay marriage, the human race would become extinct, she laughed and said that was an absurd way to look at it. She actually laughed.

He hated it when women looked down on him. He thought back to his time in the military when he had a bitch female officer bossing him around. It was bad enough we had women in the military, now we were making them officers and letting them tell men what to do.

All of this was petty compared to what Tom saw as the overriding threat against America. There was a conspiracy of globalists in our government and corporate headquarters who dreamed of a new world order, one that put international finance and corporate profits above the interests of the American people. He had read extensively, everything from *The Turner Diaries* to online postings. He'd learned that political parties were meaningless. Democrats and Republicans could pretend to battle in Congress over little things, but in truth, they all came together at the top. Congressional leaders of both parties, bureaucrats, government agencies, and corporations, bonded to form the deep state, and all conspired to line their own pockets at the expense of the average Joe. He learned that the deep state was part of an international conspiracy that would undermine America's national interests in favor of globalist goals.

Battling all of this and more is what drove Tom's ambitions. He wanted in with groups of like-minded citizens like the Pineland Patriots, and now the entry door was opening a little wider.

Tom and Charlie Gibbs sat side by side in front of the fireplace in Gibbs' cabin, drinking beer and enjoying cigars. They had just finalized their living arrangement. Tom would pay $500 a month to rent Charlie's second bedroom. Charlie needed the money and Tom needed the space, so both were feeling good.

Privately, Tom thought the arrangement offered more than just needed living space. He and Charlie had hit it off well since they met at the shooting range, and Tom was convinced Charlie was part of R3's inner circle. If that was true, Tom hoped it would help him get inside as well.

Tom flipped what was left of his cigar into the fire.

Charlie said, “Remember, I got just one rule. Don’t ever touch my pork roll in the refrigerator. We can share everything else, beer, whatever, but do not touch my pork roll.”

Tom smiled and said, “I’ll remember that.”

Charlie said, “Your rent is going to help, but I’m still hurting for cash. How are you looking for money?”

Tom had thousands stashed in a safe place, but as much as he liked Charlie and wanted to stay on his good side, he wasn’t about to share that information. “I’m strapped myself. I need to work something out soon.”

Tom eyed his new friend. Charlie was a strapping guy, at least twice Tom’s size. He was barrel-chested, with a full beard and shoulder-length hair. Regardless of the weather, he always wore a cutoff denim jacket exposing his massive, tattooed arms.

Tom watched as Charlie blew rings of smoke toward the rafters. He looked like a man wanting to say something but not sure if he should. Finally, he shrugged and said, “How bad are you strapped?”

“Pretty bad,” Tom said.

“Bad enough to do something about it?”

Tom was wary but intrigued. “What do you have in mind? I’m not afraid to work.”

Charlie laughed. “This isn’t a job interview, at least not that kind of job.”

Tom didn’t respond, and Charlie studied him for a few more seconds. He was about to take a risk and was considering whether it was worth it. He shrugged and said, ”I know a guy who is looking for a couple of guys to make some easy money, but I have to move soon."

Tom knew what easy money usually meant. He also knew that a business arrangement with Charlie might help with his aspirations moving forward.

"I'm always interested in easy money."

Charlie looked skeptical. "Can I trust you?"

Tom smiled. "Sure you can trust me. If not, you'd know how to find me."

Charlie's expression darkened to a scowl, and he said, "You know I will."

Tom nodded.

Charlie relaxed and said, "I know a guy who knows a guy who deals with high-tech equipment, sensors, circuits, chips, all very expensive stuff. He needs it moved from his warehouse to another location. He's willing to pay $20,000 to move two van loads. Ten grand each."

Tom didn't get it. "Seems like a lot of money to move two vans of stuff."

Charlie laughed. "It depends on how you define the word 'move.' The guy is short on cash. He needs us to remove his materials from his warehouse and stage a break-in so he can collect the insurance. The stuff is worth more than a quarter million when he resells it."

Tom whistled, and Charlie went on. "He's got it all set up. It can't go wrong. They are his security cameras, so he knows how to fix them. He gave me two days to find someone, or he is gonna look elsewhere. I was gonna poke around tomorrow with some of the guys at the range but now I'm thinking, 'What the hell, why not use my roommate?'"

Tom said, “Thinking about trust, do you trust this guy well enough to believe he’s got it covered? Are you sure we’ll get paid?”

“Yeah, I trust him, and we’ll get paid. I did work for him before. He pays. He’s a pretty smart guy. Like I said, he deals in high-tech stuff. Some big deal he was working on fell through. He was left with all this surplus that he can’t handle. We’ll move it. He’ll claim it was stolen, collect the insurance and then resell the stuff at a discount to a buyer he has lined up. But the buyer is only in for a couple days and that’s where the money comes from to pay us.”

Tom thought for a minute. Ten grand would go a long way toward getting him into the inner circle without touching the money he had stashed.

He tossed it around for a minute and said, “Okay. I’m in.”

Chapter 51

Nick answered Liz’s call on the second ring and said abruptly, “Not you again? Are you stalking me?”

“Very funny, Nick. I called because I miss you, and that’s the reception I get?”

“I’m sorry,” Nick said. “I was missing you too and was just about to call.” He paused and said, “Actually, I can’t lie. I was taking a nap.”

Liz said, “Well, then, wise guy, I’m glad I woke you up. I hope I spoiled a deep sleep.”

“I was dreaming about you,” Nick replied.

Liz smiled at the thought and said, “That’s very nice.”

Nick went on. “You were in Walmart dressed like George Washington.”

Liz was disappointed the dream wasn’t something romantic if there was a dream at all. “You’re making that up.”

“You were in the food aisle pushing a cart.”

“You’re lying.”

“In the produce section picking out tomatoes and cucumbers. I think you were going to make a salad for the troops.”

Liz started to speak, but Nick plunged on. “You looked impressive. The kind of commanding presence men in uniform would follow. In fact, there was a guy in uniform following you. He looked like a security guard.”

Liz searched for a retort but Nick was too quick. He added, “You would think George would be in the hunting department buying boots and a heavy coat for the Christmas crossing. Those guys in the painting looked like they were freezing their asses off.”

Liz laughed out loud and decided to play. “It’s 2018. The roles are reversed. Martha was probably in the hunting department while George was shopping for dinner. History shows Martha actually led the crossing.”

Nick grunted. “That’s typical liberal BS. Men are under attack everywhere.” He realized his joke mimicked one of Tom’s grievances and regretted it. He turned serious. “How are you?”

Liz said, “I need to see you. Are you free?”

“Absolutely. What’s wrong? Something with Kate?”

"No, the opposite. I've dragged you into this mess and I realize we haven't had any fun lately. I was hoping we could just go someplace together."
"Sure, where?"
"Anywhere. Pick me up and we'll just go. There's nothing new with Kate. Andrew Ertz drew up the divorce papers, but he can't serve them because Tom is missing. His work says he took a two-week vacation, which is strange in early December, and he hasn't been home. Anyway, Kate and Addie are settled into their routines, Kate at the hospital and Addie at school. It's a quiet time. I thought we could take advantage of it and get together, block that mess out for a while and just have a good time."

Nick checked his watch. It was approaching 4:30. "I'll be there by 5:00. By the way. I did lie earlier. You weren't dressed like George Washington. You were wearing much less and I'm too shy to discuss it."
Liz smiled and hung up without responding.

Nick thought about the divorce papers during his drive to Langhorne. He worried how Tom would react when he received them and whether it was safe for Kate and Addie to be alone in their house. They discussed getting them an apartment, but Ertz explained that might have legal implications during a custody battle. Besides, Kate was adamant that she didn't want to disrupt Addie's life any more than it was. She belonged in her home, enjoying her room and her neighborhood friends. The house was calmer with Tom absent, and Addie seemed more relaxed.

It was dusk when Nick arrived. He pulled into Liz's driveway, and she came out right away. She wore jeans, a navy peacoat, and a knitted hat against the early December cold. She got in the truck, closed the door, and kissed him." Then she said, "Thanks for coming."

Nick looked at her and smiled. "Do you know what I like best about you?"

She thought for a moment. "My amazing personality?"

"Overrated," Nick said flatly.

"My trim and toned yoga body?"

"No, but that's a very strong second."

"My money?"

"Didn't know you had any."

"Some," she said. "I'm frugal."

"Not as frugal as the guy you're talking to who lived his life day after day in a five-hundred square-foot deli with the same three friends. I never spent a dime."

"That's not true," Liz scolded. "You weren't a recluse in your early life, and you're not one now. I've told you to focus on that."

"Sorry," Nick said. "I forgot there was another Nick."

Liz corrected him. "There was, and there IS another Nick now."

"Right," Nick said. "Was and is. I've got it."

"Okay," Liz said lightly as she slid closer in her seat. "What do you like best about me?"

"The way you decorate your house for Christmas."

Liz gave him a strange look. "That's it?"

Nick remained straight-faced. "That's it. I mean the finely toned body thing is a close second, and your personality isn't really that bad if I'm being truthful, but it's the house, hands down."

Liz was glad Nick was there. She needed a lift in spirits, and he was working overtime to provide it. “And why is that? Why the house?”

“Simple beauty,” he replied, “which also describes you, by the way. I mean, look at it. A very tasteful wreath on the door with a single spotlight. And one candle in each window. Perfect. Which also describes you, by the way. Simple beauty and perfect.”

Liz smiled. “I’m glad you like the house, and thank you for the exaggerated compliments. You’re sweet.”

“Sweet? I was in the Army Special Forces and you’re calling me sweet?”

“Very sweet.” She leaned over and kissed him again.”

Nick thought back to how exciting it was to go parking with a girl. The eagerness, the anticipation, and all that. It had been decades since his senior prom, but he remembered. “Maybe we should just stay in the driveway and fool around.”

“Nope, the neighbors would be jealous. They’re jealous already because you’re so handsome. I don’t want to put them over the edge. We’re going somewhere. Back out of here.”

Nick reversed out of the driveway and said, “Jimmy warned me about you.”

Liz looked disappointed. “About what?”

“He’s always saying relationships have complications.”

Liz interrupted and said kiddingly, “Oh, are we in a relationship?”

Nick ignored the question and went on.

“Jimmy said, relationships have complications and one of them is decorating for Christmas. He said when he worked at the Steel Mill lots of guys would complain about all the stuff their women made them do at Christmas."

Liz teased again, "Oh, am I your woman?"

Nick ignored her again, and said, "When I told Jimmy I was coming over, he said, 'Watch out. It's Christmas season. I bet she wants you to decorate.' But here we are, and your place looks great."

"Jimmy is a trip."

"He certainly is. Kind of my adopted brother. He has some needs, but there is no one more loyal than Jimmy."

"I can see that. You're lucky to have a lifelong friend, three actually, right?"

Nick thought of his high school friend, Johnny Francelli, who died in Vietnam. He wondered what Francelli would have been like had he made it home. "Yes," he said. "I've got life-long friends still around."

It was getting warm in the truck and Nick adjusted the heater. "I'm relieved about how Jimmy is reacting to you. He and I were inseparable. Now he's sharing time. I worried about it, but he's good. As long as he and I do some quality things together. He's been lifting weights with me in the basement at Angelo's, and we go to the shooting range once a week. He likes it."

"Your time together is important. I don't ever want to interfere with that."

Nick nodded. "Given the fact that I have nothing to do from breakfast until bed, I think I can handle both of you."

Liz smiled. "I'm confident you can."

"The guys loved it when you played pinochle with them. It would be great if we could do that once in a while too."

"Any time you want. It was fun, and I will enter the tournament next year."

"Just make sure you don't win."
"I'm not sure I can do that. As far as I could tell, there wasn't much competition in the last tournament."

Nick let the ribbing pass and said, "Okay, where to?"
"I don't care. I just want to drive and end up somewhere to eat. It could be for a hot dog or filet mignon. I just want to relax together. But we have one quick stop to make first."
"Ok. Where is that?"
"The Arts Society."

They parked in the lot and Liz asked Nick to come with her. He took her hand, and they walked toward the building.
Liz said, "It's coincidental that Jimmy said what he did about Christmas decorating."
"Why is that?"
"The Society is decorating the building tonight."
Nick stopped dead and gave her a wary look. She burst out laughing and said, "Don't worry. We're not staying."
Nick was skeptical. He said, "The building looks great with a single candle and wreath on every window. Simple beauty, why mess with it."
Liz smiled. "We did that last week. Tonight, the inside gets done."
Nick's shoulders sagged and Liz laughed again. "Trust me. We're not doing anything. I took the liberty of telling a little white lie that you have a doctor's appointment tonight and I'm driving you. I just thought it would be good to show my face first."

They entered the building and Nick saw a handful of women hard at work. Liz's friend Julie, who Nick had met at

the gala, saw them and rushed up. She gave them each a hug and asked how the room looked so far.
Liz said it looked beautiful and asked about the Phillips display. Julie rolled her eyes and said, “That’s next.”
Liz explained to Nick that Mildred Phillips was an elderly resident of the Borough who had an extensive collection of very old Christmas figurines that the society displayed each year. No one in the society had the courage to tell her that after several years of repeated displays, they had lost their wow factor. So, each year, the display went back up.

“I wish we could help, but you’ll be fine as always. Send me a photo when you’re finished.” Julie said she would. She gave them both another hug and said, “Nick, will we see you at the Christmas tea?”
Before Nick could answer, Liz said, “Absolutely. We’re looking forward to it.”

They left the building and Nick said, “I guess I’m looking forward to the Christmas Tea. As Jimmy would say, relationships are complicated.”
Liz laughed. “It’s not nearly as bad as it sounds. It’s actually a lot of fun.” She draped her arm through his and said, “You’ll love it.”
Nick shrugged and said, “That was a very short visit.”
“It was, but it accomplished the two things I wanted.”
“You showed your interest to Julie and the others, but what was the second thing?”

“I wanted you to know that if it weren’t for you, I’d be in that building figuring out how to arrange Mildred Phillips’ Christmas figurines. I love Julie and my other friends, and I enjoy my work there, but I wanted you to know that you've added another dimension to my life, and I'm grateful for it. Now let's go eat and have some fun."

Chapter 52

It was the same meeting room R3 used for his weekly speeches, only this time there were just ten in attendance. It was the inner circle, and Tom felt a mixture of pride and apprehension for being there. The thought crossed his mind that he might have gotten in over his head, but he quickly brushed it aside. This was where he wanted to be, and he convinced himself he belonged there. Besides, R3 had warned him that once he came there was no going back. Still, his heart was pounding, and he used his sleeve to wipe the sweat from his brow. He reached for his beer and realized his hand was shaking. His nerves were in overdrive, and he hoped no one noticed. Charlie, sitting next to him, obviously did because he leaned closer and said, "Relax, Buddy. You're in, and R3 likes you. He was surprised you made the truck runs with me. He said it proved you have some balls, and he didn't mind the money either."

Tom nodded and took a breath. He had surprised himself with the truck runs. He'd been jittery before the first one, but it went smoothly. So, when Charlie offered him another gig, with a promise of more money, Tom said yes right away. The jitters were gone by the second run, and he found it exhilarating. He told Charlie that if any other opportunities popped up, he was game. All in all, he was feeling pretty good about himself.

They were waiting for R3's arrival, and Tom decided that moving around might calm him. There was a beer cooler on the side of the dimly lit room. He took the last chug from his bottle and stood to get another. He asked Charlie if he needed one, and Charlie nodded.

He steadied his breathing and scanned the room as he walked to the cooler. There was no barbecue spread tonight. This wasn't a recruiting meeting. This was business. There was a large television mounted on a table with the chairs arranged in a U shape so everyone could see. Someone he hadn't seen before was hooking up a lap-top to the screen.
Tom grabbed the beers just as R3 entered the room. There were a couple of other guys standing in the back and R3 told everyone to take a seat. Tom scanned their faces. Aside from Charlie, he only recognized two others from seeing them at the range bar.

R3 greeted the group and Tom noted a change in his demeanor. He was no longer the happy recruiter looking to expand his audience for his weekly propaganda talks. He was talking to men who were already in, and it was time he told them what was coming. R3 stood with his hands on his hips and said tersely to the guy adjusting the computer, "Finished?"

The guy said he needed one more minute. The screen came to life and the guy nodded. R3 said, "Next time come earlier. I'm not paying you to make me wait."
The guy nodded again.

R3 turned his attention to the room and said, "We have a new member, Tom Baron." Tom gave a half-wave to the group, but no one responded. It was obvious they were naturally wary of any newcomers. They didn't know what R3 was planning, but they were sure it was big. If it went sour because of a snitch or someone's incompetence, they could all go down, not just him.

R3 read their faces and said, "He's good. He proved himself, and Charlie vouched for him." Charlie nodded and said, "The guy is solid. We've worked together."
There still weren't any hugs and kisses, but a few guys nodded their greeting. They knew that part of passing R3's test of proving himself meant he'd paid a chunk of money for the cause, just like they did, and probably got the money in a similar way.

R3 decided that was enough about Tom. It was his group, and if he said Tom was in, then Tom was in.

He turned his attention to the guy with the computer. "This is Joe Crane. He's our guest speaker." Then he added sarcastically, "Where are you from, Joe, Princeton, Yale?"
Joe shook his head and said, "Not quite."
R3 laughed, which gave everyone permission to do the same. Then he said, "Joe is part of a militia in York County,

Pennsylvania." The men nodded their approval and R3 went on.

"Now I know we've never had a guest speaker before, but I'm sure you guys have heard one at your local library meeting or at the monthly gathering of your garden club."

There was more laughter.

R3 said, "Joe learned his computer skills in the army before they bounced him. Why was that again, Joe? Why were you discharged?"

"I was in a company where white guys were in a minority, just like America is becoming. Let's just say I didn't like it and did some stuff."

R3 smiled and said, "I bet you did. Good for you." He added to the group, "So now Joe is defending his country the same way we are, on the outside where we can get something done."

He paused and added, "And we will. But until the big day comes, we have work to do. There are groups like ours formed with different interests. Some are primarily anti-immigrant, some anti-black, some know the Jews have a stranglehold on our finances, some are anti-gay and this new trans bullshit, whatever the hell that is. Others focus on the fact that women are taking over society and pushing men aside. Some, like us, are pissed off about all of that.

"There is a growing movement to unite these groups. To talk to each other, to build a network through the internet, because the one thing that bonds all of us is our anger over what's happening to America, and our determination to do something about it.

"Joe has put together a collection of websites for many of these groups. He's going to give you an overview and then we'll send you a link to his program that includes all the sites. Once you have it, spread the word. "

For the next forty-five minutes, Joe highlighted scores of hate groups and their causes. It was empowering for Tom to see what was out there and how their causes made sense. Tom was getting the feeling that there were far more like-minded people out there than he realized. He decided that he and the others Joe was mentioning weren't the fringe that the media liberals talk about. The real fringe were the liberal snobs who were ruining the country. They had no idea what America was about. Tom glanced at R3 as Joe spoke and felt admiration for the man who had the vision and the dedication to set things right.

He perked up when Joe got to the sites that focused on women. He listened as Joe talked about hiring and promotion practices that discriminated against men, about Hollywood's depiction of men as dumb, fumbling idiots in commercials and sit coms. Joe shared statistics about the growing number of lesbians and his view of what that meant for men. He pointed to abortion as a growing trend to reduce the importance of motherhood. If women weren't going to have babies, then why did they need men? Joe saw abortion as a way to free women to remain in the workplace and compete with men for jobs. He said that kids were being turned against men and being indoctrinated toward liberal causes in school.

Tom listened intently to every word. It was true, all of it, and he saw how it was all linked. For the first time in a long time, Tom felt good about himself. R3 had even given him a job tending bar. This was his new home. Kate had looked down on his views for so long, even mocked him. He was sure she was peddling her views to Addie when he wasn't around.

He missed Addie. She was a good kid. He didn't know how long she'd stay that way before her mother's influence would ruin her. He'd already seen some subtle changes in the way she viewed him. He decided to see her soon.
His thoughts returned to the meeting. R3 thanked Joe and dismissed him. Then he said, "It's time to do something big. Let's talk about what that might be."

Chapter 53

Sam Culligan rented a room at a small motel on Route 72 in Manahawkin. The place was a relic of the 1970s but it was clean and served its purpose. For two days he cruised past the shooting range looking for Tom Baron's car. He had gotten the plate number from a contact at the Pennsylvania Department of Motor Vehicles.
The Triple R shooting range consisted of a cluster of buildings that appeared to have been added in stages with little regard for aesthetics. There was a main building that most likely housed the indoor shooting range, a small snack bar that advertised hot dogs, and a bar connected to the main building by an enclosed walkway. There was a

three-walled shed that housed quad ATVs advertised for rent. Behind the buildings was a dirt trail that led into the Pinelands and a berm used for outside shooting.

On the evening of the third day, he saw Tom's vehicle parked on the gravel lot. Sam parked and debated whether to look for Tom at the bar or at the shooting range. He decided there wasn't a strategic advantage to either choice, so he opted for the bar.

The place was dimly lit with rustic furniture. There was just one patron at the bar, but behind the bar pouring the patron a shot of whiskey was Tom Baron. Sam hadn't won anything since a raffle in 7th grade for free tickets to a roller rink, but he was lucky now.

Tom watched him as he crossed the room. Culligan wore jeans, a flannel jacket, and work boots. Tom thought he had the hard features of ex-military or maybe a cop.

Culligan sat two seats down from the other patron and scanned the beer choices on display. There weren't many. He thought Bud would be the best fit. He put a twenty-dollar bill on the counter and ordered one.

Tom nodded. He pulled a beer from a case below the bar and placed it on a paper coaster in front of him.

Culligan thanked him and said, "You can ring me up. I only have time for one. "

Tim took the money to the register and returned with his change. He glanced at the other customer and said, "Need another, Frank?" Frank had kept his eyes on Culligan since he walked in. It was clear to Culligan that the guy was more than just a customer.

"One more shot and beer," Frank replied.

Tom served him, moved back to Culligan, and finally spoke. "How's it going?"

Culligan, nodded. "I'm good. How about you?"

Tom ignored the question and asked another. "Where are you heading?"

"I'm working on a job on Long Beach Island. I'm a plumbing sub-contractor."

Tom asked where he was located.

"I live in Burlington. A friend landed a contract on a hotel project on the island. It's big so he subbed out part of it. The work is good, but the hour commute each way is a pain in the ass."

Tom wasn't sure he was buying the story. "Not many people stop here for just a drink. There're other places on this stretch. Most people stop here if they want to shoot or rent a quad. The drinking is extra."

"Same with me," Culligan said. "I'm here to shoot. I noticed the sign yesterday on the way to work. I haven't shot in a long time, so I packed my piece this morning and planned to stop. Thought I'd have a beer first."

Tom nodded. He was beginning to relax. "What do you use?"

"I've got a few. I brought my Glock 19 with a thirty-three-round magazine and laser optics."

"Nice piece."

"I'll need some ammo too. The sign said you sell it."

"Whatever you need."

Culligan extended his hand across the bar and said, "Sam Jackson." He had no intention of using his real name.

Tom shook his hand and said, "Tom Baron."

Sam said, "I know."

Tom looked perplexed.

Culligan reached inside his jacket for a folded manila envelope, slid it across the bar, and said, "Tom Baron, you've been served."

Frank slammed his hand on the bar top and said, "Son of a bitch!"

Culligan smiled as he slid off his bar stool and said, "Yeah, from what I hear, he really is."

Tom recovered enough to say, "What the hell is this?"

"You can read it yourself, but I'll help. It's your divorce papers."

Tom looked at Frank, and Frank started to stand. Culligan gave him a hard stare and said, "Sit down or I'll put you down."

Frank froze as he weighed what the outcome would be if he took Culligan on. To save face, he didn't sit, but he didn't move either.

Tom looked at the envelope and pushed it away. "You've got a lot of balls coming in here."

Culligan grinned and said, "You're right. I do."

He walked to the door, turned back, and said, "See you in court, asshole."

Culligan drove to the edge of the property parked on a cluster of pine that concealed his location but gave him a clear view of the bar. He knew from the sign posted inside that the bar closed in a half hour.

Twenty minutes later, Frank left, got in his truck, and drove away. Twenty minutes after that Tom Baron did the same. Culligan waited and followed at a safe distance. Less than three miles down Route 72, Baron turned onto a dirt drive that ran through the Pines and led to a cabin. The cabin was dark except for a dim porch light. Culligan parked at the road and edged closer to the cabin on foot. He watched Baron leave his truck and use a key to enter.

Culligan waited. A single light came on. Five minutes later it went out and another in a side window came on briefly before going out as well. Culligan surmised that Baron let himself in, did something in a front room, maybe got a drink from the kitchen, entered what was probably his room, turned out the light, and went to bed. Culligan smiled. He had found Tom Baron's new home. But who did he live with? Who owned the place? Did the other vehicle belong to a girlfriend?

Brian had asked for a report as soon as there was any news. Culligan called him on the way back and reported what he had. Brian asked for the license plate number of the other vehicle and the cabin's address. It was late, but he wasn't going to wait until morning to find out more. His best computer "researchers" had all the equipment they needed at home. He'd awaken one if he had to and get some answers.

Fifteen minutes later Brian called back. The vehicle was registered to the address of the cabin, and the owner of both was Charles Gibbs.

Within twenty minutes, as Culligan was crossing the Burlington-Bristol Bridge, Brian called again. Gibbs was a veteran, divorced, unemployed, and in the final weeks of his unemployment compensation. His social media postings were filled with far-right rants and conspiracies. Apparently, Baron had found a friend and a place to live.

Chapter 54

Nick and Liz thought it would be best if they each honored their Christmas traditions. Nick thought it was important to spend time with Jimmy, especially this year. Liz felt the same way about her Arts Society friends. She also thought Kate would appreciate private time with her mom and daughter.

On Christmas Eve, Liz would join some friends from the Arts Society to sing Christmas carols in the neighborhood and then gather at their building for drinks and a candlelight dinner. The idea was launched years ago by members who lived alone and wanted to be with others for the holiday. It caught on and grew over time. The next morning, she would drive to Feasterville for Mass with Kate and Addie and then back to Kate's to open gifts and spend a quiet day. This year would be even quieter with Tom gone.

This year, like every year, Angelo would prepare the Christmas Eve Feast of the Seven Fishes for Donna, Nick, Jimmy, Big Frankie, and whoever else was available. This year, Johnny, Carrie, and Gracie joined them. After dinner, the guests would leave and the guys would drink until it was time for midnight Mass. They'd meet again for breakfast, exchange gag gifts, and at ten o'clock on the dot, they would call Tish Moyer, the wife of their former teammate and friend, Billy, who perished in the 9-11 World Trade Center attack.

Although they hadn't seen her since Billy's funeral, they'd been calling each year for eighteen years out of respect and to offer her support. The truth was that she boosted their spirits as much if not more than they boosted hers.

From the time she delivered the eulogy at her husband's memorial service until now, her courage and resilience had been an inspiration to them all. She had remarried ten years later and recently retired from her practice as a psychologist.

Nick remembered the day they watched as the towers burned and came down. They called Jill to check on Billy's status. She was terrified and promised to call as soon as she heard from him. The call never came.

As the hours passed and Billy's outcome became more apparent, Nick remembered Jimmy sitting by himself and mumbling, "Not Billy," over and over. More than any of them, Jimmy needed that yearly phone call to Tish to ensure she was okay. It was one of the reasons Nick felt he had to be with him at Christmas.

After the call, they'd watch football all afternoon. That was Christmas.

At Liz's suggestion, Nick bought Addie a Barbie doll house for Christmas. The plan was that she would FaceTime Nick and then open the gift while he watched. Nick had no idea what FaceTiming was, so Liz practiced with him until he was confident he could use it.

His phone rang at 4:15 and Nick answered on the first ring. Jimmy and Big Frankie were with him, eager to see if he did it right. He pushed the button and was thrilled when Addie appeared on the screen.

"Hi Nick," she said with her usual enthusiasm. "Merry Christmas!"

Nick smiled broadly and said, "Merry Christmas. Did you get some nice gifts?"

"Yes. Mommy-Liz got me an iPad. Mommy is mad at her because she said it will spoil me. But I don't think she means it. But I had to make a zillion promises that I'd clean my room, do my homework, brush my teeth, and take out the trash every day if I want to use it. Geez. They take the fun out of it."

Nick laughed out loud, and Addie went on. "I see commercials on TV where a man gives a girl a diamond for Christmas. He doesn't say, 'I'll give you this diamond, but you have to empty the trash each day.'"

Nick loved it when she got wound up. "You've got a good point there, Addie. But you should do those things even without a gift."

Addie sighed. "I know. Anyway, I got lots of nice gifts from Mommy and Santa. But!"

She stopped, and Nick asked, "But what?"

"But," she continued in an exaggerated scolding tone, "there is one more big, beautiful present that I've been looking at all day. Mommy-Liz said I couldn't open it until your dumb football game was over so we could FaceTime."

"I'm sorry, honey. We could have done it at halftime."

"I don't know what halftime is. Mommy-Liz said it would give me something to look forward to, but the wait is killing me."

"Well, the good news is, the wait is over, and you have something to look forward to. Let's do it."

"Okay, here we go. Mommy Liz said she wants to talk with you when we're finished."
"Good."
"She said you are going to exchange gifts tomorrow. Did you get her a diamond?"
Jimmy and Big Frankie were in earshot and howled at the question. Jimmy whispered to Big Frankie, "Relationships bring complications."
Nick gulped and heard Liz scold her in the background.
"No. I didn't get her a diamond."
"Why, don't you like her anymore?"
Jimmy and Big Frankie covered their mouths to suppress their laughter.
"I like her very much, but…"
Nick heard Kate laughing in the background and Liz said, "Addie, open your gift now!"
"Okay, here goes." She started to tear off the wrapping and Nick lost the image as the phone moved. He heard her shriek with delight when she saw what it was. She came back into view and said, "Thank you so much, Nick. I love Barbie stuff and I don't have the doll house."
Nick felt himself tear up. You're welcome, honey. I'm glad you like it."
"I really do. Mommy-Liz wants to talk now."
Just like the abrupt endings Nick had grown used to, she was gone.

Nick cherished his time with his deli family. They were his brothers and they faced the struggles of life together. But now, hearing the laughter of a little girl who has exploded into his life so suddenly and completely and brought so much joy, he felt he had two families and was grateful for both.

Liz and Nick had spoken Christmas Eve and Christmas morning, but she said Merry Christmas again when she took the phone.

"Merry Christmas," Nick replied. "God, I love that kid."

Liz said, "I think it's obvious she loves you back." She paused and said, "I've missed you, but I'm glad we're getting together tomorrow night."

They made a reservation at Itri. Liz said she was tired of all the big meals over the holidays and was in the mood for a simple night of pizza, wings, and beer.

"Me too," Nick said, "but I have a little problem with the gift exchange."

"I said you didn't need to get me a gift. "

"It's not that. I got you a gift, but I got confused after it was wrapped. The doll house Addie unwrapped was actually for you."

Liz laughed and said, "I'd have a hard time getting it back from her now."

Nick grinned. "I'm looking forward to tomorrow night."

"Me too," Liz said. "I like Christmas, but the day after Christmas is my favorite day of the year. All the stress and hustle and bustle are over and we can just relax."

Nick was about to respond when he heard a pounding sound in the background. Liz said, "Oh my God."

Nick heard Addie say, "It's Daddy." She sounded more frightened than happy.

Nick heard a commotion and Kate was raising her voice, but he couldn't make out what she was saying.

Nick said urgently, "Talk to me, Liz. What's going on?"

Liz sounded panicked. "Tom is at the door. It's locked and he's pounding on it."

"Stay on the phone, Liz. Tell me what's happening."

He heard Kate say in a raised voice, "I think it's best if you don't come in today."

There was more pounding and muffled shouting.

Liz said, "Tom just realized that Kate had the locks changed. He said he wants to see his daughter on Christmas and will break down the door if Kate doesn't let him in."

Nick could hear Addie crying and Liz said, "Come here, Addie. Sit with Mommy-Liz."

Nick cursed the fact that he wasn't there. He said to Liz, "Stay on the phone, but give me Kate's exact address. Big Frankie will call 9-1-1"

Liz gave the address, and Nick repeated it to make sure Frankie got it right.

"What's happening now, Liz?"

"He is enraged. I think he will break in the door. Kate is telling him she'll unlock it if he calms down first. She's pleading with him."

Nick's mind was racing. He said, "Okay, tell Kate to stay with that. She'll open the door if he calms down. Try to stall him."

Nick wasn't sure how Liz could do that and calm Addie at the same time. He was grasping at straws.

He looked at Frankie who gave him a thumbs up. "The police have been dispatched. Stall as much as you can and when he gets in, do everything to defuse the situation."

Nick heard Kate trying to reason with Tom. Then he heard a loud smash followed by another, and Kate, Liz, and Addie shrieking at the same time.

Liz screamed, “He kicked in the door! He’s in the house.”

Nick repeated, “Keep the phone on Liz and try to diffuse. Don’t confront.”

Nick heard a male voice scream, “Bitch, you keep me from my daughter on Christmas! You changed the locks to my house! You filed for divorce a week before Christmas. No warning?”

There was another scream and Liz said, “He just slapped Kate and knocked her to the floor.”

“I’m putting the phone down but leaving it on.”

Addie was hysterical, and Nick heard Tom say, “Don’t cry, honey. It’s Daddy. I just want to say Merry Christmas to my little girl.

Addie kept crying and Liz must have been shielding her because Nick heard Tom say, “Let her go, Liz. Come to Daddy, honey.”

Nick heard Addie say she didn’t want to. She was afraid.

Tom said, “What have you done to her to make her afraid of her own father? Get out of the way, Liz.”

Nick heard Liz cry out in pain, "You’re hurting my arm.”

He had a flashback of the Vietnamese villager abusing his wife as he watched from his prisoner cage. Then, as now, he was powerless to help.

Nick could feel his blood pound at his temples as his heart pumped harder and harder.

He looked at his friends and saw the same fear and anger on their faces he was feeling and through her sobs he could hear Addie repeating, “Daddy, no!”

Frankie's phone rang and Nick watched as Frankie's eyes widened. He slammed his palm on the table and screamed into the phone, "Feasterville, not Trevose!"
Frankie told Nick there were two municipalities with the same street name in the county and the dispatcher had confused the two.
Nick felt sick. He heard scuffling and Kate screaming again. She must have gotten up and gone after Tom.
Addie screamed, "Don't hit Mommy again."
Tom screamed, "Be quiet, Addie. You're just like your mother and grandmother."
Tom must have noticed the phone on the coffee table with an active screen and yelled, "Who the hell is this? Who were you talking to?"
Then the call ended.

Chapter 55

The tension was palpable as Nick and the others raced toward the hospital. No one spoke, as each was lost in his own thoughts of concern for the girls' condition and anger over the attack.

Jimmy found it strange that his thoughts turned to football. On Thanksgiving Day of their senior year, they played in one of the biggest upsets in Bristol football history as the Warriors defeated the undefeated Morrisville Bulldogs on the game's last play. There were plenty of heroes on both sides of the ball that day, but if you asked Jimmy, he'd say the unsung hero was Nick. Jimmy would never forget the look in Nick's eyes during that final drive. It was the same look Nick had now as they drove to Jefferson-Aria Hospital in Oxford Valley.

Big Frankie drove his F-150 with Angelo riding shotgun and Nick and Jimmy in the back. Halfway to the hospital, they broke the silence as each tried to reassure Nick, but Nick just nodded without saying a word.

Angelo noticed Frankie's flushed face and the bulging veins in his neck. He thought back to the night of Johnny Francelli's funeral. All of the guys had gathered at Johnny's house to console his mother, Anna. They'd been drinking, and one of their classmates, Vince Morelli, said out loud that Johnny's death was a waste and the whole stinkin' war was a waste. He obviously didn't intend it in a disrespectful way, but to emphasize the tragedy of what he saw as a senseless loss. But the comment upset Anna, and Johnny's sister fired back that her brother was a hero, and his death wasn't a waste.

Morelli, obviously drunk, doubled down, and said, "Yeah, but a hero for what?"

With that, Anna burst into tears, and Big Frankie stood and told Morelli to leave. Morelli got up, and Big Frankie led him by the arm to the door. He went reluctantly, but not before making one more cutting remark. "I loved Johnny as much as anyone else, but get your heads out of the sand. This war is a waste and Johnny died for nothing."

Big Frankie knew it was the beer talking, but it didn't matter by then. The last thing Frankie heard as he walked Morelli out was Anna crying. Big Frankie pounded Morelli so hard that it took half the guys at the gathering to pull him off.

Angelo didn't want to see a repeat of Big Frankie's temper and said, "We all feel the same way, Frankie. Stay cool." Frankie just stared ahead.

Jimmy whispered, "I don't know what to say, Nick. You know I would say something if I knew what to say. But I don't."

Nick nodded.

Angelo said he made phone calls to Johnny and Brian. "I figured you'd need them at some point."

Nick gave another slight nod.

They made it to the hospital and parked in the emergency room lot. The four of them rushed through the door to the ER where they were met by a security guard who raised his hand to stop them.

"Easy, fellas. How can I help you?"

Nick was looking over the guard's shoulder hoping to see Liz. He said softly, "Liz Ambrose."

The guard gave an understanding look and said, "Okay, let me call someone." Nick looked as if he was going to walk past him. The guard put his hand out again and said, "Listen, I know Liz. A lot of us remember her from when she worked here. Just let me do my job and make a call. We'll take care of you."

Nick took a step back and said, "Thank you."

The guard returned to his desk, used the phone briefly, and told them a nurse would be out in a minute.

A nurse arrived quickly. She scanned the group and said, "You're all here for Liz?"

Nick nodded.

"I'm Nurse Lake. Liz is an old friend."

Nick had to gather himself before speaking. "How is she? Can I see her? How are all of them? The little girl?"

"Are you Nick?"

Nick said he was. Nurse Lake smiled and said, "Liz said you'd be here. I'll take you back." Then she added to the others, "Sorry, only one at a time. The rest of you will have to wait here."

She led Nick by the arm and said, "They are assigned to ER bay number six, and I'll bring you there to wait, but they aren't there right now."

Nick stopped and took a breath. "Where are they?"

The nurse took his arm again and walked. "Please don't let your imagination get the best of you. Given what they've been through, they are going to be okay. The doctor ordered a precautionary CAT Scan for Kate to ensure her orbital bone isn't fractured. That's the bone around the eye."

Nick knew that.

"She was struck in the face and it's very swollen. If it is broken, and I don't believe it is, the usual protocol is to ice it, rest, and allow it to heal. Other than that, and a few bruises, she should be fine physically. Emotionally, we gave her something to calm her. Moving forward, she might want to talk with someone."

Nick thought of Dr. Braun, but Kate wasn't a veteran so it wouldn't work.

Nurse Lake continued. "Liz has a strained shoulder and a nasty bruise on her bicep. I'm told she was holding the little girl and wouldn't let go of her. The man apparently yanked at her arm to free the child."

Nick balled his fists and struggled to control his anger.

"We placed her arm in a temporary sling to relieve the strain. Anti-inflammatories and ice for a couple of days and she'll be fine."

Nick was afraid to ask the next question. "What about Addie?"

"She was unharmed physically. Thanks to Liz, I don't think he touched her, but she is significantly traumatized and worried about her mom."

Nick cursed.

"Fortunately, we were able to get her some time with the hospital psychologist while Kate was being tested. Liz is with her for that."

Nick had a distant look as if he was thinking of something else. Judging by his clenched fists and the tightness in his arm she was holding, she had an idea of what he was thinking.

She said, "I get your anger. Everyone here who knows her is angry. But the police are on top of this. The most helpful thing you can do is focus on the emotional support they need."

Nick didn't respond.

The ER six curtain was open, revealing that Liz and the others weren't back yet. There was one gurney, one chair, and the standard monitoring and IV equipment.

"You can sit there while you're waiting. It shouldn't be much longer."

Nick remained standing. He rubbed his face and mumbled, "She's just seven years old. This shouldn't be."

The nurse agreed. “This was a lot, and like her mother and grandmother, she’s going to need time to work through it.” Then she smiled and said, “But she is a brave little girl with an amazing personality. Very bright, and very inciteful. She managed to say some things that cracked us up.”

Nick forced a smile and said, “That’s her.“

“Again, it shouldn’t be long. They’ve been gone for a while. Please come to the nurse’s station or press the pager on the bed if you need anything at all.”

She left, and Nick gave Jimmy a call to update everyone in the waiting room.

He hung up and began to pace. The phone rang and it was Jimmy calling back to tell him that Brian and Sam Culligan were on their way.

Nick saw Liz and Addie approaching. Addie was holding Liz’s good hand and walking with her head down. Liz saw Nick and smiled. She said something to Addie. The girl looked up, saw Nick, and broke into a run. He squatted to greet her, and she locked her arms around his neck. “Next Christmas you’re going to watch your stupid football game at my house.”

He squeezed her tighter and said, “Okay.”

“We needed you today.”

They loosened their grip and she started to cry. “It was so scary.” Between sobs, she said, “Daddy hurt Mommy and Mommy-Liz. That’s not the way Daddy used to be.”

Liz made it to the room and watched as Nick consoled Addie. “I know, Honey,” Nick said. “That was scary. But it’s over. Mommy and Mommy-Liz are going to be okay, and you’re all safe.”

Addie was smarter than that. "What if he comes again?"

Nick had an answer to that question that he couldn't share. Instead, he said, "I don't think he will. The police won't let him. "

She seemed to accept that for now. Nick said, "Let me say high to Mommy-Liz."

He stood and hugged Liz awkwardly, avoiding her injured arm. He could feel her shaking. A tear ran down her cheek, and he wiped it away.

"I'm fine," she said. "It's a minor sprain. We just have to wait for the radiologist to read Kate's CAT-Scan."

She took Addie's hand again and said, "The doctor thinks everything is ok. He just wants to be sure."

Addie smiled bravely.

The nurse returned and said, "Good news. The scan was negative. Nothing is broken. They are wheeling your daughter back. The doctor is doing the paperwork to release everyone. When he's finished, I'll review his instructions with you and any meds he may prescribe, and then you can go."

She handed Liz a card. "This is the number for social services. The counselor recommends you do a follow-up for our brave little girl."

Liz thanked her.

"Take good care, Liz. I wish I had seen you under different circumstances. Let's do lunch when you're ready."

Liz promised she would.

They found Angelo, Big Frankie, and Jimmy waiting for them in the lobby.

Liz was moved by their show of support and introduced them to Kate. "This is no way for you to spend Christmas night," Kate said. "You should be with your families."
Jimmy said, "We are."

Chapter 56

Brian and Sam Culligan entered the ER lobby just as Liz and the group were leaving. Jimmy, Angelo, and Big Frankie had never met Kate before tonight, and they were saying their goodbyes.

Brian said, "I'm glad we caught you. We're so sorry about all of this." He looked at Kate's swollen face, Liz's arm, and Addie's eyes puffy from crying, and he shook his head. "I guess it's a good sign that you've been released."
Liz said, "It's so nice of you to come, but you shouldn't have. It's Christmas night."
Brian smiled, "Trust me, between the Christmas Eve partying, the Stella waking us at 5:00 AM to open presents, and overindulging in Christmas dinner, I've had all the Christmas I need for one year. Besides, Jenny insisted I come."

Liz looked at Culligan, and Brian caught her meaning. "Sam has no family in the area, so he was our guest for Christmas dinner and more than eager to come."
Culligan's smile confirmed Sam's explanation and Liz said, "Well, thank you both."
Culligan replied that it was his pleasure. He scanned the group, saw the hard look in Nick's eyes, and nodded knowingly. Nick nodded back.

They were standing in the ER entranceway, and Brian said, "Can we slide off to the side for a moment? I called Andrew Ertz and..."
Liz interrupted, "You called our lawyer on Christmas night!"
Brain laughed. "He's Jewish, and he didn't mind. In fact, he became engaged right away, which is why we're here."

Jimmy asked, "Is it true that Jewish people eat Chinese food on Christmas because all the other restaurants are closed "
Brian ignored him and Big Frankie gave him a slight jab to the ribs.
Brian continued. "I'm sure this is the last thing you want to hear after the day you've had, but Mr. Ertz strongly recommends we do a couple of things tonight if possible."
He looked at Kate and added. "If you're up to it."
Kate asked what kind of things.
"He wants photos of you taken by a credentialed forensic photographer before the swelling goes down. Sam can do that. He wants photos of Liz's arm as well."

Angelo wasn't sure this was a conversation Addie should be hearing. He interrupted Brian and said, "Addie, there's a vending machine right over there. I bet you'd like a snack."
Addie knew Angelo from a visit she and Liz made to the deli a couple of weeks earlier. She looked at her mother for approval and Kate said it was a good idea. "But no sugar," she added, "it's too close to bedtime." Angelo took her hand and led her away.

Brian continued. "As I said, he'd like photos of Liz's arm and Addie."

Kate, said, “We’ll see about Addie, but I doubt it.”
Brian said, “I understand. Ertz asked me to remind you that his primary interest is about future custody. Tom dug himself a giant hole today, but Ertz doesn’t want to take any chances. Are you up to it tonight?”
Kate said, “If it keeps my out-of-control husband away from Addie, I’m up for anything.”
“Good,” Brian said, “because there’s more.”
Kate waited.
Ertz wants a step-by-step video recording of your account of everything that happened today, from the time Tom showed up at the door until he left. He wants three separate interviews, one with you, one with Liz, and one with Addie.”
Liz put her hand up to stop him. “Addie is out. She’s been through enough. Not negotiable. She’s out for the photos too.”
Brian nodded his understanding.
“I’ll do all the rest,” Kate said, “whatever you need. But is it necessary? The police already have our statements, and they took photos.”
Brian shook his head. “What they did might be good to have, but Ertz doesn’t want to rely on the thoroughness of the officers or lack thereof. Memorialized statements like this from you, taken soon after an event, are valued by the courts. We’re not leaving anything to chance.”
“Where will we do this?”
“At your house. Ertz wants film of the physical damage too.”

Angelo, Big Frankie, and Jimmy made their last good-byes, wished Liz and Kate well, and went home. Brian drove everyone else to Kate's.

Ertz knew he'd get more information if Kate and Liz were interviewed apart from each other. It forced each to search their memory instead of relying upon the other person telling the story.
It was late, and they decided Kate would go first while Liz stayed with Addie in her bedroom until she fell asleep.

Culligan asked Kate open-ended questions and interrupted only when Kate had stopped and needed a prompt. She filled in the details that Nick had only heard in bits and pieces over the phone. As he listened, the flashes returned of his abusive father and the Viet Cong villager striking his wife.

His anger grew with every detail, a blow to the face so hard that it knocked Kate to the floor. A second blow, a violent push actually, that sent her to the floor again when she was trying to pull Tom away from Liz and Addie.

Nick watched Culligan skillfully lead the interview. He remembered that Culligan was ex-special forces and Brian had said he was a solid guy. Coming from Brian, that was high praise. Brian had also shared Nick's service record with Culligan. Even though they barely knew each other, it seemed clear there was an unspoken level of mutual respect.

As the interview progressed Culligan's face revealed the same reaction as Nick's. The few times Culligan and Nick made eye contact, Nick felt a bond growing.

After a series of very detailed facts, Kate ended the interview with an opinion. "Something has gone terribly wrong with Tom. The man who came today wasn't the man I married. It's like something has snapped. I learned over the years that he had a temper. His frustrations about politics and his rants grew to the point where I wanted a divorce, not just for my sake, but for Addie's. She loved her Daddy but was becoming increasingly frightened by him. But today wasn't just an angry Tom. It was an angry Tom on steroids. I definitely think he needs psychiatric help."

Liz gave a similar account of the basic facts and added what was going through her mind as the action unfolded. She'd been torn between taking Addie by the hand and running, but not wanting to leave Kate alone with Tom. After his first vicious strike that knocked Kate to the floor, Liz was afraid he would kill her.

She also recounted the terror Addie experienced. Sitting on Liz's lap, the little girl was shaking like a frightened rabbit, and Liz could feel the child's heart racing.
She described Tom's effort to get Addie away from her and his violent tug of her arm while Addie clung desperately to Liz's neck with both arms.

She ended the interview with details about her phone. "When Tom saw the phone, he assumed I'd already called the police, and that's what saved us. He needed to get out of there before they arrived. When he noticed the phone was on and I had hit record, he became further enraged and destroyed it with his foot before running. "I wish we had the recording."

Brian said, "We'll get it from the cloud once we get you a new phone."

Nick had no idea what the cloud was and didn't care. He didn't care about legalities either.

Brian had Ertz on speakerphone, and he was explaining the complications of arresting an assailant from another state. There were jurisdictional issues involved, extradition agreements between states, and more. Nick didn't care about any of it. Pennsylvania might have trouble with a suspect in another state, but it didn't matter to Nick. For him, justice could be exacted easily with a quick ride and a $2.00 toll to take the Burlington- Bristol Bridge to Jersey.

The interview work was over and Culligan was packing up his equipment. Kate and Liz had walked Brian to the door, and Nick was alone with Culligan.

"The bastard," Culligan said.

Nick nodded.

Culligan stood there looking as if he was wrestling with a difficult decision. Finally, he shrugged, took a card from his jacket pocket, and handed it to Nick. "Baron's address in the Jersey Pines. He shares a cabin there with another jerk from the Pineland Patriots."

Nick had felt a connection with Culligan as soon as their eyes met at the hospital. They looked at each other now, and held the stare for a few seconds, two former special

forces guys, one young and one old, but apparently on the same page about how to deal with Tom. Nick's expression didn't change, but he extended his hand, and they shook. Finally, Nick said, "Thank you."
"Just don't get either of us in trouble, and call me if you need anything. Take good care of those girls."

Chapter 57

Gabe Karmer, Johnny Marzo's informant, and three other guys were having a beer at the R3 Bar when R3 came storming in breathing fire. Charlie Colson was tending bar and R3 barked, "Where's your buddy!"
Charlie wasn't sure who he meant. "My buddy?"
"Baron, dipshit. Where is Tom Baron."
"I left the cabin to open the bar, and he was still sleeping."
R3 headed straight toward the back room and told Colson to follow him. He waited at the door for Colson to pass by and then slammed it shut.
"I'm away for a few days to spend time with my sick mother over Christmas and when I get back, I find out this shit happens."
Colson froze. Tom Baron stumbled into the cabin drunk the night before and told him what happened with his family. Colson knew how much R3 hated anything that might draw law enforcement's attention, but he couldn't figure out how R3 could know already. He was about to speak but R3 thundered on.
"I saw Frank and he told me some cop-type guy came in last week and served divorce papers to Baron."

Colson had forgotten about that and felt relieved. Getting served with divorce papers wasn't as bad as what Baron did the night before. Colson tried to calm R3 by saying it wasn't that bad, that men get served divorce papers from their bitchy wives all the time.

R3 exploded. "I don't want it. I don't want any shit near this place. Get him on the phone and get his ass in here. I'm trying to launch Boom50 and I have plans for him. Now I don't know. Get him!"

Gabe couldn't pick up all of the usually super cautious R3's rant, but he heard one phrase loud and clear, Launch Boom50.

He had no idea what it meant but it sounded important to R3. Whatever it was, he would pass it on to his handler at the FBI.

Chapter 58

Tom Baron showed up at R3's office an hour later and the militia leader lashed out as soon as he entered the room. "It's been a friggin hour, Baron. Did you take a God damn bubble bath first? When I say get over here, I mean now."

When Charlie Colson awakened Tom with the call to summon him, he also alerted him that R3 was fired up about the server coming to the bar, but didn't know about Baron's confrontation the night before. Colson advised him to be quiet about it. Now, Colson sat in the corner trying not to make eye contact.

"Get your head up, Colson. Baron is your guy, you vouched for him, and now I'm not so sure about him."

He lit a cigarette and seemed to calm down. He took a deep drag and exhaled slowly, directing the smoke toward the ceiling. He rubbed his eyes with his free hand and then stared at the two men. There was a long silence. When he spoke again, his voice was lower. "These are tense times. There's a lot going on and a lot that needs to be done in a hurry. I don't need anything, and I mean ANYTHING interfering with my plans."

Baron and Colson nodded their understanding.

R3 got quiet again, and he looked as if he were weighing an important decision. He took another drag and then snubbed out the cigarette.

"Because the two of you worked together on your private heists and really showed some balls under pressure, I had you guys pegged for the Launch of Boom50. Now, I don't know. Can I trust you not to screw it up and land us all in jail?"

Colson and Baron responded enthusiastically. They wanted in.

R3 nodded. "Okay, I paid big money for the explosive device you'll drive to Trenton. Charlie, you'll drive the car that will be detonated and park where I tell you. Baron, you'll follow and bring him home."

Both men smiled, and R3 filled them in on the details.

Chapter 59

The office of Lynn Sellers, Regional Director of the FBI, was located in the Federal Building on Arch Street in Philadelphia. Johnny Marzo was ten minutes early for the nine o'clock meeting. He hated pre-meeting small talk, so he lingered in the lobby a few minutes longer. Besides, he knew Director Sellers would be the last person to enter the room.

He thought about his last meeting with her when he received the "do not shave" notice. He was sure then that he'd be assigned undercover. Carrie was equally sure that he would miss Christmas. But the meeting came with no change of assignment. Director Sellers thought there wasn't enough intell to risk inserting him yet. Instead, he would continue his normal duties but would increase his monitoring of his informant for daily updates.

Now, still unshaven, Marzo was ready for anything. He knew when he passed on the new Boom 50 intell, the reaction would be quick and significant.

He entered the conference room at 8:57 and greeted the group that included several faces he didn't know. He took an empty chair next to Mark Rice from Washington DC. Rice was a special assistant to the Director for Domestic Terrorism. Marzo liked Agent Rice. He was competent, practical, and assessable. Most of all, he was part of a direct line that flowed from Marzo to Sellers, to the Director of the FBI, to the president.

"Bad to see you, Mark."

Rice smiled. "Bad to see you too."

It was a game they started a while back. Since they only saw each other when bad things were brewing, they changed the customary good to see you greeting to one that better reflected their reason to meet.

Rice leaned in and whispered, "Good job with the intell."

"The CI is solid," Marzo replied. "He's been hanging with the militia group for months. He can't get all the way in, but he's on the periphery. Not sure what this will amount to, but I had to send it up."

At exactly nine o'clock, Lynn Sellers entered the room. Marzo had researched her profile three years ago, after she was appointed Regional Director. She was fifty-eight then with over thirty years with the Bureau. She'd come up through the ranks, with an impressive record of fieldwork before jumping to the administrative side. Marzo liked and respected her. She was smart, insightful, and a straight shooter.

She wore a dark blue skirt and matching jacket with a starched white blouse. She had allowed her short hair to go grey and kept it stylishly cut. Her normally pleasant smile was absent as she greeted everyone, took her seat, and lost no time getting started.

"Good morning. We have a potential attack that could take place less than five days from now, so we have work to do. She went around the room and introduced everyone at the table, which included various Bureau and Homeland Security officials, Rice, Marzo, and ranking state police supervisors from Pennsylvania, New Jersey, and Delaware. A large screen on the wall facing her held scores of faces she introduced collectively as state and homeland security officials from across the country who were attending the meeting virtually.

She began with a recap of how the intell was obtained. "We acknowledge there isn't much to go on, but we've had our eyes on Boom 50 for a long time, and minimizing the threat could have dire consequences."

From there she reviewed what Boom 50 was all about.

"For over two years there has been chatter on the dark web about an idea called Boom 50. We believe, I stress believe, because we don't have solid evidence, that the idea was hatched by a nut-job militia member from Indiana named Roy Mathew. The plan was to stage an explosion at the same hour in every state capital in America on New Year's Day. The idea was that such an event would be a catalyst for all militia groups to recognize that the time for concerted action had arrived.

"Mathew was smart enough to know that killing innocent people would cause a backlash, so he stressed that the targets would be easy to access physical targets rather than human ones, hence, on a day when the capital ground would be vacant."

She scanned the room for a moment and continued.

"Fortunately, there is no organized militia network, so it was difficult to put together such a coordinated attack. As time passed, there was some anger expressed on the web that Mathew had a good idea but wasn't making it happen. During the height of the criticism, Mathew died in a motorcycle accident and the idea has been dormant. Now intell has surfaced that may indicate it could have new life."

Bart Messenger sat directly across from Sellers. He was a public response analyst whose job was to hypothesize the public's response to a crisis. There was a time when Marzo considered the position frivolous, but not anymore. He'd seen enough useful analysis from the young agent to change his mind.

Sellers looked at Messenger and said, "Bart, I want you to assume for a moment that the full Boom 50 plan is in effect. What are your thoughts on how that might unfold?"
Messenger didn't delay his response. "I think the Boom 50 plan is brilliant. Think about it. They are aiming for easy targets. Imagine the public's reaction to the bombings. The press and social media will be hysterical. Fifty Bombs in one day! Fifty state capitol grounds damaged. People will be terrified, even with the assumed low death toll."
Messenger paused briefly for effect.
"Almost fifty years ago we were deeply embroiled in a difficult and costly war in Vietnam and were told repeatedly that we were winning. Then, the Viet Cong emerged from virtually everywhere to attack every provincial capital in Vietnam simultaneously. It was called the Tet Offensive because it was launched on the Lunar New Year. Eventually, they were repelled, but the attack's psychological impact was devastating. It was the defining moment that turned millions of Americans against the war, and it emboldened the Viet Cong.

"Boom 50 would be the militia movement's Tet Offensive. It will inspire and energize extreme right anti-government elements. Meanwhile, the public will question our ability to protect them."

Heads were nodding, and Messenger said, "But it gets worse. A frightened nation will demand action, and Congress and the President will give it to them. Congress will pass legislation giving law enforcement much broader powers and more funding. It will be like the Patriot Act on steroids. The President will issue executive orders to do the same.

"The public will like this, but the militias will like it even more. We'll be playing right into their hands. One of their biggest gripes is the abuse of government authority. In their eyes, the new legislation will make it easier to prove their point when recruiting."
Someone said, "That makes no sense. They can never win that argument. Public sentiment will turn against them even more."

Sellers put a hand up to signal she wanted Messenger to finish uninterrupted, but Messenger decided to respond. "It depends on how you define winning. They want chaos and division. They want to let it rip to split the country even more. They believe they'll emerge stronger out of that chaos. But it gets worse."

"With the increased power and mandate to keep America safe, the FBI and other agencies will go after the militias. There will be conflicts and shootouts like Waco and Ruby Ridge. It will unleash a cycle of unprecedented domestic turmoil. Disaffected people not affiliated with a militia per se, lone wolves as we call them, might take it upon themselves to plan attacks as well. In the end, we will win, as you say. But at what cost? American law enforcement waging an all-out war against citizens who consider themselves patriots."

Sellers waited until she was sure Messenger was finished and let the implications sink in. Then she said, "There you have a worst-case scenario of what could evolve if Boom 50 was fully implemented. My gut reaction is that it won't be, but if it was, then I see Agent Messenger 's assessment as very plausible.

"Now let's hear an assessment of how narrow this attack might actually be. It was Agent Marzo's informant linked to the Pineland Patriots in Ocean County, New Jersey who provided the intell that opened this assessment, so I'll ask him to update."

"Thank you, Ma'am." He nodded to the aid who was operating the technology and a photo of R3 appeared on the split screen. "This is Richard Raymond Rogers, better known as R3, the leader and mastermind of the Pineland Patriots militia. I don't want anyone in the room or those watching from remote locations to let down their guard because of what I'm going to say. And I agree with Agent Messenger 's assessment of what could happen if fifty capitals were hit. But here are some reasons why I think R3's group will be acting on its own and focus on this area." An image of the shooting range complex appeared on the screen and Marzo said, "The Pineland Patriots, operate out of a bar and shooting range complex owned by R3. He also lives on the property. He is the one our informant overheard during an argument Rogers thought was private. The informant was confident that he heard Rogers say, 'I am about to launch Boom 50.' It would not be possible to pull off nationally without increased internet chatter, and there is no evidence of that."

"Point number two is that R3 is not a nationally known figure, and there is no evidence that he enjoys any special status in the world of militias. This may be semantics, but if the Patriots were part of a national effort, one would think he would have said, 'we,' meaning affiliates across the country, are about to launch, rather than 'I' am about to launch.

"Our best guess is that he's a wannabe leader who sees the opportunity to make a name for himself by kick-starting the plan Mathews never had the chance to implement. Since our monitoring shows nothing about Rogers having any national profile and the web has been dead quiet about the plan, our speculation is that he is planning to bomb a capital by himself. in the hope it will inspire others to do the same later. In short, I think R3 is planning an attack in Trenton, NJ. If he follows the Mathews plan, the attack will come on New Year's Day and will be somewhere on the capitol grounds. It's speculation, but it's the best we've got."

Sellers waited for a response. When there was none, she said. "I agree with Agent Marzo that the Trenton scenario is much more likely, but every field office and state police agency across the country should be on quiet alert. On the other hand, I want a full court press on the Pineland Patriots. We're putting together a joint task force of federal, state and local law enforcement to provide the manpower we need. Agent Marzo will run point on this. I want every member our CI identified followed around the clock. I want helicopter support available. I don't want to see a single sedan involved in this. You'll be in the Jersey Pinelands. I want no vehicles except trucks, jeeps and motorcycles.

She turned to the Superintendent of the New Jersey State Police seated at the table and asked that added manpower be placed under Marzo's direction. The superintendent agreed. "I want photos of R3 and his associates, as well as shots of the compound sent to the phone of every stakeout team."

She tapped her pencil on the yellow pad in front of her. Then she added,

"I want frequent updates on this. Hourly, if necessary. Call me day or night."

Marzo agreed.

"This meeting is over," Sellers said.

As the meeting broke up, Sellers said to Marzo, "I checked before the meeting, Brian Kelly still has his security clearance. We won't be bringing him on board for this. As you know it takes time we don't have to get the approvals for using a civilian company for an operation. But you are cleared to pick his brain informally if you'd like."

Chapter 60

There wasn't any question that Nick would ask Jimmy to go with him to confront Baron. Jimmy would never forgive him if he didn't. Jimmy agreed to drive, and after Nick called Culligan for more details, they made a dry run on December 27 to scope things out. Now, a day later, they were on the road for the real thing.

On the way, Jimmy said, "Two trips to the Jersey Pinelands in two days. That's a lot of gas, Nick."

Nick, whose nerves were on edge, exploded. "Now! In the middle of all this, and you're worried about gas? I'll give you the damn money. I can't believe you."

Jimmy laughed out loud. "I knew it. I planned the whole thing in my head. I knew if I complained about gas you would blow up. I even guessed the things you'd say. 'Time like this..." and all that stuff. I did it because I was nervous, and you weren't talking. I wanted to break the ice."

Nick smiled. "You're an idiot, Jimmy."

"I know," Jimmy said proudly. "But you picked me to come with you."

"Yes, I did. Hope it wasn't a mistake."

"It wasn't. I swear."

"Okay, then let's rehearse."

"Again? It's been like ten times."

"Make it eleven."

"Okay, then let me tell it. "

"Go ahead but include everything."

Jimmy cleared his throat. "First of all, we leave the guns in the car."

"Absolutely, I don't know why you brought them in the first place. We're not gonna shoot anybody."

"Baron works at a shooting range. I thought we could practice," Jimmy said. "We could go to the range to see him and pretend we're practicing."

Nick dismissed the idea. "Just leave the weapons in the truck. And I told you. We're going to where he lives, not the range."

"I know. I just thought it was a good idea."

"This is no time to change a plan, so convince me you know it."

Jimmy went on. "So, the plan is, we park right in front of the cabin, not like we're sneaking up, but like we have a good reason to be there. I follow you to the porch and you knock. I don't say a word except for the line you gave me. "

"That's right, not a word."

"You still haven't told me what you're going to say."

"That's right," Nick said firmly. "I haven't, and I don't intend to."

"Once we're inside, I still don't say a word."

"Right."

"Once you get him on the ground…are you sure I can't help with that?"

"I won't need any help."

"I'll be there if you change your mind."

Nick had been struggling since Christmas night to channel his rage to the mission he had in mind. He learned in Vietnam that rage was a distraction. He saw many a soldier gunned down because they had a friend die in their arms or saw someone right next to them lose a limb. Rage caused them to act impulsively in response and their recklessness often cost them dearly.

Nick conceded that rage was a strong motivator, but thinking things through, visualizing the plan over and over, and utilizing his Special Forces training are what yielded results. That's why he didn't race off to New Jersey as soon as Culligan gave him Baron's address. It took a lot of will power not to, but he knew his day would come.

He listened as Jimmy resumed his summary.

"Anyway, you're gonna pretend we are robbers and we're not there because of what Baron did to the girls."

Nick said for emphasis, "That's the most important part. If you say the wrong thing that tips him off that know we know the girls, then we'll always have to worry that he'll come back for revenge."

"Not if we kill him," Jimmy said casually.

Nick was startled. "Jimmy! Kill him? Are you crazy? We don't kill people."

"Except in Nam," Jimmy replied.

Nick didn't respond.

Jimmy thought back to his time in Vietnam as a tunnel rat. Each time his platoon found a new tunnel, Jimmy was ordered to go in, and each time he went in, he was convinced he was going to die. But, Lieutenant Timmer, the sadistic bastard who led the platoon, ordered him in time after time. It seemed as if Timmer was actually enjoying it. After a while, Jimmy began thinking about killing Timmer. He was amazed at how easily the idea came to him. Convinced he was doing to die if the tunnel searches continued, Jimmy considered it a matter of kill or be killed.

His plan was simple. The next time the platoon was in a firefight and everyone's attention was focused on the enemy, he would shoot Timmer in the head so the others would think the VC got him. The rumor was that things like this happened more often than people realized, especially if men thought their officer was inept and exposing them to needless danger. He wondered if he would ever have the courage to do it, but with each passing day the decision became clearer. Fortunately, he never had to act on his plan because fate took care of things for him.

Many officers in Vietnam chose not to wear their officer bars on their uniforms because it made them attractive targets. The VC strategized that taking out the officers first in a confrontation would create confusion among the ranks. But Timmer was an arrogant bastard who wore his bars proudly until one day, while the platoon was on patrol, a VC sniper took out Timmer with one shot. Jimmy never went into a tunnel again and never knew for sure if he would have acted on his plan.

Finally, Nick broke the silence and said, "Vietnam was different. Everything there was different. That's not who we are. Remember that."

Jimmy said he would and then continued his narrative.
"After you get him on the floor, I'll help with the zip ties. Then you're going to ask him where he keeps his money. Most likely, he's not going to tell you, and we're going to search his place. Then when you give the thumbs up when he's not looking, I'm going to say, "Charlie said this guy has a lot of money hidden and I want it."
"Right," Nick said. "And I'm going to tell you to shut up and keep Charlie out of it."
"We want Baron to think Charlie put us up to it, right, Nick?"
"Right."
"That's it. I don't say anything else."
"Nothing. Just do what I tell you."

Nick did a mental review of the details Culligan gave him from his own surveillance and what Brian had learned from the informant. It was information Brian was not authorized to share, but with a wink and a nod, he left the file on his desk in plain view for Culligan to see while he stepped out to the restroom. Brian had never done anything like that before, but this was personal.

Nick had the notes Culligan had given him but didn't need them because he committed the information to memory. Charlie Colson tended bar at the Triple R until eleven each night. He drove a '95 Dodge Ram pickup with Jersey license plates 863-H27. Baron usually left the bar around nine and went back to Charlie's cabin. Baron's Pennsylvania plate on his Ford pickup was HG9-R31. The notes also contained the names of a handful of guys that frequented the range and went to R3's meetings. Nick already selected the name he would use to get in the door.

Nick and Jimmy arrived at the bar at 8:20 and confirmed by the vehicles that both men were still there. They parked at a distance and waited.

At 9:15 they watched Baron leave the bar and walk to his truck. He drove out of the parking lot in the direction of the cabin and Jimmy followed at a safe distance.

"Fall back," Nick said. "Give him time to get into the house before we arrive."

Jimmy slowed until they saw Baron's taillights turn. Nick told Jimmy to pull over. "It's too soon. I want him to get in."

They waited a few minutes until Nick said, "It's game time, Jimmy. Remember. Just one line."

"Don't worry. I remember."

They parked in front of the cabin next to Baron's truck and walked to the porch. Nick knocked hard and waited.
Baron said, "Who is it?"
Nick said it was Steve Massy looking for Frank Jones. Massy was a made-up name, and Frank Jones was the guy in the bar when Culligan delivered Kate's divorce papers. He saw Baron pull back the curtain to check them out.
Baron didn't know a Steve Massey and had no idea why he was looking for Frank at his house, but when he pulled back the curtain, he saw two older guys who looked harmless. He'd just been with Frank a few minutes earlier and he decided it would hurt to give them directions to the bar.

As Nick heard Baron fumble with the lock, he summoned all of the rage he'd held in since Christmas. Baron had the door open halfway when Nick stunned him with a quick jab to the face followed by a vicious chop to his throat. Baron staggered back trying to regain his breath when Nick landed a full fist to his face that put him down. Baron was dazed enough for Nick to stop, but he thought about Liz and gave him one more shot for good measure.
He pulled the zip ties from his back pocket and told Jimmy to help him hold Baron's arms together. Baron recovered enough to resist before they had the zip ties secure, so Nick placed his forearm on Baron's neck and applied pressure until he started to choke. That worked for the arms. Next, they zip-tied his legs. Once he was fully secured they took a break. Jimmy looked at his friend with admiration and was about to speak when he caught himself. It wasn't time yet.

Nick just took down a man half his age, but he wasn't feeling that great. His hand hurt from the punches, his arthritic wrist was throbbing, and his breathing was labored. He stayed on the floor next to Baron and took several long, deep breaths as Baron thrashed around to break free of his ties.

Nick's breathing returned to normal just as Baron gave up struggling and looked at them wild-eyed. His face was a bloody mess and he smelled like he pissed his pants. "Who are you? What the hell is this?"

"I don't have time for your questions," Nick said in a menacing voice, "and I only have one question for you. Where is the money?"

"What money?"

Nick sighed and gave each of Baron's ears a hard simultaneous clap that left Baron moaning.

Nick looked at Jimmy and said, "Pull the place apart. Nick waited while Jimmy searched closets, drawers, and under the furniture without success.

Nick gave him the nod and Jimmy shouted, "Charlie said the money was here, and I want it!"

Baron looked incredulous. "Charlie?" He mumbled through his pain, "He sent you here?"

Nick said to Jimmy, "You idiot. Charlie didn't want his name mentioned."

Then, out of nowhere, Jimmy said, "That won't matter if we just waste this guy."

Nick was stunned by the comment. He looked at Jimmy in disbelief and wanted to strangle him, but he recovered quickly. The damage was done, and he decided to play along with Jimmy's improvisation. Nick saw the panicked look on Baron's face and whispered, "My partner is getting impatient. Sometimes I can't control him when he gets that way. If you make us play hide and seek all night, you may not leave here alive."

Jimmy hadn't intended to ignore Nick's instructions. The remark just popped out, but he liked what Nick did with it and felt proud to be a bigger part of the plan. He continued tossing things around and Nick said to Baron, "You can save yourself more pain and my friend and me valuable time if you tell us where it is."

Baron said, "There is no money."

Nick gave him another jab to the nose that already appeared to be broken, and Baron let out a scream. Nick told Jimmy to search the bedrooms. "Start with the one on the right."

Nick could hear Jimmy rummaging through the bedroom wall while Baron moaned in pain. Nick leaned closer and said, "One way or another, we're going to wrap this up in ten minutes. My preference is that we leave with the money and with you alive. But..."

Baron was whimpering and Nick said, "C ome on, Buddy, act like a man. You are a man, aren't you? I'd better check." He gave Baron a quick jab to the balls and Baron howled.

Jimmy came out of the bedroom and said, "Nothing." He was heading for the second bedroom when Nick noticed Baron make a furtive glance at a set of keys hanging on the

wall. He told Jimmy to stop. "Grab those keys and see if they work for the truck."
Jimmy looked perplexed "The truck? Do you really think. .."
"Yeah, I do. See if he has one of those stationary locked contractor's toolboxes."
Nick could tell by Baron's eyes that he had figured it out. He smiled at him and waited.
A couple of minutes later Jimmy was back holding a duffle bag. He dropped the bag next to Nick and did a little jig.

Baron had managed to prop his upper body against a kitchen cabinet, but he sagged back in frustration as Nick unzipped the bag. It was loaded with cash. Nick smiled and said, "I don't feel like counting it. How much is here?"
Baron shrugged. Nick placed his hand on Baron's thigh and said, "I feel another gender check coming on."
Baron grimaced and said, "Thirty-one thousand give or take."

Nick thanked him and said, "It looks like our visit here is over."
Baron noodled enthusiastically, obviously wanting them to leave, but Jimmy said, "What do we do with him?"
Baron looked at Nick pleadingly, and Nick said. "Nothing. We've got no gripe with this guy except that he wasted a lot of our time."
Jimmy feigned disappointment but said nothing.

Nick leaned into Baron again and said, "Listen, Buddy, I have no idea who you are and I don't give a shit, but let me give you some advice. Your buddy Charlie likes to gamble, and he's not good at it. He is into us for much more than what's in this bag. He set you up. He said we could get most of what he owed from his roommate, as long as we make it look like a random robbery. My friend here screwed that up, but I don't care. Seems like you and Charlie have some things to iron out."

Nick stood. He thought about the girls and wanted to give Baron one last shot, but his hand hurt from the previous blows and his wrist was still throbbing. He said, "It was nice meeting you," and then kicked him in the ribs.
As he moved to the door, he added, "Hopefully, Charlie will untie you and you two can work things out."

Chapter 61

After a long day, Carrie had finally gotten Gracie to sleep, and she and Johnny were relaxing with a good movie, a brick of St. Stephen's cheese, from the Forager, her favorite cheese shop, and a glass of wine. At ten-fifteen Johnny's secure phone rang and he saw it was Dan Pelligrino, one of the agents on stakeout. He answered on the first ring and said, "Hold a minute, Dan."
He gave Carrie an apologetic look and said, "I've got to take this." She knew their night was over.
He left the room and said, "Go ahead, Dan."
"Sorry to bother you, but we have some developments at the Charles Colson house that I thought shouldn't wait until morning."
"Good," Johnny said. "Let's hear it."

"I'm here with Mitch Lyons. As you know, we're assigned to tail Tom Baron. Because he and Colson live and work together, we handle both unless they split, in which case we hand one off by radio to another team."

Johnny knew that.

"We used one of the quad trails in the area to stake out the bar waiting for Baron to leave as spelled out in his pattern profile. The strange thing is, there was a pickup truck across the road with two guys in it. It was like they were staking out the place as well. As expected, Baron left the bar at nine-fifteen, and the pickup followed. When Baron turned into the property, the truck hung back and then turned as well. That made things difficult for us to track undetected, so we parked in another quad trail and walked the rest of the way. By the time we had the cabin in sight, we could see that the pickup had parked in front of the cabin, right next to Baron's truck. It was empty so we assumed the two in the second truck were already inside.

"We settled in to wait because Colson was still due back a little after eleven when he closed the bar. While we waited, we ran the plates on the mystery truck, which is why I called you. The vehicle is registered to James Wright. He lives at 629 LaFayette Street in Bristol, Pennsylvania.

Marzo sat frozen, his eyes widening in disbelief. The room spun for a moment before he said, "Please repeat."

Pelligrino did and added, "About twenty minutes later one of the men left the cabin and opened the tool storage box in the truck. It looked as though he might have taken something, but we can't be sure. Then he went back into the house."

Johnny's mind was racing. What the hell was Jimmy doing at Baron's place? What was he looking for in the truck?

Marzo composed himself enough to say, "Then what?"

We waited another fifteen minutes and two guys left. The guy who had gone to the truck and another guy."

Johnny asked for a description of the second person, although he was sure who it would be. As expected, Pelligrino described Nick.

It didn't take a genius to figure out what was going on. Baron beats up Nick's girlfriend's daughter. Nick and Jimmy visit Baron. He shook his head and wondered what they were doing, fearing what they were doing was more accurate.

"Any evidence of foul play?"

"Not from our vantage point. They left casually and headed west on 72. We didn't want to leave our assignment so I took the liberty of radioing for a tail on them. A team of undercover Jersey state troopers from the task force picked up the tail. The last report, they were still heading west toward the Burlington-Bristol Bridge. If they cross the river, the Jersey guys will have to break it off. Should we call for a pickup at the Pency side?"

"No need. I'll handle that from here."

Pelligrino said, "Colson gets off work in forty-five minutes. I'll check in then."

Marzo said, "I don't like how this sounds. I'm on my way. Call me with any updates."

Carrie knew the drill and had his jacket waiting for him when he hung up. She had no idea what the issue was, and Johnny had no intention of telling her. He kissed her goodnight, asked for a raincheck, grabbed his weapon and ID, and was out the door.

Once in the car, he dialed his father's number. It was late and he didn't want to scare him, but he needed to do it this way. He needed to reach out to Jimmy but didn't want evidence of direct contact with him tonight. He loved Jimmy like an uncle and wanted to protect him, but he didn't want to ruin his career in the process. He needed time to think.

Angelo answered and said immediately, "Johnny, what's wrong?"

"Hi, Pop. Don't worry, everything is fine. Sorry to call so late, but it's important."

He heard Angelo tell Donna that everything was ok.

Johnny said, "I need you to call Jimmy now and tell him I need his ass at the deli at eleven tomorrow morning. and it's not a social call. Tell him he had a busy night so he should get some sleep."

Angelo began to question, but Johnny cut him off. "Please, Pop. I can't say any more, but I need you to do that."

Angelo said he would.

Next, he called his long-time friend and partner, Zac Taylor. Zac was black, and there wasn't much opportunity for African-Americans to work undercover when infiltrating a rightwing militia so Zac had been reassigned for the duration of this operation. But Marzo sensed something was blowing open and he wanted Zac nearby.

Chapter 62

Colson entered the cabin after his shift and stopped dead. The place had been ransacked. Then he saw Baron on the floor, bloodied and bound at the wrists and ankles.

"Holy shit! What happened?"

Tom was conscious but stared at him blankly.

Colson went to a drawer and came back with a pair of scissors. He bent over and snapped the ankle ties. "Jesus, what happened to you?"

Baron didn't speak. He tolerated what he thought was Colson's act. He needed his hands free before letting Colson know what he knew.

Colson sniped the wrist ties and Baron struggled to his feet, gingerly, wincing at the pain in his ribs where Nick kicked him. The room was spinning and Tom leaned on the kitchen counter for balance.

Finally, he said, "Robbed."

Colson looked genuinely surprised, which infuriated Baron more. When Colson turned away to return the scissors, Baron grabbed an iron skillet from the counter and struck a vicious blow to the side of his head. Colson, staggered, fought to keep his balance, but lost. He fell to the floor in a heap. Baron was on him screaming and pounding him with the pan as a dazed Colson fended off the blows with his arms. Colson managed to push him off and tried to roll away, but Baron was lunging for him again. Colson reached for the scissors which had landed at his feet. He held them up as Baron pounced on him. He could feel the scissors puncture Baron's chest. Baron gave out a moan and went limp.

Colson pushed Baron away and slid back in horror at the sight. He surmised that he must have punctured Baron's aorta because there was blood everywhere. Colson's clothes were soaked with it, as were Tom's. He was still dazed from the blow to his head and he sat motionless, waiting for the room to stop spinning. He felt a sudden wave of nausea and vomited on the floor beside him. He was sure he had a concussion, or maybe it was the site of Baron that made him sick. Baron's wound sprouted more blood as his heart took its last beats and then stopped. Baron's open, lifeless eyes were fixed on the ceiling. It was all over in seconds and Colson had no idea who attacked Baron or what set Baron off against him.

He was shaking uncontrollably, and his heart raced. He wiped his bloody hands on Baron's pants and reached into his pocket to retrieve his phone. He needed to tell R3. He'd know what to do.

He cursed when the call went straight to voicemail. Panicked, he grabbed his keys and stumbled out the door. He sped out of the parking area, but his pinning head forced him to drive slowly as he headed to the Triple R. He parked and was relieved to see the light was still on in R3's apartment. He pounded on the door and waited. R3 swung the door open while holding a pistol in his free hand. One look at Colson and his blood-soaked clothes and he lowered the weapon. "Jesus, what happened?" He was about to let him in but thought better of it. He didn't want blood in his apartment, especially until he knew whose blood it might be and why it was shed.

R3 told him to step off the porch. He closed the door and joined him in front of the building.

"What the hell is this?"

Colson told him everything. The more R3 heard, the angrier he got. He preached over and over that he wanted nothing to draw attention to who they are or what they do. In impulse, R3 cuffed him on the side of his head. It wasn't a vicious hit, but given Colson's condition, it was enough to send him reeling. He caught himself on the hood of his truck and regained his balance.

R3 was enraged. "You stupid shit! What are you doing here?"

Colson said sheepishly, "I didn't know what to do."

"So, you decided to drag me into it? Beautiful. Look, you brought Baron into the group and vouched for him. He's your mess, go clean it up."

R3 could see Colson was clueless. He said, "Get rid of the body. Dump it somewhere away from the road. Deep in the pines."

"What about his truck?"

"Jesus, the truck!" R3 shook his head. "Ditch the body tonight. Tomorrow I'll have Frank follow you. You'll ditch the truck someplace an hour away. Remove the plate."

He looked at Colson with disgust. "This screws up Trenton too. I'll have to get Frank to follow you in place of Baron."

"I'm sorry, R3. I'll make it up to you."

"Damn right you will." He cuffed him again and said, "Now get the hell away from here. This is not my problem."

Colson drove back to the cabin. It was cold but he was sweating, and his head was throbbing. He lowered his window for more air, just in time as more nausea hit and he vomited again.

He was angry with R3. He had idolized the man and was there whenever he was needed, but now, when he went to him for help, all he got was humiliation. And R3 was wrong about it not being his problem. He killed Tom in self-defense. All he had to do was call the cops and explain. The only reason he didn't is because R3 didn't want any cops snooping around, any attention at all. Colson didn't like it, but he'd do it R3's way. R3 was smarter and maybe he had a reason that Colson hadn't considered.

Chapter 63

Marzo's GPS indicated he'd get to the Triple R area at 11:35. Jimmy, and most likely Nick, had stumbled into an operation with major national security implications, and Marzo had no idea what to do about it. He was about to call Brian for advice when his phone rang. It was Pelligrino again. The clock on the phone read 11:21.

Marzo answered and said, "Go ahead, Dan."

"This is wierd. Colson must have closed a little early because he got home at just a little after eleven. With everyone buttoned up for the night, we walked to our vehicle to watch from there. But here's the crazy part, "I was just about to call you to say everyone is tucked in when Colson stumbled out of his house to his truck and kicked up gravel as he took off toward the Triple R. We didn't know whether to stay at our post or follow him. I called the team watching the Trible R to have their eyes out for him heading their way."

Marzo shook his head. The joint task force had multiple teams positioned in the area, but it was getting difficult to coordinate the logistics. He said, "You did the right thing. Stay put. I'm ten minutes out. We have to find out what's happening in that cabin. Marzo was about to hang up when Pelligrino said, "There's one more thing. We can't verify, and I didn't have as good a line of sight as Agent

Lyons did, but Mitch says he may have seen blood on Colson's clothing."

Marzo used the tracking device on Pelligrino's phone to get close. He parked behind a gas station that was closed for the night and walked the last quarter mile. He joined Pelligrino and Lyons in their vehicle.

He called Sellers to brief her and discuss the next steps. Should they hit the cabin and risk blowing the cover of the entire surveillance effort or should they wait? Sellers said, "I made you the Agent in Charge for a reason. You're in the field. You make the call as events unfold."

Marzo hung up and Pelligrino's phone pinged with a text message. He read the screen and said, "It just keeps getting better. Colson visited R3's residence. They spoke briefly out front. They may have had an altercation. Hard to tell from the distance. Colson left and is heading back this way."

Marzo exhaled. He was focused on his job, which seemed to be heating up, but he couldn't shake the concern he had for Jimmy and Nick.

Chapter 64

Minutes later Colson was back. He parked and had difficulty exiting the truck. He moved gingerly and was stooped over, favoring his side. He struggled to keep his balance as he entered the cabin.

“Pelligrino said, “He looked a lot better than that forty-five minutes ago.”
Marzo watched the door, wondering what the next move should be. Then it opened, and Colson appeared straining to drag a body.
Lyons said, “Jesus, this clown is having a bad night.”
“Not as bad as the guy he’s dragging,” Pelligrino said.
Marzo had seen enough. Sellers said it was his call, and he was making it. “I think it’s time we introduced ourselves. They left their vehicle, spread out among the pine trees, and converged on him from three sides with weapons drawn.
Marzo said, “Can we help you with that body?”

Too weak and light-headed to carry Baron, Colson was dragging him by the legs. At the sound of Marzo’s voice, he released him, sighed with resignation, and leaned against the porch post for balance.
Marzo said, “Get on the ground slowly and put your hands behind your head.”
It was obviously painful for Colson to move, but he got down and Agent Lyons stepped forward to frisk and cuff him. He removed a Glock stuffed inside his belt and a cell phone from his pocket.
Pelligrino said, “I’d say you had a pretty bad hour.”
Colson said, “I didn’t do nothin wrong.”

The last thing Marzo wanted was for Colson to lawyer up. He needed information now. He said, “Stop talking. Isn’t that what you guys are taught?” He mimicked a gangster’s voice and said, “Don’t say nothin to nobody. For now, that’s good advice. Keep quiet, but listen carefully because I'm only going to say this once."

Colson was beaten, sick, and scared. He didn't have the energy to resist, so he nodded his agreement.

Marzo told Lyons to remain with the body and crime scene while he and Dan spoke with Colson in the jeep. Then he told Colson to get up, which he couldn't, especially with his hands cuffed behind his back. Lyons helped him to his feet and did a double take on the amount of blood on his clothing.

The door to the cabin was still open. Marzo peeked inside and saw blood everywhere. "Wow, Colson, this looks bad for you. Real bad."

Colson protested. "It was self-defense."

"I told you not to say a word. I think I can help you with this mess. If you're smart, there might be something in it for both of us."

They piled into the Jeep and Marzo told Pelligrino to remove the handcuffs.

Marzo said, "As things stand now, your life as a free man is over. Forget about the murder which you allege was self-defense."

"It was!" Colson insisted.

Marzo said, "Shut up and listen. Let's assume we accept the self-defense thing. We'll discuss that later and you'll have the chance to explain, but I want you to know you have so much more to deal with.

"Take that cabin, for example. As a crime scene, I could search the cabin right now, without a warrant, but I don't need to take the risk. We've got a federal magistrate and county judge on speed dial so we'll go the careful route and use a warrant to make sure we're on solid ground."

Colson rubbed his face and probed the side of his head for blood. He said nothing.

"So, when we do the search, it's gonna be like a treasure hunt. I think there is a pretty good chance we'll find weapons violations."

Colson knew he would.

"I'm also sure we'll find drug violations."

Colson cursed to himself as Marzo went on.

"But you know what? Disposing of a corpse and tampering with a crime scene isn't good either, is it?"

Marzo let that sink in and then said, "Are you good with math? Because I'm adding up the years in prison, and it's a high number. Remember, one violation is one count and one jail term. Two violations are two counts and two jail terms. So, each illegal weapon is a crime in itself. When we're dealing with terrorists, judges like to run the sentences consecutively."

Colson shouted, "I'm not a terrorist!"

Marzo replied calmly, "Please don't talk. You'll have plenty of time to do that in a minute."

Colson nodded and Marzo said, "So let me explain this terrorist stuff. There are more FBI agents and state and local cops in this area tonight than there are deer in the Pines. We saw you come home. We saw you leave. We saw you meet with R3. We saw you come back. We saw you try to remove the body.

We have eyes on everyone linked to R3. One way or another, he is going down tonight. That Boom 50 bullshit is over."

Colson winced at the reference. Marzo obviously knew stuff. Marzo noticed Colson's reaction and went on. "Once you are linked as a coconspirator to a terrorist attack, your life is over. My guess is that the phone Agent Lyons took from your pocket will be a gold mine of information. Our technicians will be on that like the California gold rush."

Colson looked very sad, and Marzo said sarcastically, "Let's see if we can turn that frown upside down, maybe get a nice smile out of you. See, here's the thing that's really good for you. I've also got the Assistant US Attorney and the State Attorney General on standby. These are the kind of people who can make deals.

"They don't give a damn about you. They could put you away for life and not lose a minute's sleep over it, or they could let you walk if they get what they want in return. It's very easy to make the weapons and drug charges go away. We can even make the dead body go away if your self-defense story is plausible."

"It's the truth," Colson said.

"Please be quiet," Marzo said, "I said your story might be plausible. We'll find out soon when you explain, but right now, all the evidence points to you. I'm sure they could get a conviction if they work at it.

"What they want in the worst way is Richard Raymond Rogers. You give us what we need to get him and Boom 50, right now, tonight, and I get you a signed immunity deal. We won't put you in the witness protection program, but we'll get you a plane ticket to wherever you'd like to live and a few bucks to start over."

Colson was thinking.

Marzo said, "Now you can talk. Tell me about this self-defense thing."

Colson went through it all step by step, and Marzo found it plausible. "I think we could work with that. As long as you know we could just as easily reject it and get a conviction. We could jam you up pretty well.

"One more thing to think about, guys like R3, don't give a rat's ass about you. I've been in this game a long time and I guarantee you that shit runs downhill. R3 would write you off in the blink of an eye."

Colson would never admit it, but he got a taste of the real R3 tonight.

Marzo said, "You've got five minutes. Take door number one and you're a free man living in Idaho or Maine or wherever the hell you want. Take door number two and you are in an orange jumpsuit for a long, long, time."

Colson said, "I get a signed immunity statement tonight before I say anything."

Marzo smiled and nodded to Pelligrino who said the communications truck had been on standby and was on the way.

Within minutes Marzo and Colson were in the FBI communications vehicle complete with fax machines, printers, video, and electronic surveillance equipment. The US attorney faxed over a signed immunity agreement laying out what was expected of Colson to exercise the agreement. Once Colson crossed the line to be a snitch, the government made it clear he had to be all in. Satisfied that Colson understood, he took Colson's video confession regarding R3, Boom 50, and other members of the inner circle in real-time.

Once they had enough to arrest R3. They faxed over an arrest warrant and gave Marzo the go-ahead. As for Colson, he would owe them additional hours of questioning after he got cleaned up and received medical attention.

Chapter 65

By 2 AM federal agents had executed simultaneous arrests on five of the six inner circle members whose names were provided by Colson. They would each be charged with conspiracy to commit a terrorist act. They'd be held and questioned separately with the goal of offering a deal to anyone who provided additional names or information regarding weapons storage or planned attacks. But the main focus was at the Triple R compound where more than twenty federal and state agents had converged.

Colson had said the truck loaded with explosives destined for Trenton was stored in the barn behind the shooting range and a bomb squad was on hand to move in when ordered to. An arrest warrant for R3 had been faxed along with search warrants for the entire compound.

Marzo's partner, Zac Taylor, was already on the scene setting up the command center when Marzo arrived. Zac had been seriously wounded during the famous shootout in Bristol years earlier when he and Marzo entered the old power station where a potential assassin was holed up. Marzo shot and killed the perpetrator and Taylor made a full recovery. The men were more than just partners. They and their wives dined together and hosted playdates for their kids. Marzo remembered the hours in the hospital waiting for the surgeons to say Taylor would pull through. It wasn't an experience he wanted to repeat.

A cluster of black SUVs had delivered tactical teams wearing body armor and carrying specialized weapons. The command vehicle had drawings of the compound obtained from the building code department of the township months earlier when the Triple R was first placed under surveillance. The drawings were supplemented by information provided by Marzo's confidential informant.

Marzo, Taylor, Pellogrino, and Lyons gathered with the tactical leaders to review how R3's living quarters would be breached. Teams would approach from front and back with a third team securing the truck in the barn and allowing entry for the bomb squad.

With the teams in place, Marzo gave the green light for the tactical leaders to go when ready. The teams smashed the front and back doors and breached the building. There was no gunfire and Marzo listened on the open channel as they cleared the rooms one by one. Marzo sensed something was wrong. There had been no confrontation and no sign of R3. Marzo double-checked with the surveillance team assigned to monitor R3. They swore that they never lost eye contact with the front or rear door. R3 did not leave the building since his visit from Colson three hours earlier.

The next radio contact reported that the assault team had found what appeared to be a tunnel facing the east side of the building. There was a small shed in that direction and Marzo began to move toward it. Suddenly, the shed door burst open and a black-clad individual, presumably Richard Raymond Rogers, R3, emerged from the shed and raced toward the quad rental pavilion that housed six ATVs. Marzo shot out after him.

R3 reached the pavilion, fired up an ATV, and raced toward the dirt trail that ran away from the building and into the forest. Marzo was seconds behind and hoped that all the rental vehicles had keys already in the ignition. He hopped on the first vehicle he came to and was relieved to see it had a key. He started his vehicle and sped off in the same direction. He could hear R3's vehicle but couldn't see it. R3 was traveling with the lights off, and following him was treacherous because R3 knew the trails, and Marzo didn't. He felt he was losing ground.

Marzo had a decision to make. He could pick up speed if he turned on the headlamp to illuminate the trail, but the headlamp would make him an easier target if R3 began to shoot. He decided he had no choice. He flipped on the headlamp and gunned the engine. He could faintly hear more ATV's behind him which he assumed were additional agents giving chase. The added speed allowed with the headlamp on worked, as the sound of R3's vehicle grew louder.

A shot rang out, and then another. They missed but Marzo killed the headlamp and slowed his speed. Then he sensed

something had changed. There was no longer a sound coming from ahead. R3 had stopped. And Marzo was racing toward him, presenting a much easier target. He killed his motor, got off the quad, and used it as a shield. He waited. He had no idea how far up the trail R3 was.
The sound of the backup ATVs was growing louder as the agents were driving with their lights on.
Marzo notified Zac Taylor to launch the helicopter and overhead floodlights on the trails. Next, he told Agent Lyons to put someone on a computer to find a map of the trails. "I'm gonna want a vehicle at every point where someone could exit the trail."

Marzo saw the lights of the backup ATV's approaching and he radioed for them to go dark to avoid becoming targets. He wished the drivers were from the tactical team because they'd be wearing infra-red goggles. But he knew the tac guys wouldn't have been out of the building fast enough. Most likely, it was Pelligrino and Lyons. He asked them to confirm, and they did. Like him, they had a sidearm, radio, and ear pods, and that was it.
He ordered them to turn off the ATV's and stay put. He estimated they were thirty or forty yards behind him.
The helicopter approached with the floodlights illuminating the area and causing Marzo to reconsider. He decided that it would expose their position to R3 as much as it might expose R3 to them. He made a quick decision and radioed Taylor to have the pilot kill the lights and switch to the infrared camera feed back to the command vehicle
"Zac, you're gonna have to walk me through this. Check the infrared signal, figure out who is where and guide me to Rogers."
Zac listened.

Marzo said, “From our end, we have three ATVs in a row on the trail. You’ll get a heat source from the still-warm vehicles and the agents who are with them. Mine is the lead vehicle. I’m off it and about ten yards to the right. Whatever other images you see will be Rogers and his vehicle. Talk to me.”

Taylor relayed the order to the pilot and waited. “I’m not sure I like this, Johnny. Dangerous.”

“I have no other option. You relay what you see. That will give us eyes on him, without him having eyes on us. Just don’t screw it up.”

“Thanks, partner. No pressure.”

Then Taylor said, “Okay, I’ve got the feed. Judging by this, R3’s quad is about twenty-five yards ahead of you on the trail. R3 has moved away from the vehicle. He’s about ten yards away from it and moving south, deeper into the woods.”

“Ok, I’m moving southwest to meet him. Pelligrino and Lyons, you head southeast in case he changes direction. Do not fire unless ordered to. I don’t want you shouting at me.”

He said to Zac, “I’d like to know why R3 stopped. I guess he thought he’d be harder to track off the trail and without the noise of his vehicle.”

“Or maybe something else. We have your CI on the line. He said the rental quad gas tanks are filled before a rental, not after. So, whatever gas they had was what was left from the last use. He said they were usually pretty empty after a day’s rental. The perp may have just run out of gas.”

“Ok, So where am I?”

“You’re drifting a little too far west. Stay due south. That’s what he’s doing.”

Marzo picked up the pace. It was impossible to run because the denseness of the trees required a slight direction change every couple of feet, but he took faster and longer strides.

Taylor told Pelligrino and Lyons they could make up ground by walking on the trail since Rogers was heading away from it.

“Got it!” Pelligrino replied.

Marzo kept the pace and Taylor reported he was closing to maybe fifteen yards.

Marzo would have liked to shoot him and get it over with, but two things were preventing that. He couldn’t see him, and the trees were so dense that there wouldn’t be a clear shot from that distance.

He continued to close. Taylor said, “You’re ten yards behind and to the right. Soon you’ll be able to smell his cologne.”

Marzo said, “Is he still heading away from me, with his back to me? “

“He’s heading away, so the assumption is yes,” Taylor said.

“Okay, here’s the plan. Tell the chopper to be ready to turn on the floodlights. On the count of three, turn them on. Hopefully, I’ll see him before he can turn to see me behind him.”

“That’s it?” Taylor said. “That’s the plan?”

“No time, Zac. Just do it.”

“Roger that, partner.”

Taylor conveyed the plan to the helicopter pilot and got confirmation.

Marzo steeled himself to prepare for the abrupt change in the lighting. He knew R3’s first instinct would be to look up for a precious second or two. That, plus the time it would take to turn to look behind him and pan for a target would hopefully give Marzo the time advantage he needed.

He told Taylor to start the countdown.

He used his free hand to form a shield at the base of his forehead to soften the change in lighting when it came from above and steadied his Glock with the other.

Taylor said, Three, two, one…"

The lights came on and Marzo winced at the glare, but there was R3, closer than expected, maybe twenty feet ahead. Surprised, RD3 froze, then looked up briefly as if he expected machine gun fire from above. Rejecting that, he began to spin to search for the next danger. Marzo fired round after round, knowing half would hit trees. R3 got off two wild shots before he went down.

Marzo approached cautiously, making a wide arc to approach him from the rear. R3 was lying still on his stomach. As Marzo got closer, he realized R3 was wearing body armor just as R3 turned and raised his weapon. Marzo shot him in the throat before R3 got off another shot.

Chapter 66

The follow-up interview and initial paperwork, especially after an agent-involved shooting, took hours, and it wasn't until just after seven AM that Marzo would be able to call Regional Director Sellers.

He wrestled with how to handle Nick and Jimmy's visit to Tom Baron's cabin shortly before he died. Pelligrino had been the agent on surveillance and would expect the written report to include what he saw. Marzo didn't want to put Dan Pelligrino in a bad position by asking him to forget the visit. Like Marzo, Pelligrino did things by the book, and Marzo wouldn't compromise him.

Ultimately, Marzo decided to be truthful with his boss, or at least ninety percent truthful, and ask for consideration. He was pleased when he received a text from Sellers an hour earlier asking him to call when he was free. Now he could broach the whole Nick and Jimmy thing without it being the main purpose of the call.

He called, and for the first five minutes, Marzo was as humble receiving her praise as Sellers was effusive in giving it. She had read the early faxed report from Taylor and had some minor technical questions which Marzo answered. Then, out of character for her, she joked about it being December 29 and how Marzo had thwarted the planned attack almost seventy-two hours before the January 1 target date. "If this were a movie, the writers would have had you stopping the attack in the final seconds. I prefer that it ended this way."

Marzo said, "That's usually how the script is written."

Sellers said, "Another part of the Hollywood script is that the supervisor holds a high visibility post-operation press conference where he or she gets most of the credit." She laughed and added, "I'll be doing mine at 11:00 this morning. You belong there with me front and center for some well-deserved praise."

Marzo didn't respond because he knew what was coming next. "Of course, we know that we can't do that because your visibility would blow any chance of future undercover work. But I want you to know that Washington will know the role you played."

He replied, "Thank you, Ma'am. Without the work of Taylor and the crew in the helicopter, I'm not sure what would have happened in those woods."
"Noted," Sellers said. "Now, aside from a few days off that I'm giving you now, is there anything at all I can do for you?"

Marzo said, "Actually, there is one thing on my mind. As you know from the initial report, Rogers wasn't the only person who died last night. Thomas Baron, one of Rogers' men, was also killed."

"Yes. I'm aware of the Colson character. Flipping him quickly made last night's success possible."

"What you may not know is that Thomas Baron was a wife abuser. I didn't know him, but he's from my hometown. Totally unrelated to any of this, two men, friends of mine, who are also friends of the abuse victim's family, paid Baron a visit just an hour or so before he died, to dissuade him from harming the woman again. I won't go into details about that."
Sellers surmised they did more than talk with Baron when they visited and she was wise enough to say, "Please don't. But go on."

Marzo got her message and saw it as a good sign. "My point is that with Colson's confession, we know that the two visitors played no part in Baron's death. I see them as just two good samaritans wanting to protect an abused woman but stumbling into a mess on the very night things were going down. I'm inclined to write it off as that and move on."

Sellers said, "I told you before, I put you in charge of this project for a reason. If it is your judgment that we should do what you just said, then interview the men for the record, put the interview in your report, and close that piece of the investigation."

Marzo felt a weight lifted from his shoulders. "Will do."

Sellers said, "You might want to advise your friends that while their intentions were admirable, they should let law enforcement handle things in the future."

"Rest assured we will have that conversation."

Sellers said, "One more thing. You've been gone all night and I'm announcing the operation in a couple of hours. I met your wife at my welcome reception, and she's a smart cookie. It won't be hard for her to figure out where you were last night. You better tell her before my press conference."

Marzo smiled into the phone. Their pattern was clear. Carrie would learn of another of his dangerous undercover operations and get upset. Marzo would ask Angelo and Donna to watch Gracie for two days while he and Carrie went on a getaway. At first, she would sulk in the car on the way to their destination, and Marzo would remind her of the lives saved and the families spared the loss of a loved one. She would nod her head in understanding and mumble disappointment over why it had to be him doing the work. They'd talk more and she would slowly lighten up. By dinner that night, they'd be having a ball.

Marzo said he was on it. Sellers wished him luck and signed off.

Chapter 67

Nick texted Liz on the way home from Manahawkin and asked if he could see her early the next day. She replied, "COME FOR BREAKFAST. WHERE HAVE YOU BEEN?"

Nick wrote back that it was a long story, and he'd see her soon. He wished he knew which version to share when he saw her. He didn't want to be untruthful, but he didn't want to drag her into something that was not her doing. He was beginning to second-guess himself about what he and Jimmy just did. Maybe he didn't need to take that last kick. Maybe he should have left the whole thing in the hands of the law. He also had no idea how he would get the money back to Kate? How would he explain it?

For all of Jimmy's limitations, he showed keen insight every now and then. He must have read Nick's mind because he gave Nick a tap on the arm and said, "That son-of-a-bitch deserved what he got, maybe more. He sent Kate to the hospital, hurt Liz, and scared the daylights out of Addie. It might have taken months to get him if you waited for the cops. And even if they did arrest him, he'd never get the ass-kicking he deserved.

"As for the money," Jimmy went on, "it belongs to Kate. He got off easy. He stole forty thousand and you're giving back thirty."

Nick appreciated Jimmy's words, but it still just didn't feel right.

Jimmy added, "I'm proud of you. For an old man, you showed you've still got it. The creep was half your age and a badass militia member, and you put him down like BAM! It was lightning quick. You're the man, Nick."

Nick thought about that and wondered whether Jimmy had hit on the real reason why Nick was feeling conflicted. Maybe the trip to Manahawkin wasn't only about seeking justice or retrieving Kate's money. Maybe it was more about Nick wanting to prove something to himself. Whatever it was, he had about seven hours to figure out what to say to Liz.

Nick arrived at Liz's house shortly after seven the next morning and rang the doorbell. She greeted him in the doorway with a long kiss before pulling him inside. Nick reflected on how important doorways had become for him lately. She was still wearing her robe and hadn't applied any makeup, but he thought she looked great.

She said, "I'm sorry I'm still in my robe." Nick eyed her up and down and said, "I'm sorry too, but we can change that." She smiled at the comment but didn't respond.
Nick said, "I smell bacon."
"When you say you want to meet this early you either get the food or the glamor. I figured you'd opt for the food. "
Nick said, "I got both," and kissed her again.

"What's in the bag?" She smiled teasingly and said, " Are you staying overnight?"
Nick had dropped the bag by the door when Liz pulled him inside and looked down at it now.
"I wish it was that simple." She looked perplexed by the comment, and Nick said, "I'll explain later."
She took him by the hand to lead him to the breakfast table and he winced.
She asked what was wrong and then noticed. "Nick, your hand is swollen. Let me see." She lifted it gently and the nurse in her took over. "Your knuckles are bruised. What did you do?" She added kiddingly, "If I didn't know better, I'd say you were in a fight."
Nick didn't smile.
Liz looked concerned and said, "What's going on?"
"I'm starved. Let's eat. I have some things to tell you."

Nick sat and Liz brought out eggs, bacon, toast, coffee, and a plastic sandwich bag filled with crushed ice.
"Put this on your hand to reduce the swelling."
Nick put the bag aside and looked at her.
She said, "Okay, you have your food and my full attention. What's up? What's in the bag?"
Nick took a sip of his coffee before responding. "You and I have a deal to always be honest."
"Yes we, do," Liz said emphatically. "So, what's in the bag?"
"I've really been struggling between totally lying, telling the whole truth, or doing a little of both."
Liz said, "Well, that struggle is over. Tell me the whole truth or get your breakfast at Denny's."
"I just don't want to drag you into something."

Liz lifted the ice bag and gently placed it on his hand again. "I'm all in. What's the big deal?"
Nick looked apologetic and said, "I should have told you first, but I knew you'd say no."

Liz was losing her patience. "Nick, I got up early. I made a nice breakfast. I greeted you with a kiss. If you don't stop beating around the bush, I'm going to tell you where you can put your eggs."

Nick got up and retrieved the bag. He placed it on the table and unzipped it, revealing stacks of cash."
Liz recoiled and said, "Sweet Jesus, what is that?"
"That is roughly $31,000 of the $40,000 Tom Baron took out of the joint bank account he held with Kate. The creep must have spent the rest."
Liz looked at him in disbelief. "How did you get it?"
"I asked him for it."
"Where?"
"At a cabin in Manahawkin that he shares with a guy from the shooting range."
"How did you find him?"
"You can ask me that a thousand times, but I won't tell you. Not negotiable."
Liz accepted that and said, "So how did you get the money?"
"I already told you. I asked him for it."
Liz looked doubtful. "You asked and he just handed it over?
"Not right away."
She glanced at his hand. "Is that why your knuckles are swollen? Did you fight?"

Nick smiled. “I wouldn’t exactly call it a fight. It was over pretty quick.”

Liz frowned and said softly, “Oh, Nick, what did you do?”
Nick thought for a moment and then said, “Short version?”
“The truth! The whole truth.”
Nick wanted to ease the tension. He grinned and said, “You want the truth? You can’t handle the truth.”
She smiled briefly at the famous movie line and said, “Thank you, Jack Nicholson.” Her smile disappeared just as quickly. “No time for jokes, Nick. You just put $31,000 on my table, and you’ve been in a fight. I deserve to know what happened.”

Nick said, “You’re right.” He glanced at his eggs, shrugged, and told her everything.”

Liz sat mesmerized as he told the story and was speechless when he finished. She took a sip of her coffee, declared it was cold, and took their cups to the counter to pour two fresh ones. Finally, when she sat, she rubbed her temples and said softly, “What were you thinking?”
Nick shook his head. “I’ve thought about that all night. One easy answer is that I wanted Kate’s money back. Now that we have it, I’m not sure how we handle that, but that’s a discussion for later. Another reason is that he deserved to have his ass kicked. I’ve got a special thing about men who abuse women and frighten kids, so there’s that.”
Liz scolded him. “I saw the expression on your face after his attack, and I hold you to stay calm.”
Nick replied, “I tried, but it only worked for a while.”

Liz ignored that and said, “You left him zip tied?”
“Only for ninety minutes when his buddy would come home from work. Not a big deal.” Liz shook her head. “Look at you Nick, banged up hand, bag full of money, maybe some second thoughts about the whole thing floating around. I’m so sorry. You did this for me, and it’s my fault.”

Nick looked at his breakfast plate again and pushed it away. His appetite was gone. “It’s not your fault. If you want the truth, I felt as if I had something to prove.”
She leaned closer and rubbed his forearm. “You don’t have anything to prove to me. I think we’re great just as we are.”
Nick nodded and said, “I think so too. But I didn’t do this to prove something to you or impress you. I did it to prove something to myself.”
“To yourself?”

Nick took a long pause before saying, “You are the best thing that’s ever happened to me, and this is as good a time as any to say that I love you. I really do and that should be enough to make me content, but I still have stuff swirling in my head, stuff that my VA shrink says I have to work through.”
Tears welled in Liz’s eyes. “I love you too. I love you very much, so what kind of things do you have to work through?”
“Maybe it’s the POW thing, or the long rehab, or my self-imposed exile from the normal world. I wasted so many years isolating myself from everyone and everything except three guys in a deli. Now, I’m having a real problem accepting that I’m growing older, and my internal clock is ticking. I resent everything I’ve missed in life.

"That's why I searched for you and I'm so damn happy I did. I had an impulse to recapture the person I was before Vietnam by finding the person who could fill the void in my life. Unfortunately, that same impulse is what also made me go after Tom, to recapture the feeling of strength I had when playing ball or serving in the army."

Liz said, "I don't get it."
Nick tried to explain. "In my youth, I would have gone after him ten minutes after I heard what he did. But this time, I let my anger build until I questioned whether I was too old, whether I had what it would take to deal with him."

Nick took a long breath and exhaled slowly. Then he rubbed his face and said, "This may sound a little like pop psychology, but I wasn't fighting Tom Baron last night. I was fighting old age, raging against it."
Liz's tears were flowing now, and she wiped them from her cheeks.
Nick went on. "My knuckles are swollen, my arthritic right wrist and shoulder are throbbing, and I was breathing harder than I wanted to admit when the skirmish with Tom was over, but I did it. My body was telling me that I'm not the man I used to be, but my head said yes, I am, damn it!"
He went on. "I hear more and more news about people my age, my classmates, dying or dealing with serious medical issues, and it gets to me, makes me think."
Liz interrupted. "Our age, Nick. Those people are our age not just yours. We are growing old together."

"Right," Nick said, "Our age. Sorry. Anyway, I hear the clock ticking and I'm wondering when it's my turn. I want to slam the damn clock against the wall."
Now it was Liz's turn to try to lighten the mood. "I think you've done enough slamming for one day."

Nick shook his head. "I want to do things, Liz, with the time I have left. I don't mean see the God damn Eiffel Tower. I mean I want to accomplish things. Do something meaningful. I thought getting the money back would be meaningful."

Liz put her hand up to stop him. "Ok, Big Guy. I've had enough of this. First, I hear the same clock ticking as you, and it seems to tick faster each year, but my reaction is to be grateful I found you and I want to spend the time I have left enjoying my life with you. I'm at peace and wish you were too. As for wanting to accomplish things, you saved a pilot's life. That's quite an accomplishment. You won the Distinguished Service Cross. That doesn't happen often, and you've helped hundreds of veterans. You testified before the United States Congress for God's sake. If you want something meaningful, keep helping vets. I'll help if you like. We'll do it together. I have some experience, remember?"

Nick started to respond, but Liz interrupted. "Here's one more thing you've overlooked. You've filled a very big void in a special little girl's life. Addie's not crazy about you because you can prove that you're still a badass tough guy who can beat people up, or because you were in special forces and were awarded the Distinguished Service Cross.

She's crazy about you because you are kind, funny, dependable, and caring. Throw in that you are handsome, and it pretty much sums up why I'm in love with you too."

Now Nick's eyes were filling as Liz added, "Please stop looking back at what you missed, or who you used to be. Look forward and plan your future. We both may go tomorrow, or we may still be kicking until we're ninety."

Nick listened.

Finally, Liz said, "I said you didn't have to prove anything to me or yourself, but there is maybe one thing you can do to prove you're the man I think you are."

Nick raised his eyebrows and said, "What's that?"

Liz smiled through her tears and said, "Will you marry me?"

Chapter 68

Liz's phone rang before Nick could respond. She saw the call was from Kate, so she playfully put the call on speaker. "Hi Kate. I'm sitting here with Nick discussing a very important question. How are you?"

When Kate spoke, it was obvious she was crying. She said, "Mom, I have terrible news. The police were just here to tell me that Tom is dead. He was killed last night."

Liz and Nick looked at each other in disbelief. Nick wondered how it was possible. He was sickened when he saw the look on Liz's face that implied Nick must have done it. She stared wide-eyed as Nick shook his head no. She recovered enough to respond to her daughter. "My God, Kate. What did they say?"

Kate ignored the question and said, "I couldn't stand Tom any longer and wanted him out of our lives, but this is terrible. I mean, he's Addie's father. How do I tell her? What do I tell her?"

Liz didn't have an answer.

Kate said. "Thank God she had just left for school before the officers came."

She was sobbing now. "My daughter will have to grow up with the thought that her father was killed. That's horrible."

Liz glared at Nick with a look that said, "What have you done?"

The look stung him, yet based on what he had told her, it was understandable why she'd assume that.

Nick began to panic about others who might make the same assumption if they ever learned that he was at the cabin. Worse than the assumption was the possibility that his final kick did some internal damage that caused Baron's death. Could there have been an after effect from the blows Nick landed to Baron's face and throat? Nick didn't think so, but he had no other explanation and he needed one. He said, "Kate, this is Nick. I'm so very sorry to hear this. What exactly did the police say?"

"They said Tom was stabbed last night."

Liz looked horrified. She scowled at Nick and turned away.

Kate continued between sobs. "They said the man he lived with did it. He already confessed. They said it was determined that the roommate did it in self-defense."

The words hung in the air. The roommate did it. Nick breathed a sigh of relief as his anxiety eased. He had no idea what happened after he and Jimmy left the cabin, but he was grateful for the confession.

Liz looked apologetic and put her hand on Nick's. She turned back to the phone and said, "I'll be there in 45

minutes." Then her yoga experience took over and she said, "Take deep breaths and exhale slowly. Sit quietly and meditate like I taught you. Don't let your mind wander."
"That's easy to say, Mom, but the man that I married was stabbed to death. My daughter's father. I couldn't stand him, but I didn't want him dead."
"I know, Kate, but you need to pull yourself together."
Kate persisted. "What am I going to say to Addie?"
"I don't know. But we'll figure it out together. I'll be there soon. Remember, deep breaths."

They said goodbye and Liz hung up. She looked at Nick with tears in her eyes. Her guilt was oppressive, matched by her fear that she had shattered their trust and damaged their young relationship so quickly.
"Nick, I'm so sorry. Please forgive me. After you said you were there last night, and came here with money…" She trailed off and then started again. "When I heard Tom was dead, I just put things together, but I should have never jumped to that conclusion."

Nick hated seeing her looking so pained. He put his hand on hers. "Don't worry. Anyone in your place would have reached the same conclusion. I was scared stiff when I heard he was dead because I knew everything could point to me. It's okay, I understand. Worry about your daughter, not us."
"It's not okay," Liz said emphatically. "I feel as though I've ruined something between us."
Nick shook his head. "Don't say that. You haven't ruined anything."

"Yes, I have. I've been so happy with you, and then, in one moment, I thought I lost it all, that I didn't really know who you are. That it would all come crashing down."

"But it didn't," Nick said. Liz cried openly. "Wrong. You'll always remember that I thought the worst of you."

Nick stood and walked to her side of the table. He took her hand, guided her to her feet, and wrapped her in his arms. He said softly. "Please don't do this. I need you, Liz, and nothing is going to change what we've found together. Please."

She doubted the moment would fade as easily as Nick thought, but she raised her head from his shoulder and forced a smile. "Okay," she said. "It never happened."

"That's right. Never happened. Now go to your daughter."

Chapter 69

While driving home from Liz's house, Nick's phone rang. He answered in time to hear Jimmy in full panic.
"Nick. This is Jimmy. I have trouble. My phone died last night, and I didn't charge it until this morning. When I did, I saw that Angelo tried to call me four times, starting late last night. I called him back and he said Johnny Marzo wants to see me at the deli at 11:00, and I'm supposed to bring you. Angelo said Johnny was very mad but wouldn't say why." He stammered and added, "Why do you think, Nick? Why is he mad? Do you think it's because of last night?"

Nick's mind was racing. He couldn't think of a reason other than last night, but how would Johnny know, especially so soon?

"Keep calm, Jimmy. I don't know, but Johnny is our friend. It'll be okay. Let's just wait and see what's up. I'll pick you up when I get back to town."

They arrived at the deli and found Brian waiting for them. Angelo was behind the counter and Brian nodded to him, which seemed to be his cue to leave. "I'll get out of here for a while. Call me when you're finished. He flipped the sign on the door to "closed," and left through the back to his residence.

Nick sensed a chill in the room and said, "Hey, Brian, good to see you. Where's Johnny?"

Brian said tersely, "Johnny can't be here, so he sent me."

Jimmy said, "Angelo said Johnny wanted to see us."

Nick was becoming annoyed by all the mystery and asked what was up.

Brian hadn't smiled yet and there was no indication he was going to. "What's up is what the hell were you thinking last night?"

Nick wondered how many more times he'd be asked that question today. He hoped it was the last. He stared blankly and Brian said, "Last night you walked right into a major FBI operation against an imminent domestic terror attack. A surveillance team saw you entering the cabin owned by Charles Colson and shared by Thomas Baron. The same cabin in which Baron's dead body was found shortly after."

"Dead body!" Jimmy blurted. "Sweet Jesus."

Nick hadn't told Jimmy about the phone call from Kate. He didn't want to worry him if didn't have to, at least not until he found out what this meeting was about. Now he knew.
Jimmy said, "Oh, boy. That's not good."

"I think we can agree on that," Brian said. "Johnny's not here for two reasons. First, although he loves you guys, he would seriously consider lunging for your necks if he saw you face to face. Second, he used Angelo to deliver the message and sent me here because he can't have any record of talking with you except for a formal phone call which he'll make later. Now, I want you to tell me everything that happened in that house last night, from the time you entered until the time you left."
Nick told the story, and when he finished Brian said, "Jesus, Nick. This isn't the wild west. Zip ties? A kick to the ribs?"
"We're sorry Brian. We had no idea about the FBI."
"Of course, you didn't. But you being there put Johnny in a very difficult position. If it were anyone else, your asses would be in federal custody right now answering a ton of questions, and most likely facing charges."
Jimmy got wide-eyed and looked to Nick for guidance. Nick didn't have any yet.

"Here's the problem. The agents on surveillance made a record of the two of you entering the cabin. They traced the truck's plates back to Jimmy."
Jimmy looked startled and said, "Oh, boy, that's not good."
"They didn't know who the second guy was, but once Johnny heard the report, he assumed it was Nick. So, this is the FBI. They are known for their thoroughness. The

agents will expect to see your visit in the final report, which no doubt would lead to your investigation. Here are just some of the crimes you committed: breaking and entering, aggravated assault, false imprisonment, and grand theft."

Jimmy was chewing his fingernails and Nick was shaking his head in embarrassment.

Brian said, "There will be a press conference today at noon during which the Regional Director of the FBI, Johnny's boss, will explain that a task force headed by Agent Marzo, thwarted a major domestic terror plot last night during which several of the participants were arrested and the ring leader, Richard Raymond Rogers, was shot and killed by Agent Marzo."
Jimmy said, "No shit?"
"Yeah," Brian repeated, "No shit! Johnny was a hero again, and he cashed in on his achievement by asking his boss for some leeway. He told her he knew you both and was aware of a domestic abuse situation involving Tom Baron and a friend of yours. He told her his assumption was you visited for that reason, and it had nothing to do with the terror plot. He said if that was the case, he would recommend closing that part of the investigation. As I said, any other circumstance and she would have said to drag you in anyway, investigate, and see where it leads. Instead, she said he was to interview you informally and, if it was still his recommendation to close that thread, it was fine with her."
Jimmy clapped and Nick kept his head down. Brian said, "So, when Johnny calls, you are to limit your comments to only his very specific questions. Volunteer nothing extra

and keep your answers short. It will be over in five minutes. He'll be able to say he conducted the interview and reached his expected conclusion. One more thing. Johnny doesn't know about the money. I don't see how anyone else knows. Technically, you could argue it wasn't theft, but it could be messy. Just keep that quiet until I figure out how to deal with it. In the meantime, I'll keep helping Kate with her bills as I promised."

Nick cleared his throat and said, "There's something else I should tell you. Liz knows about the money. I gave it to her this morning."

Brain rolled his eyes. "Damn, Nick. You're not making it easy. We can't deal with that now. Make sure she sits on that knowledge until we work it out."

"Thanks, Brian. I will. I'm sorry about all of this. None of this is Jimmy's fault, by the way. He was along for the ride as a friend."

Brian smiled. "If I wanted to make Jimmy nervous, I'd tell you that as an accomplice, he'd be equally guilty."

Jimmy turned pale and Brian laughed. "No worries, Jimmy. I'm just bustin.' You're both safe."

"So, we're finished here?" Nick asked.

"Almost. As soon as you answer the question I asked earlier. What the hell were you thinking?"

There it was again. Nick sat quietly until Brian said, "I'm not asking that question rhetorically. I mean it. What were you thinking?"

Nick cleared his throat again, and said, "I had two goals. I wanted to give him the ass-kicking he deserved, and I wanted to get Kate's money back."

Brian said, "Admirable goals. Can I suggest that next time you let law enforcement handle things?" He added with a smile, "I know it might be slower than your method, but…"
Nick allowed a smile of his own. Brian softened his tone and said, "There are few guys I admire more than you, Nick. So, tell me, what's a guy in his seventies doing going after a guy half his age? Talk to me, Nick. I'm here for you."
"I know you are, Brian, and I appreciate it." He paused and said, "The truth is, I was trying to prove to myself that I could still do it."
Brian sat back and rubbed his face. He let out a long breath and said, "Nick, for as long as I've known you, you've been in a perpetual state of unease. Much of it is understandable considering what you went through; nevertheless, you've been unhappy, and unfulfilled. But all that changed when you found Liz. You're happy, positive, I bet you even feel better physically." He smiled and said, "Run with that, Nick. Run with the life you found with Liz. You should have no need to prove anything to us or yourself. It's time to feel at peace. An NFL Hall of Fame player doesn't have to step back on the field in his seventies and play again. People evolve into a new game, a new chapter in life. Liz and her family are your game now, Nick, and it's a great one."

Nick smiled and said, "Thanks, Brian. I've got it. And thank Johnny for me too."

Chapter 70

New Year's Day passed peacefully. There were no explosions or attacks to inspire copycats across the country. A search of R3's safe revealed names of militia leaders from multiple states who were contemplating future Boom 50 operations, and the US Attorneys in their respective federal districts were exploring conspiracy charges. Three of R3's inner circle arrested during the FBI operation flipped and offered information that would help in Boom 50 prosecutions. Johnny Marzo received a letter of commendation from the FBI Director, and the Chief of Staff to the President of the United States called to offer the President's gratitude. Marzo shrugged off the accolades and attributed much of the operation's success to luck.

Privately, one thing gnawed at him. He had been trained to block out any thoughts of Carrie or Gracie when on a mission, knowing they could be a distraction from the absolute concentration he needed to survive. He followed that maxim without fail until the last mission. During the most dangerous moments in the pitch-black woods, alone with Richard Raymond Rogers, thoughts of his wife and daughter flashed before him. He thought briefly about how much he didn't want to leave them. Looking back, Marzo knew that a two or three-second distraction could have been the difference between living and dying. He considered the irony in the belief that the best way to live to see your wife and daughter again was to not think about them, and focus instead on his training. He hoped he wasn't losing his edge.

Marzo conducted his interview with Nick and Jimmy and filed his report closing out their involvement in the events at the cabin. Brian coached Liz to hold on to the $31,000 and make deposits in Kate's account in small increments while he continued to make her mortgage payments.

Kate and Liz told Addie her father had passed away in an accident, saving her the full truth for when she got older, or maybe never. The counselor from the hospital proved to be a Godsend, helping Addie cope with the mixed feelings of losing a father whom she loved and had grown to fear. Kate and Liz smothered her with love, and she was doing okay and returned to school.

Liz saw much less of Nick in the week after Tom Baron's passing. She had spent much of her time at Kate's, even sleeping there several nights. When Nick saw her at the small funeral service, she looked drawn and tired. She told him she wanted to get together for a quiet night but couldn't until she was sure Kate and Addie were okay. Nick told her she was where she should be doing what she should be doing.

Chapter 71

Liz was having Addie for a sleepover and asked Nick to come for dinner. Addie's counselor wanted Addie to return to as much of her normal routine as possible, and that included spending time with Nick. The truth was that Nick needed to see Addie as much as Addie may have wanted to see Nick. It had been ten days since Tom Baron's death, ten days of Nick trying to reconcile his empathy for Addie's loss and his guilt for his attack on her father. He felt that, somehow, seeing her would help.

He and Addie were playing a board game while Liz prepared dinner. Liz discovered she was missing a couple of key ingredients and asked if Nick would mind running to the store, but Addie said, "We're playing a game, Mommy-Liz. Can Nick keep playing? I think I'm going to win."

Liz saw the request to spend time with Nick as a good sign. She looked at Nick for approval and Nick said, "I'm not leaving here until I win this game."

Addie giggled and said, "Not you. I'm going to win!"

Liz said, "Okay. I'll go and let you two keep playing. But don't cry if you lose."

"I won't," Nick deadpanned.

Addie almost fell off the chair laughing. "No, Nick. She meant me. When I was little, I used to cry if I lost. Mommy-Liz said we couldn't play anymore if I cried, and I stopped."

Liz laughed. "Now, before each game, we say that to each other."

Addie said, "So, I'm saying it to you, Nick. Don't cry if you lose."

Liz left for the store and Nick and Addie resumed their game.

Addie won, and Nick pretended to sniffle and asked Addie for a tissue.

"You're faking!" She shrieked. "You're not really crying,"

Nick smiled. "You caught me."

They were putting the game away when Addie said quietly. "My Daddy died."

Nick had been with her briefly a couple of times since Tom died, once at a gathering at Kate's after the funeral service. He felt bringing it up again signaled she wanted to talk. The counselor had advised the adults in her life to let her get her feelings out and to let her guide the conversation.

Nick said. "I know, Honey, and I'm very sorry."

"Did you know him?"

Nick wasn't sure how to answer. "Not really. I only met him once."

Addie said, "Sometimes I have funny feelings about him."

Nick wanted to tread easily. He said, "In what way?"

"Sometimes I miss him because we used to have fun together and sometimes I don't because he used to scare me ."

Nick searched for something to say. The counselor suggested keeping responses open-ended so the child would talk if she wanted to. She said to use what she called door openers, and a good door opener was to parrot the child's comment. This was a little heavy for Nick, but he gave it a shot.

"So sometimes you feel both ways."

"Yes. Is it okay to feel like that?"

"I think a lot of people would feel the way you do."

"Why did Daddy get so mean?"

Nick wished he had gone to the store. He knew it was healthy for Addie to talk about her father, but he didn't want to say the wrong thing. He shrugged and decided to go with his gut. Remembering his abusive father, he didn't want Addie to go through life with a similar memory.

"Sometimes people get sick, and it makes them act a different way. I think that's what happened to your father. I know he loved you very, very much. When you think of the fun you had together, that was your real dad. When you think of the times you were scared, that was when he wasn't feeling well and it made him different, even mean sometimes. But people who knew him said he was a wonderful man."

Addie said, "Oh."

Nick said. "I have an idea. It's like a game. Do you want to try it?"

Addie said, "Sure."

"Okay, close your eyes and think of a time when you had a really good time with Daddy."

Addie thought, and said, "When we went to the circus and the elephant pooped. Daddy and I laughed, especially when the clown scooped it up. Daddy said he was a pooper scooper." She laughed at the memory.

"That's a great story. Can you think of another?"

"He used to tuck me in and tell me stories. Sometimes we'd make up stories together. I'd start and he would add something and then I would add something. The stories ended up sounding silly, but it was fun."

They went through a few more stories and then Nick said. "It sounds like you had a wonderful dad. When you think of him, think of all the fun things you did. I know there are lots more. And when you have sad thoughts from when he was sick, just try to replace them with good ones."

Addie smiled and said, "Okay."

Nick squeezed her chin gently and said, "You know that if you ever want to talk about Daddy you can do it with Mommy, or Mommy-Liz , or even me if you want to."

"Okay."

Nick tried to change the subject by asking about school.

"It's okay, I guess. I don't like it."

"You don't like it?"

"Ever since Daddy died my teachers and friends are treating me different."

"Different?"

"Yes. They are being extra nice to me. I don't like it. It makes me feel funny. I just want them to be the way they were before."

Nick made a mental note to tell Kate. He replied, "Sometimes when people feel bad about something they don't know how to act or know what to say. I think they'll be back to normal soon."

Addie nodded and Nick tried to lighten the mood.

"What about that little boy who used to stare at you and then run away? How is he doing?"

Addie laughed. "He's different. Like you said, I think he's in love with me."

Nick smiled. "I never said, he's in love with you. I said he probably likes you."

Addie shrugged and said, "Same thing. Anyway, he doesn't just stare at me anymore. The other day he said, 'Hi Addie' and then he ran away."

"He actually said 'Hi Addie' before running?"

"Yes."

"Well then, maybe he does love you after all."

They laughed again then Addie's expression turned serious. She said, "I love you, Nick. Is that okay?"

Nick was stunned and looked at her as tears welled in his eyes. His voice choked as he said, "That's more than okay, Addie. It's the best thing in the world. I love you too."

Liz came through the door in time to see Nick wipe a tear from his cheek and she said, "Did Nick lose the game?"

Chapter 72

While Liz brought Addie upstairs to read her to sleep, Nick poured her a glass of her favorite dessert wine. On his way to the fridge to get his beer, he stopped and thought for a moment. Though he remained a devoted beer drinker, he noted that couples always shared wine in romantic movie scenes. Liz had been introducing him to some of her favorites, and he found some he liked. He decided to pass on the beer and share the bottle with her. He put some nuts in a bowl, put the bowl, the glasses, and the bottle on a tray, carried it to the living room, and settled back to wait for Liz. She arrived half a glass later saying that Addie must have been exhausted because she fell asleep sooner than usual.

Addie captured all of the attention during dinner, so Nick was finally able to take a moment to admire Liz. She looked great in nice-fitting jeans and a white blouse untucked. The color had returned to her face and she wore just the right amount of make-up. Best of all, she was smiling.

She noted the tray on the coffee table and thanked him. She sat next to him, took a sip of wine, and put down her glass. She snuggled closer and curled her legs up under her. She rested her head on his shoulder and said, "I've been waiting for this for a week."

Nick said he was glad she was back.

"Kate and I have been laser-focused on making sure Addie is okay."

Nick said, "I think she will be."

"You seemed a little misty eyed when I got back from the store. What was that all about?"

Nick recounted his talk with Addie, and Liz said, "You're so good with her. She's crazy about you." She lifted her head from his shoulder and added, "So am I."

She kissed him long and gently, and it was as if the tension of the past week was melting away.

She sighed and said, "All week I've been waiting for this chance to tell you again how sorry I am for doubting you about Tom. I really don't want it to ruin…"

He interrupted her and said, "Yes."

She lifted her head from his shoulder so she could turn to him, and said, "I'm sorry, what did you say?"

Nick smiled. "I said yes."

She didn't catch on and gave him a quizzical look, so he explained.

"A little over a week ago you asked me to marry you. I was too stunned to respond. Then we learned Tom was dead. Then you thought I did it. Then you went on a guilt trip when you found out I didn't. Then I had some concerns about the FBI, and you've been worried about Addie. That's a busy week, and none of it offered a good backdrop for me to say, 'Hey, about that question you asked.' Now, things have calmed down. So, if you're still interested, my answer is yes."

Liz said. "Oh my God. I'm sorry. I didn't know what you meant at first. So, you're saying yes?"

"Yes."

She smiled broadly. "So, you think we should get married?"

"No, I think it's crazy. Nuts. I have no idea what we'll do or how we'll do it, but if you're asking if I'm happier than I've ever been and if I wish I was with you at the times when I'm not, that I miss you when I'm driving home, ten minutes after I leave your house, not to mention you make me feel

like a teenager, and you're the sexiest girl in the world, then yes, I guess that means I want to get married."
She shrieked, wrapped her arms around his neck, and kissed him again.

When they parted, Nick said, "I've seen enough wedding stuff on TV to give me the shakes when I think about planning a wedding. I mean pick a date, a place, the food, the guest list, the dress, the flowers. Scary stuff, right? And then, what do they call those girls who go over the top? Bridezilla? That's a pretty cool term, whoever dreamt it up. You don't impress me as a bridezilla. You're not, right?"
Liz laughed. "If it makes you feel better, I don't care when, except soon. I don't care where. I don't care what we wear or what we eat. As for the guest list, if we don't see someone often enough so we can say by mouth, 'Hey, we're getting married, wanna come?' Then we shouldn't worry about it."
Nike grinned and squeezed her shoulder. "I'm starting to like you, Liz."
"You should," she teased. "I'm perfect for you."
Nick snapped his fingers as if he had forgotten something. "I have to get a ring. I didn't know your size and I didn't want to sneak into your room to get a sample. No more breaking and entering for me."
Liz smiled. "I have my mother's rings and they fit fine. If you don't mind, I'd love to wear them. I can give them to you and then you can give them to me."
"Sounds very nice, but I feel like I should be buying your rings." He grinned and said, "How about if I pay you for the ring?"

"Absolutely not, That is a terrible idea." She thought a moment and said, "I don't have a ring for you either. Why don't you get your own ring? You can give it to me and I'll give it to you. We'd be even."

"Perfect."

They raised their glasses and Nick said, "To wedding planning."

They sipped and Liz said more seriously, "How is Jimmy with all this?"

"He's trying to be positive. But he's a little down. He thinks he and I are breaking up. He'll need some hand-holding, but I think he knows I'll never leave him."

"You better not. I love Jimmy."

"I won't. Same with Angelo and Big Frankie."

"We're not giving up the lives we know; we're adding to them."

"That's a good way to put it," Nick said as he refilled his glass.

Liz took his hand, and he thought she was being sweet until he saw that she was examining it. "No new bruises," she deadpanned. "You must have made it through the week without a fight."

"It's been all peace and love."

"Can I get a promise you'll keep it that way?"

"You've got it."

Liz asked for more wine, and while Nick poured, she said, "We do have one decision to make tonight, and it's yours to make. We need to set a date. I'm good with whatever you pick."

Nick rubbed his face and cleared his throat. "My decision?"

"Yup. I don't want to be a bridezilla and dominate things."

Nick said, “I need to tell you something. I think you know I was a pretty decent football player in my day, and a damn good soldier too. But for me, the game or the mission wasn't the hard part. The hard part was the nerve-racking wait for the game or mission. So, if we're getting married, let's do it next weekend.”

“Next weekend!”

Nick said, “Today is Tuesday.” He started counting days on his fingers but gave up. “It's like a week and a half away. Any longer than that, and I'm a basket case.”

Liz pretended to be deep in thought. Then she smiled and said, “People might say we're rushing into it. I'll just have to tell them that almost fifty years is a long enough wait. Next weekend it is.”

Chapter 73

Liz put aside any impulses about what a bride should be doing to prepare for wedding preparation and decided to enjoy watching Nick plan instead, or at least try to. Nick decided to have some fun and test her commitment to his plans. He started with the food. “I want the same kind of food that was served when my friends and I crashed wedding receptions as kids.”

“You crashed wedding receptions?”

“All the time. Didn't everyone?”

“Maybe. I guess I missed out. Okay, and what kind of food is that?”

“Roast beef sandwiches, potato salad, and a sheet cake.” Liz raised her eyebrows. “That's it?”

“That's it,” Nick said smugly.

Liz smiled. "Did I ever tell you I went to a wedding once where they served duck, couscous, and kale? I was hoping for something like that for us. But I like roast beef, so we're good. What about appetizers? Did they serve appetizers when you crashed weddings?"

"Chips and pretzels."

Liz suppressed an urge to laugh and said, "Perfect. Where will we be having this reception?" She had an idea of what was coming, and Nick didn't disappoint. "I was thinking of the deli."

Liz remained straight-faced and said, "Angelo's deli?"

"Of course. I was thinking of a small wedding. I went over my guest list, and I'd invite thirteen, the guys, plus Johnny and Brian and their families. It all comes to thirteen. I'm thinking if you do thirteen, we'd fit. We've had more than that for the Pinochle tournament."

"You mean the tournament Julie and I are going to win this year?"

"It'll never happen, but yeah, that's the one. "

She smiled. "I'll have to check my guest list to see if I can get it down to thirteen."

"No stress," Nick said. "If we need a slightly bigger place," he emphasized the word slightly, "I'll try to find us something."

"What about entertainment at the reception?"

"I'm thinking a good radio station and maybe some records."

Liz laughed out loud. “Records? Do you still call them records? Would I be too pushy if I suggested music from the internet?”

“Not at all. Great idea. Would you handle that? I’m gonna be swamped with all the other arrangements.”

Liz said flatly, “It’s the least I could do.”

“I forgot to tell you, with all these decisions mounting up I decided to hire a wedding planner.”

Liz had been sipping a soft drink through a straw. The comment caught her by such surprise that she snorted soda into her nose. When she stopped coughing and cleared her throat, she said, “I don’t blame you. You’ve taken on a lot.”

“It’s Brian.”

“Brian is the wedding planner?”

“He volunteered. I think he’s capable.”

“He hunts terrorists, Nick. Seems like this might be under his pay grade. Speaking of pay grade, you know he’s going to want to pay for things.”

“I know. He already said he wants to pay for everything as our wedding gift. I told him I’d have to talk to you. I didn’t think you’d want to do that.”

“I don’t. I mean, it's very nice, but I wouldn’t feel right.”

Nick shrugged. “You know, once he wants to pay for something there’s almost no stopping him.”

Liz said, "I know. Would you be offended if I called him? Maybe he'd listen to me."

"Fine with me. Give it a try."

"Are you sure? I don't want to step on your toes with this."

"I'm positive. I've got my hands full anyway."

She waited and said, "What about church?" They both wanted a Catholic ceremony but were striking out with churches. Both Liz's parish in Pendel, and Nick's parish in Bristol were already booked for weddings the following Saturday. Liz's parish actually had two scheduled an hour apart.

"Brian inquired about doing a second at St. Mark's. They balked at first but finally agreed. We can get married Saturday if we can wait until five o'clock."

They were standing in the kitchen. She put her arms around him, kissed him, and said, "Do you know how nice that sounds, that we can get married on Saturday?"

Nick smiled and kissed her back. "It sounds pretty good to me. So, you're good with five o'clock?"

"Five o'clock, midnight, I don't care as long as we do it."

"Great. Tell Brian when you call him. I have to talk to Big Frankie about the trucks."

Liz decided to bite. She hadn't had this much fun in a long time. "The trucks?"

Frankie has the newest truck of all of us. "I asked him to drive us for the wedding. Jimmy and Julie will be in Angelo's truck as best man and maid of honor. Then everyone else can follow behind. Anyway, Big Frankie had agreed to make sure all the trucks shine."

"That's very nice, but aren't you forgetting someone?"

Nick scratched his head in thought.

"How about our flower girl? How is she getting around?"

Nick smacked his head. "Addie! How could I forget about Addie? See, there's so much to do. That's why Brian is helping. Which car should Addie be in?"

"Don't worry. I'll ask Kate what would be best." She brushed his hair with her fingers and said, "You're doing too much, Big Guy. I want you to relax so you enjoy this. I'll call Brian to tell him we don't want him paying.

Liz called but had less luck with Brian than Nick had. "Liz," Brian said, "I've known Nick since I was in high school. I love the guy. Johnny and I consider him an uncle. Jenny and I would really like to do this for you. Besides, when I hear Nick's plans, we're not talking about a lot of money."

Liz laughed. "Okay. It's so nice of you and Jenny. Actually, as the wedding planner, I do have one request of you."

"Anything you need, Liz."

"I'm having fun watching Nick plan this wedding, and I don't want to change a thing about the food, the music, the vehicles we'll use. Promise me that?"

Brain made a face. "Roast beef sandwiches, potato salad, and sheet cake? Really?"

"Really. No deviation and no multitiered cake. Sheet cake like the man says."

"You got it. But it will be the best damn roast beef you've ever tasted."

"That's a deal. And no band or DJ. We'll do the music the way he wants it. But, having the reception in the deli," She shook her head. "I know how important that space is to him, and I don't want to hurt his feelings, but I have some friends who would like to come, and they won't fit. Think you can gently move him away from that?"

"I'm glad you said that because that was my plan. I know he wants things simple so I looked into the Ancient Order of Hibernians Hall here in town. It's available and can hold one-hundred and twenty-five. I'm going to pitch it to him tomorrow that we move to the bigger room and have a bachelor party at the deli the night before the wedding."

Liz beamed. "That's a perfect idea. Thank you."

Brian looked relieved. "I'm glad you like it. Actually, it's a bachelor party with a twist. I'd like you to be there near the end. If all goes well, there is something I'd like you to see."

Chapter 74

What Brian called a bachelor party turned out to be a private dinner for the deli guys, Johnny Marzo, and Brian. Whatever promises Brian made to Liz about keeping the

wedding reception simple apparently didn't apply to the party. After Angelo reluctantly agreed to allow outside food, Brian had it catered and provided a five-course dinner with lobster and filet mignon as the main course.
Nick started off with a few jokes and after that, the banter was non-stop. The beer and wine flowed, and so did the stories. Nick couldn't remember feeling so relaxed.

At Brian's request, Donna had invited Carrie, Jenny, and Liz to meet at her apartment behind the deli at eight o'clock, two hours after the party began. It was all very mysterious, but Brian asked that they trust him. Shortly after eight Brian called Donna and asked the girls to join them.

Nick beamed when he saw Liz, and the other men ensured that their wives had a chair and something to drink. Liz saw the remains of the lobster shells and gave Brian a scolding look. He smiled and said, "Tonight's menu wasn't in our agreement."
She laughed. "I guess that's why we have lawyers."

The small talk continued, and Liz noticed Brian checking his watch. Whatever he had planned was either late or would be happening soon. Judging from the faces around the table, Liz got the impression that everyone else was as much in the dark as she was, even Johnny. A few minutes later, Brian received a text that made him smile.
He left the table and walked to the door. The conversation stopped as everyone turned their attention to Brian. He unlocked the door and welcomed a man and woman who stepped in. They looked to be in their early seventies. The

man was trim with close-cropped hair. The woman was smartly dressed and held onto her husband's arm. Both looked nervous. Brian whispered to them and then turned and gestured toward Nick.

They crossed the room, the woman forcing a smile and the man looking apprehensive. When they reached the table the man said, "Sergeant Hardings?"

Nick was surprised by the sergeant reference. He nodded and the man extended his hand and said, "Adam Gregory ."

Nick shook his hand, looked at Brian, then back to the couple, and said, "I'm sorry. Do we know each other?"

"No," Gregory said haltingly, "but I wish to God we did."

Nick looked perplexed and Gregory said, "I was a Navy pilot shot down over North Vietnam over forty-five years ago. I was captured and imprisoned by local villagers."

Nick was stunned.

Gregory said, "I was beaten, tortured, and deprived of food. I had no hope of living, and then, one night all hell broke loose. There were explosions everywhere and weapons fire. Then someone made it to my cage, his face covered in camouflage paint, and said the most beautiful words I've ever heard. He said, 'Did anyone order...'

Nick joined him to finish the sentence. "Did anyone order a taxi?"

"Yes. That's what you said, 'Did anyone order a taxi?'"

Nick covered his face with his hands and sobbed while Gregory and the woman watched and cried openly.

The rest of the room sat in stunned silence as Gregory said, his voice choking, "You saved my life. For over forty-five years I've been tortured not knowing who you or the others were who rescued me."

Nick couldn't speak and Gregory was too overcome to continue. Brian asked the couple to sit, and everyone scrambled to find them chairs.
Gregory took a seat next to Nick, and the woman, presumably his wife, sat beside him.

The woman rubbed her husband's back, and Liz motioned for Jimmy to give her his seat so she could sit on the other side of Nick.
Brian said, "Let me share some things while we give Nick and Adam a chance to absorb this. First, this is Amanda Gregory , Adam's wife." She forced another smile while she continued to console her husband.

"You may remember a while back Nick was interviewed by a journalism student about his thoughts as a former prisoner of war."
Liz said to Nick, "That's the girl we met at the Arts Society. She's the girlfriend of my matron of honor's son." Nick nodded and said quietly, "I remember."

Brian said, "When I read the part of the interview about Nick and the pilot never having contact, I decided to use my company's connections at the Pentagon to search their database for the name of the pilot who was rescued on the date on Nick's Distinguished Service Cross citation. Once I had the name, it wasn't hard to discover that Adam Gregory was alive and living in Chicago. I reached out and he told me his story."
By now Gregory had composed himself enough to continue. "Let me tell this, Brian. I've been wanting to for so long." He turned to Nick, "All these years I've had this

nagging feeling in the back of my mind that I was never able to thank the man who saved me. I wondered about him and wondered what his life was like. It wasn't until Brian found me and told me the story of you being captured that I really lost it. I had no idea. When Brian offered to fly us here at his expense to meet you, I said, absolutely not. We're going and paying our own way."

"Nick Hardings," he corrected himself and said, "Sergeant Hardings, we're forty-five years late, but my wife and I are here to say thank you."
Nick was regaining his composure as well and mumbled, "You're welcome."

At first, Liz questioned Brian's judgment for arranging this meeting at this place and time, before the entire group, but scanning their faces now, and sensing their emotion, she realized they were the people who had been with Nick all along. They had loved him and suffered with him, and it was appropriate that they be present to share the moment.

Gregory said, "Please give me a minute to share my experience in the hope you'll understand why I never reached out.
Nick said, "It's okay. It's not necessary."
Gregory replied, "It is for me. Please give me a minute." He took a breath and went on. "When you rescued me, you'll remember I could barely walk. I was in your presence for maybe ten minutes at most, when you ordered the two men with you to get me to the chopper while you provided cover fire. I never learned your name. The other two rescuers got me to the chopper and handed me off to the crew, so I never learned their names either. The chopper transported

me to base where I was transferred again and medivacked to a hospital ship off the coast. Everything was complete chaos for those twenty-four hours. I was sick, wounded, in tremendous pain, and shuffled from one place to another and one person or team to another. Eventually, I went through two months of medical care and then was discharged."

"Honestly, by then I just wanted to go home. Yours was just one of a handful of faces I saw that night, and while I would have occasional thoughts of gratitude to the man who saved me, I had no idea who he was or how I would even go about finding him. By then, I just wanted to put the war behind me. Then, when Brian called and I learned that the man who saved my life spent two years in a POW camp, I couldn't bear not seeing you and thanking you in person. My God, what happened to you was so unfair."
He broke down again, and this time it was Nick who rubbed his back whispering it was okay.

Amanda Gregory said, "I insisted on coming with Adam because I wanted to thank you personally for the life you gave us. Her hands trembled as she removed an envelope from her purse and said, "Adam and I didn't meet until after the war. Adam became a pilot with American Airlines, and I worked at a ticket counter at O'Hare airport. She removed two photos from the envelope. "These are our sons, Chad and Robert. Chad graduated from Northwestern and is a pharmacist. Robert went to Loyola and works in real estate. They each have wonderful wives and gave us five adorable grandchildren." She slid their photos in front of him, paused for emphasis, and said, "If you didn't rescue Adam from that cage in that jungle…" She trailed off, omitting the obvious.

With that, Nick completely broke down, and there wasn't a dry eye at the table. Liz put her head on Nick's shoulder, and he took her hand.

Mrs. Gregory said to Liz, "Brian explained to us that you're getting married tomorrow. We agreed two weeks ago to come today, before anyone even knew that was happening. When you announced your wedding, Brian suggested we postpone the trip, but I insisted on coming now because I wanted to tell you the remarkable thing your husband-to-be did for us."

Liz smiled and said thank you.
Amanda looked at Nick and said, I hope we didn't do the wrong thing.

Nick looked up, rubbed his eyes, and said, "I used to tell myself it didn't matter that I never heard from the man I rescued. Now I know that it did, and I can't thank you enough for coming."

Gregory said, "Nick, you and I are the only people in this room who know what it feels like to be held captive in a bamboo cage in the jungle, with no hope of freedom or survival. But I'm the only one who knows what it's like to be freed from that. Forgive me if I'm overstepping my bounds, but I wonder if in some ways you're still not completely free. You were released when the war ended, but maybe not really freed. I hope your wedding tomorrow to this beautiful lady finally allows you to live the rest of your life experiencing…" He searched for the right words and settle on, "experiencing something good."

Nick managed a smile. He squeezed Liz's hand and said, "I promise you, it will."

Chapter 75

Brian, now kiddingly called the wedding planner by everyone at the deli, took some liberties with the guest list. Once Nick gave his approval to move the reception to the Hibernian Hall, Brian took that as approval to expand the list. He asked Big Frankie to comb Nick's veteran database and email an invitation to the most frequent correspondents. He and Jimmy went through Nick's high school yearbook and added another handful of names. To provide balance, he encouraged Liz to send an invitation to the Arts Society in addition to the family and friends she intended to invite.

The bottom of the invitation read, "Casual Dress. No reply needed. Just come. No Gifts."

The church was half filled, more than Nick expected. At exactly five o'clock, Nick and Jimmy left the sacristy to join the priest, Father John Eagelton, at the altar. Nick looked handsome in the only suit he owned. He added a tie picked out by Carrie. Jimmy wore a sports jacket he found at the same thrift store where Nick purchased his suit. He looked uncomfortable and kept fidgeting with the sleeves, but his exaggerated smile never faded.

Nick scanned the pews and was moved to see several veterans he helped over the years as well as a handful of friends he had lost contact with. Liz's guests were seated on the opposite side of the church. He recognized a scattering of faces from the Arts Society.

There was activity in the church vestibule as the girls arrived by trucks driven by Big Frankie and Angelo. They exchanged hugs with the girls before walking up the side aisle to sit in the first pew reserved for them. Nick watched them and his memory went into overdrive, flashing pieces of over sixty years of friendship filled with school pranks, football, times at the deli, and the friggin' war that impacted them in so many ways. He knew his messed-up life had weighed heavily on them, and the guilt they held for not serving when he did. He hoped the visit by Gregory would somehow be as much of a catharsis for them as it was for him.

Finally, the girls were in full view. Addie looked adorable in a powder blue dress. Her mother fussed over her hair one last time before giving her a kiss for encouragement and then walked up the side aisle to join relatives. Nick knew that flower girls often had the jitters, but Addie looked just as confident and self-assured as he expected. Julie, the Matron of Honor wore a knee-length dress of the same color that looked great on her slim, yoga instructor figure. Nick was glad that Liz had such a good friend, even more so because he liked her. He hoped she wasn't as good at Pinochle as Liz claimed. The guys could never handle a women's team winning the tournament.

Finally, Liz came into view. She looked perfect in an off-white pants suit with a powder blue blouse that matched the girls' dresses. She was beaming from ear to ear, and she waved when their eyes met. Nick had never seen a bride wave to the groom from the back of the church before, but he waved back.

Brian had found another proverbial loophole in their wedding contract. Nick had spelled out the music he wanted for the reception, but he never addressed the ceremony music. Brian hired a full horn ensemble to position in the choir loft, and they played Pachelbel's *Canon* as the wedding procession moved forward, led by Addie.

Nick watched the little girl as she headed down the aisle with her head held high and a smile worthy of the occasion. She was dropping petals that were no doubt from the most expensive flowers Brian could find. She was spreading them nicely, not in clumps, not too sparsely, but in just the right amounts, at perfect intervals, and with poise and grace uncommon for a child her age. She reached the altar and winked at Nick.

Julie came next, and Nick reminded himself that his life with Liz wouldn't only be spent at the deli. He suspected he'd be devoting a fair amount of time at the Arts Society and was grateful that Julie would be there to make him feel welcome.

Finally, he had an unobstructed view of Liz. He wanted to think that she looked better than ever, but he couldn't because she had always seemed perfect to him, whether in a nurse's uniform decades ago, a sweat suit working in her garden, or an elegant dress at the society gala. But as she drew closer, he conceded that maybe her smile was just a bit more radiant than usual.

His mind drifted to another time. Nick is in a hospital bed. The room is dark, and Nick's mood is even darker. A female voice stirs him from his semi-sleep with a cheerful, "Good morning." She's humming a light tune as she opens the blinds and the sunlight floods in. He blinks to adjust to the glare and sees a nurse at the side of his bed. It was a new nurse, one he hadn't seen before.

"Good morning," she repeated cheerfully.

Nick mumbled, "I prefer it dark," to which the nurse responds in the same upbeat tone, "Not anymore."

Nick snaps back to the present as Liz reaches the altar. She winks, and Nick wonders whether she and Addie had a plan.

Once by his side, she whispered, "Hello, handsome. I see you wore a tie."

"Is it okay?"

"It's nice for the wedding but take it off for the reception. It's not you."

Nick whispered back. "You look nice."

"Is the suit okay?"

"It's nice," he whispered with a broad grin, "but take it off after the reception."

She thought about elbowing him but decided against it.

The music ended and Father John began the ceremony. Liz had opted for a full Mass, which Nick welcomed, but it wasn't long before his knees were killing him from the kneeling.

The homily was just the right length and included touching comments about the bride and groom gleaned from interviews with the Best Man and Matron of Honor. Toward the end, Father John said, “All weddings are nice, but I put them into two categories. The first is of the bright-eyed, young couples filled with optimism and bubbling with energy, making the standard transition from dating to engagement to marriage, as friends and well-wishers cheer them on. Their life horizon is presumably long, with endless and exciting possibilities. I call these the fairy-tale weddings, and they are a celebration of youth.”

He paused and said, “But there is a second category. Maybe it's my age, but I have a special place in my heart for when mature couples come along who have found love later in life, people who have seen so much of life’s joys and challenges and have weathered life’s storms if you will. Their apparent time horizon is shorter, and they appreciate that the time they have is precious. They know that marriage, like life, requires effort and acceptance of each other’s imperfections. I call these the reality weddings.”

Heads were nodding as he continued. “So, fairy tale or reality? By now, you’re probably thinking that Nick and Liz belong in the second category. But if you think that, then you don’t know Nick and Liz.”

He smiled and raised his voice. “I’m here to proclaim to the world, or at least those present, that this a fairy tale couple if I ever saw one. Meeting with Nick and Liz, to prepare for this ceremony, I felt as if I was meeting with two teenagers, and trust me, they are gaga about each other.”

The congregation laughed and the priest continued. "Yes. They may have a few years under their belts, but I assure you this love affair that began almost fifty years ago and will be consummated today in marriage is indeed a fairy tale." He raised his voice even louder and said, "Let's get these two married in the eyes of God and all of us!"

The congregation cheered.

The couple faced each other to prepare for their vows. Jimmy and Julie stood at their sides, leaving Addie alone in her pew.

Nick had gone through some of the most rigorous combat training of any military force in the world and went on countless combat missions before his last, ill-fated one, but through it all, he earned the reputation of having ice water in his veins. He never faltered, never hesitated. But as it came time for the vows, he felt his heart racing.

He looked at Addie alone in her pew and beckoned her to come to him. She did, and he lifted her to hold her in his arms. Father John looked at him and shrugged. He patted her cheek gently and said, "These young couples are so unconventional."

Addie wrapped her arms around Nick's neck, and Nick felt himself relax. He winked at Liz and whispered, "I'm ready." If Liz had any doubts about marrying Nick, which of course she didn't, they would have vanished at that moment.

Father John read from the nuptial rites of the Catholic Church. The couple exchanged vows and Father pronounced them married. Nick's arthritic wrist ached from holding Addie and he had winced as he struggled to share

rings while holding her. With the ceremony complete, he put her down and told her to return to her pew.
Nick and Liz knelt side by side and held hands through the Offertory and Consecration. Nick watched the faces of the guests as they passed by on their way to Communion. He saw so many that meant so much to him, and he couldn't wait to talk with them at the reception.

Father John gave the final blessing and the ensemble played Mendelssohn's "Wedding March," as the couple left the church to the wild cheers of their friends.

Chapter 76

Brian and Johnny Marzo's families were seated together. Carrie said kiddingly to Julie, "What has gotten into your husband?"
Jenny laughed out loud. "Beats me. He advises the FBI, CIA, and Homeland Security, and discovers what he really wants in life is to be on stage. Look at him."

Brian was using Spotify to play music while everyone waited for the bride and groom's arrival. When Jenny reminded him that the couple didn't want a DJ, he replied that he was the self-appointed Master of Ceremonies. He used their daughter Stella, and Johnny and Carrie's daughter Gracie to visit tables to solicit song requests.

Big Frankie delivered a message and Brian smiled. He said, "Everyone please take your seats. I'm told the bride and groom have arrived. "
Jenny leaned closer to Carrie and said, "Normally, I'd be mortified by Brian's behavior, but I know you're a good

friend who knows I had nothing to do with this. Besides, he's having fun."
Carrie joked, "You know I'm here for you if you ever need to talk. "

Brian introduced Addie who was escorted by Kate. Next came Jimmy and Julie. Jimmy was greeted by good-natured catcalls from his veteran friends. He replied by discretely running his middle finger along his cheek.
Liz and Nick were introduced to thunderous cheers while Brian played the theme from *Rocky*.
Jenny said, "Oh my God. *Rocky!* I swear I didn't know about this. I would have stopped him."
Carrie said, "Look at Liz. She may want to kill him. "
Liz was glaring at Brian, but halfway across the room, she burst out laughing and rolled with it.

After the introductions, the guests mingled and Liz said, "Introduce me to some of your friends."
"I'd like to, but this isn't my reception. It's ours. I want to meet your friends first."
"Okay, let's do that." There were no seating arrangements since RSVPs weren't required, but the guests had pretty much segregated themselves on opposite sides of the room. She draped her arm through his and they moved toward her guests. They chatted with relatives of Julie, and Nick told them how much he liked her.

They moved from table to table. Nick recognized some of the people and met others for the first time. He sensed her friends were over the moon happy for Liz. At one table, Liz said, "Nick wants to get involved at the Society, but he's made it clear he will not hang Christmas decorations." Everyone laughed and Nick felt relieved.

They had visited almost every table when Liz said, "Not him. I was hoping he wouldn't come."

Nick followed her line of vision and saw Seth Wagner.

He said, "I didn't notice him at church. Maybe he came late."

Seth caught their eye and started moving toward them.

Liz whispered, "Here he comes. Be nice, I guess."

Nick teased, "Can I just knock him out?"

"No! I promise I won't try to change anything about you, with one exception. No more tough guy stuff. No more punching."

Seth worked his way through the tables and reached them. He appeared to be drunk, which had to mean he had started drinking elsewhere.

"There's the newlyweds," he bellowed. He leaned in to embrace Liz, but she stepped back and said, "Hi, Seth. Nice of you to come."

"I wouldn't miss congratulating the new couple." He turned to Nick and said, "And here's the man who has every mature gentleman in Langhorne wondering what Liz sees in him. Of course, I mean that as a compliment."

Nick glared at him, and Liz said, "Look, Nick, there's my friend Beth. I'd like you to meet her. She walked away expecting Nick to follow. Instead, he lingered another moment weighing his promise to Liz against his desire to drop Seth where he stood. He thought it would make a good memory for the guests. For years to come people would say, 'Remember that wedding where the groom decked one of the guests?' It's things like that that make events stand out.

Seth either had a death wish or was too drunk to realize he was flirting with danger. He said more quietly, "An old guy like you better get a bottle of those little blue pills. I hear she's hot stuff."

Nick decided to count strikes, and that was number two.

Liz had taken a few steps before she realized Nick hadn't followed. She went back, pulled on his arm, and said, "Come on, Slow Poke. We have lots of guests to meet."

Nick said nothing about Seth as they visited a few more tables before heading toward the other side of the room. On their way, they stopped to say hi to Stella and Gracie, who had bonded with Addie. The three girls had taken their shoes off and were dancing and sliding on the polished dancefloor. Liz was happy to see them getting along. Addie had no siblings or cousins, and Liz hoped they could adopt each other as relatives.

They made it to the other side when Nick stopped dead as a couple approached them. He stared for a moment and said, "Tish?"

She nodded that she was, and he locked her in a long embrace as tears welled in his eyes. When they parted, he said, "My God, you're as beautiful as ever."

"Hardly," she replied. "It's so good to see you, especially today." She looked at Liz and smiled.

Nick said, "I'm sorry. Liz this is Tish...." He paused before adding her last name. She helped him. "I'm Tish Kane, and this is my husband, Bob." Everyone shook hands, and Bob said, "So nice to meet you. Tish has talked so much about you."

Tish said to Liz, "I was married to Billy Moyer, one of Nick's high school football buddies. Billy passed away eighteen years ago at the Twin Towers. Bob and I married ten years later. I talk to the boys every Christmas, but I haven't seen Nick or the other guys in a long, long time."
Bob said to Tish, "Why don't I get us some drinks while you guys catch up a little?" He turned to Nick and Liz and added, "It's an honor meeting you, and good luck to both of you."

While Bob headed to the bar, Nick's head was swirling with memories. Billy was a regular on the street corner when they were kids. He was probably the fastest player on the football team and came up big at big moments. But what Nick remembered most was that Billy was intelligent and focused on his career goals. He followed his long-time dream of attending college, excelled in his studies, graduated with a degree in finance, and went to work in New York. At the time Billy enrolled at Penn State, the government was giving draft deferments. Many went to college for that reason, but Nick knew that Billy was simply doing what he always planned to do, long before Vietnam was on anyone's mind.
He married Tish, a psychologist, and they bought a Bed and Breakfast on Long Beach Island, New Jersey. They would invite the deli guys to spend an occasional day at the beach, and although she never treated him, they had many long and helpful talks.

The guys were devastated by Billy's passing, especially Nick. Once a full supporter of the war, Nick's views soured after his return from Walter Reed, and he was always grateful that Billy managed to escape the war without physical or emotional damage. The irony of Billy perishing at the hands of a new enemy was difficult to handle.

Nick said to Liz, "Billy worked in New York and died on 9-11. We were all devastated, but Tish was an inspiration to me when I saw the strength and grace she showed in the face of her loss." He turned to Tish and continued. "I wish I could have had the strength you did, but I want you to know I thought about you a lot. I'm so glad you're here and Bob seems like a nice guy. I'm glad we finally got to meet him."

Tish said, "I'm so happy to see you happy. We wouldn't have missed this. I'm so glad your DJ helped Jimmy track me own for the invitation."

Nick and Liz smiled at the DJ reference. Tish added, "As for Bob, I never thought I'd find someone to share the rest of my life with, but I have." She smiled at Liz and said, "I guess we all have." She added, "Go on, you have a lot of guests to greet. I have some catching up to do with Jimmy and the others. By the way, we sold the apartment in Manhattan and retired to that place on LBI that you remember. We're only an hour away. I hope we can see each other."

Liz said that would be great.

Liz watched them walk away, grateful that she had learned another piece of Nick Hardings' past.

Nick introduced Liz to various veterans he had helped over the years and each one had a different story of gratitude. At one point, Liz told Nick, "I'm beginning to like you more and more."

Nick said, "Wait until you hear the bad stuff."

They reached Ralph McGinnis's table and Ralph jumped up to greet them. There was another long embrace and a lot of good old boy back-slapping. Nick said to Liz, "Remember when I told you I testified before Congress?"
Liz said, "Yes, of course."
"Ralph is an old high school buddy. He later became an undertaker, and he used his limo to drive all of us to the hearing."
Ralph said, "We couldn't have been prouder of you. And the whole scene, the hearing room, the congressmen, and the reporters, was one of the most important days of my life." He directed his comments to Liz. "He wrote one thousand letters to his congressman. Pestered him so much on behalf of veterans that he was invited to speak." Then he repeated. "This guy addressed a committee of the United States Congress."
Liz knew much of that but was still caught up in Ralph's enthusiasm and pictured the scene in her mind.
Ralph said, "I'm so glad to be here. I wish you guys much happiness."
Nick gave him a second hug and said, "Please *get* your ass back to the deli sometime soon."
"You bet. I already promised Angelo I would."

As they walked away Liz said, "He seems very nice."
Nick said. "He's a great guy. I've always felt a little sorry for him because he never played football. None of us cared, but he did. When he hung out with us you could tell he didn't feel like he belonged. Like I said, none of us cared, but he was always doing things to get accepted, even

years later. It's funny. Here's a guy with a very successful and lucrative business, and there's a part of him that wishes he hung out at a run-down deli with a bunch of misfits."
"You're not misfits. Maybe just a bit eccentric."

As they moved on, a woman approached, with Jimmy, Big Frankie, and Angelo behind her. She looked their age, maybe a couple of years older. She seemed familiar, but he couldn't place her. She noticed the look on his face, smiled, and said, " I guess I can't blame you; it's been almost forty years since I last saw you. I've changed a little."
Jimmy couldn't hold it in any longer and blurted, "It's Cissy."
It didn't register right away and then Nick said, "Cissy Francelli?"
She nodded yes and he immediately broke down. They hugged and he rocked her back and forth seemingly forever.
Liz watched and Big Frankie explained that Cissy was the sister of their dear friend Johnny Francelli, who was killed in Vietnam. The guys had hung out at her house all through high school and her mother Anna treated them as her sons. Of all the emotional weights the gang carried through life, the heaviest, even heavier than what happened to Nick, was Johnny Francelli's death. They all believed Johnny was destined to do good things and the hardest part was watching Anna grieve. She had been their surrogate mother for so long, and they remained loyal to her until she died.
Liz already knew some of the story and was getting misty eyed herself.

When Cissy and Nick broke their embrace, they exchanged quiet words for some time before Nick said to Liz, "Remember I told you that we all went to Washington to walk by President Kennedy's coffin when he was shot?"

Liz said she did.

Nick said, "Cissy stole her mother's car that night and drove us."

Cissy added, "I'll never forget it. I got in lots of trouble but would do it again. Besides, I think deep down, Mom was actually glad I did it. She loved JFK and was glad we went."

Nick smiled at the memory. "It was one of the most memorable times of my life. I think that went for all of us."

The guys behind Cissy agreed.

Cissy said, "I'm here to deliver a message from Johnny. He speaks to me in dreams sometimes and I don't give a damn if you don't believe it."

Nick said. "I believe it."

"Johnny wants you to know that he was really pissed watching you miss so much of your life and would have kicked your ass if he was here, but he couldn't be happier for you now." He also said, 'Tell him to live his friggin life.'. His words, not mine."

Nick held her gaze for some time and then said, "Tell Johnny I will."

Cissy shook her head and said, "Tell him yourself. Don't you pray?"

"Yes, I do."

"Then tell him. He'll be listening."

They left Cissy as Brian announced that the buffet table was open. He was pumping up the quality of the roast beef, but Liz wasn't ready to eat. She said to Nick, "Would you mind if we just sat in a quiet corner for a minute or two?"

"Not at all. I apologize that it's been one person after another taking our time."

Liz said, "Don't be silly. I've appreciated every piece of information today. It wasn't always pleasant, but it shed light on who you are. And you have amazing friends."

"Still, we need more time for you and your friends."

"Trust me, I'm fine. It was just very emotional hearing those stories and I needed to breathe. Let's sit."

They sat side by side, far enough away from everyone that it was obvious they wanted a moment alone.

Liz said, "We did it, Nick. We're married. Is it possible for a bride to get married at five o'clock and fall in love all over again by seven? That's what happened to me at this crazy reception."

Nick smiled and hugged her. They sat quietly for another minute or so until Liz said, "I need to powder my nose. Let's sample Brian's roast beef when I come back."

Nick scanned the room. Some guests were eating, others were dancing. He noticed Julie walking across the floor toward the food as a slow song was playing. She passed near Seth. He stopped her and took her hand as an invitation to dance. From her body language, it looked as if she begged off as she pointed to the food table. He held on to her hand and pulled her toward him. He placed both arms around her and pulled her closer as he started swaying with the music. She was pulling away slightly,

trying to avoid a scene, when his one hand dropped to rest on her backside.
Nick started walking their way just as she gave Seth a hard shove, broke free, and walked away.

Seth laughed and called after her as if it was all just good fun, but she kept on walking. Nick stopped when he saw she was okay, and waited for Liz. When she came out of the restroom he walked to the head table where Julie was sitting with Nick's friends and Kate. Addie was still off playing with the girls. Julie looked flustered. Nick helped Liz to her seat, winked at Julie, gestured in the direction of Seth, and said, "I'll be right back."

He walked toward Seth as Julie explained to Liz what had just happened. Nick reached Seth by the time Liz got the gist of the story. Seth saw him and slurred, "There's the lucky groom. "
Nick said, "I've been meaning to tell you something. I have a bad temper and recently got scolded by my wife for punching someone. I promised her no more punches. But I have a promise for you. If you ever fondle, touch, squeeze or make any other physical contact with any woman from the Society, I will slap you silly. If you make any inappropriate comments or tell inappropriate jokes in their presence, I will slap you silly. And if I find you retaliate in any way because of this conversation, I will slap you double silly. I know that's a lot to remember. Is all that clear?"
Seth hesitated, then nodded.
"Say, it," Nick demanded.
Seth said softly, "It's clear."

"One more thing. I hear you are a great patron of the arts and a generous donor to the Society. I commend you for that and I expect you'll be just as generous as ever."

He turned to leave just as Marzo walked up. "What's up, Nick?"

Nick led him back toward the head table and said, "Not much. Just catching up with my friend, Seth."

Marzo said, "Liz was concerned you were getting into trouble."

"Me?" Nick smiled. "Not at all."

The roast beef was a unanimous hit, as was the potato salad. Several guests commented to Liz that they thought a casual wedding with outstanding food was a very cool and unique idea."

Brian was back at the microphone, and Jenny was still rolling her eyes about it.

He said, "We have some comments, and the first is from our flower girl, Addie Baron, the granddaughter of the bride."

Kate gave her daughter a kiss and pointed her to the stage.

"She took the microphone from Brian and said, "Hi everyone. I was going to ask Nick to sing a song with me, but Mommy-Liz said he is a terrible singer."

The guests laughed and Nick whispered to Liz, " That's not true. I was pretty good in my day. He gestured to his friends and said, "We all were."

"I just assumed you wouldn't want to sing so I covered for you."

"You assumed right."

Addie was about to continue her comments when she saw a familiar face enter the hall. She did a double-take, pointed to the back, and said, "Mommie, Mommie-Liz, it's Uncle Peter!" Everyone turned as Liz and Kate jumped to their feet. Liz put her hands to her mouth and said to Nick, "It's my son." She rushed to meet him, and they hugged. Then she took him by the hand and led him to the table.

Nick had met him once before at Baron's memorial service a few weeks earlier, and they hit it off well. But that was before there was any talk of a wedding. When he received the invitation, he said he had an important meeting that he couldn't miss and it would be impossible to fly out again so soon after his last trip. He said he hated missing the wedding and promised to visit within a month.

Liz was ecstatic. "You said you couldn't come, but you're here."
"I really wanted to all along but thought I couldn't. My boss saw I was bummed about something, and when I told him, he insisted I come. By then it was short notice to get a straight flight. I got a ticket with a connection in Chicago. Of course, that was delayed which is why I'm late."
Liz bubbled, "Well you're here now, and we're just getting started."

Nick waited until Kate and Addie finished their hugs and kisses and then shook Peter's hand and thanked him for coming.
Peter said, "I'm so glad I'm here." Then he looked around and said, "It's been a long day and I could use a drink. Which way is the bar."

Nick pointed and Peter said, "Why don't the two of us go get one?"

Nick said, "Sounds good."

When they were alone, Peter said, "I really wanted to be here for my Mom's wedding, but I also wanted to come to talk with you in person. I know that sometimes adult children can get a little crazy when a new man comes into their mother's life."

Nick nodded.

"Mom and I either talk by phone or text each other almost every day. I want you to know that I've never seen her happier. That plus the wonderful things Kate tells me about how you treat Addie sealed the deal for me." He put out his hand and said, "Welcome to the family."

Nick ignored the hand and reached out to hug him instead.

When they broke, Peter smiled and said, "Normally I'd add that if you ever hurt her, I'd come after you, but Mom says you're a badass, so I guess I'd have to hire someone."

Nick laughed. That won't be necessary, but I admire your point. I think you're my kind of guy."

Chapter 77

Once the excitement of Peter's arrival calmed down and Nick and Peter returned to their seats, Brian was up again. "Before we get to the comments from the Matron of Honor and Best Man, Addie Baron is going to try again to ask her question."

Addie returned to the stage and said, "I actually have two questions. I asked my mom what a honeymoon is, and she said it's when people take a vacation after they get married. So, my first question is, 'Where are we going?'"

Liz and Nick laughed and Nick said loud enough for the room to hear, "We?" The guests had fun with that.

Kate called out to her daughter, "Just ask your next question." Addie wasn't sure why she wasn't getting an answer, but she shrugged and said, "This one is for Nick. Everyone knows I call my grandmother Mommy-Liz. Since you're married now, would it be okay if I called you Daddy-Nick?"

Nick flashed a wide grin. "Yes, Addie," he said above the cheers, "it would be great if you called me Daddy-Nick."

Brian was back to introduce Julie Hall for the Matron of Honor speech. Julie leaned over to kiss Addie on the forehead on the way to the stage.

She smiled nervously and began. "Good evening. I'm Julie Hall, the proud Matron of Honor of my best friend Liz. I can tell you now that it will be impossible to convey adequately the amount of joy I feel tonight for this marriage of Liz and Nick, but I'll do my best.

"Before I get to my prepared speech, I want to say that Liz and I met years ago as volunteers working at the Langhorne Arts Society. As lovers of art, we appreciate the unique and the unconventional, and those are the words that come to mind about today's marriage celebration. Usually, it is the bride who does most of the planning. But I'm told Liz deferred to Nick for much of today, and Nick, in turn, hired a wedding planner. Let's show our appreciation to Brian Kelly for his efforts."

Brian stood and waved proudly as the guests cheered and jeered good-naturedly and Jenny rolled her eyes again.

Julie said, a bit tongue in cheek, "I understand wedding planning isn't his primary job, but he assured me tonight that he's having business cards made." Those who knew Brian's profession burst out laughing, and Jenny wanted to crawl under the table.

Julie continued, "In an unconventional move, the wedding party was driven to the church and reception in pickup trucks, nice trucks I can assure you, but trucks, nonetheless. I want to thank Angelo Marzo for driving me, Jimmy and Addie, and Big Frankie for driving Liz and Nick."

The guests clapped.

"Also, music is important at any wedding, and the contrast between having a full brass section perform at church and relying upon internet music at the reception was certainly cool and unique. And let's talk about food. Serving roast beef sandwiches at a wedding is certainly unconventional, but, as Brian explained, when it is pure Angus beef cooked to perfection and dripping with delicious gravy, it might set a standard for future receptions.

"But most unconventional of all is the love story of these two people we celebrate tonight, and how they arrived at this place together, and I don't mean by truck."

"You know, you can go through life thinking you know someone pretty well, especially when that person is your best friend. Three months ago, if you asked me to describe Liz I would have said, she is strong, independent, self-assured, and comfortable, even content with her life. I would have said that marriage would have been the absolute last thing on her mind. Not that she had a lack of desirable suitors over the years. As the most attractive and coolest person her age that I know, she had many. It was just that she seemed to have everything she needed.

“Then one day about three months ago she came bouncing into our yoga class bubbling like a schoolgirl about the man who showed up on her doorstep the day before. She proceeded to tell me one of the most wonderful love stories I've ever heard.

“I mean, you had to see her that day. She went on and on about Nick being funny and handsome, and strong and kind. I thought she might have been a bit overblown with her praise, but I know now, if anything, she was understating things.

“Nick, you knew Liz way back when, I mean way, way back when, and you know her now, but I can tell you in the years between, at least the more than twenty years I've known her, she has been a remarkable mother, grandmother, and medical professional, always caring for others. In my case, when I lost my husband in Afghanistan fifteen years ago, she became my rock, and she's been so ever since. From what I've learned about you, I'm confident you'll be a rock for each other.

“I wish I could find words that aren't cliche to describe what your marriage symbolizes, but I can't. So, at the risk of stating the obvious, your relationship is a testament to the resilience of the human heart and proves that love knows no age boundaries.

"So, to all of the guests here, please think of the wonderful things you're thinking tonight about this couple and imagine I've said them all because I wish I could.
Liz and Nick, I wish you much laughter, joy, and good health in your years together and I look forward to our continued friendship."

She left the stage to applause and gave Liz and Nick a brief hug. As she left Nick noticed a piece of cake had fallen from the table and icing landed on his shoe. He quickly snagged a cloth napkin and wiped it off. He looked up and saw Liz watching him. He smiled and said, "Carrie and Jenny gave me these shoes before our first date. This is my first time wearing them. I want to make them last a long, long time."

Brian took the microphone one last time. He winked at his wife who smiled and shook her head. She never liked his work in counter-terrorism, but decided it was preferable to what she was watching tonight. He glanced at Johnny Marzo and wondered how much longer he and his buddy would be fighting terrorists. He concluded it would be quite some time.
After checking to make sure that his wait staff had distributed champagne to everyone, he introduced Jimmy to give the best man speech and toast.

Jimmy took the stage looking nervous and uncomfortable. He fidgeted with his sports jacket for a moment and then just took it off and tossed it on a nearby chair. He looked at Liz and Nick and said, "You know I love you guys and would do anything for you, but that it for the jacket."

The guests cheered. Jimmy paused, smiled bravely and began. "I was going to start this by saying all you need to know about Nick is that whenever he sees a kid selling lemon aide, he stops his truck and buys some. Every time. If the kid is charging a buck, he'll give him two. He doesn't even like lemonade. Sometimes he'll take a sip and then pour it out after we're out of sight. Anyway, that's the kind of guy he is.

"I think that's a nice thing to know about Nick, but not the best opening for a Best Man speech, so I'll try again."

"For the benefit of Liz's friends, I'm Jimmy. Those who know me will tell you that I'm not very smart, and I can't argue with that. That's why I am so honored that Nick picked me to give this speech because he doesn't care how smart I am, and I know he doesn't care if I screw it up. The fact is, he's never cared if I screwed up. He's been there for me our whole lives, grade school, high school, football, defending me, encouraging me, helping me, picking me up. The only time we've been separated was when we went to Vietnam. I was terrified, not just because of the Viet Cong who wanted to kill me, but because Nick wasn't there to help, to tell me what I should do.

"I guess you know that Nick was a prisoner of war. He came home in worse shape than you can imagine. I remember the day when Angelo, Big Frankie, and I sat in Marzo's Deli and watched the news coverage of the POWs landing at the airport in Washington. It was the happiest and saddest day of my life. Happiest because Nick was back in the United States. Saddest because it was obvious how hurt and sick he was. While most of the POWs walked off the plane or maybe needed a crutch or wheelchair, Nick was wheeled out on a gurney, with an IV tube in his arm. It broke our hearts."

"It also killed us knowing it would be months before he'd be out of the hospital. We wanted him here so we could care for him, and we worried about how he'd be treated. We know now that he was in the hands of an angel who gave him much more than medical care." He smiled at Liz before going on. "So, at a time when we thought he was going through his worst hour, Nick was actually falling in love."

"Now, all these years later, Angelo, Big Frankie, and I have fallen in love too with the same girl as Nick." He paused and said, "Liz, remember that movie where the football guy gives this long speech at the end to the girl he loves, and when he stops talking the blond girl says, 'You had me at hello?'" Someone called out, "That was *Jerry Maguire*."

"Whatever," Jimmy said. "It doesn't matter. What I want to say, and I know I speak for Big Frankie and Angelo too, Liz, you had us the day you walked into the deli, grabbed a beer, and sat down to play cards."

Liz smiled and Jimmy waved a finger at her. "I know you expect Nick to spend time at that art place in Langhorne, and that's fine, but I need you to promise us that you'll spend time with him at the deli too."

Liz said she promised and blew him a kiss.

"As for Nick, I want you to know that there is no one better to have with you when times get rough than Nick." He paused to gather himself and said, "I have a story. We had a big football game in high school. It was late in the game, and we were losing. Nick threw me a long pass and I got clobbered when I caught it. Looking back, it was the greatest moment of my life. But at the time, I was woozy as I walked back to the huddle. When he saw me, he started laughing. Here we were, at a crucial point in the game, the catch set us up for a possible score, everyone is nervous, and Nick, our team leader is laughing. He looks at me and says, 'Jimmy, I've heard of people getting the snot knocked out of them, but I've never seen it in person. Wipe your nose with your sleeve.' Everyone in the huddle laughed. It kept us loose and we went on to win. So, what's the point? The snot part was funny, but what Nick said next made me so proud and I think inspired the team. He said…"

Nick finished it for him by calling out, "But you held on to the football."

"That's right," Jimmy replied. "You remember it. You said, 'But you held on to the football.' It made me so proud. That's Nick. Keeping it loose and always encouraging. I promise you Liz, you're in good hands."

Turning to Nick, one last time, he said, "Nick, when I saw you on the gurney forty-five years ago, I knew it would be a long recovery, but it turns out, you needed the girl who treated you at first to bring you back to full health. In my professional opinion, you are officially cured and Angelo, Big Frankie, and I are releasing you from our care."

There weren't many dry eyes in the room. Jimmy said, "I like that last line like we were doctors or something, but I have to be honest. Angelo made up that one. The rest was mine, except for the part about Nick falling in love at the hospital. Big Frankie wrote that. I thought it was pretty nice, so I included it."

Jimmy turned serious and said, “Nick, I know you’re worried about me, with all these changes. You know that change is rough for me, but if I could survive a miserable, horrible, stinkin’ year in Vietnam without you, I’ll do my best while you’re hanging art in Langhorne. Congratulations on finding Liz. Congratulations on finding each other. I love you both. We all do.”

Acknowledgments

My long, good, and talented friend, Bert Barbetta, has edited all of my books. I've referenced him so often that I've run out of ways to say thank you. Let me just say that the completion of *Lost Time* would have been impossible without him.

Equal thanks goes to my wife and fest friend Karen who read my previous night's work each morning and gave valuable criticism and support.

Lost time is the last of the Anna;s Boys series. The books are listed here in order.

Till the Boys Come Home (prequel)

Anna's Boys

Stealing Tomatoes

Homegrown

Lost Time

.

Made in the USA
Middletown, DE
23 January 2024